MW01138674

All characters and other entities appearing in this work are fictitious. Any resemblance to real persons or other real-life entities is purely coincidental.

Fancy People

The Jet Set Chronicles

By

K. Cooper Ray

Prologue

That last night at Moomba was a tectonic shift, he said. Yes, there was the physical beating from the accident, or as his therapist kept correcting him "the attack", but more than the assault on his body was the assault on his mind, his life, his ambition and ultimately his delusion. I met him, if met is the right word -- we were never properly introduced — at the Charleston Library Society where he had, by his own admission, sought asylum. He'd just moved to Charleston from Manhattan and came every day to the Library for what I did not know. He was not here for research or study. He did not bring a laptop or notebook. He never requested a book. He never met anyone for business and rarely spoke to the staff. He just came to sit. And stare. He avoided eye contact although his eyes must have scanned every nook and cranny of this old building from marble baseboard to crown molding. He examined stacks and displays as if he were a documentarian of minutia all from his chair at the corner table. To my eyes he looked lost, confused, and perhaps drug-addled. If not for his natty dress and well-groomed good looks one could easily mistake him for a vagabond. We get vagabonds here. Some of the clerks call them tourists, but they are vagrants looking for a bathroom or respite from the heated streets. They are not here to bask in the architecture or inhale the mellifluous ether of old books. And they certainly don't come to read.

After a couple of weeks, slowly, like a tranquilized lion stirring from anesthesia he began to approach the desk to ask questions, but only when I happened to be there. None of the clerks or other staff was approached. The questions were not any odder than the myriad questions we get on any given day, but his were odd in that there was no logical line. If his eyes were nets for catching the visuals of the library, his questions seemed dropped from a fortune cookie.

"Are these the original marble tiles from 1748?"

"Was the piano a gift from a patron and is one allowed to play it?"

"Is there a cleaning lady after hours or do the clerks sweep the floors?"

Like I said not particularly odd queries but no rhyme, no reason. He certainly wasn't applying for a job. The only rhyme, the only pattern, was his schedule. He arrived every day at two o'clock and would leave ten minutes before closing at 4:50. He never talked to anyone, except these queries to me. He did not seem to own a cell phone. He was a real oddball in a town where eccentricity is an art form. He seemed to appear from out of the blue with a mist of gloom surrounding him. He always wore dark suits, white shirt without a tie and his dark hair was always slicked back sharply. I had the notion on more than one occasion that he was a haint, perhaps the son of a grand old family who died too soon. It was later I learned his story and it was revealed in one busted-dam, tidal wave of words hurled at an accidental exorcist.

One afternoon he lingered past closing time. It was a hot day in mid June. The humidity was not yet at wet-sponge state but the heat was beating down in pelts. I thought he may have fallen asleep because he hadn't moved toward the door. I could set my keys on his departure. When he stood to leave I began my closing duties, but not this day. I walked from my desk to the table where he had uncharacteristically slumped over his folded arms, head cradled inside.

"Sir?" I said gently. "The library is closing."

He jerked his head so violently one thought he must never have heard sound before. I apologized for startling him, but he stood abruptly and darted toward the door. As his hand touched the door handle he turned and looked back at me and asked, "May I buy you a Scotch?"

No Charleston man has ever turned down a drink, even from a half-crazed stranger. Hell, that's how many a friendship begins! We walked out of the library down King Street to the back bar at the yacht club. This act alone was not discussed, he was silent during the 10 minute walk, and I assumed he was a member. I am not. The bar was empty except for a trio of silver-haired gentlemen and a bartender. I remember being agog at entering the sacred club so casually, yet he seemed right at home in the bastion of what is referred to as Old Charleston. He received a welcoming nod from the men we passed. We found a seat in the billiards room and began drinking scotch from glasses which silently appeared, unasked for. He began to tell his story as if it was a performance, and I was a camera recording him. It was an intimate telling, confessional yet dramatic. He did not look into my eyes but seemed to slip into a trance as the words fell deliberately from his lips. The recitative seemed rehearsed, with appropriate rises and falls of emotion and volume. The scotch glasses never ran dry as the bartender quietly added ice and more pours. When he finally finished speaking it was well past midnight. The bartender switched off lights in the other room. I sat stunned. Not merely at the tale but at the performance. It was part Shakespearean soliloquy, part poetry, even a nod to a modern musical or opera. We were both very drunk, but for the first time since the first day he appeared in the library, he smiled. His heretofore stony countenance changed with that smile. He was suddenly a movie star, radiant and handsome and full of grace. I sat still, wondering if he expected applause. Then he stared straight into my eyes as he stood and pulled me to my feet.

"By the way, what's your name, Sir? I am Judge. Judge Mender. Pleased to make your acquaintance."

He bounded for the door. I followed thinking I was in the trail of Icarus, fallen, damaged but still brightly scorched from his brush with the sun.

Act One   Rise & Fall

Chapter 1   Buddy Russ & Miss Lucinda
Chapter 2   Perfect Day for Banana Hammocks
Chapter 3   Showdown & Shining Achievement
Chapter 4   The Scarlet Lamb
Chapter 5   La Goulue, Save Venice, Doubles
Chapter 6   Young Frick & Victoria's Frost
Chapter 7   The Photo
Chapter 8   Recklessness & Reckoning
Chapter 9   The Season's It Girls Announced
Chapter 10   The Walkers Take Manhattan
Chapter 11   The List

Act Two   The Players

Chapter 12   Judge's Call of Duty
Chapter 13   Victoria Stokes
Chapter 14   Maxwell Gloats
Chapter 15   Scarlet Floats
Chapter 16   Moomba Found
Chapter 17   Jet Set Exposed
Chapter 18   Scarlet Rises, Victoria Reigns
Chapter 19   Lucy & The Wonder Ball

Act Three   Season in the Sun

Chapter 20   Into the Shining
Chapter 21   The Announcement
Chapter 22   Flea Market Affair
Chapter 23   Last Night at Moomba
Chapter 24   The Photo Reveals
Chapter 25   Myths & Muses at NYY Ballet Gala

Act One

Rise & Fall

I had taken two finger-bowls of champagne, and the scene had changed before my eyes into something significant, elemental, and profound.

F. Scott Fitzgerald

Chapter 1

Buddy Russ, Lucinda Walker

December 25, 1999

Judge barreled down Lee County Road 154, letting the heavy sedan shake the cobwebs out of her engine. He pulled a drag from a cigarette and then used it to mime a little drum solo on the black steering wheel. He adjusted the side mirror and opened the sunroof. The sun flooded the interior of the twenty-year-old Mercedes promoting a thin layer of dust on the dashboard. In the glare of this new light he checked his reflection in the rearview mirror. Good, but too pale, he thought, New York ghostly.

It must be seventy-five degrees by now, he reckoned. "CNN says it's sixteen degrees in New York City," his little sister Clarkson announced that morning. "God Bless Alabama," he'd responded sleepily. It actually felt good to be home and in the country. He was surprised that he was so content and relaxed.

Judge pressed the buttons to open all the windows on his old car and shifted into fourth gear. This was his car from college that sat un-driven and unloved in his mother's garage most of the time. The Auburn University decal was still in the back window, the one he picked up at the university bookstore when his uncle handed down this car to him his sophomore year. The black 240D was his jack-booted pride and he now remembered how much he loved driving the old tank. He wrapped the memory around him of this car and those times and wanted to hear something to make the trip in his mind complete. He fished in the door pocket for a cassette tape, the pocket a potluck of memory. He landed on a beat-up white cassette with the name Alabama barely legible and snapped it into the player. The tune blared through the back speakers and he couldn't believe this is where the tape had last played.

> My home's in Alabama.
>
> No matter where I lay my head.
>
> My home's in Alabama.
>
> Southern born and southern bred.

He careened through the countryside of alternating cattle farms and pine forests, eager to see his old bud Russ and smoke a joint. The much dreaded Christmas was behind him now and it wasn't horrible. The family opened the presents and gorged on the orgy of food and he was now free to visit his friends. He thought back over the morning and smiled to himself.

Judge re-wound the Alabama song and sang it over and over until he got closer to town. When he arrived at the main road, he turned the volume down. Since the windows were open, he didn't want anyone to hear what he was listening to. He fished around the door pocket for another tape and found one marked Cool Tunes, black sharpie on masking tape. He ejected Alabama and chunked it in the floor board and popped in the second tape. It was a Dave Matthews song.

Judge joined Dave on the stage in his mind, singing full-throttle loud until he rolled up on the edge of town. Again he reached for the volume, lowered it and searched through the windshield for something familiar. He turned right onto Eighth Street at the Historic Downtown Ophelia sign and rolled through the three blocks of dilapidated houses to the edge of downtown. Today being Christmas, the bright and cloudless sky cast a particular loneliness on the antique brick streets. But lonely was not in him today. It was as if someone had left the door open just for him to look around and he liked the fact that no one was there to disturb him, not a person, not a vehicle, not even a stray dog.

He punched the accelerator, shifted into higher gear and continued up Eighth Street across the railroad tracks and up the hill into the historic district. He was on his way to Russell Walker's house like it was eleventh grade and nothing had changed between them, or him and this town. He pulled the car into the driveway of the Walker's stately old antebellum house; big white Corinthian columns guarded the place like Confederate soldiers. He expanded into a greater sense of home, more than he'd felt when he pulled into his own driveway two days before. He jogged up the stairs and opened the heavy, creaking door and smelled the melody of holiday scents: the fourteen-foot tree in the parlor and the miles of cedar garland over every door, mantle and banister; the cinnamon from the kitchen won over the other smells of meats and casseroles; and finally, the unmistakable Walker's family smell, potpourri that Mrs. Walker stashed in bowls and plates and vases all over the house, managed to rise above the other smells and stake its claim in his memory.

The lady of the house -- Lucinda Walker -- rounded the corner on her way up the stairs and stopped dead in her tracks, her face lighting into an expression of pleasant surprise. Mrs. Forrest Walker was a five foot four peacock of a woman with naturally brown hair she had to dye only every other month, which she wore shoulder length and carelessly styled. Judge remembered from the time he could notice such things that she was always incredibly turned out. While most of the other women in town succumbed to the plantation diets of their maids, Lucinda Walker always minced her little meals with tiny little forks. She maintained a figure so dainty that her maid tried to stir bacon fat into every dish to fatten her up in fear that she might blow away. But she did breeze about. Her tiny feet scurried quail-like from corner to corner, barely touching the floor as she moved. Judge had always basked in the generosity of her admiration.

On this day, Christmas day, Lucinda Walker wore brown and crimson plaid trousers and a grey cashmere twin set, a halo of heirloom pearls at her neck. She stood there staring at Judge and her expression of wonder soon melted into sheer joy as she put down a straw basket overflowing with Christmas cards and colorful ribbons.

"Judge Mender! As I live and breathe!" She rushed toward him and hugged him and kissed him on the cheek. Judge inhaled her scent deeply and smelled the good and decent past.

"My goodness, just look at you," she said. "You're a grown man, more handsome than ever. I swear you look more like your dear gorgeous daddy every time I see you!"

She stood back, at arm's length and looked him over from head to toe. "Russ! Mimi! You all get down here and see what Saint Nicholas has delivered to our parlor!" she yelled up the stairs as she pulled him to the kitchen toward the back of the house. "Let's have a drink. This occasion calls for champagne."

"If I remember correctly, even the opening of the mail at Walker House is an occasion that calls for champagne," Judge said with affection.

"Well, don't tell all you know, Judge Mender," Lucinda said, "The Baptists would call for a lynching. Besides, there are a few cultured men left in the world who appreciate a woman of fine tastes and charming eccentricities."

"I hope to be counted in their number," he said, his heart swelling with every second passed.

"You've always been my number one admirer, Judge," she said as she strode down the hallway, her chestnut hair impeccable, even in motion. "Lord, why is it whenever there's a handsome man in the house, I start to babble like Blanche DuBois? Damn that Tennessee Williams for making our language so poetic."

Judge followed her into the kitchen and still more memories flooded over him and almost tripped him. He had spent his adolescence in this kitchen. Lucinda Walker and this house had been his refuge when his father died and his mother had shocked the town by marrying the shiftless Ranson three months later. When life was not going in the direction he wanted it to, he found home in this house and in this kitchen.

"Where's Birdie?" Judge said, figuring to find the Walker's maid at the stove where she always stood, especially in his memoir of this house.

"Oh, she spends Christmas with her daughter in Montgomery. She will be beside herself that she missed you."

"Please give her my love," Judge said wandering around the room, smiling as he found clay molds of all of the Walker children's hand prints on the wall next to the door, his own pair holding equal space with those of the Walker's. He read the carved inscription. Judge Mender, Fifth Grade, 1982. He placed his hands on top of the smaller ones in the clay. "It would have been nice to see her."

Lucinda closed the refrigerator and handed Judge a bottle of Moet Chandon to open. She plucked two crystal flutes from a silver tray on the counter. Only Lucinda Walker would have a sterling silver tray full of crystal flutes ready for company at Christmas, he noted admiringly.

"So tell me how it feels to be a big shot big city journalist." She held the base of the flutes waiting to be filled. "I've kept up with you, you know."

Judge flashed on another memory of seeing Jet Set for the first time in this kitchen. He reckoned she had been a subscriber since the magazine started.

"Is that a fact?" he said toasting her and noticing the dance in her eyes. "And what do you think of my little career?"

"I love it!" she pronounced grandly. "I tell everyone who'll listen that you are a smashing success and I am responsible for making you such a snob. I knew a few of my keen observations were bound to rub off on you if you hung around long enough. It was inevitable."

Judge laughed and took a long swig of champagne. "You were my first taste of pompous high society, you know."

"Well, be sure to thank me in the book when it's written."

"Without a doubt."

Lucinda pulled up a stool and perched elegantly on the edge. She pulled a cigarette out of an ivory case on the island and waited for a light. Judge quickly produced his lighter and extended the flame.

"Now, tell me," she said and exhaled a long plume of smoke. "Who is this Chase Peters and where is he now?"

The kitchen door swung open and Russell Walker bounded through.

"Well, if it isn't a carpet baggin' Yankee right here in our own kitchen."

"Hey, buddy." Judge turned and the two embraced, affection overflowing.

Russ finished hugging Judge with three slaps on the back and pulled back to look him over.

"Oh damn," Lucinda said. "I had hoped for a few minutes of gossip before the bruising bear descended on us."

"Lord, has mama got you drinking that sissy champagne?" Russ sidled up to his mother and kissed her on the cheek. "Let's have a man's drink, goddammit. You still take a scotch, Judge, or you too high falutin' to be seen without a champagne glass?"

"You pour the scotch, buddy," Judge laughed. "I'll drink it."

"Russ, let poor Judge drink his champagne. We were celebrating his triumphant return." Lucinda said as she winked at Judge and adjusted her pearls.

"Oh forget all that. Here." Russ shoved a clinking scotch-filled glass into Judge's hand and removed the champagne flute from the other. He looked Judge up and down and said, "What the hell are you wearing?"

Judge flushed. He looked down and saw that he was wearing a black cashmere Prada v-neck, dark blue Helmut Lang jeans and black Tod's driving shoes.

"What are those? Sissy shoes?"

"You leave Judge alone, Russ. Those are Mister J.P. Tod's fine Italian driving shoes," Lucinda said as she cocked her head to await Judge's acknowledgement.

"Well, you better leave those things to the eye-talians because we're about to stomp in some mud."

"I'll be fine, Russ." Judge said. "If you remember, I'm the one who jumps over the mud. You're the one who always fell in,"

"Oh, that's right. Russ do you remember the time…" Lucinda started.

"Yeah, yeah, yeah. We all remember," Russ interrupted. "Come on, Judge, let's go out back."

"I'll let you go, Judge, only if you promise to reconnoiter with me before you skip town for another five years."

He kissed her on the cheek. "I promise, Miss Lucinda."

Judge followed Russ out the back door, across the deep porch and down the back stairs.

"You boys come back before dark." she said as they hit the bottom of the stairs. "I don't want to have to get a call from Sheriff Tate again."

"Ha ha, mama." Russ said. "We're not thirteen anymore."

"We'll see," she said. "Don't think I don't know what you're going to do. I still think it's best to mow the grass, not smoke it." She turned and went back into the kitchen to finish her champagne.

Judge raised his head and spotted the tree house at the edge of the winter woods and felt thirteen years old again.

"I can't believe that thing is still in one piece." Judge said.

"What you talking about?" Russ said. "You don't trust our tree-house building skills?"

"Yeah, dude. I know you're a big shit contractor now, but back then we weren't so great at swinging the hammers. If I remember right we were stoned most of the time."

"True dat. I guess it is a miracle it's still here. Hell, we've even had a couple of hurricanes through here. You know what, bud? I'm a damn good builder."

Russ shot up the ladder and bounced through the door in the floor. Judge followed him up and took a seat Indian style across from him on the plywood floor. Russ was already firing up a joint and inhaling deeply when Judge closed the door between them. Russ passed the joint to Judge and he took a long, slow drag.

"So what are we doing tonight?" Judge exhaled and passed the joint back to him.

"Having a party, dude." Russ took the joint. "The parents are going to the Curry's and we have the place until midnight. We'll do some shots and raise some hell here then go over to Harry's."

Judge noticed a faded but legible red magic marker scrawl on the ceiling. Leigh was here. Party On!

"Good God!" he said as he passed the joint to Russ and got to his feet. "This can't be from that night, can it?" He said examining the writing, which was millimeters from his nose, the ceiling height measured for thirteen-year-olds, not twenty-seven.

"What are you talking about?" Russ said, inhaling and holding.

"That night, summer of eighth grade when Robert brought that girl home from Tuscaloosa," Judge said almost trance-like.

"Oh dude. That was the greatest night of my young life," Russ said, stretching his arms wide against the tree house walls. "Man, that was my first real blow job, you know. I think about that night sometimes."

"Man, I haven't thought about that night in years." Judge said, as he rubbed his hand over the scrawl like it was Braille and his rubbing would release more details.

"What a kinky skank she used to be, huh?" Russ said and tapped Judge on the leg to pass the joint. Judge sat down and took the smoking stick.

"Kinky skank? What are you talking about?"

"Dude, she was, like, twenty and she was my brother's girlfriend home for a weekend to meet my parents. And she shimmies up the ladder when he goes to sleep to blow two thirteen year olds camping out in a tree house."

"Well, when you put it that way," Judge laughed. "It does seem a little tawdry."

"Hot as hell, though. I still jack off to that skank."

"I wonder where she is now," Judge said as he took the joint from Russ.

"Don't have to wonder no further, dude," Russ said. "She married Harry Watson and moved back here to Ophelia. Hell, she's a Bible thumper now, always preaching about somebody going to hell. Whenever I hear about her preaching on somebody, I think, yeah, you didn't talk so much with my knob in your mouth."

Judge laughed hard in the middle of an inhale and started choking so hard his eyes started shedding tears.

"Don't cry, Judgie. I'm sure you'll get a blowjob once more before you die." Russ punched Judge hard on the arm and lifted the door in the floor and descended to the ladder. "Come on, I need a drink. Hey, are you going to be here for New Year's? We're all going up to the lake house. Hell, everyone's going. Even Lella. She divorced Jason last year, you know. Jesus, have you even talked to her since you've been back?"

"I haven't talked to her since I moved to New York."

"You're kidding; you haven't talked to her in, what? five years? You were on the verge of getting' hitched, man. How crazy is that? You ever think what your life would've been like if you'd married Lella?" Russ started walking out of the woods toward the house.

Judge hadn't thought about Lella since he escaped to New York. Now the memory warmed him like a fever. He remembered the weekends and summers at the lake with Lella and he took off on a magic carpet. They were the best times of his life, he thought, and Lella, well Lella was the first girl who saved him from himself.

"Judge. Yo, Judge, you in there?" Russ stopped in the yard and Judge continued walking past him, lost in a recollection. 'Hey, Judge!" he shouted.

Judge stopped and turned around. "What?"

"Are you stoned? I was telling you about New Year's at the lake. You gone be around?"

"Nah, man." Judge said. "I'm going to South Beach tomorrow and then Palm Beach for New Year's."

"Well hootie hoot hoot. What's going on down there?"

"Just some friends and a little work."

"Man, tell me about the women," Russ said. "I want to hear about the women."

Judge smiled. "Man, you wouldn't know what to do with yourself."

"Yeah, I would. Tell me."

"No, really." Judge said. "They are so damn beautiful and they dress, damn! you can't imagine the way they dress. I am continually amazed at the beauty that is woman. They all try to outdo each other and it is a fantasy to behold. Honestly, I think their beauty makes us better men."

"That sounds like pure poetry," Russ said dreamily. He stopped and was trying to picture what Judge was saying. "And hot, huh? You gettin' your share?"

"Yeah, I do alright."

"Yeah, dude." Russ punched Judge in the arm again. "You always were a pussy magnet. We're going to get laid tonight."

They loped back up the stairs and into the house and Lucinda Walker sat on her perch at the island in the kitchen pouring champagne for Mimi, the youngest Walker.

"And here he comes now," Lucinda announced.

"Oh my God! Judge Mender!" Mimi squealed and ran up and threw her arms around his neck. "You look hot."

Judge hugged her tightly, noticing that she had filled out nicely since the last time he saw her.

"Look at you, Little Mims. How old are you now?" Judge said admiring her.

"Nineteen. I'm finally old enough for you."

"Mimi! Stop flirting with poor Judge," Lucinda said. "It's too early in the day."

"Where are you in school?" Judge asked.

"Alabama."

"She pledged Kappa, just like her mama." Lucinda boasted.

"Did I have a choice?" Mimi said to Judge.

"You must be having a blast right now." Judge said.

"Yeah, I love it. They love me up there and mama's too far away to get on my nerves."

"Not too far away to check on her though." Lucinda said. "I have my spies on the Capstone."

"That's the damn truth," Russ said. "For one skinny little southern lady, mama sure gets some inside information. She made my life hell in college."

"Who're you kidding?" Judge said. "We were hellions."

The four of them stood there laughing and drinking and a warm wave rose in Judge that found its origin in scotch and marijuana, but crashed over him in the affection of this family.

"Well isn't this a charming reunion of the old gang?" Lucinda said, happy to have all of her children back in her kitchen.

"Yeah, and it's just getting started," Russ said slapping Judge on the back. "It is just getting started. Yee ha!"

"Yee ha!' Judge yelped with a laugh. "It's been a long time since I let out a rebel yell."

"Well, we got more work to do than I figured, Judgie boy. First you lose your southern accent and now you tell me you ain't rebel yelled? What's next? You goin' gay?"

"Why?" Judge said, imitating Russ's deep accent. "You feel yo'self attracted to me?"

"Yeah, baby doll." Russ said wrapping Judge in an embrace of exaggerated passion. "Gimme some of that Yankee love."

"Oh, you two. I always knew you'd end up together." Lucinda said then turned to Mimi with a raised eyebrow. "They were very close when they were boys."

"Ha ha ha," Russ said sarcastically, letting go of Judge. "Damn, boy. You did give me boner."

"Russ!" Lucinda screamed and laughed.

"Gross, Russ," Mimi said.

"Alright. I've got to get dressed." Lucinda said. "When the conversation denigrates into boners it is time for this woman to leave. Come here, Judge. Give me some sugar."

She hugged Judge tightly. He felt the best he'd felt in months.

"Good to see you, Miss Lucinda." He said with a smile. "I'll try to come by and see you before I leave tomorrow."

"No you won't." she said as she put her glass in the sink. "Y'all will be out all night raisin' Cain and you'll barely make your plane tomorrow. I'll see you when I see you. Who knows? I might just catch a plane to New York City and make you squire me around to some fancy parties." And she walked out the door.

"I'd like that!" he yelled after her.

"Me too, honey" she yelled from the hallway.

"I think your mama is a little drunk" Judge said to Mimi.

"I wish I was." Mimi answered.

"Well, hell." Russ said. "Stop standing around bumpin' gums and start drinking.

"What time is it?" Judge asked.

"Six o'clock," Mimi answered. "Why?"

"I was going to go home and change."

"Into what?" Russ asked. "more Eye-talian clothes? Fuck that. You can borrow some of my shit. I want to raise some hell tonight and don't want to have to worry about fightin' nobody 'cause they took you for a homo."

"Easy, Bubba." Judge said with a smile." I can still kick your country ass."

"Oh baby waby, Judgie." Russ said wrapping his arm around Judge's shoulders. "Don't get all defensive about your sissy clothes. They might be alright up in New York City, but down here we still dress like men with balls."

"I swear you too should just make out and get it over with." Mimi said downing her glass of champagne.

Russ ran around behind Mimi and grabbed her arms while Judge picked her off the ground by her feet, repeating a torture they had perfected from years of terrorizing Mimi.

"Y'all, put me down," she wailed. "Mama! Russ and Judge are messing with me!"

"Come on," Russ said. "Let's throw her in the pool."

"Maaaaaaaaaama!" Mimi screamed so loud that Judge started laughing uncontrollably and dropped her feet. Mimi turned and snatched away from Russ's grip and punched him as hard as she could on the arm. She then turned to Judge and said, "You're company tonight, Judge. That was your one freebie."

Chapter 2

A Perfect Day for Banana Hammocks

Judge idled at the curb outside of the Miami airport, taking sweet time smoking a cigarette. He wasn't in any hurry to catch the cab to Maxwell's place. He'd never been to Miami or South Beach and after five winters in New York, he understood why so many New Yorkers came down. Even here, in between the exhaust fumes of the covered airport drive, he felt the tropical breeze's seduction. He hadn't been completely comfortable with the idea of making this trip. Judge only knew Maxwell in the Manhattan party-circuit style: telephone calls and black-tie parties, dinners at trendy restaurants and gallery openings. Now he would be Maxwell's house guest, and they would see each other morning, noon, and night. Maxwell promised him solitude and it was only when Maxwell informed him that his room would be in a separate residence next door to Maxwell's own, did Judge confirm. "You'll have your own residence with your very own entrance, Lord Mender," Maxwell teased. "You will only see me at cocktail hour, which in your case will be quite often."

Judge stubbed out the cigarette in the little pebbles of the ash can, threw his leather case in the trunk, and handed the driver the address. "2421 Lake Pancoast Drive, oh, the Helen Mar," the driver grumbled gaily. "No problem."

As the taxi pulled away from the bustling concrete grid, a passionate sun filled the taxi. Judge opened the window and stuck his head out and his unruly hair danced and whipped his mouth, his ears, his nose. The racing air felt balmy on his face. He sucked in a mouthful and held it like a bong hit.

The taxi pulled up to the Helen Mar, and Judge was relieved to see that the place was one of the beautiful, old deco buildings and not one of the high rise monsters he'd feared. He called Maxwell from the taxi and was surprised to see him standing on the portico of the building, grinning and waving.

"Welcome to the Helen Mar!" he shouted. Maxwell was dressed in white linen, from head to toe, big Chanel sunglasses, a straw hat in the porkpie style and white Gucci loafers. He was already much tanned from the weeks he'd been in residence. From his exuberant appearance, Judge gathered that he was ready for some company. "How was Dixieland? How was the flight? Don't you hate flying commercial? It's a terrible shame that Victoria's father's plane wasn't available."

"Hello, Mr. Jones," Judge broadcast grandly, "What a beautiful place. And the weather!" The driver placed his case on the sidewalk and Judge paid the man and picked up his case and followed Maxwell through the lobby.

"This is the famous lobby were Valentino used to waltz through after a night of concupiscent carousing. And Greta Garbo! She lived on the top floor for years. She may still be up there for all we know. I swear she faked her death just to throw us off the scent."

"Only you would buy a place because Greta Garbo was cosseted away in it." Judge said, admiring the lobby.

"The pool is just past those doors. But let's get you settled first. Are you hungry? What time is it? I lose all track of the day down here, and I wouldn't have it any other way. Tell me all the gossip in New York since I've been gone."

Judge filled him in on all the news. There wasn't much to relay since most people left town after the Winter Wonderland Ball and New York had felt deserted. At least as far as their crowd was concerned.

The style of Maxwell's apartment was high bachelor -- if perhaps the term bachelor should be set off in quotation marks, Judge mused to himself as if her were writing the place up for Jet Set. The snippy tone of his recent writings was seeping into his private editorial. He wondered whether this was positive portent or if he was becoming what he feared most, an effete aesthete. Then he wondered what would be the harm in striking that pose. This weekend he would ape the manners of his host, the ultimate aesthete in the Oscar Wilde tradition. This would be an opportunity to walk around in different skin for the weekend. After all, he would have to return to himself soon enough in Palm Beach as Victoria's house guest. This would be amusing.

"I bought this place for nothing a few years ago," Maxwell continued. "You can't imagine what disrepair the old girl had fallen into. While the Euro trash and piss-elegant queens were discovering South Beach, this sweet little gem of a building was crumbling away. Can you imagine? One of my clients had owned this entire floor, during the heyday, of course, and was too old to endure the renovation process, so I picked it up for a song. I don't have to tell you that it has quadrupled in value in seven short years. Quadrupled! Can you imagine?"

Judge took note. White walls and a painted white concrete floor were the canvas, painted on by Zebra skins and other African pelts from an animal that Judge couldn't immediately identify lay systematically strewn on the floor. There was an enormous silver mirror above the mantle, climbing the wall to the twelve foot ceiling. Two gilded French torchieres with gilded flames spitting skyward flanked each side. A cream canvas sofa abutted two worn brown club chairs seated across from each other, punctuated with Jonathan Adler pillows. In the center, a low white marble table was piled high with glossy photo books. The vignette was crowned with a towering white orchid above yet another, taller stack of books. There were windows around the room, and the shades were pulled high to reveal the buildings next door, the pool and the canal beyond and finally, a glimpse of the ocean through the high rises across the canal. Through the double glass doors was a wrap around terrace overlooking the pool with teak furniture shaded by the umbrella-like leaves of towering banana plants in oversized terra cotta pots. It was a tropical dream unlike anything he'd ever felt and Judge allowed himself to breathe deeper, inhaling something he wasn't quite sure of but growing ever more comfortable in this exotic climate.

As Maxwell's narration continued unabated, Judge followed him next door to the guest apartment which was decorated in a similar style on a smaller scale. Judge laid his weary case down just inside the door and exhaled, exhausted but content.

"I'll leave you to unpack and freshen up before you come over for cocktails. Are you hungry?" Maxwell beamed. "I am so glad you're here. We are going to have such a grand time."

"I'm glad to be here; thank you for having me, Maxwell," Judge said with gratitude. "I'm not terribly hungry, so drinks will do nicely, thank you. I'll be over in say, twenty minutes?"

"Perfect. See you then. This is going to be such fun. I can't wait to show you my little paradise." As Maxwell closed the door Judge was already prostrate on the bed falling into a spell.

Judge knocked on the door of Maxwell's main apartment and waited for him to open the door. The door swung open wide and Maxwell had experienced a costume change. He now wore a very oversize, white terry robe with his initials swirled in hot pink on the breast pocket. He wore matching white terry slippers with the same colorful monogram and a crown of oversize Chanel sunglasses perched on his slick-haired head.

Judge laughed as Maxwell stood back and struck a pose.

"Well, hello, Madame Jones," Judge managed between laughing. "I can honestly say you have never looked gayer."

Maxwell pouted disappointment. "Didn't you find your gift?"

"What gift?" Judge asked.

"I purchased this identical look for you, too. It's in the box on the little gold chair in the bathroom, along with a very sexy bathing costume."

"Oh, well I'll have to trot back over and check it out before I go down to the pool."

"But wait!" Maxwell opened his robe with a flourish and he flashed a skimpy swimsuit with an animal print and gold chains. He put a leg forward, model style, and held the pose. "I got you one of these!"

Judge burst into laughter. "There is no way in hell I am going to wear a banana hammock, Maxwell."

"Banana hammock?" Maxwell said deflated. "I swear sometimes you are still such a hick from Dog Patch. It's not a banana hammock, darling. It's Versace!"

"Well, la tee da, but I repeat. There is no way in hell I am wearing a Speedo."

"But Judge, I got you a red one. I knew you'd poo poo the pink and green."

"I'm flattered that you know me so well, and I thank you for your generosity, but my Vilebrequin will do just fine."

Judge laughed again as Maxwell cinched his robe in mock disgust. He scuttled behind the bar and presented a pink frozen drink in a large martini glass with a pink orchid on the rim for decoration. "Ta da!"

Judge looked at the proffered drink in his hand.

"Here, have a fagarita." Maxwell handed the concoction to Judge.

"And the drink just made it gayer," Judge laughed, took a sip and smacked his lips. "Do I eat the flower?"

"Only if you want to die," Maxwell said. "Not because it's poisonous, but because I'm test driving this new drink for a dinner party tomorrow night, and those orchids are impossible to find at this time of year."

"Well, it's beautiful. And delicious."

"Thank you. Are you hungry? There's a cold mini buffet on the bar and, well, that's it really. All we ever do down here is drink. You shouldn't have a problem with that."

"That will be fine," Judge said as he looked over the bar. "So what's on the agenda today? There is an agenda, I presume."

"Absolutely not!" Maxwell shouted as he adjusted an orchid on a different glass, stood back and pursed his lips. "Too much? Don't answer. So, I thought you might enjoy the pool this afternoon. It's very nice. Or the beach if you prefer, but I am not a beach person. You're on your own over there. Sand and squealing kids are not my idea of a pleasant afternoon."

"And yet you own a place in South Beach, go figure." Judge took another taste of the drink. "The pool sounds nice. I actually might take a nap."

"A nap? Good lord! And technically, we are on Miami Beach. South Beach starts just across the canal. You can sense a discernible drop in class."

"Well, I'm exhausted, but I promise I will give you Judge concentrate tonight. I will entertain to beat the band."

"Beat the band?" Maxwell teased. "Good Lord, that's even too corny for me. At any rate, I thank you for your gift of yourself."

Maxwell stooped down under the counter then said, "Oh, wait, I forgot to tell you. I have a few friends coming over soon and they'll be joining us for dinner. We'll be at the pool, but we will not disturb you."

"That's fine," Judge said a little disappointed. "I really only need a half an hour to recharge. I'll be fine." He picked at the cold cuts and cheeses. "These olives are amazing. So who's coming?"

"Well, let's see. There's Gilles Dumond and his lover, Pierre de Carre. Bruce Babo and his gorgeous new boy toy, that new Polo Ralph Lauren model, what is his name? And I think John Marco is coming with his boyfriend du jour and, ta da! My date for the week arrives today."

"Your date? Well, when the cat's away and the mouse is frolicking on the beach…"

"I believe you know him. He works for me. His name is Caleb Johnson."

"Caleb Johnson? No, I don't think I do."

"You'll recognize him when you see him." Maxwell flashed a grin so wide his eyes closed, but Judge didn't see it. He had turned and walked out the door.

Judge found an empty pool deck scattered with white chaises longues circling the perimeter. It was now after three in the afternoon. He figured most of the residents were at lunch or off at the beach. He found a chair in the direct sun and shucked the robe Maxwell had laid out for him. The sun felt good on his body. He looked at himself stretched out in the chair. He punched his solid stomach with the bottom of his fists and felt good about his body.

His eyes drooped and he laid his head back and lowered his shades to shut out the season, the season that had started with such promise and high hopes and had now turned to exhausted routine. He had returned to New York fully charged in September and was ready to dive into his work. He recounted the continual nights of parties and stressed-out hung-over deadlines. The Winter Ball almost killed him. Judge didn't sleep that night as he struggled through a cocaine-jacked drunk to finish the story. He felt like he hadn't slept in months. Even in Ophelia, Russ had him on the run. His last night at home had ended this morning at daybreak when Russ drove him to the Atlanta airport. He closed his eyes and was asleep in five minutes.

Judge was awakened by a whoop, and he raised his heavy head to see Maxwell and company clucking out of the lobby, onto the pool deck. They were all wearing the identical robes and slippers, carrying the same silly pink drink like torches of a haughty mob. Judge lifted his sunglasses and propped up on his elbows as they approached his side of the pool.

"Lord, give us strength," Judge said as Maxwell plopped down in the chair beside him.

"Don't judge, Judgie. Line up, everyone, let me introduce you to my famous house guest, Mr. Judge Mender."

Judge stood up and shook hands with each as Maxwell said the name. Pleased to meet you. Pleased to meet you. Pleased to meet you. Judge sat back down in the chair and Maxwell handed him a drink.

"Ah, you brought me a fagarita," Judge said. "How thoughtful." The men shucked their robes and they all, to a man, were wearing the same Versace bikini that Maxwell had modeled.

Maxwell screamed. "Glorious. We look like a Busby Berkley musical. Where is Esther Williams?" he shouted.

Judge thought, thank God no one else is on this pool deck.

"Gilles, would not you kill to see this gorgeous boy in one of these Versace's?" Maxwell said motioning to Judge.

"Oui!" Gilles poofed. "He has very nice legs. He should show them off." Gilles returned to smoothing out his towel on the chair, fabric stretched across his double-wide French ass.

"He refuses to wear one," Maxwell pouted. "He calls them banana hammocks."

Judge saw their faces scrunch up as they figured out the slang. The Americans laughed first, then, whispering to the Frenchmen, causing a small sensation on the pool deck.

"Banana hammock! Ah ha! ha, banana hammock."

"God, take me now," Judge mumbled to himself. How would he get through the next two days? He began to reassess his earlier discovery. This wasn't such as escape as he'd hoped. Maxwell was so relentlessly social that this was the same drive just a different cast. This was his homo high society, the one he did not mix with in New York. Maybe he'd call Victoria and head up to Palm Beach one day early. Damn, he didn't have a car, he remembered. He settled in his chair and pulled his shades over his eyes. Oh, the oppression of being a house guest, he sighed. He lifted the pink drink in the air and toasted the Versace mob.

"Here's to a perfect day for banana hammocks," Judge said to himself.

The sun waned with Judge nodding and joining the conversation only when directly addressed. He glided off to sleep again, the chuckle and clucking of the poolside posse notwithstanding. He couldn't help himself and he knew he was quickly approaching rude -- or at the least ill-bred -- but he couldn't keep his head up or his eyes open. Maybe someone on the plane slipped a roofie in my drink. He laughed at the thought but inspected the French men to see if they were ogling him. In and out of sleep he nodded as the sun disappeared behind one of the taller buildings. The ocean breeze took a turn for the cooler.

"You gorgeous boy. Look everyone! It's Caleb come to treat us all with his heroic physique." Maxwell shouted as Judge jarred into waking. Caleb was smiling and waving as he strode on to the pool deck wearing black board shorts and sunglasses. Judge watched as all the pink posse adjusted themselves and waited for this treat of the trade. Judge slipped into envy for a moment. Up to that moment, Judge and the Polo model were the beauties at the pool, catching the lip licks and eyebrow dances. Now, Caleb pulled all focus and Judge wondered if he shouldn't go up and try on the Versace.

Caleb came astride Maxwell and lifted him off the ground like a stocky bride across the threshold. All of the men clapped and hooted. Maxwell fluttered down to the ground then twisted his mouth in a little pout and said, "Caleb. You didn't put on your present. I can accept that from Judge, but not from you. Back up stairs this instance and put on the Versace."

Caleb stepped back from the group and untied the black ribbon at the waist of his board shorts. A symphony of giggles and gasps went up from the gallery like tiny bubbles from a champagne flute. Caleb gave the waist of the suit a yank and pushed them to his ankles and kicked them over Maxwell's head. There, in all its big basket glory, was the Versace bikini.

Squeals, whoops, claps and bravos peppered the air in a fireworks of approbation as Maxwell stepped up to give the boy a hug. "Thank you, for the suspense. And the show!" Maxwell then turned to the group, his arm wrapped hopefully around Caleb's firm muscled waist. "Gentlemen, the incomparable Caleb Johnson." Maxwell shot Judge a side look then went back inside to fetch more drinks. Judge closed his eyes and tried to drift, but in less than a minute he felt a bump and the sensation of skin on skin, and Caleb was sitting next to him, on the edge of his chair, his muscular thigh brushing against Judge's side.

"Hey, Judge. You remember me?"

"Hey, Caleb," Judge said without turning his head or opening his eyes. "That was quite a show."

"Well, they seem to love it, and it doesn't hurt to give out some little thrills. Besides, Maxwell's good to me. I know he appreciates a show."

"That's the understatement of the week."

"So, you hung-over or what?" Caleb said as he stood up, realizing Judge wasn't as enthralled with his semi-strip tease as were the others.

"Something like that. I'll be livelier later. I'm sure Maxwell has something extravagant planned."

"Alright." Caleb snapped to attention and stood up. "Good to see you, dude."

"Yeah, you too."

Judge slept a few more minutes until the men began yelping and splashing into the pool. Caleb organized a volleyball game, of sorts. Judge managed to slip off the deck without drawing too much attention and slipped into his room undetected.

He heard the rat a tat tat of Maxwell's knock at the door, it was nine o'clock. He'd slept for four hours. Jesus, I'm groggy. He opened the door and there stood Maxwell in a turquoise shirt and yellow pants with a pink belt, his extended hand offered a tiny, steaming cup of espresso.

"Wake up, Judgie Boy. Dinner's in an hour and you'll need to pull yourself together."

"You didn't drop a roofie in here, did you?" He couldn't think why he would be so groggy.

"What the hell is a roofie?" Maxwell stepped around Judge and into the apartment. It was pitch black because he'd passed out at five. "Good God, Dracula, turn on some lights in here."

Maxwell clucked around the room switching on lamps, pulling down shades, fluffing up pillows. In five minutes the place looked like the center-fold of Metropolitan Home.

"Get dressed," Maxwell said. "We eat at ten. I can't wait to get your opinion on this new chef I'm test driving tonight."

He waltzed back out the door, shutting it behind him. Judge stared at the closed door, then the steaming coffee cup, the well-lighted room with the fluffed, plush pillows and smiled with wonder. A shower, a shave and a crisp white shirt later, Judge knocked on the door of Maxwell's apartment and found himself face to face with Caleb.

"Hey." Judge said and brushed past him.

"Hey," Caleb said, bemused, and let him pass.

Maxwell's guests were seated around a big round table in the middle of the room that heretofore had held piles of books and a huge candelabrum. Now it was set for a casually elegant dinner for ten bachelors in a stylish condo on Miami Beach.

"Judge! You're alive!" Maxwell stood and swept his arms wide and directed Judge to the empty chair. "And how handsome you look with all that south Florida sun."

"Hello, everyone," Judge said. "I apologize for my tardiness."

"Oh, it's okay, Judge. I've explained to everyone your grueling social schedule and that you are here to rest before it all cranks up again in the New Year." Maxwell sat and motioned for the server to bring them the first course.

"I don't see how you do eet." said Gilles. "I mean, all dose pahties. Eet would make me tres fat tee gay. Bon. Eef I were you, I would keel myself."

"Oh, Gilles!" Maxwell said. "You have such a way with our language."

Judge looked tenderly at Maxwell. This was the Maxwell he'd never seen: relaxed, funny, flamboyant, yes, but sweeter and warmer. He seemed to expand here in this hothouse environment away from the cold calculations in Manhattan. This was where he can finally be himself, Judge thought. He was surrounded by his real friends, and he didn't have to cater to their every whim. Yet he did take care of them. He treated all of the visitors at his table -- especially Judge -- like guests at a grand hotel, every need taken care of before one could think to remember what he needed. Judge looked at Maxwell who listened intently to some inane story from the Polo model and Judge thought, I should remember to tell him how good he is.

The party finished dinner with a round of quiet applause, and Gilles told Maxwell the new caterer was worth whatever dimes he paid him. They adjourned, with some of the party taking up residence on the terrace, while the younger men, Caleb, Polo Boy, and Judge, settled into the deep cushions of the sofa and began drinking the barrage of concoctions Caleb chucked their way.

"Try this," he said and thrust a caramel colored drink in a shot glass in front of them. "It's called a buttery nipple."

"Here. A red-headed slut."

"A Blow Job."

"Up All Night."

"Sex on the Beach."

Maxwell crossed behind the sofa on his way to the loo and yelled, "Who's having sex on the beach?" The boys erupted in unrestrained giggling and Judge realized, momentarily, how silly they must look, but then, he didn't care.

"I'm going skinny dipping!" Polo Boy shouted as he stood, ripped off his shirt and headed to the door.

"I'm with you," followed Caleb. "You coming, Judge?"

"Have fun!" yelled Judge after them as the door slammed.

Maxwell came back into the room. "Goodness! What is all that ruckus?"

"The boy toys just went skinny dipping." Judge said laughing at nothing.

"Why didn't you chase after them?" Maxwell said as he sat down next to him.

"Because," he said and turned the shot glass up to get the last drop of sex on the beach.

"Because...?" Maxwell pursued and lifted the shot glass to his nose and took a big sniff.

"Because I'm on holiday and I am not getting drunk and carousing until dawn." He slammed the shot glass down on the low wooden table.

"I hate to break this to you, darling pie, but you are already drunk." Maxwell mimicked Judge and slammed the shot glass on the table. "You might as well carouse until dawn."

"I don't think I can." Judge said, absently spinning the shot glass.

"Well. You're on holiday, you may do as your heart desires." Maxwell sighed.

Judge leaned up and kissed him on the cheek. "I think you're the most interesting person I know, a real sweetheart." He slurred, drunken yet sincere.

Maxwell laughed. "I can't think of a finer compliment from a finer gentleman. Even if you are three sheets to the wind, I'll take it as it was intended." Maxwell stood up to return to his guests on the terrace. "Do you want to join us on the lanai, frolic with the bucks in the pool or stay where you are?"

"Honestly?" Judge surprised himself. "I think I'll go to bed." He stood up unsteadily and kissed Maxwell on the cheek again and said goodnight.

Judge fumbled to the bed in the guest apartment, shucked his clothes on the floor and fell face first, naked on the bed. He fell deeply into sleep and didn't know what time it was when he felt a hot hand on his ass, and he jumped awake. "What the hell?!" he shouted and tried to find a light, fumbling under the lampshade.

"Hey, dude. It's okay. It's me. Caleb"

Judge jumped out of bed and turned on the light switch. There in the full blaze of bright light lay the irrepressible smile of Caleb in all his naked glory. "What's wrong?" Caleb said. "Come on. I'm horny."

"Caleb, first of all get the hell out of here. Second, what are you, high? You're Maxwell's guest and if you're horny, that's where you should be climbing into bed in the dark."

"Yeah, right. Like I'm gonna sleep with that old troll," Caleb said. "Stop hyperventilating and get over here and blow me."

Judge climbed back on the bed and Caleb smiled, "Yeah..."

Judge didn't slide in with him. Instead, he took his palms and, placed them on Caleb's sides and shoved him as hard as he could. The boy sailed off the bed and slammed into the closet making a loud clatter as the doors popped off the track and smacked the back wall. Judge jumped off the bed and stood over the dazed Caleb. Judge was red hot.

"If you ever talk that way about Maxwell again, I will beat the shit out of you." Judge sought to control himself. "You better make your excuses to him in the morning because I'm going to tell him to throw you out if you don't leave on your own. You're nothing but a shiftless hustler."

Caleb was getting to his feet and Judge stood there staring at him, the two of them naked and tense, like stags in the field. At that moment the front door swung open and Maxwell burst into the apartment, which offered an unobstructed view of the undressed goings on in the bedroom. "What happened? Is everything oh..."

Judge flushed with embarrassment and Caleb smiled in his sexy drunk haze.

"I'm sorry," Maxwell flustered, and turned around and went back through the door.

"Maxwell! Wait!" Judge shouted and ran after him into the hall. He got to Maxwell's door just as it slammed shut and he heard the lock turn and click.

"Come on, Maxwell, talk to me. It's not like that, I promise." Judge went back to his bedroom and Caleb was stretched out diagonally across the bed, rubbing his chest.

"Well, we're caught now, may as well enjoy the rest of the night." And he patted the empty space beside his naked thigh.

"Fuck you, dude."

Judge yanked the pillow from under Caleb's head and jerked the coverlet off the bed from under his legs. "You better be out of here in the morning. Or I'm selling you out to Maxwell and you'll not only be out of a vacation pad, but a sweet gig in Manhattan as well."

Judge curled up on the sofa. How did things get so fucked up he wondered?

The morning came and went and Judge awoke to a tap tap tap on the door. He stirred on the sofa, buried under a pile of pillows. He heard the door knob turn and the lock click and last night hit him in the face.

"Judge? Are you risen?" Maxwell poked his head around the half-closed door.

"Yeah, come on in." Judge sat up squinting and redirected one of the pillows to cover his nakedness.

Maxwell pushed the door open wide and bent down and brought up a tray. He whistled as he crossed the room and set the tray on the coffee table in front of Judge. There was coffee and toast and orange juice, all presented under a bright pink peony so perfect and round it looked like a long-haired Chihuahua. Maxwell handed Judge his sunglasses.

"Good morning, Mr. Mender. I trust you have finally caught up on your sleep?" Maxwell walked over to the blinds, which although closed offered little protection from the stampede of high noon.

"May I?" He reached for one of the blind's cord.

"Sure." Judge said as he sipped the coffee black and slid his shades on.

Maxwell pulled the blinds up one by one around the room then backtracked opening the windows wide. "It is an unbelievably beautiful day out there, time to rise and shine."

Judge gathered his strength, letting the coffee stir his nerve. "Maxwell…"

"So, Caleb came in this morning and told me what happened last night," Maxwell interrupted. "I apologize for my dramatic departure. I was a little drunk from all those cocktails by the pool and free flowing wine at dinner." Maxwell sat down in the chair opposite the sofa.

"What did he tell you?" Judge asked.

"He said he was drunk and when he came up from the pool, he went into the wrong bedroom. It was dark and he slid into bed with you and you jumped out of your skin and he hit the floor. It all sounds rather hilarious. Now he's gone to town to do the shopping for tonight's dinner. How do you feel?"

Judge looked at Maxwell and ¬¬-- for the first time -- felt sorry for him. He had never seen him so vulnerable. He looked so innocent and as preposterous as Caleb's excuse had been, Maxwell wanted to believe, had to believe that the boy he was courting would not humiliate him. He also had to believe that Judge wouldn't disrespect him in his own house.

"Yeah," Judge said. "He scared the hell out of me."

"Well, I guess there's a first time for everything," Maxwell said with relief. "Judge Mender kicking someone out of bed."

"Well, I guess there's a first time for everything." Judge imitated Maxwell, pursing his lips and smiling. Maxwell had put their world back in order and Judge silently agreed this was best.

Maxwell wanted to talk about the dinner from the night before and get Judge's impressions of his friends. They discussed the food and the wine and the anecdotes, all the while, Judge sat comfortably naked under a single pillow, drinking his coffee. Finally, Maxwell popped up and said. "Okay. Time to get ready. I want to go into Bal Harbor today see if the new Gucci slide came in. You may come with me, though I know you detest shopping and Gucci even more. Or you can lounge by the pool and soak up the sun. I'm leaving in twenty minutes, so tap on my door when you decide." Maxwell closed the door behind him.

Judge began to think about how little he really knew about the people he called his friends. Was it a New York way of life that he was only beginning to see the machination? The people he ran with were polite and amusing and witty and great dinner companions, but were any of them real friends? His relationships with people used to be just that: real. Now he was surprised when he felt emotion or vulnerability in one of them, or the discovery of real character. When did his requirements for friendship get turned inside out?

Chapter 3

Coconut Showdown & A Shining Achievement

Judge excused himself from the lunch table early. The tables on the deck of the Palm Beach Bath & Tennis Club were beginning to fill, and he started to recognize New Yorkers. It wouldn't be long before the table hopping started and he wasn't ready to enter the fray, not just yet. He had taken a break from it all, first in Ophelia then in Miami and though he knew he would be thrust back soon enough, he wanted to postpone the re-entry. He explained to Victoria that he needed to do a little shopping before the party that night. It wasn't true, but it was language she understood. He certainly couldn't afford anything at Trillion on Worth Avenue, but he would wander around and get the feel of the town. He needed to get away from house-guest hell. His stay with Maxwell had been a nice distraction but there was still the regiment of his host's agenda and now he was here with Victoria getting in step with hers. Rise and shine, get dressed, go to the B & T for lunch, kiss, kiss, be attentive, on your toes. Being a good house guest was exhausting.

He wanted to explore Palm Beach on his own. He wished he'd rented a car. Victoria said feel free to take hers, which he did, but he disliked being completely indebted to anyone. He drove down County Road and parked the car on Worth. He had not taken two steps on the sun-soaked sidewalk when he heard a squeal from behind. He turned to see Rhea Brown standing there with Frankie Haynes.

"Judge Mender! I can't believe it. You are the sexiest man on Worth Avenue, next to this gorgeous thing, of course, but never mind, you look hot."

She approached and gave him a big showy air kiss.

"There are so many New Yorkers in town right now. Everyone is staying at the Brazilian. Funny, I never pictured you for a Palm Beach pussy, society does strange things to handsome men. Next thing we know you'll be listed on the Fanjul's Christmas card. Then you'll know you've really arrived. I swear, if I catch you wearing Lily Pulitzer, I will rip them off you. Although, now that I think about it." She smiled a cocked, half smile. "So tell me: Who, What, Where?" She telegraphed.

"Hello, Miss Brown", Judge said courtly. "Hello, Frankie." The two men shook hands as Frankie nodded behind big dark sunglasses. "I just got into town last night. I drove up from Miami. I'm staying with Victoria Newton."

"Well, well, well. How's things over at WASPville?" I hear the pool is so cold you have to wear a wetsuit to float on a raft." She laughed at herself and Judge smiled. Frankie scanned the avenue, bored and ready to move on.

"Listen, we are in a crazy rush, but what are you doing for New Year's?"

"I am going to the Coconut's party with Victoria."

"Oh God, kill me. Are you serious?" She rolled her eyes. "Well, when you're completely drained of all life and blood at the dinosaur dance, come over to Mia's house on Island Drive. We'll be bringing in the New Year New York style."

"I don't know if Victoria would allow it," he said joking.

"Tell her Lucy Shining will be there. She'll let you come. Bye lover." She leaned in and kissed him on the lips, turned around and led Frankie away to a black Mercedes 300SE. Judge thought at first glance that she was dragging him away by his crotch, but then realized their hands only met there.

Lucy Shining will be there. The words ricocheted around his head. He hadn't seen her since the Winter Ball. He figured that she left town with the migrating geese. He had put that night out of his head. He knew that it was a once in a lifetime and he had blown it. He was fine. He could not get off track with a hopeless infatuation with Lucy Shining. She was out of his league. He walked on and changed the subject in his head.

Judge wanted to check out the shops on the famous Worth Avenue, but with the Rhea run-in and the news that there were many New Yorkers in town, he headed back to the car. South Beach had been good for him. After straightening out with Maxwell after the Caleb mess, getting away from the same crowd, the same conversations, the same expectations, was welcome respite. He knew that he wasn't ready to step back on the carousel. He figured it would be unavoidable soon, but he wanted to postpone the air kisses. He turned the car around and took a left on County. Maxwell told him of an eccentric little thrift shop, The Church Mouse, and he wanted to check it out. He figured there would be little chance of running into the Park Avenue set there. He spotted the sign and pulled around back to the parking lot. Damn, he thought. I could have walked.

Entering the tiny shop, Judge was assaulted by rows of Dynasty-style cocktail dresses and gowns -- all sequins and beads -- and he couldn't help but laugh out loud. Typical, he thought. He quickly catalogued the store and saw men's shoes through an opening in the back.

He checked out the shoes and, seeing nothing that suited him, landed on a rack of sport jackets, most of them navy blue with gold buttons, but a few variances caught his eye. There was a brown, cashmere blazer. Size forty? Italian? Loro Piana? Hell yeah, he thought. He checked the price. A hundred and fifty dollars? Not bad.

He slipped the coat on and closed the button and was turning to find the mirror when a voice behind him said, "Perfection. You couldn't have gotten a better fit with Cesana."

Judge turned, and smiling there six feet away, stood Lucy Shining. He felt the breath leave his body like an expelled gasp, quickly and quietly.

"I see you've discovered the best shop in town."

She came up and kissed him on the cheek. "I've missed you since our date. When did you get to town?"

"Hey beautiful." He smiled and hugged her tight. "I just got in last night. What a nice surprise."

"Wow," Lucy said. "That's the greatest hug I've had all year."

"There are plenty more," he said. "You just give me the word."

"This jacket is really good for you. So handsome. You absolutely should get it." She smoothed the shoulders of the jacket. "How was your Christmas?"

Judge was already lost in her. He didn't want to move. She was so close that her scent blanketed him. Her hair, her body, her perfume, every piece blended into a bouquet around her. He was buzzing in the car on the East River again.

"Christmas?" He snapped back. "Oh, fine. Lot's of country cooking. And yours?"

"Gorgeous. I went to my mother's, which is why I'm here. Rhea called and said to come down for New Year's. They're all staying at Mia's. So I drove over. My mother only lives forty-five minutes from PB. Where are you staying?"

He was almost embarrassed to tell her. "I'm staying with Victoria Newton."

"Weeeell, isn't that fancy. Is her house really as huge as they say?

"It's enormous. I have to put out bread crumbs to find my way back from the pool."

Lucy chuckled and put her hand on his arm. "I'm glad I ran into you, Judge Mender."

"I'm glad you did too," he said with cool affectation.

She looked at him and narrowed her eyes. "I hope to see more of you." She stepped away and held up a long cashmere scarf of the brightest, deepest orange. "Look what I scored. Isn't it beautiful? And for fifty dah lahs. What a bah gan."

"I'll say. I wished I'd found it first."

He couldn't keep himself from smiling. Ever since that night in the car when she asked him about the Chase story, he had seen inside her. She sat stripped of bravura and sass and now he was swimming in that night, in that feeling. Now he wanted more. He wanted to love her. He wanted her to love him. He felt his heart swell

"Don't be greedy, Mister Mender," Lucy said. "You have the find of the century in that snappy 'schmere jacket. I think we both did very well at the Church Mouse. Don't you?"

She turned toward the door leading into the rest of the store. "I have to go meet Rhea and Frankie for a late lunch. Would you like to come?"

"I would love to," he said much too quickly, then deflated. "But Victoria took me to the B & T for the early bird special. She gets up at the crack of dawn, so lunch is at noon sharp."

Suddenly he felt embarrassed at the mention of the Bath & Tennis Club, at the fact that he was having lunch there. He saw that everything about him looked pretentious and she would think him silly and boring, but he couldn't help asking, "Do you ever go there?"

"The B & T? Oh, all the time with my mom, but not this trip. Not with Rhea, you know."

"Why not with Rhea?"

"No Jews, babe. No Jews at the B & T."

Judge flustered. He was always surprised to find out someone was Jewish. Not for any anti-Semitic nonsense, but growing up in Alabama, he had no grasp of the cultural road signs. He could only tell someone was Jewish if they were named Stern, Silverman or Stein.

"Oh, yeah. I forget about the Jews," Judge said adopting her easy tone. "And people think southerners are messed up. That's crazy, huh?"

"Stupid." She flipped through the rack of navy blazers, brass buttons twinkling in the store's bright light like diamonds in a mine.

"So you're staying at Victoria's?" Lucy said. "That sounds nice. Tell her I said hello. I like her, you know. She's always so nice to me."

Judge smirked to himself. Of course she likes you, he thought. Lucy Shining is the only girl in New York who doesn't give a damn about her or how much money she has.

"I will give her your regards," Judge said, trying to regain composure.

"Why thank you kind sir," she said as she bowed, then curtsied. "So where will you be tonight to ring in the millennium?"

Judge was not going to risk telling her the Coconut truth, not after Rhea's reaction. "Oh, Victoria has something planned, but I ran into Rhea who invited me to Mia's. So, hopefully I'll see you tonight."

"Well, in case you don't make it until after midnight," she leaned in and kissed him softly on the lips. "Happy New Year, Mister Mender."

She turned around and walked out the door. Judge was impaled.

Judge headed back to the Newton house in a daze. He was relieved that no one was home. He was able to slip up the stairs and into his guest bedroom and close out Palm Beach. He lay down on the bed and tried to sleep, but Lucy kept running through his mind. What is going on with me he wondered, Can she really be interested? Yes, they had a healthy flirtation, but that was what was expected of them. They were both players on the same field. He was grateful that they hadn't slept together the night of the Winter Ball. He was unnerved around her to begin with and that would have made the future impossible.

After an hour of the running loop of the Church Mouse kiss and the revelation car ride and the Winter Ball wearing out his brain, he drifted into sleep and didn't wake up until a tap on the door.

From the other side, came the muffled announcement: "Meester Meender. Please. Sorry to disturb. Mees Newton says to kindly awaken. You are expected for deener in half an hour."

He fumbled for his watch. Damn, I slept for four hours. Judge pulled his tuxedo out of the closet and gave it a quick once over. It'll do, he thought. He showered and shaved and slicked his hair back in his best Palm Beach impersonation. He put on the tuxedo, for the first time in three weeks, and groaned as he tied the tie. How nice it was to be out this monkey suit for a while. He looked in the mirror and said aloud, "Smile!"

He heard the music from the floor below. Victoria enjoyed her boom boom and there was the incongruous blare of Maria Carey's Dream Lover running up the chintz covered walls. When he descended the stairs, he found Victoria's other guests already assembled. He wondered how they were talking, the music was so loud.

They were a small gathering, Victoria and Andrew, Sweetie and her date, Jameson, Victoria's cousins, Marissa and Taylor, Elizabeth Pilgrim and himself. Victoria was in full plumage with her chicks clucking around her. She'd had a girl come up from South Beach to do her hair and makeup, and Judge noted that all she needed was a big diamond crown to set it all off. She wore her patented de la Renta gown, this time in black organza, with black opera gloves. She'd pulled the diamonds out of the vault and hung the ornaments on her ears, her neck and both wrists. Judge was dazzled.

"Well, his lordship descends," boomed Victoria. "Enter, enter. You know everyone here. Champagne for Mr. Mender, Adalis. Judge, caviar and bellinis are on the piano."

Judge made his way around the room, greeting everyone and exchanging handshakes and air kisses. God, he groaned. He couldn't bear Elizabeth Pilgrim. She was as rich as Lucy, maybe more, but such an utter bore. She was tall and thin and beautiful, but possessed the personality and disposition of overcooked pasta. He prayed he wouldn't have to sit next to her, but he knew that prayer was in vain. Victoria would consider it the highest honor for Judge to sit next to the railroad heiress and he would have to spend the next two hours pulling teeth to get through it.

"Your coverage of the Winter Ball was fabulous, Judge." Elizabeth offered with constipated delivery.

"Thank you, Elizabeth," Judge returned. "It was a terrific party. You should all be very proud."

"Except!" Victoria boomed. "For that god awful Lily von Reynolds. I still have not forgiven you for running a picture of her in that ridiculous costume."

"I told you, Miss Newton," Judge said laughing. "I had nothing to do with the photographs. I was on a plane to Dixie."

"Well," Victoria continued. "It was enough to ruin the mood. I still have one question. What the hell was she wearing?"

The group sent up a chorus of laughter and the maid served another round of champagne.

"Oh," Victoria said when she finished laughing at herself. "I hear you ran into Lucy Shining today at the Church Mouse," Victoria boomed across the music from the stereo. "She's staying at Mia's, with that wretched Rhea Brown, I suppose." She leaned into Elizabeth and Judge, "that house is a travesty. Gauche, gauche, gauche."

"Yes," Judge said. "They've invited us over, if we find time." Judge said.

"Well, that's something to consider if we find the time to go slumming. Down your champers, everyone. Let's eat."

Dinner was as Judge had imagined. Prime rib, whipped potatoes, haricot verts and corn soufflé. He ate heartily for the first time since Christmas dinner at his mother's. The dinners at Maxwell's had been a little on the fou fou side because he was trying to make the Frenchies feel at home. But here on Victoria's table, she served what she wanted to eat. "You can never depend on these mink-y caterers." She pronounced. "They splash three beads of caviar on a Bellini and announce 'dinner is served'. Well not in my house. We eat real food here. Elizabeth, dig in. You're too anorexic. I want to see that plate cleaned."

When dinner was cleared, Victoria stood up and said, "Coconut time. Let's go show these old men how to party. We'll take two cars. Judge, Elizabeth, you will ride with me."

On the drive to the party, Victoria filled them in on the history of the Coconuts. They were a group of bachelor men who had held this New Year's Eve party for as long as anyone could remember, long past the point when their bachelor days were assigned to memory. Now they were all in their seventies but carried on the tradition in a state of amusing nostalgia. The party needed a little new blood, which is why Victoria's mother insisted that they go and why her mother told her to invite Judge Mender. The thing could use a little mention in Jet Set, if he knew what she meant.

Victoria charged up the steps of The Colony with the skirt of her gown clinched in her fists, elbows out. The party followed like little goslings, scurrying in her wake. Judge held back, lit a cigarette and allowed the group to make the entrance he was so sure was their intent. He waited until the last of the party had disappeared inside before stubbing out his butt and mounting the stairs.

"Mr. Mender. Welcome to the Coconuts Ball." The voice boomed from none other than Victoria's mother, Cecilia Newton. If Victoria gave the air of a Hapsburg princess, her mother was imported from the reign of Queen Victoria. She stood at the top of the stairs swathed in pale yellow satin and organza. She was wearing a headband of diamonds that told every arrival who was the real queen of Palm Beach. She was a plump woman with large fleshy arms and a helmet of blonde hair with silver streaks. Judge stopped in front of her and she extended those arms, grabbing his biceps and pulling his cheeks toward her protruding lips.

"We are so pleased to have you here," she said grandly. "I haven't seen you since Corrina's Animal party at the Waldorf."

Judge had been at her house for a day and a half and had not seen her once. Tennis and shopping and lunches had kept her away and now she descended upon him in full glory. "I hope all is comfortable with your rooms?" without waiting for an answer, she turned to the row of silver-haired, dapper gentleman standing in a receiving row to her left, each with a bright red carnation stuck in the lapel of his black tuxedo. "May I present the Coconuts? Gentlemen, this is the famous journalist from Jet Set, Mr. Judge Mender."

Judge nodded in their direction as one by one, Mrs. Newton introduced him down the line. Once he reached the end, exhausted from the hand shaking and small talking, she released him. "Find Victoria, darling. I'll be along in a while."

He turned back to the end of the line, and there, magically and suddenly stood Maxwell Jones, grinning like a madman. "How do you do, Mister Mender."

Judge burst into laughter. "What are you doing here you old queen? Tell me you're not a Coconut."

"Oh God, no. I just saw Victoria, and she told me you were lollygagging outside. I had to witness your introduction to these cadavers. And P.S. Ix-Nay on the Een-Quay talk. The wifey is here. Let's show some respect."

"Of course, Mr. Jones. Where is the little woman? I guess you abandoned Caleb on the beach."

"Ix-Nay," he scowled.

Judge smirked. It was amusing to see Maxwell squirm for a change. "And how is it in there?"

"Oh, the usual," he sighed. "Don't even ask about the b-rate décor, a few garish arrangements and some red film on the up lights. There are quite a few younger people here this year, so that always makes it lively. I do hope something scandalous happens, that doesn't include me, of course."

"Of course," Judge said, scanning the room. "Anyone I should note, or run from?"

"Both! That horrid Lily von Reynolds is here and she's already got Victoria cornered. It is priceless." Maxwell said, motioning toward Victoria. "And, our special guest this evening is none other than your banished friend and mine, Chase Peters."

"What?!" You're kidding." Judge's eye darted around the room. "I do not want to see him, Maxwell."

"Too late," Maxwell chirped. "He slithered up to me already, 'Well hello, Mr. Jones, how are you Mr. Jones, how have you been Mr. Jones.' I wanted to smack him. He's as un-chastened as ever."

The two men stepped out of the crush of the entry way to look around the room. Judge searched for a bar, but Maxwell pulled him behind a forest of potted palms.

"Do you know that he's brought some television crew to town with him?" Maxwell said.

"Who?" Judge asked still looking for the bar.

"Chase! Pay attention please," Maxwell nodded and smiled at a very old and very distinguished looking lady and lowered his voice. "Evidently, he's filming some new reality show about the idle rich and he's been pulling a camera crew around all week. It seems that little Chase has anointed himself some sort of spokesman for high society and is busting into parties all over town. Of course, Cecilia Newton wouldn't let the varmints in here, so he's solo tonight. The rub is that no one of real value will have anything to do with him, so he's ingratiated himself with a bunch of climbers like himself. You should see the drips he's attached himself to tonight, I mean, really low rent. It's too tragic, yet hilarious at the same time." Maxwell paused and nodded a silent greeting to a

Coconut. "Even so, it seems your little article made him famous, which is why I had to puncture his little hot air balloon."

Judge, who heretofore had been surveying the room and only half-listening to what he figured was another one of Maxwell's hen-house rants, suddenly turned to face him. "What did you do?"

Maxwell, basking in Judge's attention, said. "I turned to him and said, 'Our good friend Judge Mender is expected tonight. He's staying with the Newtons.' I don't know which made him squirm more, the fact that you were coming or that you were staying with the first family of PB. No matter, let's go to him."

"Are you crazy?!" Judge sputtered.

"My dear," Maxwell said patiently. "Everyone in this room knows who he is, knows who you are, knows about the story, and is waiting for this confrontation. This little contretemps is the evening's featured entertainment. Your reputation will be made or lost in this moment, and you must make the move. You will stride boldly up to him and wish him Happy New Year. It will brand him forever and that will be that. By the time the story gets back to Manhattan, it will be legend."

"Jesus, Maxwell, I don't know."

"Don't disappoint me now by being spineless," Maxwell said and flicked a speck of ash off the black satin lapel of Judge's jacket. "Come. I'll clear the path."

"Can I get a goddamn drink first?" Judge said.

Maxwell plucked a bubbling flute of champagne from a passing tray and handed it to Judge. "Let's go."

Maxwell maneuvered around the perimeter of the room. Judge hadn't seen Chase yet, but he spotted Victoria and her eyes pierced his skin. Had she set him up? There was no way she couldn't know that Chase was going to be there, he thought, her mother was greeting people at the door. Was this Maxwell's revenge for Caleb in South Beach? He felt like an unprepared actor being shoved on to the stage, all bright lights and a full house. He refused to believe that this could all be sport, so he stepped in line with Maxwell's pace and raised his chin. He would do this. He would sing for his supper.

"There he is," Maxwell whispered, "cowering in the corner."

Judge looked up and locked eyes with Chase Peters. Chase raised an eyebrow as if to say, don't come any closer. He was in a huddle with three, blond, middle-aged women that Judge quickly concluded were of no distinction, and they all turned their heads when they saw him. In thirty seconds, Maxwell and Judge were upon him. Maxwell stopped short and stepped aside. The three women scurried for cover.

"Chase Peters," Maxwell said haughtily. "You remember Judge Mender."

Judge imagined that the music stopped and every head turned in their direction. Did a plate crash? He wondered. He felt his cheeks burn, but did not allow any emotion to cross his face. Chase, on the other hand, was a ball of red fury.

"Hello Chase," Judge said, one hand tucked gallantly in his pocket.

"Hello, asshole."

Maxwell burst into laughter, "Nicely put, Chase, nicely put."

Judge smirked and said, "I haven't seen you in a while. I hope all's well with you."

Chase reached into his full drink and removed the lime clinging to the side and threw the contents of the drink in Judge's face.

"Fuck you, Judge Mender."

Judge licked his lips and smiled at Maxwell. "Hmm, cheap vodka."

Maxwell exploded with a laugh that rocked the room. Chase pushed past Judge and walked toward the door. Judge's back was to the room. He pulled out his handkerchief and wiped the vodka from his face and patted the lapels of his jacket. He turned and winked at the destroyed Maxwell.

"How was that, you conniving old queen?" Judge said in his best Cary Grant. "Will that do?"

"That was the greatest single moment of my life. He's completely ruined. Thank you."

"Now can I get a real drink?" Judge asked. "I seem to have vodka in this one."

"Absolutely!" Max said loudly. "To the bar, conquering hero, to the bar."

Judge looked over Maxwell's shoulder and caught Victoria's smile. She nodded and raised her champagne flute, her victory complete.

Maxwell instructed Judge to stay at The Colony for an hour and a half to let the room get over the incident, let them settle down and see that he was not shaken. Maxwell said he should dance with some of the old dames and then make a respectable exit with the Newton party. Judge was on autopilot now. He couldn't believe what had happened tonight. It was so Dynasty. Was that the theme of the day? He was embarrassed to be in the middle of such a cat fight. What would his friends in Ophelia think if they heard he'd had a drink splashed in his face by another man? Russ would eviscerate him. Hell, he thought, I'm so far from their comprehension, why should this event be the shocking blow? All he wanted was to get out of there and see Lucy. How long would it take? He drank glass after glass of champagne but could not get drunk.

Judge did as Maxwell instructed and danced with the ladies he presented. Small talk and waltz he could do with his eyes closed. When Victoria announced the party was leaving, Judge was in such a state that he never noticed the passing of midnight. Had he been outside smoking?

Victoria decided they would all go to Mia's house en masse. Great, Judge thought. I have to show up to the cool kid's party with Lady Astor and the court of pretension. He told himself it couldn't be any worse than what Maxwell had put him through. Their little party arrived at the Wilson house around one a.m. where the gravel driveway was full of expensive cars no less impressive than the Mercedes dealership. The lights in the castle-like home were in full blaze, in every window a flicker of light or a shadow dance. There are actually turrets, Judge noticed.

"Where's the moat?" Victoria sniffed. "Have you ever seen anything so tacky?"

Mia Wilson appeared on the doorstep. "Victoria Newton, my goodness, don't you look beautiful."

"Mia, dearest, what a gorgeous house," Victoria boomed. "Happiest of New Year's!"

"Mwa! Mwa!" The two heiresses exchanged loud airy kisses, new money smacking old.

Rhea Brown appeared in the door. "My god, all the rich white people just arrived. You all look like a spread from Town & Country."

Victoria sniffed again and waltzed past Rhea without speaking.

"Well, Happy New Year to you too, fat ass," Rhea said under her breath.

Judge gulped. Oh god, he thought. This was a mistake to mix these two groups. He took a look at the eight of them. They were dressed incredibly formal, while Mia and Rhea — and the rest of the party he guessed -- were casually dressed like a normal New York night out.

He stopped to greet Mia and Rhea, allowing the geese to migrate inside without him. Rhea wrapped her arms around his neck and said, "Kiss me, you fool."

Judge pecked her on the lips and said, "Happy New Year." He pulled away and gave the same to Mia. Mia held on, wanting more.

"Where's Lucy?" Judge asked.

"Probably fucking my boyfriend," Rhea said carelessly. "If you see them, tell them I'm pissed. Come on, Mia. More champagne." Rhea pulled Mia into her arms and they stepped through the door in lock step. Rhea turned and looked at Judge. "You coming?"

"I'll meet you inside," Judge said, looking through the windows above him.

Judge made his rounds around the room, nodding to those he could get away with, and stopping and saying hello to those who arrested him, all the while scanning the rooms for Lucy. He had been through most of the house and caught no sign of her. He stepped out onto the pool deck and walked across the damp, dark lawn to the edge of Lake Worth. He lit a cigarette and, just as he exhaled the first drag, heard what sounded like a screaming Indian crossing the lawn behind him. He turned and saw Lucy, who upon reaching a distance of no less than five feet from him, left the ground and sailed toward him. She wrapped her arms and legs around him and the knotted pair fell to the ground. Judge and Lucy lay laughing on the edge of the seawall, inches from the dark, cold water.

"Smooth move, ballerina," he said as he stubbed his cigarette in the grass. Lucy nuzzled beside him. The two of them propped up on elbows and stared into each other's eyes.

"I've been looking for you all night," Lucy said a little too loudly. "These people are so damn boring."

"Yeah, I've been in a little fresh hell myself."

"So kiss me and make it all better."

He looked at her, but couldn't tell if she was sincere or drunk.

"How drunk are you?" he whispered in her ear.

"Oh, I'd say I'm about a five. How drunk are you?" she whispered back, mocking him.

"I'm only two and a half."

"Well, kiss me dammit, kiss me."

Judge ran his hands through her hair and held her neck. He traced his thumb along her lips as she closed her eyes. He closed his eyes and kissed her. He felt his heart pound, his stomach flip. And then he stopped because she stopped.

Lucy sat up straight and looked at him with surprise.

"Are you in love with me, Judge Mender?"

"I think so," he said unguarded. "I can't stop thinking about you."

"Good, it took you long enough. I don't think I've waited so long for any man. I need to be loved, but I have a sneaking suspicion that you're gay. It's okay. Gay men are always falling in love with me," she said laughing.

Judge adjusted quickly.

"It's New Year's, babe." Judge said mocking her. "You're my first kiss. I had to make up for lost time."

She laughed and grabbed his neck. She kissed him again and got up and ran into the house, screaming Indian and waving arms. He fell back on the ground.

After an eternal minute of counting stars, he stood up and walked back toward the house. Piano music wafted through the open doors as the lights within provided a warm glow to the dark back lawn. Judge swung around the edge of the pool and entered the living room. He made a lap and discovered Victoria in the library holding court. Mia's parents, and many of the adults from the Coconuts party, had arrived and someone famous was playing the piano. Was that Shirley MacLaine? Judge found a bathroom and decided to pull himself together. He found a half-smoked joint sitting next to the sink. Thank God. He fired it up and smoked it down to the ash. He held in the vapor as if it were life itself. He had to change his head, his mood, the evening's direction, nothing was working for him.

He left the bathroom realigned. He looked around for a bartender. If Lucy is going to fuck with me, I'm going to get drunk, he decided. He went to the bar and asked the bartender to give him a full bottle of champagne. He grabbed two glasses and headed for a spot near the piano. People were singing. He didn't know the song so he poured champagne. He looked up and Lucy stood there smiling.

"Who's the other glass for?" she said as she picked it up and waited for him to fill it.

"For you, crazy lady."

"Thank you," she said. "I like it like that."

Judge felt relieved and comfortable now. He had hit the place he wanted to be, reinstated his cool and relaxed in the comfort of this class. The rest of the night they sat and talked, Lucy sang, danced, jumped up and down on his lap, drank champagne and kissed him a million times. After the third bottle of Veuve, he finally caught up to her and felt on equal drunk footing.

When they had drained the third bottle, she looked at him and said, "I'm bored."

"Let's go to your room then," he said.

She smiled and cocked her head.

"Do you think that's such a good idea, considering how in love with me you are?"

"You let me worry about that," Judge whispered. "I can handle a broken heart."

"Now I think I love you, Judge Mender."

Lucy took Judge's hand and they crossed the room and disappeared down the hall. Victoria snapped Andrew on the shoulder.

"Well, it's time to go home." She stood up, straightened her skirt and walked to the door. Mia hunched in a chair talking to Frankie Haynes, who had his hand on her knee as her skirt slid away.

"Sorry to disturb you, Mia, uh, excuse me boy," Victoria had no need for boys like Frankie. They didn't chase after her and they had no money. "Thank you for a lovely party, Mia darling. Good night." Victoria kissed Mia loudly on each cheek and glided through the door and out onto the gravel drive.

"What a miserable evening," she said as soon as they were in the car. "If it weren't for the Chase Peters drink fling, I should have stayed home. But oh, I guess we can't rehash that until the morning when dear Judgie finally makes it home."

Victoria looked over her shoulder into the back seat and shot Elizabeth a glance. "Looks like Lucy Shining will be our next Jet Set profile." And she burst into laughter and slapped Andrew on the knee.

Judge slowly opened his eyes into the bright sun streaming through the sheer curtains. He scanned the room but couldn't figure out where he was. He was much drunker last night than he intended. He prided himself on alcohol control, especially here in a place he'd never been, as a house guest no less. She had made him nervous and unsure. He was thrown off his game and wanted to get drunk fast. The race to catch up to Lucy hit him all at once. And then he remembered the joint.

He remembered climbing the stairs and sneaking into this room. Was it this room? They kissed in the doorway. He took off his jacket, his tie, his shirt. He winced. A picture flashed in his brain. He and Lucy became much more adventurous than he intended. It was supposed to be beautiful, hot, passionate, yes, but beautiful, sweet. Damn. Why had he drunk so much? He looked at the sheet-shrouded figure next to him and felt at first pride, then shame, then panic, then calm. Judge needed some water. He needed a cigarette. He needed a Vicodin.

He slowly crept out of bed and searched for his underwear. Clothes were strewn everywhere. He couldn't find his boxers so he slid on his tux pants and walked out onto the balcony. He found their shoes on the ground and realized they must have been out there at one point. Had they been naked on the balcony? Who'd seen them? Who knew? Who cared?

He stood smoking, thinking, replaying what he could remember. His head hurt, but not unbearably: he'd had worse hangovers. He was glad he stuck to champagne last night. What was he going to do now? He alternated between recall and fast forward. What happened? What now? What next? Judge heard her rustle in the bed behind him. He turned and crossed his arms over his bare chest.

"Hey, babe," Lucy said. "Who knew you had that body beneath all those tuxedos."

"Funny, I had no trouble imagining yours," he said through a sly smile. The panic and pride and pain evaporated.

He stubbed out the cigarette in a dirty glass and climbed back into bed with her. He wrapped her in his arms and kissed her until she sighed. She let her hands find the waist of his pants and pushed them toward the foot of the bed, kissing him between rumbles of laughter. The door opened and Rhea screamed as her eyes fell on Judge's bare ass.

"Oh. My. God."

Frankie peaked over her shoulder and echoed the sentiment. "Oh. My. God."

Rhea closed the door, laughing and repeating, "Oh. My. God."

Lucy laughed. "Well, Mr. Mender, looks like you've got to marry me now. My reputation's been ruined and my daddy will hunt you down with a shotgun."

Judge laughed and pulled the sheets up into a low, mounding tent. "I'll protect you." He snuggled into her neck and began lightly kissing her there in the place she responded without discretion. The pressure was less intense there, him holding her, kissing her, not talking or thinking or putting this together.

A cell phone bleated from the bedside table.

"Oh shit!" he snapped.

"What?"

"Mrs. Newton is having a thing today. What time is it?" He reached for the side table, turning the clock around. It was eleven AM. "Hey, sexy lady, can you give me a ride?"

"I guess so," Lucy said confused. "Let me brush my teeth." Lucy kissed him lightly and slid across the big, disheveled bed and stood before him, naked. "This isn't some hump and dump excuse to get away from a snuggle is it?" she teased.

Judge pulled her back to the bed on top of him and kissed her again. "Yeah, I'd get out of bed with the most beautiful girl in the world to go have breakfast with some old lady. Damn, I guess that's what I'm doing, so yeah, gotta dump."

She laughed and jumped out of bed. He watched her tanned, dazzling body disappear into the bathroom.

"Damn," he said out loud. "This sucks."

The drive back to the Newton's was a manic ride for Judge. He fumbled with thoughts and sentences in his head, searched for anything, the right thing to say. The panic returned and he thought how stupid he was. Why did he get out of bed? They could have stayed another hour or two. Hell, even a half an hour instead of his ridiculous excuse to meet Mrs. Newton.

Lucy stared at the road ahead. Finally, she said, "I am not pulling into the driveway, lover boy. You're making that walk alone."

"Ah, come on," he managed to match her tone. "You don't want to come in and have breakfast with the family?" He reached around and put his hand around the back of her neck.

"Oh yeah, that's my lifelong dream."

Judge searched again for the right tone, the right delivery. He landed on the one that seemed interested, but nonchalant.

"I fly back to New York in the morning," Judge said. "What are you doing tonight?"

"I'm going back to my mom's today as soon as I get back and pull it together."

"But, when will I see you again?" he pleaded in mock panic.

"You won't, baby. I leave on Safari the day after that and I plan to be eaten by tigers."

"Yeah right," he said sarcastically.

"Seriously," she said. "I'm in New York for a day before I head to Arusha with my dad. I'm away the entire month of January."

"Jesus," he said exasperated. "Now who's getting the hump and dump."

"What can I say?" she smiled. "I'm a player. I'll bring you back a zebra skin or something."

Judge laughed because that was what she expected, but his throat closed and his breath shortened and he realized he had blown it.

She pulled up to the hedge just before the gate to the Newton's house. He leaned over and kissed her lightly and jumped out of the car. He pushed away the panic and decided to play it light. "So Happy New Year, babe," he said. "See you when you get back to town."

"Uh, okay," she said, nonplussed.

He shut the door and walked around to the driver's side. He leaned down and stuck his head through the open window.

"I had a great time last night, I really mean it."

He put his open palm lightly on her cheek and pulled her toward his lips and felt the joy at the top of the mood swing, where everything was beautiful and warm. He pulled away and looked into her face. She opened her eyes and shook her head to awaken. Lucy looked at him with narrowed eyes and a little smirk. She tapped the gas pedal and gave the engine a small roar.

"Happy New Year!" she yelled and hit the pedal and threw her arm up and gave a slow, sexy wave.

He stood there, motionless until the car was out of sight. He turned and walked across the crunchy gravel toward the house. His heart pounded, his head hurt and his panic doubled his pulse. He had to be alone fast. He had to get to his room undetected. He felt like he might vomit and that scared him even more. He did not notice Victoria in the upstairs window, brushing her hair and smiling.

Chapter 4

The Scarlet Lamb

Judge avoided Richard Hadenfield for the third day in a row. The heat generated by his Chase Peters story back in November now sat like a dried out turkey. Winter arrived rude and sudden in New York and pushed the warm relief of South Florida into a hazy memory. Judge landed back in the city longing for the relaxation and revelry of the Christmas break. Ophelia and his visit home grew sweeter to him and he wondered if he wouldn't have been better off staying there instead of hobnobbing with the vacationing social crowd down south. Ah, but he always came back to Lucy.

He spent the first day back in cold, dark New York comparing the contrast of his high life in elegant houses in resort climes to the confinement of his studio apartment in the city. He replayed New Year's Eve over and over, second guessing his action and reaction. He couldn't stop thinking about the ridiculous scene at the Coconut party with Chase, Maxwell's delight in setting it up, and Victoria's glee at the outcome. Then there was Lucy. Elation and despair were bundled intricately together in his recollection of Lucy. He savored the night with her only to be stabbed in the gut at how it ended and his ineptitude at post-coital denouement.

He scurried in and out of the Jet Set offices rodent-like, selecting the spaces of time when his editor would most likely be out and about. Before the break, Richard informed him that his past two fuzz pieces on writers and painters were not his best work. Scandalous stories not only brought the writer mention but also the publication; Jet Set had been the talk of Park Avenue for the past two months thanks to his Chase story. Richard wanted more and it would be time for another socialite story soon. Richard left several voice mails calling Judge into his office, but Judge feigned sick and said he was working from home. It was now Tuesday, a week after his return from Palm Beach, and Judge knew he could no longer avoid him. He gerrymandered toward his cubicle, walking the longest way around the newsroom.

"Well, Happy New Year," Leah, his assistant, mumbled as he passed. "Richard wants to see you as soon as you're in."

"Am I in?"

"Looks like it."

Judge dropped his bag and turned toward Richard's office. He stood sheepishly in the editor's doorway until being waved in. He hadn't taken a seat before Richard blurted:

"What have you got in mind for March?" Richard skipped the how-have-you-beens and how-do-you-feels.

"Well, I was thinking about Lily von Reynolds. She's..."

"Kill it. New York's already got that in the hopper, coming out next week."

"Who's writing it?" Judge was pissed. Society was his beat and he hated when New York scooped him. Victoria Newton had been pitching that story to him for months. Did she pitch it to New York?

"Some new girl over there – Julie Whitaker, I think -- trying to make a name for herself. I hear Hollywood's interested. She's already got an agent and talking huge advance." Richard said, twisting the little knife into Judge. "So what have you got for me, Golden Boy"?

"Well, there's this thing I was thinking of on the Hiltons."

"Boring. What else?"

"What about Steven Sanders?"

"The decorator?"

"Yeah, evidently he's having an affair with Sugar and James Le Baron. And neither one knows about the other."

"No shit?!" Richard was interested.

"Yeah, they've been carrying on at the Palm Beach estate while Sugar's in New York and then back at the New York apartment when James is in Palm Beach."

"Unbelievable," Richard said. "Do you have sources?"

"Yes. I heard it from three different sources in PB."

"Well, I'll be damned. That's good."

"I think I can get some folks on the record. It appears he's made some enemies."

Judge was relieved. He could write this story with ease. He had no respect for any of the parties involved. The decorator, the husband and his wife were all unbearable, new money snobs with terrible tastes and zero personality. Plus, Mr. Le Baron's business on Wall Street was shaking up. It was a well-timed story of international interest.

"No," Richard said, lighting a cigarette. "You can't write it because we can't publish it."

"Why not?" Judge said aloud before he could edit himself.

"For one thing, James Le Baron is an old friend of Mr. Whitmore, Sr. - our esteemed publisher and boss. And Le Baron is the number one donor to Whitmore's charity."

"Oh, I guess that's that then."

"What about Victoria Newton?" Richard asked.

"Victoria Newton?" Judge sputtered.

"Yeah. She's old money, extremely private, and never been profiled. She's come out of nowhere all of a sudden. And you're getting along well with her it seems." Richard prodded. He'd been through many a stable of young buck writers and this was always the story they never saw coming. It titillated him to watch the gears turn.

"But Victoria is..." Judge knew he couldn't say friend, Richard would crucify him with ridicule. "Victoria is one of my best sources."

"Exactly. She should have no trouble talking to you. I hear her apartment is a ridiculous homage to Mrs. Astor. How was the Coconut Ball, by the way?" Richard needled. Judge squirmed.

"I cannot ask her to do it," Judge stammered. "She'll think I'm crazy. She's always been very up front that her attention to me was not proffered to land her in the magazine."

Richard exploded with laughter. He could not hold it in any longer.

"It's true, Richard." Judge was getting angry. His face was hot, and he knew that he was showing it.

"Judge, I realize that you are handsome and charming, but if you think for one moment that your presence at Victoria Newton's dinner table or her mother's Palm Beach estate is not directly related to your position at this magazine, you need to wake up and smell the blue blood. She wants to be written about. She's aching to be profiled. And you, Golden Boy, are the one to write it."

Judge needed time to process. Would Victoria be flattered or offended? Would she cooperate? Surely she would trust him to write a positive piece. Would Richard accept that or would he want Judge to stir up some dirt? He had to get out of this office and pull his head together.

"I really don't feel comfortable doing that right now, not enough time to do it justice. She's hosting the Frick thing next month. We can get it in for April, but, wait! I know! Can we postpone it until the fall when her charity benefit takes over Newport?" This is good, he thought, keep going, keep spinning. "Every member of the junior set will be up there for the weekend and it promises to be a grand old drunken weekend with grand old scandal. I'll lobby her to give us another exclusive."

"That sounds good. I like it. Start your research, though. Get to know her background. So who else is there to write about now? Is there any dirt on Lucy Shining?"

Damn, he thought. What does this old vulture want from me? He barely had time to tie his goddamn shoes this morning and now Richard was drilling him for story ideas. He racked his brain.

"Well, there's a new girl in town that's making quite a stir. I sat next to her last month at Victoria's dinner. Her name is Scarlet Goodman. She's supposedly from some wealthy, old plantation New Orleans family, really lovely. She's only been here four months and already on some high profile benefit committees and spending a lot of money. She's being sponsored by Victoria it seems."

"Oh yeah?" the editor said half-interested. "Is she worthy? I'm not enthralled by another cotton candy piece on some southern deb. Do you think there's an angle?"

"I think so. I'd like to talk to her a bit more, find out what she's about."

"Okay. Get to it. I want a draft by Monday." Richard stubbed out his cigarette and turned to his telephone. The conversation was over. Judge wandered out into the hall toward his cubicle. He was shaken by Richard's bluntness. Monday? Fuck him.

※ ※ ※

"Sweetie, it's Victoria. Pick up." Victoria stood in her usual morning position, in her robe in front of the papers, coffee and bagel in hand, barking into the telephone.

After a couple of muted taps of her slipper on the hard wood floor, she heard the receiver pick up.

"Good Morning, Tory. Sorry, I was in the other room..."

"You are not going to believe this!" she interrupted. "Judge Mender is doing a sniff around on Scarlet Goodman. I mean, Scarlet Goodman! I invite her to my house for one dinner and then put her on the Frick committee and now suddenly that little cracker is about to be profiled by Judge Mender? What the hell is going on in this town? I mean, nobodies are becoming somebodies and evidently I am the goddamn publicist. Who am I, the new Rhea Brown? I'm going to jump off the Brooklyn Bridge."

"What do you mean? I thought you wanted that. I thought he was going to take her down." Sweetie was trying to keep up.

"He's doing a fucking fluffer! I know the tone of his questions by now, honey and I can tell which direction his articles will go even before he knows and this one is going in the wrong direction. I wanted an assassination not another goddamn coronation!"

"What could there possibly be to fluff about? Who is she?" Sweetie was all ears now. She loved when Victoria got so flustered she fell into foul language.

"She's nobody, that's who. I met her on Sally's disease committee, whatever that flop was, and I saw immediately what she was." Victoria was rummaging through her cabinet looking for something; she knew not what.

"And what is that?" Sweetie asked.

"A fake!" She barked. "Ah, here it is."

She found a little brown box from La Maison du Chocolat and untied the Hermes looking ribbon to find two gold covered pieces remaining among the crumpled brown wrappers. "She said she was from New Orleans and went on and on like she was some deb of the year down there. I got suspicious when she didn't know Bunny Brewer, I mean, who doesn't know Bunny Brewer in New Orleans? She's the Brooke Astor of Hooterville, for Pete's sake."

"Oh, I adore Bunny Brewer. How is she doing?" Sweetie, distracted, "I haven't seen..."

"That is not the point, Sweetie. Focus! The point is, she didn't know Bunny and after a few telephone inquiries, it appears nobody knows little Miss Scarlet, at least not her family. They seem to know her as some little cracker from the sticks who latched on to this New Orleans boy named Harrison Jackson. His mother and sister do not approve. It appears she went around town dropping his name and spending his money and now she's here, in New York pulling the same routine. Can you imagine the audacity?"

"She is pretty, though. I can see why she's popular. She was so charming at your dinner. I'm always fascinated by those southern belles: they seem to be raised in a hothouse."

"Oh please shut up! Are you trying to get on my nerves, Sweetie?" Victoria barked. "Hothouse, snot house. It sounds more like a whore house."

"I'm sorry," Sweetie said laughing, then changing her tone into uncharacteristic sarcasm. "I meant to say, even though she appears pretty, it's easy to see that her beauty is cheap and her charm insincere."

"Ha, you are a boneless little filet, Sweetie." Victoria punched her clinched fist into the air with a stumpy Ha! "Anyway, your interruptions notwithstanding, as I was saying, here it is exactly one month later and Judge Mender is calling asking for her number and I am about to fall down with palpitations."

"What did he say? What was he asking?"

"Oh hell, I don't know. He was saying how pretty she is and how charming she is and how stylish she is and asking about her family and her money and New Orleans and I couldn't answer any of that because I don't know the girl. I'm so upset I can't talk about it anymore. Let me go. Talk to you in a few. I've got some calls to make."

Victoria hung up the phone and immediately picked it back up.

"Hello operator, New Orleans please. Yes. The Peyton Brewer residence. Yes, on Garden Street," she said a little annoyed. Why didn't the operator know where the Brewers lived? Weren't they all related down there? She unwrapped the little chocolate ball hiding beneath the gold foil and popped it into her mouth, chewing it with vengeance and swallowing it in a gulp

Chapter 5

La Goulue, Save Venice, Doubles Entendre

Judge navigated the expensive sidewalk outside La Goulue feeling like the stiff clapper inside a clanging bell. It was high noon on high society: lunch time on Madison Avenue. Women wearing varying colors of Chanel tweed jackets with high fur collars pecked and preened in the tiny entry of the restaurant while they waited to have their coats checked in the opening act of this daily performance. Judge pushed his dark glasses higher on his nose, flat against his face like a mask, as usual, wishing only to speak to those he chose. He wore a delusion of anonymity, but he was more famous here than any of the other diners.

Craig, the maitre d'hôtel, gave a giddy hop when he saw Judge Mender walk through the door of his establishment. A handsome Scot with premature gray hair, Craig had a taste for the good life offered by being at the helm of such a popular restaurant with the uptown crowd. Unlike most of the lunching ladies of a certain age, the women in Judge's wake were young, sexy and, in Craig's dreams, available. He had a taste for the divinities, and from his post at La Goulue's magnet for well-preserved women, Judge must have seemed like Hugh Hefner wearing a tailcoat of bunnies.

"Hello, Judge," Craig boomed as Judge passed from the sidewalk of hellos and how-are-yous into the ritual of tuna tartar, small salads and soufflés.

"Good morning, Craig. I'm meeting...

"I know who you're meeting and she's already seated in the corner banquette. Is that good for you today?"

Judge looked over the room and saw Scarlet beaming and waving. The front room at Goulue is bright and light when the sun is full at midday. The entire front of the restaurant is comprised of windowed doors in the old French bistro style. Inside it is all warm wood and brass railings all displayed on a patterned tile floor. The clatter chatter bouncing off those floors can be deafening. Judge usually liked to sit in the front where one could smoke if the doors were open, but it was much too cold today for open windows.

"That'll do, Craig, thanks."

"You'll have to fill me in later on whom that delicious treat is. I don't think I've ever seen her before."

Judge wondered whether he should tip Craig for his service. I'm not one of the Palm Greasers begging for a table, he reasoned. Judge mentioned this place every other column, which was tip enough.

After noting the notables around the front tables and deducting that there was none he needed to bow to save one, Judge made his way toward the corner banquette exactly diagonal across the room from the front door. Half way across the packed little room, Mrs. Newton dined with Corrina Samuels. He pulled to a stop as he came astride the table.

"Judge, darling, how are you?"

"Hello Mrs. Newton, Hello Mrs. Samuels. Don't you two look lovely today?"

"Why thank you darling, and you," she laid a manicured hand on the sleeve of his jacket. "Mmm, cashmere."

"Loro Piana. I found it in Palm Beach, actually."

"It's very nice. My Wilson used to have one just like it. I gave it to the Church Mouse last Christmas. It's important to help the underprivileged."

"Your generosity is appreciated."

"Your story on the Coconuts was just splendid. They were very pleased. We must do it again next year. You will be our guest. So, will we see you tonight at the Save Venice Gala?"

"Yes, Ma'am. I'll be stopping by for cocktails. Then to Victoria's dinner, then on to dessert at yet another dinner further uptown. There are too many events tonight. But duty calls."

"Well, I'll miss you at dinner, but it'll be good to see you at any rate. It should be very glamorous, you know. Gowns! Gowns! Gowns! I haven't dressed up since New Year's Eve. I can't wait. So who are you lunching with today?"

"A friend," he said. "I look forward to seeing you both tonight. Enjoy your lunch."

Judge wasn't sure if Mrs. Newton knew who Scarlet was and didn't want to waste any more time explaining her.

Judge made his way to Scarlet in the corner and she squealed hello as she stood to kiss him. Judge noted that a lady should never rise to meet a man. The scorecard had begun in the negative.

"Hello, Scarlet, I hope I haven't kept you waiting too long."

"Oh, no. Judge. I just love this place. Was that Victoria's mom with Mrs. Samuels?"

"Yes, do you know them?"

"Only by reputation."

"Well, it's quite a reputation."

"I know! She's involved with some very nice charities. Are you going to her Save Venice party tonight?"

"Yes, will you?"

"Oh yes! I can't wait. I have a gorgeous Valentino all ready and waiting."

"Valentino? Very nice."

Judge looked at her lovely face then down her long white neck and into the plunging cleavage of her silk blouse. The waiter appeared with menus and took their drink order and disappeared just as hastily into the choreographed swirl of waiters and customers and busboys.

"I did a little research on this place," Scarlet said abruptly. "Did you know that La Goulue was a famous dancer from the Moulin Rouge? It means The Glutton. La Goulue, I mean. She got the nickname because she finished off all of her customers drinks." Her bright eyes blinked rapidly, telegraphing her interest in this subject more keenly than the words tumbling carelessly from her lips. "She was a poor little girl in

92

Montmartre and her mother ran a laundry business. She borrowed the customer's clothes at night and would prance through the Moulin Rouge pretending to be someone she wasn't. She became really famous until she was eventually regarded as the queen of Montmartre.

"Impressive."

"I know! It has a tragic end though," Scarlet said wistfully. "She ended up broke and crazy, an alcoholic loony. She wandered around the streets of the Montmartre crying 'je suis la Goulue, je suis la Goulue' but nobody cared anymore and she died dirty and poor and crazy. It's a terribly sad story."

Judge looked deep into those six carat eyes to see how deeply this story resonated, but it was like the sun flashing on a clear blue lake, seen only as reflection. She blinked and smiled, "I can't wait for the Frick party! It's going to be such fun!"

"I've heard you girls are working hard. So tell me, Miss Scarlet. How did you come to New York?"

Scarlet went on with her meandering story and he sat there feeling a new sweetness. It was warm inside his cashmere jacket and his eyes began to blur and he fell into the sweet haze of day dream, lulled into a state of suspension by her voice, a story, a memory. There was a faint recollection of his high school girlfriend Lella on Waverly Lake, her father's boat, the August sun. He took few notes and trusted that his tape recorder would record this unexpectedly pleasant journey. He smiled and snuggled deeper into his daze and had the sense that this was the beginning of something new and good in his life. There was a hint of home, a pleasant memory, a time gone by but not forgotten or irretrievable.

Judge stared out the front window as Craig helped Scarlet into her coat and whispered a seed of seduction into her ear. Then, suddenly, Judge saw Lucy. Bundled in the bright orange cashmere blanket of a scarf high on her neck and hood-like over her head, she hurried past the aquarium view of Goulue, headed uptown. She wore dark glasses that covered most of her face and she clutched a big book close to her breast like a school girl scuttling across campus. Every girl, woman and man of their set who passed this window slowed to see and be seen. Some peeped nonchalantly while others peered deep into the room. The cocksure and connected stopped to say hello and present themselves for scrutiny. Whatever their speed, social rank or degree of inspection, they noted who was at Goulue. Not Lucy. She walked briskly past, huddled against the cold. Judge wanted to bolt after her, but Scarlet was taking sweet time getting into her coat and Craig practically snuggled in beside her.

"Judge old boy, you and Scarlet will have to return for dinner soon, my treat."

"Oh, that would be wonderful, wouldn't it Judge? Let me check my book and see when I can come."

"Yeah, yeah. That sounds nice," Judge said pulling Scarlet in his mind. "That sounds nice. Thanks a lot, Craig, see you soon, I'm sure."

"Goodbye, Craig," Scarlet said, as he leaned in to kiss her cheek.

"Very nice to meet you, Miss Scarlet. Be sure to call me when you are ready to collect." Craig handed Scarlet his card.

"Oh, I will, thank you."

"Thanks, Craig, so long," Judge mumbled anxious to get outside.

Judge gently guided Scarlet through the doors and out on to the windy sidewalk. He looked up the walk in the direction Lucy had hurried, but there was no sign of her anywhere, on this side of Madison or the other. She had vanished. Again. When he returned he was disappointed to find Scarlet at his side, her recent ascendance squashed by the vis-à-vis proximity to the ideal of woman.

Judge leaned against the sink in his kitchen, waiting for the car to fetch him. He finished his shot of confidence and set the glass down next to the near empty tequila bottle. He wondered if he should eat something. When was the last time I ate? Lunch with Scarlet?

Scarlet had been a quiet revelation for him. He walked away from the interview unsure of his impression. She was beautiful, absolutely. Was she smart? He couldn't decide. He was impressed with her Goulue research, but after that presentation she retreated back into southern belle platitudes, which was as carefully a crafted act as any he'd encountered. Judge never revealed his Alabama roots to her, effortless because he had learned long ago to suppress his accent. He allowed himself to be lulled into chivalrous romanticism on the trill of her song. She regaled him with visions of New Orleans society and Mardi Gras balls and he felt like he could fall in love with her. Judge held New Orleans in a special place, as did most southerners. There was a land of voodoo magic and Mardi Gras Indians, sultry jazz and foot-stomping zydeco, mystical dreams and literary muse. Tennessee walked those streets. Capote was born there. Judge dreamed of moving there one day, maybe soon. He'd been there for many a New Year's Eve and Sugar Bowl football games, but his New Orleans experiences were limited to collegial drunken jags on Bourbon Street. New Orleans society and

Mardi Gras seemed as exotic to him as a Sultan's court, or a page out of Gone with the Wind.

Scarlet did make a few missteps. Her questions were unguarded, her ambition a little transparent. But, he thought, fuck it. She's pretty, she's charming and she obviously has money. I'm going to let her in. And with that, he'd begun the article, written in a haze of southern romanticism, moonlight and magnolias. He created an idealized dream of little miss Scarlet Goodman and posited her on the antebellum pedestal of divine womanhood, a hackneyed and historically misogynistic angle he was aware, but good enough to please Jet Set's readers and his editor. It was a done deal.

He pressed, once again, into his dinner jacket. He swallowed a splash of scotch, only now it was taken for tolerance, not courage. He pulled a black cashmere scarf around his neck to push away the cold. This was all the protection he would need as his hired driver would deliver him door to door tonight and a winter coat would only weigh him down. Judge was aware of a new belief that waiting in a coat check line was beneath him.

His first stop would be the Metropolitan Club for the Save Venice Gala. Judge entered the cavernous room of orchestra sounds and cocktail chatter and was dwarfed and deflated. His first impression was depressing. He unwittingly approached a group of women he didn't know or care to, the result of entering a party solo, he was unprotected before the lionesses. This pride were blown out blondes with Palm Beach hides wearing dresses so revealing, he had one word at the front of his brain. Hooker. What is it with these middle-aged women and their cleavage he wondered? After his afternoon with Scarlet, he had journeyed to a place of Old South splendor only to be assaulted with big hair and pushed-up breasts.

"Hello, Judge. I'm Buffy Harrell and this is Serenity Johnson. We're friends of Corrina's from Palm Beach. We just loved your story on the Coconut party."

Judge couldn't take his eyes off the bead-accented breasts, until, like a bass catching a glint on the lure, he was drawn to the flash on their fingers. Each woman wore a diamond so large, it nearly covered two knuckles. Hands posed on protruding wrists, splayed fingers rocked slowly like tiny boats. The stones sought the light and flashed each woman's worth. They pointed the rocks at each other, weapons of the duel. These displays were not for him or for any man for that matter. He was an innocent bystander caught in the cross fire. Women whose husbands paid them little attention retaliated with Uzi diamonds, shooting each other to reclaim small dignities. He now knew why they were standing there on the outside of the throng. They had moved into position under a direct beam of light falling from the fifty foot ceiling onto their crude theater of diamonds and breasts. This was pure display of their most treasured assets. He was amused now as the scotch warmed him inside, and his eyes followed the dance of diamonds and breasts.

Mrs. Newton appeared abruptly between two pairs and kissed him on the cheek, bumping the burlesque aside.

"Judge, you're late! Victoria warned me that you arrive late and depart early, so I forgive you. Come let me introduce you to a dignitary or two and then you'll be free. Are you heading directly to Victoria's dinner at Doubles?"

"Well, good evening Mrs. Newton," he said as he snapped into character. "You look absolutely ravishing this evening."

"Oh you flatter," and she pulled him away toward some Venetian royalty. He hadn't even found the bar.

"Welcome to Save Venice, Mr. Mender," the organizer said and launched into the group's latest philanthropic pose.

Fuck Venice, he thought. I'm out of here.

Judge excused himself from further introductions and elucidation and headed for the door. He looked up and saw Scarlet and her escort walking in. Judge felt a shade overwhelmed as he took in the grandeur of her entrance. She wore a long black Valentino gown in a clingy fabric draped across the front. It had a gracefully draped neckline that asymmetrically showcased her milk-white shoulders. Judge made quick inventory and noted that none of the junior set were at this party. Even Victoria was hosting a rival dinner next door and her mother was the host of this thing. It struck him as very odd that unconnected Scarlet would be at this party.

"Hello, Gorgeous."

"Hello Judge! What a gorgeous room!" Her blues blinked up the walls soaking in the splendor. "This is Harrison Jackson."

"Nice to meet you."

"A pleasure," Judge said distracted.

"Are you leaving?" Scarlet said as confusion wrinkled her forehead.

"Yes, I'm running over to Victoria's dinner. Aren't you coming to that?"

"Uh, why no, I thought everyone would be here? Victoria is having a dinner? Now?"

"Yeah, she's over at Doubles. I'm headed over there. In fact, I'm very late. I'll see you later. Nice to meet you Harrison."

Scarlet stared after Judge, shook it off and walked confidently into Save Venice where she soon realized that she did not know a soul.

Judge strolled out of the Metropolitan Club on Sixtieth Street confused as well. Why would Scarlet go to Save Venice instead of Victoria's dinner? It was a very strange party choice. None of the juniors went to that event. Judge only went as a favor to Victoria's mom and to mention it for the column as a thank you for his stay at her house. He'd only stayed long enough to say hello to Mrs. Newton and some board members. The juniors had their own version later in the spring, Young Friends of Save Venice. Very strange that Scarlet would go to that party. Maybe she really loves Venice, he mused.

He walked the half block down Fifth to the Sherry Netherland Hotel. Victoria Newton had put together a casual dinner dance at Doubles, the private club in the hotel's basement. He descended the red stairs – those stairs! It looks as if you're about to be transported through time to a speakeasy bordello, he mused. The reality couldn't be further from the impression. These red stairs went straight to the heart of WASP Manhattan. He was greeted at the desk by an attendant seated before a table of tiny envelopes with names he did not recognize. He was almost surprised to find his own and quickly put the little cream card in his pocket. He walked directly to the bar to order a double scotch. Doubles is a private club of the oh so WASP variety, and alcohol lubed the room. Judge had been to enough parties at Doubles to know not to enter the dependably all WASP stiffness until he was at least two insurance drinks into a good time.

This was Victoria's real stamping ground, he thought. These were her school chums and neighborhood buds from Newport and Palm Beach.

And it was high contrast to the beaded breast and diamond show at the Metropolitan Club. These girls were blond and prim and pearled. They wore little ribbons in their hair and held their mouths in little purses. They talked confidently in pinched accents and danced stiffly with bland boys with slicked back hair in navy business suits and moneyed futures. These were the children of the first party and they were in reverse roles of their less inhibited parentage.

Victoria spotted him as he entered the dining room and waited for him to cross to her. She had been chilly since he'd called about Scarlet, but he would not discuss it with her tonight. He figured since he showed at this dinner dance, this was allowance enough. He approached her on the outside of the band of Buffies and bowed slightly when she noticed him.

"Good evening, Mr. Mender," she said with plastic formality. "So glad you could join us this evening. Did you pick up your seat card?"

"Yes, thank you. What a nice gathering you've assembled on this chilly night." He responded with equal aloof.

"Well who wants to sit home on a Tuesday night? Please, enjoy yourself." She turned her back to him and walked away.

Hmm, Judge thought. She's a cold fish tonight. What the hell is going on? He walked toward the center table, assuming he would be seated next to Victoria but did not see his name. He walked around the room confused, a little lost. He pulled the envelope from his pocket and pulled out the card from the envelope. Number 32.

"Judge! Hello!" Sally Banning was at his side. "You're at my table! Victoria was so kind to give you up. We're in the back corner. I've been so busy with the Frick I haven't seen anyone lately. You will be in town, I hope."

Judge looked in the direction of her finger toward the furthest table from the dance floor – Siberia – and inventoried the drips already seated staring blankly into space. Well, that confirms it. His first thought was to walk out. Show her. But he chickened out and followed Sally to Table 32. If he'd gotten there earlier, he could have done the unthinkable and switch his seat. He shook hands all around with puffy young men who looked prematurely jowly in their banker suits and chubby women in pastel sweater sets and pearls and headbands. These were the types of people so far removed from the Jet Set crowd that he didn't recognize a single face or name. And they had no idea who Judge Mender was.

"Everyone, this is Judge Mender," Sally Banning boomed. "Judge, this is my book club from Rumson."

Judge nodded as she introduced each of them, but did not recall one of their names. He took his seat next to Sally and nodded hello to the Buffy at his right. He looked at her place card. Constance something.

"Hello, Judge. That's an interesting nickname. Where are you from?" Constance asked.

"Originally from Montgomery," he said. He had no desire to explain where Ophelia was. He sunk lower in his chair and realized he was about to have to practice the fine art of small talk with someone he had zero interest in. He glanced toward the dance floor and Victoria's table. She nodded at him and smiled stiffly.

"I was named after my grandfather who was chief justice of the Alabama Supreme Court. I've been called Judge since I was born."

"Isn't that fascinating," Constance said. "And you're a lawyer?"

"A lawyer?" Judge laughed abruptly.

"Yes. Aren't you following your grandfather's path?"

"Uh, no. I'm a journalist."

"Oh. For whom do you write? The Journal? The Times?"

"Uh, no. I write for Jet Set Magazine."

"Oh," she said deflated and embarrassed for him. "I'm afraid I don't read that."

Judge looked at her and felt a shade of her embarrassment at how suddenly lacking his place of employment had paled in comparison to her expectations of serious journalism. Fuck it, he thought. What do I care what this chick thinks.

"I write a column called Seen."

"How nice," she said in the Yankee equivalent of the southern "Bless your heart". A condescending dismissal if he ever heard one. She shifted in her chair and withdrew from the conversation. Judge didn't mind. He let her go. He turned back to his left for redemption but Sally was engaged with the fellow on her left. He looked up to find everyone at the table engaged in conversation, other conversations. He was socially stranded. He looked around the room. These were Victoria's people, he thought. She had only recently begun to circulate in the Jet Set crowd, but she was the grand dame of this group. Old wasp money, old rules, old clubs. He had a crystal realization. She's as new to the Jet Set world as I am, or Scarlet. She is making her stride just like the rest of them. He looked back at his table mates. They were still engaged. Outrageous! He laughed to himself. At no other table in this city would he be so completely ignored. Hell, even at Save Venice he would've been fawned over. Maybe I should head back there for dinner. He thought Constance had turned to him, but she merely reached for her water glass. He looked at her place card again. Constance Peters. Peters! Is she related to Chase? He looked up and over at Victoria again. She raised her glass and winked. What a bitch! He resolved to make the most of it. I can talk to these people. He dusted off his small talk arsenal and gently tapped Constance's arm. She turned stiffly in his direction.

"So what is your club reading, Constance? I find book club dissection to be the best way to really get at the meat of the matter. Don't you agree?"

Chapter 6

Young Fellows Frick & Victoria's Frost

Judge pulled the silver flask from the breast pocket of his dinner jacket. He swigged a healthy dose of scotch and slumped deeper into the backseat of the town car stuck in traffic. Funny, he thought. He used to have to take a snort to calm him. Tonight he swilled for energy and to soften the dread of the evening in front of him. The car was cold and he asked the driver to turn off the radio. It was very dark and very quiet. The well-insulated car dammed the river of sound on the other side of the window. Madison Avenue pulsed. It was a little past eight o'clock on this February night and the sidewalks of Madison throbbed with people, scurrying like rodents in the cold.

It had been two weeks since Judge called Victoria Newton asking for Scarlet Goodman's number. Victoria never returned his call, and her treatment of him at her Doubles dinner confirmed that she was less than thrilled about his sudden interest in Scarlet. It didn't matter. Since his interview with Scarlet at lunch last week the story was basically written. He only needed to arrange the photo shoot and extract a couple more quotes from quotable people. That was what he planned on getting from Victoria, but now she stonewalled him. He did not understand why her ire was so aroused, but he knew that he did not like the feeling of being on the other side of her. She sent him a note thanking him for the chocolates he sent on their return from Palm Beach, but he hadn't seriously conversed with her since New Year's Day.

He would corner her tonight. That was his solitary motivation for attending tonight. She was a host of this thing, after all. If nothing else, she would have to talk to him if she wanted this inaugural party written up in Jet Set. He couldn't figure it out. Was she jealous? He was only writing about Scarlet because he thought that was what Victoria wanted. Why had she seated him next to her at her dinner party? He had learned enough about the order of things to know that there were no accidents or mistakes: Calculation was Queen. Had he misread the game plan?

Judge churned over this latest story. Why is this becoming so difficult? He slowly boiled this story down and the reduction was sour. He realized that he didn't give a damn about Scarlet Goodman's rise. He didn't give a shit about Victoria's disappointment. Who cared? Why does Jet Set care? Why do the readers care, more specifically, why do the so-called socialites care? What is going on in there tonight? Another stupid party with the same people and the same conversations, the same girls being photographed for the same magazines. What is it worth? Who cared?

East Seventieth Street was tightly packed with yellow cabs and black town cars buzzing, vibrating, generating heat and fumes. There must be a lot of interest tonight, Judge reckoned. Tonight's blue bird special was The Young Fellows of The Frick Collection Gala. In addition to being the first big party of the new year, the event had big deal buzz because the stuffy Frick board had never succumbed to the junior revolution going on around town. Now it was decided to open the former robber baron manse up to disco dancing and binge drinking. He took another swig from the silver flask and slid it back into his pocket. He closed his eyes and laid his head back. The car stopped and his door opened.

"The Frick, Mr. Mender." The driver stood on the sidewalk, which was ablaze with light flooding the museum's triple-arched entrance.

"Thanks," Judge said and slowly swung his feet out and stood before the marble steps, another monument to be admired and preserved, another alter to be subjugated before. Here you go, Judgie boy. Pay the fiddler.

"I won't be longer than a half an hour, at most."

"I'll circle the block and wait on Madison," the driver called after him. Judge didn't acknowledge the driver and side-stepped the eager guests making their way up the stairs.

Judge took the climb slowly, looked up at the halfway point and saw Maxwell coming out of the door. He was relieved.

"Hello Judge, my boy. You look miserable, if you don't mind my saying."

"I feel like hell tonight."

"Sorry to hear that. I would offer to lend you a piece of my abundant joy, but I am off to a dinner party. I just stopped in to check the final details. It's not my best work, but these children get what they pay for. You know, a little fabric and a smattering of votives can go a long way."

"I'm sure it's beautiful. Sure you can't stay and join me for one drink? I really don't feel like talking to anyone else in there tonight."

"So sorry to say I cannot do it. I am very tardy as it is. You'll be fine once you get in. I saw many of your friends inside. Goodbye, Pet. Call me tomorrow."

"Bye, Maxwell," Judge said dejected and dove deeper as Maxwell scurried down the stairs. "I don't have any friends in there."

Inside the lobby, Judge noted the press check-in and the other journalists and photographers hustling to have their names checked off the list. Judge stood arrogantly in the flower-accented room waiting to be recognized. Sally Banning scampered over in a dream of bright red organza stitched together from the imagination of John Galliano.

"Judge Mender. Welcome to the Frick!" she shouted over the din of arrivals. "I am so glad you could come." Three other gossamer swans breezed in behind her, all wearing similar versions of the same gown. Dior must be the sponsor, Judge thought. "You know my co-chairs: Victoria Newton, Elizabeth Pilgrim, and Lucy Shining."

Judge snapped to attention at the sound of her name. Victoria gave him her best fake smile; Elizabeth's was placid like a Valium and Lucy cocked her head and winked. How had Victoria gotten her to host this thing? Lucy was notorious for not even lending her name to a committee, much less standing up as a hostess. Judge had never seen her look so unoriginal, so a part of this background. Did Victoria have something on her?

Judge felt a wave of heat on his face and the desolate private storm of seconds before evaporated. He wasn't sure how Lucy would treat him tonight after their New Year's Eve together. He'd tried to block her out of his mind this last month because he knew the thought of her would drive him crazy. He could not love Lucy Shining because she could not love him.

This would be the first time he would talk to her since she returned from Africa. His volley had to be profound, witty, sexy, confident. She stood there smiling at him. He felt his breath shorten. He swallowed and exhaled.

"Can you believe the old guard let us in here for our little party?" Sally Banning chirped in his ear. What the hell is she saying? "I mean, this is the first time ever they've turned it over to the junior committee. I hope everyone behaves."

"That counts us out, right Judge," Lucy stepped forward and took Judge's arm. "Let's go to the bar, honey. I'm sure someone in this joint knows how to make a cocktail."

Judge caught Victoria's eye as Lucy led him away. She turned her head and tilted her nose in the air. She was, momentarily, beyond his reach. Fuck her, he thought. He had entered Lucy World where nothing else mattered.

Lucy swirled Judge around the perimeter of the cocktail reception in full swing in the Garden Court. The room had been transformed into a night in Monte Carlo and the invitation instructed guests to wear James Bond Chic, whatever that meant. There were hundreds of yards of red and black tulle cascading from the ceiling to create a tent over the fountain and reflecting pool. Yards of red fabric billowed down the columns. Thousands of red votives flickered in every corner and on every surface. Maxwell created twelve foot columns of every red flower from the market intertwined with six-inch wide shiny black and silver ribbon. Judge thought for a moment that it looked like a party in the Third Reich and almost expected Eva Braun to descend the grand staircase.

Judge heard the unmistakable sound of Peter Duchin's orchestra from the far end of the main hall. Aren't they a little old for a junior event, he thought. Oh yeah, Victoria.

"This doesn't look very Monte Carlo to me," Lucy whispered.

"I wouldn't know," Judge said.

"Oh well. It looks like an expensive party and I'm sure the two of us can squeeze some fun out of it. Thank God you're here, by the way." She kissed him on the cheek and squeezed his arm. "I only stood in that stupid receiving line waiting for you. You sure took your time, by the way. And nice bourbon breath, buddy boy."

Judge felt completely new now. His pendulum swung to the opposite side and he wanted to drink and laugh and dance into this night. They continued around the perimeter, avoiding the throng of eager and giddy guests in the middle. The well-coiffed heads turned in sync with their footsteps. Many of the girls of the lower order were disappointed that they were not in Lucy's path. The men smirked as she shimmied by wondering what she was doing with Judge Mender. Judge noticed Scarlet Goodman ahead of them, crossing the room to get into position. She dragged a plump, banker-looking boy behind her. What was his name? As they approached, Scarlet let out a squeal. "Lucy! Judge! Hello! Did you two come together?"

"Hello, how are you?" Lucy shook Scarlet's hand. She had no idea who Scarlet was, but Lucy always made them feel welcome. "So nice to see you."

"Hello, Scarlet," Judge leaned forward to accept Scarlet's double-cheek air kisses. "You look beautiful tonight."

"This is Harrison Jackson, an old friend of mine from New Orleans," Scarlet trilled to Lucy.

How do-you-dos were exchanged all around.

Judge observed that Scarlet was wearing Dior. She was on the committee, but since she was not a host of tonight's party, she had probably paid retail for that dress, and it had probably cost her around five grand. Part of him was impressed that, while these billion-heiresses were getting free dresses, this little southern debutante was shilling out the cash to keep up with them. But the other side of him, the side that identified more with this crowd lately than with his southern roots was slightly perturbed that she was trying so hard.

Suddenly the photographers from the fashion magazines found them. They had got their credentials and were hounds on the hunt.

"Lucy. Can I get one for Vogue?" shouted one.

"Lucy! Over here. Harper's Bazaar!"

Judge stepped out of the frame as Lucy pulled Scarlet toward her, wrapped her arms around her and hugged her like a long-lost sister. Harrison followed Judge's lead and stepped out of the photographers' shot. Judge looked into Scarlet's eyes to see if he could glimpse the jubilation that he knew would be dancing there. Did she know what was happening to her at that very moment? Being photographed with Lucy Shining was akin to a coronation. She would ascend like a missile with that one photograph. Invitations would flood her mailbox, committees would clamor for her involvement, publicists would dial her relentlessly to attend store openings, and designers would call and beg her to accept free dresses. Judge smiled. His Scarlet story was well-timed and would hit the newsstands first. Lucy had carelessly given him a bonus.

Scarlet was composed and gorgeous. She worked the cameras at every turn. Lucy stood comfortably numb, her gaze settling on Judge, half smiling. In near-identical red Dior dresses, the two women looked like rich and regal members of the same court. The untrained eye would not be able to determine which was estate jewel and which was costume piece. Judge was riveted. He caught the eye of his own magazine's photographer and motioned for him to capture this scene. The Jet Set photographer took his place on the firing line.

Judge thought of Fitzgerald's short story, Bernice Bobs Her Hair. This was the test supreme of her sportsmanship; her right to walk unchallenged in the starry heaven of popular girls.

"Lucy! Over here for Jet Set."

Lucy held the stance for about ten seconds then disengaged from the pose and the pack and turned toward Judge. "That's enough boys. You can have this lovely creature all by herself." Lucy gently pushed Scarlet forward and the photographers circled her.

"What's your name?" the Vogue photographer shouted.

"Scarlet," she said quietly. "Scarlet Goodman." Scarlet held her pose until the photographers spotted Rhea Brown and Mia Wilson. "Mia! Mia! Can we get one over here?"

When the photographer cloud dissipated, Scarlet looked for Lucy but couldn't see her. Judge and Lucy had slipped away. She turned to Harrison, beaming. He laughed and slipped his arm around her waist, kissing her cheek. "You look absolutely gorgeous, Scarlet Goodman."

The museum's Music Room was transformed into a disco hall for the evening and DJ Tom Finn was already spinning loudly, drowning the orchestra in the main hall. Lucy and Judge found the least crowded bar on the far side of the dance floor and sidled up for a drink. Since Maxwell produced this party -- as he had much of the junior set's parties this season now that Chase Peters was banished -- and employed the same staff at each. Judge focused too late and saw the grinning Caleb smirking at him. Lucy caught Caleb's eye and Judge felt a mix of annoyance and competition when he saw her smile at him. Caleb smirked at Judge again and flashed Lucy that stupid smile.

"Are you flirting with Caleb?" Judge asked amused.

"Who's Caleb?" Lucy said, swooshing the fabric of her skirt.

"This bartender."

"Oh, is that his name?" she said nonchalantly. "Yeah, he's my man. He makes my life tolerable at these things."

Judge laughed in spite of himself. "I guess you can't be bothered to remember his name. Easier for me though, I woke up with him once." Judge looked at her out of the side of his eye.

Lucy, without missing a beat or acknowledging shock, said, "Oh, I slept with him too, I just can't remember his name. But Caleb is a damn sexy name. That's what I'll call him."

Caleb handed Lucy her vodka and cranberry and Judge a scotch.

"Hey Caleb," Lucy purred. "Thanks for the potion."

"No problem," Caleb smiled. "Are you two here together?"

"Yeah," Lucy said with a smile. "Are you jealous?"

"Not yet," Caleb said, "but give me an hour."

"We'll give you more than that," Lucy took Judge's hand and pulled him away. She locked eyes with Judge, "Won't we, lover?"

112

Judge burst into laughter and let Lucy pull him through the growing crowd at the bar.

Lucy and Judge spent the evening drinking, dancing and avoiding people. They escaped once to the Fifth Avenue Garden where the committee had set up port and cigars. It was cold and there were too many bodies. They took one look around and went back inside. They slipped into one of the galleries and Lucy produced a neatly-rolled and now flattened joint from her décolletage. The two fugitives smoked a joint beneath a Whistler just as a security guard rounded the corner like a bloodhound, nose in the air. They laughed and scurried out of the room.

Back on the dance floor, they avoided boorish conversations by dancing in the center, arms flailing like spears. They laughed at everyone and laughed at nothing. They created a wall of laughter and intimacy so impenetrable that anyone who approached them was turned away. They laughed at each other and at anyone who tried to be serious. The DJ knew which songs kept Lucy on the floor and kept them coming.

At midnight, the blare of the junior jet set's anthem boomed from the speaker accompanied by the shrieks of the Young Fellows. Rhea Brown led the charge to the center of the floor, her hands in the air and her ass bouncing to the beat.

One More Time

We're gonna celebrate...

The dancing and drinking were taking over, and as much as Judge hated to tear away from Lucy, he excused himself and headed to the bathroom. Lucy kept dancing; it made no difference whether there was a partner or not. She was soon surrounded by Rhea and Mia and, to

113

Judge's surprise, Victoria entered the fray. Funny, he thought, I don't ever think I've seen her dance.

Judge stumbled into the cavernous men's room, relieved to find it empty. He was alone in a quiet space, and allowed himself to indulge in the emotion he'd been suppressing. He knew now that the anxiety over the way things were left with Lucy was wasted time. She was exactly the same, even more familiar and intimate. He was back on track with her and in the middle of another magical night in the city.

Judge opened his eyes when he heard the door swing open and saw his colleague striding toward him. The photographer sidled up next to Judge in the adjacent urinal. "Are you working tonight dude, or you going to fuck Lucy Shining?"

Judge felt a pang at the naked remark. Then he remembered, this is how he always talks.

"Can't I do both?" he laughed. "You know who to shoot, just hit it and quit it."

"I can leave?"

"Yeah, beat it. Nothing happens now that can be photographed. Everyone's on their way to sloppy. Go home. I'll see you in the lab tomorrow to go over pictures. Oh, did you get a good shot of Lucy with Scarlet Goodman?"

"Yeah. Who's that hot little snatch?" the photographer said shaking and zipping. "I hope she's your next star because I love taking her picture. She's different than these other cold bitches. That girl has fire."

"Yeah," Judge said with admiration. "She's on her way up. I just interviewed her for a feature for May. Get used to shooting her."

"Hot damn!" The photographer zipped up and walked out the door. "Hot new snatch!" He shouted as the phrase got lost in the music and chatter of the room outside.

Judge shut his eyes again and finally relieved himself. He savored the temporary sanctuary of the cavernous men's room. He heard the door open again and the sound of the music invaded the bathroom once again.

Judge didn't open his eyes but held onto this hazy feeling a few more seconds. He felt a hand grab a chunk of his right ass cheek and slide down the back of his thigh. Then the hot breath whispered in his ear. "One more time, music's got me feeling so free" and the voice's vendor rubbed a heavy basket against Judge's ass.

Judge turned around and smiled, breathing humid vapors of bourbon onto Caleb's lips, their bodies touching in several places.

"Is tonight going to be a good night?" Caleb whispered in Judge's ear.

Judge sidestepped him with a drunken chuckle and tousled hair. The alcohol and the time spent with Lucy told him to forget hating this hustler bartender. "I don't think so, Caleb. I'm going home with Lucy tonight."

Caleb mimicked the side step, came face to face again and kissed Judge on the lips. Caleb smiled deep and sexy, stepped back and walked to the door. He looked back over his shoulder at Judge.

"So am I, dude," Caleb said. "See you there."

Judge shook his head to focus. He walked over and held onto the sink for balance. He stood in the amber glow of the bathroom, checking his reflection in the mirror. He felt nausea and his head started to spin. Judge walked back through the Garden Court, his head tucked low to avoid conversations. The room was tightly packed, and he was able to avoid any prolonged eye contact. He scurried along the perimeter of the lobby and out onto the front steps. He stepped off to the side and lit a cigarette, letting the crisp cold air snap him back. He looked down beneath him at a small ruckus on the sidewalk to see Chase Peters with a spotlight in his face talking to a camera. Good god, Judge groaned. What a moron. Judge dropped his cigarette and squashed it with the toe of his shiny patent leather shoe and walked back into the fold of noise and revelry.

Lucy hid behind a mass of flower arranging on the back bar, waiting for Judge. In his absence on the dance floor, she found herself surrounded and stifled by a crowd of eager dancers, so she sought refuge behind the giant floral display. Caleb slid behind her in the tight space and rubbed his crotch against her backside as he returned to his position behind the bar.

"Sorry if I'm in your way," she said. "I'm hiding out and waiting for my friend." She picked up a cherry out of one of the cups on the bar and popped it into her mouth.

"S'alright, Lucy," Caleb said. "You can keep me company all night."

Lucy looked at him curiously, how did he know her name? "I'm thinking of having a big bar at my next party. Do you do private functions?"

116

"For you, yes." He smiled and winked at her.

"Well, here's my card," she said. "Email me your number and I'll let you know the dates. I'm thinking late March."

Caleb took the card and put it in his front pants pocket, drawing more attention to his money maker. He smiled at her. "I will definitely be in touch." Every move he made a studied seduction.

Judge stood across the room watching. He watched Lucy hand something to Caleb and he watched Caleb put it in his pocket. Caleb caught Judge's eye and winked. Judge convulsed. He turned toward the door and there was Scarlet, face to face, eyes blinking like Morse code.

"Hey Judge," she said. "Where's Lucy?"

He smiled.

"I don't know," he said. "Maybe in a corner with your date."

Judge slid his arm around her waist and rubbed low toward her ass. Scarlet moved lightning fast, caught his hand and pulled it in front of her. Lucy appeared.

"You trying to steal my man, little lady?" Lucy said.

Scarlet beamed and said, "Hey Lucy, isn't tonight wonderful?"

"Yeah, wonderful," Lucy said as she turned her back on Scarlet and wrapped her arms around Judge's neck, smiled and kissed him on the lips.

Scarlet stood there for a mute second, then said brightly, "I'll see y'all later. I've got to find Harrison." She turned and bounced toward the dance floor.

"When are we getting out of here?" Lucy purred.

Judge stood solid and pulled her arms off of his neck. "I've got to get home early, actually," he said abruptly, "Can I put you in a cab?"

Lucy stood there with her mouth open. She looked like a little girl, her eyes squinting to comprehend the strange words falling out of his mouth.

"What?" she said.

"Yeah, I know it sucks, but I've got a big morning so I need to get home and get to bed. You don't mind do you?"

"No, of course not," she said curtly. "Go ahead, I'll catch a ride with Rhea."

Judge stalked off the dance floor, brushing against a few black wool shoulders in his way. Lucy stood there staring in his wake. He heard his name called, but kept walking toward the door. He hit the sidewalk and a cold gust blew dirt in his eye and he cursed the air. "Fuck you!" he said out loud and headed toward Madison to find his car and driver.

Chapter 7

The Photo

Downtown in the Jet Set photo lab, Judge looked over the contact sheets of the pictures from the Frick party. He ran through the pages of glittering gowns on the usual suspects. He couldn't find the one shot he was looking for. Steve the photographer handed him an envelope. "Is this what you're looking for?"

Judge pulled the photo out of the folder. Steve made a print of the obvious best shot and there, in his hands, was the most glamorous party picture Judge had ever seen. The stark contrast of red dresses against the pale marble background of the museum created a perfect composition. Lucy was radiant and looked at Scarlet adoringly, arms wrapped around her waist. Scarlet looked at the camera dead on wearing a hint of a smile. The two never looked more beautiful or richer. Yes, this was the picture.

"You never print these up for me," Judge said.

"I figured you'd want to see it like that. It's a damn good shot. That girl is going to blow up. You going to save it for the Frick page?"

"No, no, get this to the art desk," Judge said quickly. "I want this to run in the "It Girl" story in the March issue. No text needed. That photo says more that I could write. Good job, dude, good job."

"Can it make it in that issue?" the photographer asked. "I thought that closed last week."

"It did, but they had to redesign the layout. Richard hated it. It will make it if you get it over now." Judge kept staring at the picture. "Can you make me a copy of this?"

"It's yours. I made another. Hey, check it out. I made a print of another shot of Scarlet just for personal use. Later, dude." The photographer walked away in the direction of the art director's desk.

Judge noticed there were two photos in his hand, one behind the other. He pulled the second in front of the first and laughed out loud. There in his hands was Harrison dipping Scarlet on the dance floor. Scarlet was stretched out in full orgasmic pleasure with a smile to match. The flimsy fabric of her red Dior dress had pulled aside to expose her full round breast, nipple protruding and excited. To complete the scandalous shot, Harrison leered straight into the camera with a conqueror's smirk, the nipple millimeters from his lips.

Judge laughed and yelled after the photographer, "Pervert!"

"Hell yeah," he whooped. "That girl is on fire!"

Chapter 8

Recklessness & Reckoning

Victoria agreed to meet Judge for breakfast only after he intimated that he might not run anything on the Frick party. He pulled her aside the night before at the Chopard store opening, before he got drunk, and said it was urgent that they have a talk. She agreed to meet him this morning, knowing he would miss it at best or be hung over at worst. He was already in his cups when he'd slurred the shouted request. It wasn't an outright threat, but Victoria picked up the pieces and knew what he meant when he said he had to meet with her on Saturday morning and would not take no for an answer. Not that she gave a damn about the Frick. Her reputation was on the line. She hosted that party and was expected to deliver coverage in the pages of Jet Set. So she sat at Brennan's diner on Third Street at eleven in the morning waiting for him to arrive. She had on no makeup, wore a snug cashmere turtleneck and black pants and a black trench coat, and her eyes were hidden behind enormous sunglasses. She was dressed for subterfuge.

Judge wondered why she would want to meet in such a place and not at one of the more obvious hangouts on Madison. He was also pissed that he'd made this date so early in the morning. He went to Moomba after the Chopard party and drank and danced until four. He finally ended up walking home with an actor he'd never seen before and getting into bed at five in the morning. He was very tired, very hung over, and very un-showered.

Judge arrived twenty minutes after Victoria and muttered apologies as he slid into the booth opposite her. She had ordered coffee and pancakes for the both of them and was chomping them down.

"Good morning, Mr. Mender. You look like hell."

"I feel it. Moomba was out of control last night."

"I heard you took home some L.A. actor boy. I'm surprised you could pull yourself away so early to join me." She winked that infuriating wink he was beginning to detest.

Judge took a long swig of coffee and pushed the plate of pancakes away from him. Victoria dissected the night before at Chopard, but Judge wasn't listening. He was thinking he should have stayed in bed with... what was his name?

"I can't believe we pulled it off," she said between bites. "It was a great party, don't you think? I noticed you and Lucy hitting it off on the dance floor. Did you go home with her that night?"

Judge almost spit his coffee out. "What?"

"Oh, relax, Judgie. Everyone knows what a horn dog you are and it's no secret that you worship Lucy. I never believed your reputation as a genuine bisexual and recent events have re-enforced my suspicions. I'm beginning to think it's all just an act to make you seem more urbane." She took a pat of butter and ran it over the already syrupy surface of the pancakes.

Judge's suspicion of her recent shift in attitude was reinforced. This wasn't the same Victoria who warmly welcomed him to her apartment last fall or put him up in Palm Beach for the holiday. This was the formal, stiff, lips tightly pursed Miss Newton that the outside world experienced.

"I, Victoria, I don't think..."

"Oh, I'm just giving you a hard time," she chuckled. "Tell me how much you enjoyed the Frick and tell me that you are going to write it up as the social event of the season."

Judge recovered and felt a little easier as the old Victoria re-surfaced.

"I thought it was a great party. The right kind of crowd, the DJ was phenomenal, the décor was just right. I think you all did a magnificent job," he lied. His foul mood had returned after he caught Lucy with Caleb and tainted his recollection of the night. "Were you pleased?"

"Overall, I have to say yes," Victoria said slowly. "You know I kept that guest list tight as drum and you won't believe the nobodies that called trying to get in. I told the museum and the other host girls that I would not be a part of some Rhea Brown, anyone-and-everyone party that you couldn't get a drink at, much less talk to the people you knew. So, yes. I was pleased. There were some exceptions, of course."

This is where Judge usually felt the buzz. These were the moments of this job that he had relished, the bits that made his column spicy and boosted his career. Now it was like a drug he'd grown used to and yes, he needed it and depended on it, but it didn't give him the same high anymore. He was beginning to wish he could give it up altogether. Victoria sensed that his attitude had shifted too. This is usually the point in the conversation when Judge would pop up out of any degree of hangover and hang on her words, waiting to follow any trail she laid out. She would drop the curtain and let him see whom her group was against. Who they thought was over stepping her bounds and who should be booted back to the bush. As Judge had grown closer and more comfortable within this group he began to realize that there was no consensus, this was pure Victoria and who was atop her personal vendetta list. Judge checked himself, and out of habit, leaned in as she lowered her voice and her chin.

"Well, we could hardly keep her from attending since she bought her way onto the committee, but it's the last time she'll be on the Frick."

"Who?" He grinned.

"Scarlet Goodman, of course." She let the name hit him in the face and he sat back, visibly stunned. She gloated in the effect. Finally, he was alert. Victoria waited a moment before she resumed. She let him feel the weight of the name, ricocheting between them. Her knees bounced with glee under the table.

"What are you talking about, Victoria?" He controlled the visible expression of his shock, but he was getting angry. All of the jumbled frustration of the past weeks exploded on his tongue. "You introduced me to her. You sat me next to her at your dinner. You made me think you wanted her written about."

"I did, Judge," Victoria said matter-of-factly. "I wanted you to dismiss her. She's a terrible climber, parading her ambition all over town underneath that wide-eyed innocence. Couldn't you see it? I read her as a fake right away. I assumed you had picked up on that. I mean, she's from the South! Isn't that your turf? I thought you were going to ax her, and then you called me to say you think she's fabulous. She is not fabulous. I didn't think I needed to spell it out for you. Wait a minute, have you bedded her?"

"No!" he said.

"Well, at least there's that."

"But why?" he pursued. "I don't understand."

"She's a bounder. I knew it the minute I saw her. I have heard terrible things about her from old family friends in New Orleans. I thought surely we were on the same page. I guess you're slipping now that you're famous."

Judge was getting pissed. Was he going to sit there and let her manipulate and insult him? He checked himself. His old impulse kicked in. He needed to get this story.

"Well, I guess I fucked up." He sipped his coffee and redirected. "Tell me. It's not too late. I haven't turned in the story yet."

'Well," Victoria continued, "my sources tell me she pulled the same act in New Orleans. This Harrison Jackson met her at Tulane and brought her to a few parties. She was nice enough in the beginning, even charming. It was only after she got comfortable that her true colors were revealed. They say she became intolerable, stomping her way up the social ladder. She started by ingratiating herself with the Jacksons and their immediate set. The Harrison boy evidently financed her because she has no money. I hear he's doing the same here, which is questionable enough in its own right. When I told my source that she was here now, she was flabbergasted. She said Scarlet disappeared one day, and they all wondered where she went. They assumed she was hiding out in Hooterville. My friend, uh, source was shocked to hear that she was here. They knew she was cunning, but they had no idea her

125

sights were set on New York. All this would be distasteful, but there's more."

"More?" Judge asked bewildered.

"Her hunger for money evidently rivals her hunger for climbing," Victoria went on. "I've heard, and this is the most delicious morsel, that there was an incident. It was hush-hushed by Harrison's family for reasons no one down there can figure out. It's not like he was in danger of marrying the girl. I got the story straight from the source. You will not believe this. But it's true. I stake my reputation on it."

Judge jumped into a taxi and headed back to his office, his head in a swim from the night before, the alcohol, the lack of sleep and now, the burden of Victoria's revelation. He walked into his cubicle and collapsed in his chair. Thank god Leah isn't here, he thought. I don't need to hear how much like hell I look.

He opened the file on his computer labeled "Scarlet Goodman". Fuck! He suddenly remembered the April issue with the first story featuring that beautiful picture of Scarlet and Lucy. The It Girl story had already gone to print! He tasted something salty in his mouth. What was happening to him? He was getting reckless. The chair was spinning, the room was spinning, the building. He lay down on the floor under his desk, holding his temples firmly in his hands.

He breathed deep and got back up in his chair. He refreshed the screen and looked back into the story. As he was reading, he was struck by the tone of the piece. How uplifting, how luminous and innocent, just like Scarlet, he thought. He began filling in the new details of her life as reported by Victoria. He would have to spend the next hours of his life researching these allegations, calling on unknown sources in New

Orleans all to meet the May issue deadline for that afternoon. Could he kill the story? He brightened.

He got up from his desk and headed toward Richard's office. Halfway there he imagined what he must look like. He turned around and bolted into the men's room. Confronted with his reflection, he felt worse. He pumped some of the liquid soap from the dispenser and started scrubbing his face. He splashed cold water and toweled off with the scratchy paper towels from the metal box. He wet his hair and ran his fingers through the Medusa like shrub of hair, fast and furious. He tucked his shirt in and smoothed out his jacket. There were big particles of dust and what looked like spit balls on the lapel. He brushed them off and left the reflection and headed to Richard's office.

Richard was on the phone, smoking a cigarette, but motioned him in and into the electric chair. Judge sat there looking at the hundreds of photos on the windowsill, pictures of the editor with every conceivable fashion designer, celebrity, socialite and royal.

"Goodbye, Gavin. See you this weekend." Richard shot a glance to be sure the name registered with Judge.

"What is it, golden boy? Got your Scarlet story ready for me?" The editor stubbed out his cigarette and pulled another out of the pack.

"Well, actually, Richard. That's what I'm here to talk to you about. Is there any possible way to pull the story from the next issue? I've just found some very interesting news that could make it a much better piece and I..."

"Are you drunk?" The editor shouted at him? "Close the goddamn door."

Judge shot up out of the chair and considered slamming the door behind him, but instead closed it and sat back down. "No. I'm not drunk."

"Then why the fuck would you come in here asking for something as ridiculous as killing this story the day that it's due?"

"Like I was saying, I just found out some more..."

"Tough shit. The story runs. The deadline is five o'clock. End of story. You are skating on some very thin ice here, mister. I suggest you turn in this story, and it better be blazing, or you are going to find this place a little uncomfortable. Can I be any clearer?"

"I hear you." Judge said meekly. "I just thought..."

"Stop thinking and start writing. That is what you are paid to do -- and news flash! -- used to be pretty good at. What is going on with you? Do you need to check into rehab? It's nothing to be ashamed of, hell, most of my friends have been in rehab. Could be your next story. The glamorous and gifted rehab graduates as seen from the inside. Hey, I really like that idea."

"No, Richard. I don't need to check into rehab. I'm just, I don't know. I'm just trying to do the best job I can. It doesn't seem like I'm communicating that very well."

"Your work will communicate that. How much time do you need to get it done?"

Judge sensed pity and his own imminent defeat and stiffened.

"None." He stood up. "I'll have it for you on time. Thanks for the talk. I'll have it done by five."

Judge went back to his desk and stared at the screen. He would write this fucking story. Damn them all. Who was Scarlet to him? Who was Victoria, for that matter, who was Richard? He would write this story, make another splash and walk out of this office. He'd parlay this sensation into another job and finally do the kind of writing he wanted to write. If he only knew what that was.

Judge's phone rang and he unconsciously snatched the receiver and barked, "Judge Mender."

"Well, good morning, Evil. Did you wake up on the wrong side of some trashy cooz this morning?"

"Maxwell, I'm not in the mood. It's a shit day already."

"Okay, sorry. Tell me."

"I need to get out of here for a minute. Want to meet me for a drink?" Judge looked at his watch. 12:15. "I need a drink."

"Well, I guess I could do. I'm in the car, actually, just over on Fifth. Where?"

"I'll meet you at Bemelman's in twenty minutes."

When Judge walked in to the soothing muted light of Bemelman's, Maxwell was already seated at a table, sipping on a cup of coffee. Judge slid into the banquette and put his head on the table.

"Dear boy, what has brought you so low? Tell Auntie Maxwell."

"I am fucked. Fucked, fucked, fucked. I'm going to get fired and I don't give a fuck. I'm moving back home to Ophelia."

Maxwell turned and snapped, "Waiter!" who turned sharply in his direction. "A Kettle One Bloody Mary, please, make it a double." He then turned his gaze on Judge. "The tomato juice will do you good. Now tell me, what has happened?"

"It's about a feature story I'm writing on Scarlet Goodman for the May issue. She's a new…"

"Oh I know her!" Maxwell exclaimed. "A darling little belle from New Orleans. I met her at the Frick. She is absolutely charming. What a good idea."

"Please, Maxwell," Judge groaned. "Can I get through this without the exuberance?"

"Please continue. I apologize." He turned around toward the bar. "Waiter! Bloody Mary. Tout de suite! And bring me a Manhattan."

Judge relayed the story from the first meeting at Victoria's to the night at the Frick, Victoria's news and his own impressions.

Maxwell sipped his Manhattan and pushed Judge's drink closer to him. He lit a cigarette and let Judge take a deep long sip before saying anything.

"Well, Judge. Here's the way I see it. Are you ready?"

"Let it roll, Maxie. Let it roll."

"I detest that nickname, by the way." Judge rolled his eyes and Maxwell said, "But! I am willing to let it lie apropos of your depressed state and dire situation."

"Please."

"You like this girl, Scarlet, as do I," Maxwell began. "She is one of us. Her crime is nothing to the rest of the world, but here in the kingdom, it is punishable by death. I am sorry to say it, but she has been exposed. And to none other than Queen Victoria and that is the end of it. I don't want to sound harsh and unjustly cruel, but people like Victoria Newton pay our bills, yours and mine. And Richard Hadenfield's! Yes, we are lucky that we are allowed to come up to the big house, but darling, at the end of the day, we are all field hands. It is easy to forget, especially for your generation, that we are not all created equal. For me, I never forget for a moment that I am anything other than hired help." He paused and considered for a moment, then continued. "I am sure you have heard about my own little indiscretion?" Maxwell raised his eyebrow. Judge shook his head slowly.

"Well," Maxwell lowered his voice and continued. "although it happened twenty years ago, it still gets dusted off on occasion to remind me that I am under the thumb."

Maxwell leaned in. Judge followed suit.

"In brief, I fell into a youthful indiscretion with someone's husband, never mind who. The ladies circled around my wife and I was shown the door. I was on my way to being the best events planner in Atlanta, when I was saved. Serena Robertson took me to lunch and laid out the facts. If I towed the line, I would be welcomed back into my marriage, my home, my career and their world. I made that decision, for better or for worse, and ran back into the fold. Of course, things weren't so out in the open back then as they are now. But I made my choice and I have lived with the consequences all these years."

Maxwell drifted off for a moment, the years flashing by like a slide show on the wall of his brain. Then he snapped back, sat up right in his chair and sipped his Manhattan.

"So, you see," he resumed with confidence and volume, "I have a great life, but it is comprised of the crumbs of their table. And you, Deary, are in the same boat. Until you discover oil or marry wealth, you are as dependent upon their good grace as I. It is easy to forget that fact when you are swinging around St. Tropez on someone's yacht or laid up in an estate in Palm Beach, but that is the dangerous part. Never think that it is yours for a moment. That is the mistake of many a climber. Their brittle bones are scattered all around us."

"So what are you telling me to do?"

"Throw her to the wolves, my dear. It is the only way. It is a small price to pay for your future aspirations."

Maxwell finished his Manhattan and turned to the waiter. "I'll have one more, please. Tell the new bartender that he is a magical mixer and give him my card." Maxwell produced a stiff engraved card from a silver case, handed it to the waiter and turned back to Judge. "He'd never leave this plush gig, but if he so chooses, he would look very nice at my bar, don't you think. And he can mix a good Manhattan. Wonders never cease."

Judge sat in the back of the taxi as Maxwell's words bedeviled his thoughts. Throw her to the wolves. Throw her to the wolves. Judge's thoughts agitated then progressed to the spin cycle. He felt the sides of his eyes crinkle on his face. Throw her to the wolves. Maxwell knew from whence he came. He was an animate guide to this strange world they orbited. He was Judge's trusted source. Throw her to the wolves. Write the story. There can never be good girls if there aren't bad ones. The good ones only shine if the bad ones are dirty. Lucy Shining. Scarlet Goodman. Two halves of the same whole. One, an ideal, the paradigm for all he wanted these girls to be, this world to be. The other, a knock off worming into the apple unwittingly spreading rot and disease. The one must be stamped out to save the whole, preserve the balance. It was his duty, not only his job. He was in this world now and he must guard against invasion. She was pretty but she was not welcome. That had been made clear. Get rid of her. Throw her to the wolves. He felt a sinister sneer cross his lips. He could wipe her out with words. He'd anointed her with a photograph and he could extinguish her with words. He reached into his pocket and pulled out his tiny tape recorder. He pressed play. "Je suis la Goulue! Je suis la Goulue!" Scarlet's voice squeaked out of the tiny speaker. He laughed miserably. He could extinguish her with words and better yet, her own.

Chapter 9

The Season's It Girls

Page Six: March 22. Elizabeth Pilgrim is out, Sally Banning is in, and Lucy Shining is untouchable. Those are the pronouncements made by Jet Set magazine in the upcoming It Girl issue to hit stands Wednesday. Taking into account the money, the face, the body, the gowns, the family name -- and the money! The editors of the society chronicle have bestowed their blessing on a bevy of beauties. And more importantly, stripped the banner from some of the usual suspects of lovelies, sure to alter publicists' invitation lists city wide. Who else made the cut? You'll have to buy the rag when it hits the newsstands Wednesday to be in the loop.

Scarlet read the Page Six article to Harrison, rattling off every word, comma and period with rifle-like precision through the crackle of her cell phone. "Elizabeth Pilgrim is out, Sally Banning is in, and Lucy Shining is untouchable."

"Uh huh," Harrison was in his office. "Untouchable," he murmured.

"Elizabeth Pilgrim out! Can you imagine, Harrison?" Scarlet asked in shock and seriousness. "How can she be out? She just hosted the Frick for goodness sake. I hope the board isn't going to be upset."

"Uh huh," Harrison buzzed.

"Harrison!" She blurted. "Are you listening?"

"Yeah, Elizabeth Pilgrim thrown off the board of the Frick."

"No! She was never on the board, dummy. She's out! As in over. Done. Finished. According to Jet Set."

"Scarlet. Do you honestly think that Elizabeth Pilgrim, in all her billions, gives three shits what some society rag says about her?"

"Yes! I really do," Scarlet blurted. "I think behind that hoighty toighty cucumber cool of hers, she really cares. Any girl would. I'll bet she's devastated. I would be. God! I would die."

"Well. Hopefully she'll hang on until next year. Maybe she'll be reinstated."

"Harrison. I wonder who the other ones are." Scarlet mused, running her finger over the text of the names in the paper. "Victoria Newton, for sure. And Mia Wilson and Rhea Brown, definitely. Can you think of anyone else? Those ones for sure."

"Scarlet, honey?"

"Yeah, Harrison?"

"I really have to get back to work now."

"Oh okay." Scarlet stared at the article. "I've got to call mama."

"Where do you want to go to dinner tonight?"

"Oh, I don't know. Bilboquet?"

"Again?

"Oh yes. I'm sure everyone will be there."

"Okay. I'll swing by around nine."

"Can't wait, see you then."

Victoria Newton stood in her kitchen, telephone in hand, reading the article to Sweetie with much editorial insertion. "Elizabeth Pilgrim out? She outranks all of those girls, save Lucy Shining, of course. Sally Banning? She's a horse-riding tom boy! I mean, I love the girl, but give me a break! I shudder to think who else is included."

"I wonder how Jet Set came to those conclusions." Sweetie wondered.

"Jet Set?!" Victoria barked. "That list is all Judge Mender. It's his doing. I should have known something was up when he was so frosty to Elizabeth in Palm Beach."

"Well, surely you will be in there."

"Me?!" Victoria sputtered. "I have no desire to be some stupid It Girl, Sweetie. Please! I can't imagine anything more degrading."

"Oh, I don't know. It sounds like a who's who to me, sort of like making Homecoming court. I think I would like it for a minute or two."

"Oh, please. It's just some feeble attempt to sell magazines. Nobody takes all that nonsense seriously. I can't even believe we're talking about it."

Victoria closed the paper with the suddenly offensive article.

"I have to go. I'm meeting Elizabeth for lunch at Bergdorf's. I'll call you later."

"Goodbye, Victoria," Sweetie said, confused.

"Goodbye."

Victoria reopened the paper and re-read the article. "I sure as hell better be in there" She fumed. "I let that ass stay at my house in PB. Who does he think he is?"

      Lucy Shining listened with one ear and half her brain to Rhea rattle on and on.

"You are untouchable, that's for sure, but Sally Banning! Give me a break!" She shouted. "Who cares if she makes it to a party? She wears those bedazzled Badgley Mischka dresses to every gala. Ugh! Although, I don't mind seeing that Elizabeth Pilgrim taken down a notch. She's such a snotty bitch to me."

"Rhea, who cares about all that nonsense?" Lucy was running for a taxi and her hands were full of shopping bags. She had been down to Chinatown to pick up her favorite Ginseng tea at Golden Dragon and ended up buying paper lanterns and four paper umbrellas for what she did not know. She was taken by the red and gold and fringe and the way they all crinkled when she opened and closed them.

"I care for sure," Rhea blurted. "I know I better be in that goddamn issue tomorrow or Judge Mender is going to be short two hairy balls."

"Ha!" Lucy laughed. "I'll talk to you later, girl. Goodbye."

Lucy looked up and down Mott Street for a taxi, but none were to be found. "Untouchable," she sang to the tune of Nat King Cole's Unforgettable. "That's what you are..."

Lucy had not seen Judge since the night of the Frick when he abandoned her on the dance floor. She would never have cared if any other man had pulled that on her. Of course, no other man would have the balls to do that. Judge was a strange creature. He was great in bed, at least the parts of that night that she remembered. He made her laugh. He was smart, yeah all those things, but..., she couldn't figure him out. She couldn't get inside him. He was so hard to read. He was a different animal than any other man she knew. She reasoned that was the reason he stayed in her head. And he did stay in her head. Untouchable. Ha. Lucy smiled and laughed to herself and headed north toward Houston Street, looking for a taxi to take her back up town.

Judge sat in his cubicle aching over the play he now dreaded the It Girl feature would get when the magazine hit the stands. Why had he included Scarlet at the last moment? Why did that damn picture have to be so good? He needed a drink. He needed to talk to Maxwell. He snatched up the receiver and dialed the number.

"Maxwell Jones," answered Wanda.

"Hello, Wanda. It's Judge Mender. Is Maxwell available?"

"Well, speak of the devil. Yeah, hold on."

Wanda didn't bother to put Judge on hold, she just pulled the receiver away and bellowed toward Maxwell's door. "Judge Mender's on the phone!"

Maxwell busted out laughing as he picked up the receiver.

"Wow. Those are some lungs on that girl." Judge said.

"Yeah, she's giving it to me this morning." Maxwell said. "Says she's hung-over. We must sympathize. So, tell me. I guess you've got the tongues wagging this morning. I must say, I was a little surprised you had the courage to demote Elizabeth Pilgrim."

"Forget her. She's a frigid bore. The big problem hits tomorrow when the April issue comes out."

"Hmm mm." Maxwell hummed. "Now tell me why that is again?"

"Because Scarlet Goddamn Goodman is going to be listed as this season's most promising girl, and I'm going to be made a fool of when Victoria gets done with it."

"Oh Judge. Listen to yourself." Maxwell said. "It's such a trifle, really. I don't mean to belittle your article, but honey, this kind of story gets written every decade, way before you got here and will continue long after you leave. I mean, it's a nice distraction, but please. Don't let it get you down. At least poor Scarlet will have a couple months of stardom. She'll get invited everywhere and have the pick of free dresses from the best houses. Please. You have anointed her. Although," he mused. "You will destroy her when her feature comes out in the May issue. It's all so delicious, really. I have to say I love having all this privilege to the workings of it all. Who should we destroy next? Let's see. That old bat Helen Highwater hasn't paid her bill in six months. Do you think you could put her on the hit list?"

"I'm glad that you can take such pleasure in my misery,"

It was true, Judge realized. Maxwell made him see how trifling it all was, yet, would he say the same thing if Judge weren't in misery? Would he be exalting if I were pleased with it all? He wondered.

"Honestly, Judge. I wouldn't take it all so seriously. It's all just fun and parlor games. Who's hot and who's finished? Who is the new Babe Paley and who is yesterday's news? Society is the new celebrity. It seems the starlets are no longer in Hollywood. Now they're found on Park Avenue. Why does everyone care? Because you tell them to care, my dear. You must laugh at yourself every once in a while. It isn't like you to get twisted into such a knot. Leave that to those girls who would kill each other to be called It Girl. It's a silly name, really. Don't you think? I mean what about Glam Girls or Best Dressed or hell, Party Girls. I mean, that's what they are when you get right down to it."

Judge felt a sting in this attempt to assuage him. This was his career after all. This is what he got paid to do and in his attempt to make him feel better, Maxwell was belittling what he did for a living. Surely not, Judge reasoned. He doesn't mean it that way. It's just all part of the act. He was right, though. Judge did tell them who to care about. It was all in his hands. He swelled with importance.

Judge's phone lit up. Here come the calls, he thought. "Hey, Maxwell. I have to run. Meet for a drink later?"

"Call when you're leaving," Maxell said. "I will live through the day knowing you will be calling."

"Goodbye, queen."

Richard Hadenfield flapped his feathers in a fit of elation. He sat behind his cluttered desk on the telephone with his best friend and confidant, Gavin Reese.

"We include her in the It Girl issue and them we annihilate her the very next month. That Judge is craftier that I gave him credit for. He's a real comer."

The editor hung up the phone and dialed Judge's extension.

"You really hit it this time, Judge." He boomed loudly. "The timing is perfect and Page Six just helped us sell out the April issue. It will fly off the New York stands tomorrow.

"Yes, those Page Six folks do come in handy at times." Judge said, easing into a position where he could accept this lighthearted praise.

"Have you gotten any good calls yet? Any one scalding?"

"No, not yet. They'll pour in tomorrow when the issue hits." Judge said, putting on an upbeat tone. "That's when the fun starts."

"Well. Congratulations." Richard said. "I look forward to the hail storm."

"Thank you." Judge said, settling into this new laissez fare.

"So, what do you have in mind for the next one?"

Judge felt the air leave his body. "Oh, it's a whopper. But you'll have to wait until our meeting next week. I want to surprise you."

Judge sat in his cubicle stunned and silent. He picked up the phone and pressed redial. Ring, ring, ring. "Maxwell Jones."

"Hey, Wanda. It's Judge again. Is he in?"

"Yeah. Hold on."

Judge tapped his pen on the computer screen. His eyes searched across the desk for a clue. What was he going to do next? He had no idea. He was completely bankrupt of ideas.

"Judgie, my boy. What is it now?"

"I've got to have a drink. Meet me at Fanelli's?"

"Fanelli's? It's that kind of drink, is it?"

"Yeah. I'm on my way down."

"It's all so surreptitious. I love it. Should I stop by Prada and purchase a black trench?"

"Maxwell."

"Just kidding, Judge. I'll be there when you arrive."

Chapter 10

The Walkers Take Manhattan

Judge stood at the window in his apartment dinking a short tumbler of good scotch, nervously checking his watch. Russ's plane landed at three-thirty. He called to say he was in a taxi on his way to Judge's apartment. His oldest friend from Ophelia was about to enter his new life in New York. When Russ called last week it seemed to Judge like a great idea. It would be a singular experience to show Russ around the city and let him experience his New York. But now, with Russ in a taxi minutes away from invading his life, Judge felt the flutter of small panic. Judge was anxious to see how Russ would fit in with the Jet Set crowd. Russ has never been to New York, he remembered. Judge leaned on the edge of the sofa absently looking down the street. The buzzer from the intercom jolted him upright. He looked back down to the street and saw a black Lincoln Town Car in front of his building. What? He thought. Russ in a Town Car? He crossed the room to the door and spoke into the little intercom box.

"Welcome to New York, Country!" Judge yelled into the receiver. "Come on up. It's number twenty-eight. Do you need help with your bags?"

"Yee haw!" came the response that filled his apartment. "Nah, I can handle it."

Judge laughed and pressed the button to release the lock on the lobby door and then opened his own door to await the elevator. The old car rumbled up and settled on his floor and slowly opened and Russ bounded out like a Labrador retriever. He dropped his bag and ran the twenty feet to wrap Judge in a rib-crushing bear hug.

"I can't believe I'm here, dude," Russ boomed. "This is awesome."

"Oh, yoo hoo," trilled a bird-like voice from the elevator.

"Oh, yeah, I've got a surprise," Russ said and hurried past Judge into the apartment. "I've got to see a man about a mule. Where's the pisser?"

Judge absently motioned in the direction of the bathroom and looked back down the hall toward the elevator, and there standing in the dimly lit hallway was Lucinda Walker. She was dressed in a grey Chanel suit with pearl buttons and matching grey pumps, hat and dark sunglasses.

"Well who can that be?" Judge teased, "Princess Radziwill?

"Surprise, Darling." Lucinda came fluttering down the hall and planted a light kiss on the stunned Judge.

"I made Russ promise not to tell you that I was coming. I wanted it to be a complete surprise." She brushed past him and into his apartment. "You won't hold it against us, will you?"

She waltzed into the apartment and held her arms out wide. "So this is a New York City bachelor's suite. My sainted late mother would expire from the scandal of a southern lady stepping foot in such a place, but I think we're safe from gossip now, don't you Judge?"

"I don't know what to say except welcome to my humble abode." Judge glanced furtively around her. The room was presentable for he'd called the housekeeper in yesterday to straighten up for Russ, but still, he thought, it isn't prepped to receive fine southern ladies. "If I'd known this was to be a royal visit I would have ordered lilies."

"Oh it's just as I imagined it would be, chic and masculine, just like our Judgie boy." Lucinda flitted around the room and lighted on the window sill. "I cannot believe I'm in Manhattan. It's been entirely too long. I don't look like some hillbilly do I? Am I presentable?"

"You look like a queen come to inspect the government housing and you brighten this room like a bolt of lightning," Judge said earnestly. "May I offer you a cool drink? Champagne? Believe it or not, I do have some chilled."

"I would expect nothing less, Sugar," Lucinda purred. "But no thank you. Never thought I'd say that, did you. Ha. No, I'll let the shock of this surprise wear off and we should meet for a drink later. I'm staying at the Carlyle and my car is waiting. You boys call me when you've done your re-acquainting. What time is it? Four-thirty? Goodness. Let's say you both join me at Bemelman's for drinks at seven. Is that good for you? If you don't have dinner plans, that is."

Judge racked his brain, what was tonight? The Louis Vuiton party didn't start until ten o'clock.

"Actually, that sounds perfect," he said. "We can have dinner and then I have a couple of parties to go to which I would be honored for you to join."

Her face brightened. "Parties?"

"Yes, there's a gallery opening on Madison and then a cocktail on Park and then the Antiques Show at the Armory."

"Oh, heaven! What fun, a real big city night out." Lucinda exclaimed. "I shall run now. I'll see you at seven at the hotel."

She kissed him lightly on the cheek and scurried to the door. She stopped and turned and looked him in the eye.

"Judge. Don't think that you have to entertain me every second. I know you have a job and a life and you and Russie want to re-connect. We'll just have this one night flitting around this gorgeous city, and then I will release you to Russ."

"Lucinda," Judge said with affection. "It is my greatest honor to have you in my adopted hometown and I cannot think of anyone I'd rather spend it with than you. Russ will adjust."

"Oh you rascal, you are such a charmer when you don't mean a word. Toodle loo." She waltzed out the door toward the elevator.

"Damn, that was a big load," Russ said as he came out of the bathroom. "I just gave your outhouse a Dixie christening. Where's mama?"

"She left," Judge said slightly dazed. "We're going to meet her at her hotel at seven for drinks and dinner and then I'll take you to some parties."

"Aw, man. I don't want to hang out with my mom up here. I want to raise some hell. I want to get fucked up SAE style. I want to see some hot New York City girls."

"Trust me, Russ. You're going to see more hot women at the parties I'm taking you to than you can count. Besides, all the parties will be over by one, then we'll hit Moomba late night."

"What the hell's a Moomba?" Russ said.

"It's the best club in town. Hell, it's the best club in the world at the moment. I'm there almost every night. It's my living room."

"Yee ha!" Russ yelped.

"Uh, maybe we can live with only one yee ha per hour. What do you say?"

"Yee fucking Ha! Judge," Russ yelled and yanked Judge into a head lock. "Get ready to be embarrassed by your country cousin."

Judge broke free from his grasp with a laugh and a shove and walked over to his desk. He fished through a scattered pile of twenty or so invitations to every sort of event: cocktails on Park Avenue, store openings on Fifth, gallery openings in Chelsea, benefits at Lincoln Center, all strewn on his bureau like cards after a game of fifty-two card pick-up.

"All this is invitations to parties?" Russ asked mystified as he studied one after the other.

"Those are just for this week. And not even all of them." Judge said. "More are on my desk at work."

"Goddamn, man. This is the life."

Russ held up the invitation for the Louis Vuitton event. It was a big glossy photo of a Vuitton trunk which opened on a picture of Aretha Franklin superimposed over the façade of Rockefeller Center. Russ read the invitation with mouth agape.

"Special performance by Aretha Franklin?!" he shouted. "Goddamn! Is this for real?"

"Yeah," Judge said. He enjoyed showing off for Russ and this was only a damn invitation.

"Dress code: Chic." Russ read. "Dress code chic? What the fuck does that mean?"

"Don't worry," Judge said. "I've got something you can wear."

"You gone dress me up like one of them eye-talian homosexuals?" Russ said studying the invitation again. "Aretha Franklin? I can't believe this city."

"Why don't you jump in the shower and wash off some of that country and I'll pour us a couple of drinks." Judge said as he started for the kitchen.

"Alright, Cap'n. You talk like a damn Yankee now," Russ said as he tackled Judge and threw him on the bed that dominated the large studio apartment. "Dude, I told people you were a big shot up here but wait 'til I tell 'em we went to see goddamn Aretha Franklin my first night."

Russ bounced up and went into the bathroom and turned on the shower. "What you want, ooh ooh, baby I got it," he yelped. "What you need, you know I got it."

Judge chuckled and jumped off the bed and slid open the closet doors. Judge put himself into a white shirt, navy blazer and jeans. He put on his brown suede Tod's and matching belt. He went over to the dresser and slicked his hair with a thick load of pomade and confidently put in his cuff links. He reached for a hot pink silk pocket square by Charvet and thought, yeah, even if Russ gives me shit, Lucinda will love it. He turned around to face the long mirror on the opposite wall and was pleased with his reflection. Judge returned to the closet. He pulled out a black

148

Prada shirt and black Armani jacket, dark, never washed Levi's, black Gucci loafers and a black belt. That ought to fit him, he thought. "Lord, this ought to be hilarious."

Judge stood in the kitchen pouring scotch when Russ rounded the corner butt naked toweling his hair. "Where's that goddamn drink, homo?"

Judge turned and handed Russ his drink.

Russ grabbed the drink, took a big swig and eyeballed Judge up and down.

"Damn, dude. You look chic as fuck!"

Judge laughed and walked toward the bed. He pointed at the clothes: black shapes on the white bed. "I pulled you some threads, dude."

"What's all that? Am I going to a goddamn funeral?" Russ said as he picked up the black jacket. "How come you get chic and I get pallbearer?"

"Russ, trust me." Judge said. "You are going to get laid fast when you get into those clothes."

Russ tackled Judge and threw him on the bed, crumpling the fine black clothes and rolling on top of him.

"You can tell me, Judge," he said. "You've gone gay and now you want me in the cult. That's why you laid out all them black clothes. You're a member of some eye-talian Yankee homo cult and y'all need some strappin' real southern men to do the heavy liftin'."

Judge pushed Russ off him and stood up. "Just get dressed, Country. Your mother is expecting us."

Russ picked up the jacket and looked at the label inside. "Ghee or ghee oh Armani. Ain't I a fancy fuck now?"

"Here we go," Judge groaned.

Judge and Russ hurried down Tenth Street to catch a taxi that then proceeded to crawl up Madison Avenue at rush hour. Judge started to chafe, his jaw clenched as traffic crept and crawled block by block. He turned to see Russ wide-eyed and smiling agape at the sights and sounds of the sidewalks of Manhattan and his mood lightened. He was glad they'd brought Roadies. He took a long, deep swig of the scotch Russ had poured. "Sweet nectar of life," he said to the window. "Sweet nectar of life."

They arrived at the Carlyle Hotel a little after seven and Judge asked the desk clerk to ring Mrs. Walker's room. Judge then led Russ into Bemelman's Bar where he informed Russ they would wait for his mother to order a drink.

"Damn, Judge. I can't wait until we are on our own. I didn't come all this way to entertain my mama."

Russ fidgeted with the collar of his shirt and the belt and the waist of the jeans while Judge held a pose of cool belonging, leaning back in the banquette.

"This shirt is so damn scratchy, man," Russ said.

"It's called starch," Judge said amused. "You remember starch, don't you."

"Yeah, for church and weddings, but not to go out raising hell with Aretha Franklin."

At that moment Judge spotted Mrs. Walker entering the room. She wore an Yves St. Laurent black pantsuit accented with big sparkling diamonds attached to both ears and a simple strand of pearls around her neck. Her hair was Upper East Side perfect, the brown shoulder length hair flipped under and held in perfect place. She walked into the bar with a confident jaunt and surveyed the scene looking for her escorts. There was no pretension or apprehension in her gate or her eye. She was lady of all she surveyed and Judge saturated in admiration. She spotted Judge and Russ and glided over to them. Judge shot straight to his feet to greet her while Russ groaned and slowly rose.

"I cannot believe my eyes," she said coming astride the two. "Is this my cornpone, redneck son all made up to look like a Tom Ford model?"

"It wasn't easy," Judge said. "But I think I managed to shake off the hay seeds and shine him up."

"Shine him up?" Lucinda said. "He looks like Porfirio Rubirosa!"

"Who the hell is Tom Ford?" Russ said pulling the collar of his shirt again. "What the hell is a Poor Feero? I think I look swank as..., uh swank as hell."

"And you, Mr. Mender," she said taking him all in. "You are the vision of rich success."

"Well, I don't know about the rich part," he said blushing. "The success part I can work on. But, let's tell the truth. You, my dear Mrs. Walker, look absolutely ravishing."

"Why thank you, kind sir," she said as she bowed her head. "I appreciate your gallantry."

"You know I love a woman who quotes Blanche DuBois," Judge said flirting back with equal skill.

"I am going to vomit," Russ said. "Can we get a goddamn drink?"

"Let's not keep our ill-bred Stanley waiting," Lucinda said. "Please, let's be seated."

Lucinda slid into the banquette next to Judge while Russ took a chair opposite and started craning his neck looking for the waiter. Judge was so happy he laughed out loud.

"I am so glad you're here, Lucinda."

"Me too, darlin'. I've been looking forward to this since you left Ophelia right after college."

"Good, God," Russ moaned as he emptied a tiny bowl of cheese straws into his mouth.

"Judge, my boy," a voice above them boomed and Judge looked up, startled to see Maxwell Jones. Maxwell strolled up to the table and Judge got quickly to his feet while Russ fumbled to join him. Lucinda smiled broadly.

"Mr. Jones, what an unexpected surprise," Judge said and leaned across the table to shake Maxwell's hand. "May I present Mrs. Forest Walker of Charleston, South Carolina and Ophelia, Alabama."

Maxwell bowed graciously as Lucinda said, "Pleasure to meet you, Mr. Jones."

"And her son and my best friend, Russell Walker."

Russ shook Maxwell's hand firmly. "pleased to meet you, Mr. Jones."

"Mrs. Walker," Judge continued, "This is the world-renowned Maxwell Jones."

"I know of your reputation, Mr. Jones," Lucinda said as she greeted his gaze. "And I've seen all your pictures in Vanity Fair and Jet Set. Won't you join us? We were just about to order a round of cocktails."

"I would be honored, Mrs. Walker. And please, call me Maxwell."

The waiter suddenly appeared and Maxwell instructed, "Giuseppe, please bring us a bottle of Dom Perignon '90." Maxwell pulled the chair next to Russ and took a seat.

"I regret to inform you that Judge failed to mention that he was to have such fine company in town, Mrs. Walker."

"Please don't think ill of Judge, Mr. Jones," Lucinda said. "I'm afraid we pulled a fast one on him. Russ planned this little getaway and I horned in on his plans at the last minute. We caught Judge completely unaware. And please, call me Lucinda."

"Well, Lucinda, it is an honor to meet one of Judge's lovely friends from Ophelia. So tell me, how long will you be in our fair city?"

"Oh, only for the weekend," Lucinda said. "Judge has been so kind to make room for me in his schedule. He's even asked us to the antiques show."

"Well, I am on my way there myself, and I insist that you ride with me and allow me to serve as your escort," Maxwell offered. "As gallant and civilized as our dear Judge may appear, he is worthless at an antiques show."

"Excuse me, Maxwell," Judge laughed. "I will not be exposed as a fraud in front of my home folks. I was planning on faking it through."

Giuseppe arrived with the bottle of fine champagne in a silver bucket and began to pour into the assembled flutes. Maxwell and Lucinda engaged in the name game from Montgomery to Natchez, Atlanta to Savannah, and ended in Charleston. They were deep in connections as Russ leaned across the table to whisper to Judge.

"This is the last champagne I'm drinking, dude. I want a goddamn scotch so bad I could shit."

"Just hang on, Russ," Judge whispered. "Let your mother enjoy this. I promise we'll be on our own soon enough."

"Alright, I'm warning you though, I'm expecting more from this trip than champagne and fancy farts," Russ said. "And, by the way, who is this old sissy making a move on my mother? Daddy told me to keep an eye on her. You know how flirty she likes to play."

"Relax, country," Judge said. "Maxwell's a good friend of mine and your mother is in excellent hands."

"If you say so, Judge. I don't want to have to smack him." Russ said turning up the flute and emptying the champagne into his mouth in one thirsty gulp. "I'm ready to roll." He tugged at the collar of his shirt again.

Maxwell mysteriously took care of the bill and ushered the group into his chauffeured Navigator. After a quick ride to the Park Avenue Armory and many introductions to all of Maxwell's friends, Maxwell squired Lucinda to the prime booths and introduced her to everyone they passed. The two twirled through the aisles of the antiques show like the oldest of friends and Judge was happy that the two were hitting it off. As for himself, he would probably not have shown up for this crusty party and now he knew why. There was nothing but ladies of a certain age and preening walkers. Russ and Judge soon found themselves on their own and made way straight for the bar. They staked out a corner and Russ started to shuffle.

"I know mama's enjoying this shit, but when do we see some action, dude?" Russ said tilting up his glass and draining the last scotch-soaked ice cube. Russ's eyes widened and the corners of his open mouth lifted into a smile of sheer delight. Over the top of the glass he spotted a stunning blond coming straight for them. She wore a pale pink Ungaro dress with layers of chiffon flounces and a plunging neckline and a side slit up to her thigh. Judge just noticing that she was always in pink.

"Judge Mender!" Mia Wilson shouted above the din as she came up beside the two and planted a big wet kiss on Judge's lips. "Thank God you're here. I thought I was going to die following mother all over this awful place."

Mia stepped back and looked into the eyes of the gawking Russ. "And who is this strapping hunk of man staring at my tits?"

Judge laughed and Russ smirked confidently, revealing only a shade of embarrassment.

"This is my best friend from home, Russell Walker."

"I'm Mia, handsome," and extended her hand. Russ took it, not knowing if he should shake it or kiss it.

"Nice to meet you, beautiful," Russ said.

"And you," Mia said. "And please, don't be embarrassed at staring at my tits. I mean, all of these sophisticated New York men are too cool and cultured to appreciate a woman. I take it as a compliment." She then leaned in and whispered hot in his ear. "Besides, I have a great rack."

Russ laughed and elbowed Judge as Mia turned to a waiter offering champagne.

"So," Mia said pursing her lips after a sip, "when can we get out of here? You are going to see Aretha, aren't you?"

"Hell, yeah," Russ said, before Judge could answer. "You want to go with us?"

"I have a better idea," Mia said, amused by the strapping new eager beaver. "Why don't you boys ride with me?"

Mia spotted her mother coming out of one aisle and turning up another. "Hold on, I'll be right back."

"Hell yeah," Russ said as he watched the gauzy fabric of her dress slide sensually across her ass. "Duuuuuuuuude. Who the fuck is that?"

Judge laughed at the symmetry of Mia Wilson being the first girl Russ met. This was going to be a good trip. It couldn't have been better if Judge had hired a hooker to entertain his visitor. Mia would turn him out.

Maxwell and Lucinda soon rounded the nearest aisle and came over to where Judge and Russ were standing.

"Hello, boys," Lucinda said. "Oh, Judge, Maxwell is the most divine tour guide. I've already put my name on some gorgeous things."

"Mrs. Walker has excellent taste, Judge," Maxwell said.

"That's no surprise to me," Judge replied. "I am pleased you two are hitting it off."

"We are long lost friends, Judge," Lucinda said. "We have oodles of acquaintances in common. It's a miracle we never met until tonight."

"Hey Mama. We're bored as hell," Russ blurted. "We're ready to get the hell out of here and go see Aretha Franklin."

"Well, Maxwell," Lucinda said. "For all my sophisticated airs, I am afraid my offspring gives me away."

"It's quite alright," Maxwell said. "This generation has no sense of propriety or of the finer things in life. They revel in mediocrity."

They all laughed, except Russ who was straining his neck to spot Mia.

"I have an idea," Maxwell said, "if Mrs. Walker will permit me. Why don't you boys go on over to Rockefeller Center and we'll finish up here and join you there. That is, Mrs. Walker, if you are up for an Aretha Franklin concert scheduled to begin at ten o'clock. I'll need an espresso if I want to stay awake, but it should be quite entertaining."

"Oh, my goodness, yes!" Lucinda said. "I can't think of anything more exciting."

"Oh good God," Russ moaned.

"It's settled then," Maxwell said. "You boys are released. We'll see you at Aretha."

"Perfect," Judge said. "We'll look forward to it."

Maxwell led Lucinda away to the next aisle of antiques and in their wake Mia motored back into their spot.

"Let's get out of here," Mia said.

"Yeah," Russ grinned. "Let's go," and he slid his arm around Mia's waist and to her surprise, she allowed it to stay. Judge smirked. This ought to be good, he thought.

In the car, the odd trio finished a bottle of champagne that Mia had begged off the bartender at The Armory and, suddenly, Russ didn't mind the bubbly. They arrived at Rock Center and pushed their way through the tight crowd to the VIP section, a raised square of stage, covered in red carpet with white couches and low tables. Lucy Shining danced on one of the tables and she smiled and waved when she saw Judge then turned around to face the stage.

Rhea and Frankie danced on an adjacent table singing and fondling each other. Scarlet Goodman stood in a corner with Sally Banning smiling and bopping to the music, her new status obvious to all on the raised platform. Victoria Newton held court in one corner with the non-drinking, non-dancing Wasp jury. Mia immediately grabbed Russ and the two joined Lucy on an adjacent table.

"Judge Mender!" Rhea screamed. "Isn't this amazing? It's just like Les Caves!"

Judge laughed and smiled and raised his glass. He was getting pretty drunk. They had never gone to dinner and the passed hors d'oeuvres at the Armory were pitiful. He'd been drinking scotch since three o'clock and was now grinning and glazed. He could still manage to see Rhea's allusion though. The weather was beautiful and the outdoor revelry nestled at the bottom of the mountains of Rockefeller Center did lend a certain Saint Tropez to it all. At least the crowd was exactly the same as he reported on last summer at the Mediterranean hot spot doing the same exact thing here and now: drinking and dancing on tables. He looked at Mia casting a spell and a dirty dance on Russ whose face in turn vacillated between grins of disbelief and seduction. Russ could have been at a road-side honky-tonk for all the attention he paid to Aretha, the one exception came when he drunkenly crooned you make me feel like a natural woman. Russ was found in Mia Wilson.

Judge noticed Maxwell and Lucinda step onto the VIP stage near where Victoria stood, but he did not go over to greet them. His drunken gaze was locked on Lucy. He stepped up onto the table where Lucy was dancing. It was a small, three foot table, barely big enough for two sober, well-balanced dancers. He stepped up and quickly fell forward, face first into a white sofa. Rhea and Frankie laughed loudly as did Mia and Russ. Lucy shook her head and kept dancing, hands in the air. Judge didn't move after his fall. He turned over and settled into the plush cushions and let the revelry roll over him. He fell asleep.

When the concert ended, Russ pulled Judge awake and he groggily noticed Lucy was gone. The original trio stumbled out onto Fifth Avenue and into Mia's Mercedes for the ride downtown to Moomba. Judge was so drunk that he wasn't cognizant of the ride but only of coming to in a booth at Moomba with Rhea wrapped around him. Mia and Russ were making out heavily beside him.

The sound of U2 blasted in his ear, the speaker must have been over his head. Russ disengaged from Mia and turned and sang loud in his ear. "It's a beautiful day."

Judge pushed Russ's face away as the waitress leaned down to take his order. Judge asked for a glass of water and tried to focus on the room. Where was Lucy? He hadn't paid any attention to her all night. He spotted her across the room dancing with Frankie. I've got to break that up, he told himself.

He disentangled from Rhea and stumbled over to where they were dancing, rough and rudely bouncing off people every step of the way.

"I want to talk to you," he shouted over the music.

"What about?" Lucy said, still dancing.

"Come outside with me," Judge shouted back.

"You're too drunk, Judge," she said. "Call me tomorrow. I'm having fun right now."

"I don't want to talk to you tomorrow," he slurred. "I want to talk to you now."

Lucy took Judge by the hand and led him back to the table where Mia and Russ were. Judge fell into the banquette and slumped down until he almost slid to the floor. Lucy leaned down in Russ's ear and said, "You need to get Judge home. He's drunker than I've ever seen him."

"Alright, darling'," Russ said, disengaging his lips again. "We'll take care of him."

Mia cast a look at the slumping Judge and leaned into Russ and whispered into his ear. "Are all you southern boys as adventurous in bed as Judge?"

"Hey, baby," Russ says as he rubbed her exposed thigh. "You and Judge hit it?"

"And some bartender boy." Mia said seductively in his ear. "It was my first ménage a trios and I hope not my last."

"Ménage a what?" Russ said, confused.

"You know, baby. Ménage a trios, a three way. Judge and this hot cater waiter boy whose name I can never remember."

"Hold on a minute," Russ said. "Judge had sex with you and some dude?"

"Yes darling," Mia said. "And it was the hottest night of my life, until now. Haven't you and Judge ever fooled around?"

"Hell no, woman," Russ laughed. "I ain't queer."

"Ain't queer?" Mia teased and stuck her tongue in his mouth and reached for a handful between his legs. "I can't wait to get you home. Let's get out of here."

Russ snapped his head toward Judge, leaned over Mia and pulled Judge toward him. "Time to get you home to bed, lightweight."

Judge smiled like an idiot and sunk deeper in the banquette. Russ stood up and reenacted a familiar move from their college days. He picked Judge up, threw Judge's arm over his shoulder and followed the bounce of Mia's ass to the stairwell and down to the street.

Saturday morning shone bright and hateful in Judge's apartment. He awoke fully dressed lying diagonally across his bed. He fumbled on the bedside table and found a pair of Persol sunglasses. He never went to bed without light-proofing the room. The curtains were wide open, sun blazing bright and hot. He stumbled to the windows and snatched the curtains closed. He made his way back to bed and buried his head under the thick layers of covers when the door clicked open and Russ bounded in.

"Judge, wake your drunk ass up!"

"Go away, dude." Judge moaned. "It's way too early to see you."

Russ kicked off his shoes, shucked off his clothes and slid into bed next to Judge. "Move over lightweight, I need some covers." Russ snuggled in next to Judge. "Hell baby, you're almost as fine as that sweet thang Mia."

Judge elbowed Russ in the stomach and pulled the covers further over his head. "What are you doing here? I thought you went home with Mia."

"I did, but she kicked me out this morning. Some thing she had to go to. I didn't mind. Hell, I didn't get one ounce of sleep, dude. That little girl knows how to have a good time."

"Russ, please shut up," Judge pleaded. "I have got to get some sleep, my head's killing me and I think I might puke."

"Dude, when did you get out of drinking shape? You're embarrassing The South."

"I'm going to sleep," Judge moaned. "And get off me."

"Aw, come on baby," Russ teased. "Mia says you like a little man love, why not old Russ?"

Judge fell back into sleep. Russ soon followed and the two slumbered away the day until a phone started ringing incessantly around 2:00 PM.

"Oh my god, Russ," Judge yelled as he shoved the sleeping Russ. "Either answer your goddamn phone or turn the ringer off."

"Wha..?"

"Dude, you're phone is ringing like a car alarm."

"Oh shit." Russ shot up in the bed and fumbled in his pants on the floor for his phone.

"Hey, Mama," he said. "Why you calling us so early? What time? Really? Okay. We'll call you in a little while. Yeah, I'll tell him. Love you too."

"Don't tell me." Judge said muffled under the blankets.

"Mama's been with Maxwell all morning, shopping and brunchin' and they want us to meet them for a drink in an hour."

"I'm in hell. I can't believe how drunk I got last night. It was all that scotch all day and no food. Nobody noticed did they?"

"Oh no, dude." Russ laughed. "Only everybody at the Aretha concert and all those people at Moomba. I carried you out, man. You were a sorry sight."

"Please don't talk anymore," Judge said. "I honestly don't want to hear it."

"Whatever you say, bud," Russ got out of bed and went into the bathroom. "I'm getting in the shower. You know Mama and her new beau will be hounding us soon."

Judge slid back under the cover and slipped back into the peace of unconsciousness where there was no regret.

Russ came out of the bathroom and yanked the curtains open and turned on the CD player. He put on a Counting Crows CD and started singing and dancing on the bed bouncing Judge up and down.

"I'm in hell," Judge yelled. "Fucking hell!"

"Come on Judge, you remember this one." Russ boomed. "Man, we used to love this song. Come on, sang it man."

Russ leaned down and ripped off the blankets and pulled Judge to his feet, holding him for balance on the shaky bed.

> *So come dance this silence*
>
> *down through the morning*
>
> Russ continued as Judge found a smile.
>
> *Cut up, Maria!*
>
> *Show me some of them Spanish dances.*

Judge chimed in.

> *Mr. Jones and me tell each other fairy tales.*
>
> *Stare at the beautiful women.*

Russ now, loud and boisterous, drowned out Judge's scratchy voice.

> *She's looking at you.*
>
> *Ah, no, no, she's looking at me.*

They sang the song into the kitchen as Judge searched for Advil and coffee. Russ yelled after him, "Can I wear my own clothes today?"

"Hell yeah, do what you want today. Tonight too." Judge answered.

Russ poked his head into the kitchen, "Well, uh, tonight, I'm gone need some more eye-talianizing."

Judge turned and looked at Russ's big eyes.

"That Mia chick invited me to some fancy cancer party with her and she say's I'll need a tuxedah."

"Mia Wilson asked you to the Sloan-Kettering benefit tonight?" Judge was impressed. "Damn boy, you must have given her a mighty slice of southern life."

"Well," Russ laughed. "They don't call me big daddy for nothing."

Judge and Russ fell into laughter which made Judge's head pound harder. "Dude, don't make me laugh until this Advil kicks in."

Well, hurry up and get in the shower," Russ said. "I'm hungry and Mama said Maxwell is taking us someplace swank."

"I can only imagine. I usually don't have to see these people in the day light hours. But since your mother has turned Manhattan into a royal visit for the weekend, I guess I'll have to sacrifice."

"I can sacrifice anything knowing I'm gonna be ridin' my little filly Mia again tonight." Russ beamed as he tied his bucks. "If Mama only knew what was makin' me agree to old fart and lady tours, her hair'd turn green."

Judge managed to beg off the afternoon cocktail party using his unassailable excuse that he had to work. He told Russ to give his regrets and to call him later, but he would absolutely have to go in to the office to write up last night's cavorting. So while Maxwell squired The Walkers around Soho, Judge went back to bed and put the night before behind him.

When Russ returned it was after seven and Judge was completely restored. He was dressed in his evening clothes and drinking a scotch by the window when he heard Russ's key at the door.

"Hey, bud," Russ said, "I'm fucking dead, man. That Maxwell can sure run his feet and his mouth. I don't think my ears have ever heard so much bullshit from one man."

"That's Maxwell," Judge laughed. "I bet Lucinda was in heaven."

"Are you kidding? If that man wasn't a homo, I do believe I'd be calling him daddy this time next month."

"He already has one family," Judge laughed. "I don't think he wants two."

"What are you talking about? That big sissy is married? To a woman?"

"Confirmed," Judge said, relishing his role as urban sophisticate. "And a twenty-five year old daughter too."

"Well, fuck me. Things sure are tricky up here in New York City. I don't think I could keep it all straight."

"That's the challenge, I guess," Judge said a little wistfully. "Hey, you can wear my extra tuxedo. It's hanging in the bathroom, ready to go. We have to be at Cipriani in half an hour."

"Jesus Christ. I know this city never sleeps, but goddamn."

"Jump in the shower. The car will be here in fifteen."

"If I can make it here," Russ belted. "I'll make it anywhere."

Judge entered Cipriani Forty-Second Street like he entered any benefit of the season lately: head down and focused, paying no attention to distractions like press check in and greeters. He forgot about Russ. In his growing impatience with door scenes, he lowered his chin and walked straight through the entry, ignored the PR girls outside in headsets and waited to be recognized by one of the hosts. "Judge Mender!" came his way and was ignored. He stopped, suddenly remembering Russ. He turned, and found him wide eyed and blinking on the sidewalk.

"Russ!" he shouted and walked back outside. "This way."

Russ walked through the door and stopped short. "Whoa," he said wide mouthed.

Judge stopped and looked around himself, taking in the panorama through Russ's un-jaded eyes. The main hall of Cipriani was indeed an impressive sight. The former Bowery Savings Bank, a Romanesque masterpiece, evoked a stronger sense of Renaissance cathedral than savings bank. The marble-coated building was now a national landmark wearing a recent restoration. It was bought by the Cipriani family which meant it was naturally ripe to serve as a playground for society benefits. Judge often wondered how these charities made money when the benefit parties were so lavish.

Judge followed Russ's gaze up the marble walls and gilt columns to the triumphant arch. He admired the cross-beamed ceiling with painted stars and wreaths with gargoyled punctuation sixty five feet above them. He followed Russ's eyes back down the three-tiered chandeliers to the intricate marble tiled floor. The original teller walls and windows were still in place and now served as a paddock for the philanthropists inside. Dinner tables waited to be filled around the parquet dance floor. Maxwell had taken the table setting idea from the Winter Ball and expanded it. Instead of cherry tree branches he now had placed Fichus trees on the tables and strung miniature amber colored lights. Up lighting followed the gilt columns and bathed the mammoth room in a soft light that fell like snow. Across the marble floor, penguin men bobbed in and out of beautiful women in elegant gowns, accompanied by the sweet sounds of an orchestra in the back of the room. Judge slowed down to let Russ take it all in. Through Russ's eyes, Judge experienced this world anew, if only for a moment.

"Damn, Judge," Russ said mouth agape. "I've never seen columns that big in my life, and they're inside!" When their eyes came in for a landing, Mia Wilson stood there waiting for them.

"Hello gorgeous things," She said. "Judge, do you mind if I steal this man away from you for a second?"

"I'll catch up with you later," Judge said and watched Russ being pulled away by Mia, and with him, his recent wonder of this magnificent space. Judge's momentary relapse into innocence was perfectly distinguished as the president of the board introduced him to some other board members of Sloan Kettering. Judge felt his impatience rising. He listened to inanity after inanity until he could bear it no longer.

"Excuse me, please. I see someone I must say hello to."

Judge walked away with apparent purpose and ducked behind a flower arrangement balanced upon a large pedestal. He searched for Lucinda and Maxwell. Judge spotted society's newest couple standing at the center table surrounded by Maxwell's inner circle of fine ladies and magnate husbands.

Judge was utterly impaled by the gown Lucinda wore. She stood elegantly modeling a black satin strapless bodice on a full satin skirt that gently swept the marble floor. A little beaded jacket sat snugly on her shoulders. Her hair was swept up and held in place by a diamond clip, which found its echo on her neck, ears and wrists. Where had she found the time to find that dress in between Maxwell's busy agenda?

Judge quietly circled the perimeter of the gathering. He joined the assembled in listening to the two re-tell their experiences around Manhattan like two newlyweds just returned from a Grand Tour. When the members of the coterie began to dissipate toward their own seats, Judge found his own place card next to Lucinda.

"Good evening you two," Judge said as he took his seat. "You certainly held them enthralled."

"Oh, hello darling," Lucinda hugged Judge and he inhaled her scent and sighed. "I know I carry on and on, but what good is a beautiful day if you can't share it?" Lucinda said dreamily.

"I agree, Lucinda," Maxwell said as he squeezed her shoulders.

"You are wearing the most beautiful dress in the room," Judge said. "You look absolutely stunning."

"Why thank you, Judge. I must admit I feel a bit like Cinderella. You won't believe this, but Maxwell called Mister Oscar de la Renta this morning and this gorgeous masterpiece was delivered to my hotel room today. Can you imagine? I've never felt so glamorous in my entire life."

"Doesn't she look as if she were born in that dress, Judge?"

"I would have sworn it was couture," Judge answered, amused with the banter between the two of them.

"I suppose that's the beauty in being a perfect model size," Maxwell said as he gazed at her. "That dress was messengered over straight from the Vogue closet, from Giselle Bunchen to Lucinda Walker with love"

"You look absolutely stunning," Judge said. "I'm almost speechless."

"Well, I thank you. Maxwell promises to keep me dancing until they turn the lights on."

"I'm sure he will. I apologize for not joining you today, work and all. I take it you had a good time?

"Oh, Judge," Lucinda crooned. "Maxwell has taken me to the most stunning gardens in the city, places I never dreamed existed."

"Maxwell's never taken me to any private gardens," Judge said lightly.

"Well, dear boy," Maxwell returned, "These people tend to be rather reclusive. I only press them in the case of visiting dignitaries."

Lucinda giggled with delight. Judge could see why Russ was concerned. The two were obviously in the first flush of a love affair, of the mind if not the body, but a love affair all the same. The Duke and Duchess of Windsor came to mind, only Lucinda was a far more glamorous Wallis and Maxwell a much more flamboyant Edward.

Suddenly Lucinda's eyes morphed from smiling to wide open surprise. Judge followed her gaze over his own shoulder and onto the dance floor. There in the middle of the room doing an extremely dirty dance were Russ and Mia, all hands and mouths.

"Maxwell," Lucinda said, "who is that trollop that my son is making a fool over?"

Maxwell turned and followed Lucinda's narrowing eyes. His own popped open then narrowed into disgust. "That is Mia Wilson, darling. Poor Russ is not to be blamed. That Jezebel has led many a fine young man astray," Maxwell looked over at Judge and winked.

"Judge," Lucinda said calmly, "will you please retrieve my ill-bred son and slap some sense into him?"

Judge darted to the dance floor. He grabbed Russ by the elbow and said, "Excuse me, Mia, I've got to borrow this fool."

"Hey, dude," Russ slurred. "Where've you been?"

Russ smiled at Judge as his eyes rolled in his head.

"What the fuck is wrong with you,"

"I'm rolling, dude. Mia gave me a tab."

"You dropped Ecstasy?!" Judge said loudly, then lowered his voice, "When?"

"When we got here. It's all good, brother."

"Jesus Christ, you have got to get out of here."

Judge grabbed Russ by the elbow and led him to a darkened corner of the room.

"Stand here and do not move. I'm going to find Mia."

Judge searched the room. Mia stood with a group of girls that included Rhea, Scarlet, and Sally Banning. He rushed up behind her and, with the

171

briefest of hellos to the girls, pulled Mia's elbow and whispered, "follow me, please."

"He can't keep his hands off of me," Mia laughed, "What's to do?"

Mia followed Judge to the corner where Russ now faced the wall, his head leaned against it and his body fell into an ass-swiveling groove.

"Mia, you have got to get Russ out of here. He's a fucking mess already."

"Hey, baby," Mia said as she wrapped her arms around Russ's neck, "You rolling already? Damn, mine hasn't hit yet."

"Yeah, baby. Let's go get nekkid."

"Good idea," Judge said. "You two follow me."

Judge led them to the front door, out onto the sidewalk and into the back seat of an idling taxi.

"Go home and call me later," Judge instructed Mia. "I'll meet up with you after the party."

Judge stood on the red carpet, pedestrians shifted gears to avoid him. The press and the guests were mercifully inside. He watched the taxi stop and go down Forty-Second street toward the East River.

"Jesus Christ. I can't believe that crazy bitch."

Judge found his seat next to Lucinda and told her Russ was a little drunk from cocktails earlier and that he had put him into a cab.

"Thank you, darling. I can't believe he was acting that way in public, but why should anything be different here than in Ophelia. I hope he didn't embarrass you too terribly."

"It's okay. It's just like old times."

"Judge, honey, you look tired. Are you okay?"

"I'm okay. I just need to eat."

Lucinda turned back to greet an introduction Maxwell was arranging.

Judge closed his eyes and couldn't believe how exhausted he was. His head ached, his body ached. How am I going to get through this dinner? And later? What the hell am I going to do with Russ? Maybe he'll stay at Mia's and I can go home and get some sleep.

He opened his eyes and looked at Lucinda, clearly relishing her role as Maxwell's date. It warmed him and gave him a moment's relief to have her at his side. She was a comforting balm from home. He wished they were there now, in Ophelia. When this dinner was over they would just go home and wake up in the sweet country sunshine.

Suddenly a squeal came from behind him.

"Judge Mender! Get off your ass and dance with me."

It was Rhea Brown and a gaggle of girls all dressed in jewel tone satin gowns heading to the dance floor. Oscar de la Renta was this week's sponsor and the girls were a traveling band of well-dressed fairies.

"Mia gave us all Ecstasy and we're going to drop after dinner and head to Moomba," she said excitedly. "Are you in?"

"Sure," he lied. "I'll catch up with you all there."

Judge had no intention of going to Moomba tonight. The only reason he was at this party was to see Lucinda Walker. As soon as dinner finished, he was going home and collapsing into bed. As long as Russ was safe at

Mia's, he was going to get some sleep and get away from the relentless crowd.

He searched the room for Lucy but did not find her. She is the only thing that would keep me here, he told himself. He watched Maxwell squiring Lucinda around the room. The southern aristocrat held her own beside the Manhattan ladies. He thought to himself, she doesn't need this society life to be happy, she can flit in and out and it doesn't absorb her. It's all just an experience that she can try on, like a costume, and walk away from. He felt an alcoholic's misery at seeing a casual drinker put down a drink. I can walk away from this. I can go home again dammit.

Judge excused himself after dinner -- before the dancing began -- and said his goodbyes to Lucinda and Maxwell. He slipped past Rhea and company and slid into a taxi. He called to check on Russ and Mia and found them at Moomba.

"We're fine, dude," Russ a, assured him. "Sorry I freaked you out at the party. That E hit me hard. Guess I shouldn't have chewed it. What did Mama say? She alright?"

"Yeah, I told her you were a little drunk and needed to split for a while, but I was meeting you later."

"Cool move. Me and Mia are having a good time at Moomba waiting on y'all."

"I'm going home, man. Have fun with Mia and call me in the morning. Hey, what time does your plane leave?

"What! You're not coming? Come on, man. It's my last night and I want to spend some time with you. Come on over here. Mia's got an extra tab with your name all over it."

"Yeah, alright. I'll see you soon. So what time do you have to leave for the airport?"

"Mama's picking me up at six in the morning at your place. Not to worry, I'll be there. I'm crashing with you tonight. It'll be late though, 'cause Mia just gave me another tab. Yee haw!"

Judge hung up the phone and rode the elevator up to his apartment. He unlocked the door, shed his tuxedo in a pile on the floor and crawled into bed. He remembered the curtains and groaned as he got up and crossed to the window and yanked them shut. A lot of good that'll do, he said to himself. Russ has to be up a dawn. He got back into bed and his mind raced around the room. I'm going home with them tomorrow. It's done for me here. I can't take it anymore. I'm exhausted. I've got to do something before I kill myself. Yes. I will go home to Ophelia. I can live with Russ. That's what I'm doing. Judge promised himself, mumbling out loud through his fatigue. That is what I am doing. And he fell asleep.

Judge felt a kiss on his lips and thought he was dreaming. He felt naked skin on both sides of him and he struggled to wake.

"What the hell?" he said. The room was lighted by a slash from the half open bathroom door. He focused and saw who it was.

"Hey baby, it's Mia."

"What is going on?" He turned and faced the person on his other side and it was Russ, both of them naked and wrapped around Judge.

175

"Hey, man," Russ said. "We're rolling our asses off and wanted to come and get in bed with you."

Judge leapt out of the bed and turned on the light. "What the fuck is wrong with you two?" Judge pulled on a pair of jeans and a sweater and slipped into some sneakers.

"I am going for a walk and when I get back, you better be out of here."

He slammed the door behind him and ran down the stairwell.

Judge headed west toward the river. He was the only person on Tenth Street at that hour as he navigated the dark street, relishing the sinister energy of being on the street alone. He went past a street hustler who met his eye under the bill of a low baseball hat. Judge kept walking west, across the West Side Highway and into the River Park. Damn. It's cold out here by the water. I should have brought a coat. He was so exhausted he could barely tell his feet to keep moving. He found a bench and sat down and put his head on his knees. He checked his watch. It was five thirty in the morning. The goddamn sun will be up soon. I'm going home tomorrow, he told himself. I am starting over.

Chapter 11

The List

Judge opened his eyes half-way and the dimly lit interior of a hospital room came slowly into focus. He was groggy from morphine and felt no pain, only mind-numbing reality. He was surrounded by three blond women he recognized and one well-dressed man he did not. He squinted then opened his eyes wider, still struggling for focus and identification. He closed his eyes again and drifted back into medicated sleep. There was a curtain drawn to divide the room and the snorts and stirs of an older man could be heard lofting over from the other side. The dingy and sterile room was overwhelmed with gifts crowding every surface. The room was filled with bouquets of flowers from the florists of the moment and baskets of food wrapped in expensive ribbons from Manhattan's most fashionable gourmet shops. There were little bags full of shiny and colorful candies, glossy magazines, a bottle of scotch, even a stuffed teddy bear wearing a business suit and a fedora holding a reporter's pad.

"I have a call out to Dr. Barton's office," Rhea said. "I think we should wait for him."

"Jack's dad said to call his friend at Lenox Hill," Mia Wilson said.

"Lenox Hill is fine for recovery, Mia," Rhea said, "I'm talking about plastic surgeons. He should see the best."

"What's Lenox Hill?" Scarlet asked quietly.

"Lenox Hill is the best hospital in Manhattan," Mia said haughtily. "Jack's dad is on the board."

"The best and most exclusive," Rhea added.

"And the most expensive," Mia said as she and Rhea cast wary eyes on the laid out Judge.

"He is definitely going to need Dr. Flagel for those teeth." Rhea said. "There is no doubt about that. Everyone goes there. He did Queen Noor and Jennifer Lopez and Mariah Carey just last week. I know, I planted it in Page Six."

Scarlet's eyes blazed a little detectable fire at the mention of the names, and she made a note in her mind. Dr. Flagel. She was trying to stay out of the way which was not easy in the tiny room. The jungle of flowers provided a little shelter. Her dark suit helped her blend in the low lighting. For once in her life she was happy to be a wallflower. She was engrossed in the unfolding story as if she were in a darkened movie theater. Her alert eyes riveted on the actors every move, her ears caught every word. This was a different scene for Scarlet. She was now one of the girls in the eyes of the press and other party people, but that was only at night, at parties. She had not crossed over in the daylight hours.

"I didn't know he was a client of yours. I saw that column," Mia said. "Oh my god, don't tell me you're working for trade! Is that why you're flashing those super whites around lately? I knew something was up."

Rhea flashed a Cheshire cat smile that beamed hot white in the dim room.

"Gorgeous! When do I get in?" Mia said. "Did you see Penelope Trotter's mouth after he finished with her? She looked like a fucking movie star. Gorgeous, gorgeous mouth, her whole face changed. She looks like a different person. And it is definitely a prettier person, honey, let me tell you."

"We should definitely get Judge in there ASAP," Rhea said. "I mean, the swelling and the black eye will go away, but that jacked up grill is here to stay. But that broken cheek bone thing scares me. I mean, such good cheek bones. God, what if he heals ugly? Can you imagine? What will happen to him? He was so gorgeous before. His perfect cheek bones, gone."

"Well, that's not confirmed yet." Mia said. "They're waiting on X-rays to see if he goes into surgery." Then lowering her voice to Rhea so Lucy couldn't hear, "They think he might have some brain damage."

Lucy Shining sat quietly at the side of the bed, gazing sweetly at Judge and stroking his hair. "Maybe he won't need plastic surgery," she mumbled.

"Of course he's going to need it," Rhea said. "Look at him." She turned to Mia and said, "Tell your new boyfriend to please get off the phone with his broker and tell us what the hell is going on with Lenox."

"I'm on the phone with the president of Lenox Hill, Rhea," Jack Haver said smugly. "My broker is much tougher to get in touch with, you should know that."

The nurse appeared from behind the curtain, surveyed the room and shook her head. As she walked past the gathering, Rhea called after her, "Oh, nurse." Then to Mia, "You would think that they would at least put him in a private room, I mean, it's Judge fucking Mender. This room is skank."

The nurse left the room and Rhea and Mia chased after her. Scarlet, clocking their departure, quickly followed the scene into the hallway. Jack finished his call, snapped his cell phone shut and turned to announce his findings only to find the girls gone except Lucy. Jack bolted out of the room to find them. Judge stirred and opened his eyes. Lucy held his hand and stared at his swollen face and black eye. There were still specs of dried blood on his face and she fought the urge to cry.

"Hey Babe. How are you feeling?"

"Hey, Luce. What is going on? Where the hell am I? What're you doing here?"

"You're in Saint Vincent's."

"My head is pounding. What the hell happened?"

"The police found you this morning on Tenth Street. They said you were in a daze and your clothes were covered with blood. Don't you remember anything?"

Judge thought she was speaking some foreign language.

"I don't understand."

"Mia says you left your place around five."

"When? What?"

"You were with Mia and your friend Russ, at your place, and you went for a walk. They, the police, think you were attacked. They found you close to the river."

"I thought I heard other voices, or am I really losing it?"

"We're all here for you, baby. Do you need anything?"

"Water. Or a scotch."

"No scotch for you, Judge, not for a while anyway."

The nurse entered the room again and Lucy stood to get her attention.

"Yes?" The nurse said, then noticed that Judge was awake. "Oh you're awake. I guess it's hard to sleep with all this commotion going on around you."

Lucy smiled and stepped back to make room. The nurse came up beside Judge and gave the IV tube a couple of flicks with her finger.

"How's the pain, Judge?"

"I'm okay, but I'm dying for some water."

"You still can't have water, honey. They don't know if you're going into surgery or not. Let me see what I can do. I'll be back."

"Thanks."

"How long has it been since you've had anything?" Lucy asked.

"What day is it?"

"Sunday, you were admitted this morning."

"How are you all here? Who called you? Who sent all these flowers?"

"Oh, Judge!" Rhea said much too loudly upon entering the room. "You're awake!"

She sidled in on the opposite side of the bed and planted big air kisses on each cheek. "We came as soon as we heard. Don't worry. We're getting you out of here as soon as possible. Jack's dad is going to get you transferred to Lenox Hill."

Judge looked at her with bemusement. "Whatever you say, Rhea."

"I mean, this place is fine for emergencies," she said as she fondled one of the bouquets on the nightstand. "But you need the best darling, I mean, look at…"

Jack re-entered and interrupted Rhea, "Hey, Judge. You're awake. Man, how do you feel? You look like hell."

"Jack!" Rhea shouted.

"He knows what he looks like, don't you Judge?" Jack said. "Have you seen a mirror?"

"Jack," Rhea snapped and walked toward the door. "Come here!"

"You look great to me, babe," Lucy said. "How do you feel? Are you sure there's no pain?"

"Not really. I guess the morphine is doing me fine."

"You really scared me." Tears began to roll down her bare cheeks. "I thought you were leaving us."

"I must look much worse than I feel. I'm glad you're here."

Rhea and Mia came back into the room and Rhea declared. "I was the first one here, Judgie. I brought you this gorgeous basket from Balducci's."

The nurse re-entered and scanned the room with a look of disgust.

"Okay, everybody out. We have to change his IV and the doctor is on his way."

"Excuse me, nurse lady," Rhea said. "But we are very close friends here."

"And I'm sure he's grateful, but you must now vacate this room."

"Come on, Rhee," Lucy said. "Let's go." She looked down at Judge and stroked his swollen cheek. "I'll be back in a little while, babe. I'm so glad you're okay. Is there anything I can bring you?"

"Look here, Miss Nurse," Rhea said. "I've started a sign in sheet here of all of his visitors. Make sure everyone signs this when they come in."

Judge looked at a notepad on the nightstand, nestled between three bouquets of flowers. There were twenty-five or so names on the sheet. He closed his eyes and breathed deeply.

Scarlet entered the room and stood out of the way against the wall. She waited for the prominent girls to leave the room and then stepped up beside Judge and signed the list. She scanned over the names above hers and felt a thrill at her new association with these famed names.

"I was the first one here, Judge," Scarlet said quietly but with pride. "The police found my name on your cell phone and called me this morning to say you were here."

"Thanks for coming, Scarlet. How did all the others find out so fast?"

"I called them. I got here and saw your cell phone and scrolled through and called everyone."

"That would explain why the social register of NYC has found its way to this humble room." He remembered the article he'd written about her and found some symmetry between the girl now in this room and the girl he had eviscerated for Jet Set.

"I hope you don't mind."

"No, no, it's fine. It's just a little overwhelming."

"I never realized how pretty Lucy Shining is. I mean I only see her at night and the pictures in the magazines don't do her justice. And that Rhea Brown is so pushy."

Scarlet left Judge's bedside and poked through the baskets and fiddled with the flowers, reading the notes and determining where everything came from.

"Scarlet?" he said meekly.

"Yes, Judge?"

"I'm a little tired. I think I need to sleep."

"Oh, sure. I'm sorry," she said, stuffing one of the little cards back into its little envelope. "I'll go and come back later when Lucy's here. Do you need anything?"

"Maybe some fruit would be nice."

Scarlet eyed the basket on the table next to her. "Oh of course, I'll run by Dean & Deluca."

"That would be swell."

Scarlet pulled on her coat and put her bag on her shoulder and leaned down to Judge's side for a big showy display of air kisses. "I'm so glad you're okay. I was so scared when the police called to say you were here. But don't worry. I'm going to take care of everything."

She left the room wearing a broad smile, very pleased with herself.

The nurse entered immediately as if she had been waiting impatiently in the hall for the room to clear. She carried a fresh IV package and set about to change the old one. "I've never seen so many fancy visitors in here before," she said. "Are you famous?"

"No, I just run with a fancy set, I guess."

"Well, I don't want to say anything but they sure are bossy," she said as she set about to change the bags. "The one kept asking me about your condition and your doctor's credentials. I'm not allowed to give out that information. She got a little peeved with me."

"I'm sorry about that. They are a little overzealous. I'll tell them to back off."

"Oh, it's okay, honey. I can handle them. I just wanted to make sure none of them was asking on your behalf. Do you have any family we should call?"

"I'm capable of handling it myself. Where is the doctor? I really need some water."

"He'll be here in a minute." She scanned the room full of flowers, gifts and baskets. "I've never seen so much stuff in such a short time. You were only admitted to this room four hours ago."

"These people are very competitive when it comes to philanthropy, and it looks like I'm the cause célèbre du jour."

"Cause ce what? Well. I hope they let you get some rest. You need it with what you've been through. By the way, what did happen to you? You're head looks like it was hit with a baseball bat."

"I have no idea. I left home last night then woke up here."

"Hmm, maybe you were hit by a car. Were you drunk?"

"It's not unlikely, but I don't' think so."

"Well, you better rest now, honey. The doctor will be in soon."

"Bye, Judge."

"Bye, Cynthia. Thanks."

Judge fell into a deep dreamless sleep and did not see or hear the scene that unfolded around him. It was after four now and the word of his attack had traveled well beyond Saint Vincent's and Greenwich Village. The news shot up Madison Avenue and down to Wall Street. The news was passed by the bossy Yugoslav manicurists at Nail Spa and table hopped at La Goulue. In his slumber, scores of members of the junior set had come to pay their respects and to record firsthand the multitude of flowers and gifts that were by four o'clock taking a turn toward legend among a certain group of Manhattanites and their mothers. They arrived by the dozens to see the famous guest list they had heard about and, once satisfied that it was indeed high-quality, added their names to the illustrious index. It wasn't until Victoria Newton arrived that Judge was brought back to life. He heard her booming voice in the hallway.

"I realize it is after visiting hours, my dear woman, but I am on my way to Paris for the couture and I've asked my driver to stop here on the way to the airport. I must see Mr. Mender and I will not take no for an answer. Please step aside."

Judge looked up to see Victoria swing wide the door and stride to his bedside. She wore a coral Bill Blass suit with a gold necklace with one giant diamond at her neck which glistened even here in the low light of the room. She carried a brown paper shopping bag which she plopped on his blanket covered legs.

"My god, Judge! What the hell have you done this time?" She placed her heavy Birken bag on his legs as well and put a hand on his chin. "You don't look so bad. My god, by the way Sally Banning carried on I expected to find the elephant man."

"Hello, Victoria," he said groggily, trying to open his eyes.

"Look at all this loot!" she said as she walked around to the other side of the bed, and rooted through the flowers and baskets, noting where each came from and who sent what.

"Balducci, nice. Miho, nice." She said as she picked up cards and put them back. "Who uses Gwendolyn Paster anymore? Oh, that explains it." She said as she read the card. "Marcia never has had any taste. She probably heard yesterday that Gwendolyn was trendy. Pitiful."

She walked back around to his side of the bed and pulled the shopping bag off his legs. "I knew you'd be inundated with worthless flowers and candy, so I had driver pull over at one of those little delis on the corner." She pulled a set of five magazines out of the bag. They were shrink-wrapped together. She ripped off the plastic.

"I figured this would help you more than all that crap, if I know you like I think I do."

She put the stack of magazines on his chest and sat back surveying the room. Judge pulled a hand from under the cover and picked up the first one and held it up right to the light. It didn't take long to determine that they were low rent pornography. There was a giant orange sticker on the front reading "XXX" and the cover showed a plump, pimply, naked man in full coitus with a bleached blond woman whose legs were spread as wide as the page.

"Victoria Newton. You are too fucking much."

"I got you mostly the nasty straight ones, but there's a homo one in there too, just in case you come out of this thing and want to brush up on your man skills."

"Well, I have to say that this is the most thoughtful gift I've received today."

"So, where's this list I've heard all about?" she said and spotted the tablet on the table. "This is all anyone can talk about: The Judge Mender Hospital List. I had to come down here and see the damn thing for myself."

She began reading the list and her face reacted with each line. Her eyes narrowed or widened depending on the social rank of the signer. Her nose crinkled, her lips pursed, she smiled, then frowned.

"What is she doing on here? She doesn't know you. Or her? When did he get back into town? I thought she moved to Singapore? Good Lord! I thought he was busted for insider trading? Oh, this is a good one. I am very impressed."

She pulled a fancy pen from her bag and swirled her signature at the bottom of the list. She put the pen back, placed the tablet on the table and stood up.

"Well, I've got a flight to catch," she said as she leaned in to give him a little air kiss. "I hope you're out of here when I return. You know we have that damn car show coming up and I simply won't be forced to attend if you don't cover it."

"Thanks for coming, Victoria. It means a lot."

"Well, don't mention it. I'm off to the couture. I have to host a damn dinner for Valentino in Paris. I can't believe I agreed to do this. What do I know about hosting a dinner in Paris? I sure as hell can't communicate with those tadpoles. I feel sorry for those little event planners when I roll into town."

Judge laughed. He felt sorry for them too.

"Goodbye, Judgie boy," she said as she walked out the door. "See you next week."

Judge laughed again and picked up the magazines on his chest. Too much, he thought and slowly laid them down again and drifted back into sleep.

Maxwell was the last to visit. It was ten o'clock and he had to sneak past the night nurse to slip into Judge's room. When he arrived, he was surprised by the profusion of flowers in the dark room. Judge lay in the middle of the display and looked to Maxwell like an official lying in state. He choked and felt a lump in his throat as he imagined Judge dead and a tear began to well in his eye and then his eyes landed on the images on the magazine's cover lying on Judge's chest and he burst into a bellow of a laugh that snapped Judge from slumber.

"Where in the world did you get these?" Maxwell said as he picked up the first one with the title "My First Anal."

Judge stirred and focused to realize it was Maxwell.

"Hey, Maxwell."

"Hello, Judge. What are you doing with all this raunchy porn in your bed?"

"What?" he said and looked down at his chest. "Oh, Victoria brought that. I guess I fell asleep on her."

Maxwell roared with laughter. He picked up the stack and perused the titles.

"My First Anal, Back Door Alley, Tina's Threesome, and oh, here's the Pulitzer if you ask me, The Courtship of Eddie's Finger." Maxwell hooted as he put the magazines in the top drawer of the bed table. "They will be right here when you need them."

"So tell me everything," he continued. "I couldn't get here earlier because I had that damn luncheon at Saks and the breakdown was a disaster, but not to worry. I've been in constant touch with Dr. Logerquist and relayed everything to your sweet mother."

"You called my mother?"

"Yes, and Lucinda." Maxwell said as he poked through the flowers in the room. He couldn't be bothered to critique what was beneath him. He did sniff once at one arrangement. "Hmph, carnations."

"And?"

"I told them you were in a little accident and you were checked into the very best hospital in New York, a little lie, but necessary. They were terribly upset, your two mothers, but I managed to calm them down and kept calling all day with the reports from the doctor. Lucinda and Russ had just landed when I called. Evidently Russ had no idea you weren't home, something about him and Mia going back to her place. I told them there was no need to fly back up, that I would get you home and take care of you. Everyone is very relieved and you can thank me now for sparing you the hysterics of a southern mother whose son has been attacked on the streets of New York."

"You didn't tell her that did you?"

"Good God no! Do you think I wanted to hear a woman I don't know suffer a heart attack over the telephone line? I told her you were barely grazed by an out of control bus and that you were fine and in good hands."

"Thank you, Maxwell. With all the circus going on here I don't think I could handle her too. Can you believe all of this?" Judge said motioning to the horn of plenty. "You know how this all happened?"

"Do I?!" Maxwell boomed. "That little Scarlet O'Hara has chased me up one side of the city and back. She does mean well, darling, but my God, she is a persistent little thing. Each time she called it was a Page Six report on who was here doing what before I got even one morsel of actual medical news. I finally got in touch with the doctor myself to cut out Little Miss Meddling."

"And what is my prognosis?"

"You've got a major concussion. Your cheek bone, whatever the term is I can't remember, is cracked. You've lost a tooth, which is a travesty, I know. All in all, you came out alright. The greatest news is that the cat scan doesn't show any swelling in the brain, which was the main concern, so you won't have to have surgery. I just talked to the doctor and he says I can give you some water now."

Maxwell produced a small bottle of water and unscrewed the cap and handed it to Judge. Judge swallowed the contents greedily. He looked at Maxwell. "Thank you, Maxwell. This has been the most fucked up thing I've ever done. Look at what I've been through," and Judge picked up the famous notepad and handed it to Maxwell. "The good news is that I was passed out for most of that barrage."

Maxwell took the notepad and perused over the names, chuckling and smiling all the way through. "You do realize that this is a better turn out than any gala this season?"

"I guess I should be flattered."

"Flattered? You're famous. I am not kidding when I tell you that you are the talk of the town. They tell the story of your assault first, by the way, the latest version is that you were attacked by three thugs on a stoop on Tenth Street on your way home from Moomba. Where, not incidentally, you were seen cavorting with Princess Arianna."

"Maxwell, I wasn't at Moomba last night."

"Well, do you think that matters? That's the tale that's going around. The second thing they can't stop clucking about is this list. Do you know that some reporter from Page Six called and begged me to steal it for her? It appears you are the lead story in tomorrow's column. I mean, I thought you were famous, but darling, you're Elizabeth Taylor! At least for the next few days."

"And are you here to steal the list?"

"Are you crazy? They can't afford my fee for theft. I told them absolutely not. I could never stoop so low to betray a friend's privacy." Maxwell laughed with Judge. "Besides, someone already came in and copied it while you were asleep. So, I lost anyway."

The two laughed at the theater of the absurd. Then suddenly, either through a lapse in the drugs or a surge, Judge realized of all the people that had been there that day, Maxwell was the only one who knew his family, or knew enough about him to find them in Ophelia, Alabama.

"Thanks for coming, Maxie Pad," Judge said as he drifted back to sleep. Maxwell let the detested nickname ring in his ear like the sweetest term of endearment and sat in the chair watching over him until long after Judge fell back into sleep. Maxwell charmed the night nurse to give him a blanket and then settled into the cramped hospital chair and stayed through the night.

Act Two

The Players

With an evening coat and a white tie, you once told me, anybody, even a stockbroker, can gain a reputation for being civilized.

Oscar Wilde

Chapter 12

Judge's Call of Duty

September 3, 1999

A laser beam of light broke through the heavy curtains of the West Village bachelor suite. Judge Mender blinked awake into a squint and discovered the naked bodies of a brown-haired man and a salon blonde woman tangled in his bed across the room. He discovered his own nakedness and slipped into a pair of boxers. He squinted again to focus on the wall clock across the room, the Roman numerals too delicate to be read from the distance. He pulled up-right a little too surely and his temples popped from the pain of a hammer connecting with his brain. He put his head between his knees to make the nausea flutter down. The hammer stopped. Judge skulked over to sniff around like a dog worn from the hunt. He shot a scowl at the trespassing bodies in his bed still unable to identify the faces. He turned around and spied a pink evening gown hanging on the chair, sequins dancing in the renegade stream of light. Mia Wilson? But who is the dude? Confused yet mildly satisfied that the river of last night's scotch had not affected his ability to pull the best of show from either sex, he discovered the clock and the fact that he was late for work.

Judge nudged the sleeping man with his foot as he stood surveying the scene. The man stirred.

"What's going on?" the naked man muttered and squinted through a maze of curly brown hair.

"Hey." The man smiled a cocky, fuck-you smile that sent a nervous rattle through Judge like warming an engine on a frost-bitten morning.

"Morning, dude," Judge managed. "You've got to get up. I have to get out of here and..."My name's Caleb."

"Thanks. I don't..."

"It's okay," Caleb said as he turned over onto his back. He rubbed a tan hand over the blanket where the woman's ass mounded. "You were pretty drunk."

"I feel it now." Judge detested morning conversation. "Hey, I really have to get into the shower."

Judge kicked his way through the moguls of rumpled black clothing at his feet. The trio in the room corresponding to the piles of clothing on the floor and the pink gown thrown over the back of the slipper chair, hot-pink Manolos tucked underneath. He searched for his wallet in the tuxedo pile but through his hangover eyes, all the clothes looked the same, an equal set: black jacket, another, white shirt, answered, black tie, the same, all through shoes and socks. The clothes were black and looked the same in the eye but were easily discernible in the hand. Judge's pieces were Ralph Lauren Purple Label, a gift for a favorable mention in his column. The other? The standard issue of cater waiters: cheap, unlined, ill-fitting. He pulled back the curtain to unleash the barking dogs of streaming sun on the pile of clothes.

Judge sifted through the heap and found his pants. He fished his wallet out of the back pocket and turned toward the bathroom. What if this dude robs me blind? What if he murders Mia Wilson and I have to stand

198

trial for accomplice to the trial of the century? Her death would be front page news. Millionaire party girl found slain in society columnist's bed. Judge turned around and went back to the bedside table to retrieve his Rolex, a gift from his grandfather when he graduated from college. He stopped again to take in the picture in his bed. His mind searched for commentary, something to remind him how this ended last night. At what hour? Was that the cater waiter from the Waldorf party in his bed? Were there others? Were there drugs involved? His feet pulled him toward the bathroom into the shower.

Judge let the cold water revive him. Memory was his stock and trade and when he drank too much his column suffered. Not that anyone else noticed, his editor or his readers, but he clung to that journalistic integrity he'd brought to New York with him, at least until the deadline approached and he chucked that out the window and employed a little fiction. He closed his eyes and began pulling the parts together. The beginning, the beginning, where did it all begin? When a party ended at three-thirty in the morning, followed by God knows what, Judge found it difficult to trace its beginning at a sedate cocktail gathering. Beginning, beginning, getting dressed, black-tie, shirt-not-pressed-panic, rush call to Min at Grand Dry Cleaners on the corner, "please Min, this is an emergency," he pleaded dramatically since charm failed to register with the Korean. "My career hangs on your ability to press this shirt in fifteen minutes!"

The rush and fumble in getting dressed blame landed squarely on his editor Richard Hadenfield. The editor kept Judge in his office later than usual last night to discuss his next subject of a feature story. It was time for Judge to earn his keep, the editor said.

"It's time for a hatchet job in the grand old style," Richard boomed. A parvenu had gotten a little grand and it was time for a take down. Judge was not surprised by the proposed endeavor, only by the naked presentation of the fact. He knew this was what Jet Set was known for and what the tony readership expected, yet he never imagined it was discussed so carelessly. But Judge was flush with ambition and desire and he greedily lapped up the directive.

"Richard, I'm honored," Judge said softly between the lines of a suppressed smile.

"It's time. Your work has been solid. Everyone's impressed with your instincts. You have the network to get inside and the trust once you're there. And the socialites seem to love you. All I hear is 'please send that charming Judge Mender to cover the party.'"

The editor took a long drag from his cigarette, looked over the piles of magazines on his desk and deep into Judge's hungry eyes. "You realize the seriousness of this, don't you? You are about to ruin someone's life." He exhaled dramatically, "or at least, that's what the detractors will lay on you."

"Some might say he's already ruined it himself."

"Ha," the editor chuckled. "I knew you were ready."

The men spent the next forty-five minutes discussing the evidence gathered against the intended victim. The two laid out what each knew: Biography, History, Education, Scandals. The details – some public, most private – of a curated life were now being traded like baseball cards between the most powerful editor on the Manhattan social scene and his ambitious apprentice.

It was only when Judge left the Jet Set offices that he began to fully examine all sides of the proposed exercise. He was familiar with the event that was about to take place. It was the reason he came to Jet Set in the first place. His stints at smaller publications prepared him for this day when Richard Hadenfield would call on him to write this story. It was his chance to record the sotto voce of the idle rich   and from those whose livelihood and social status derived from such gilded propinquity-- and present it transformed through his sensational prose. The press -- most notably the scandalmongers at Page Six -- would pick up the trail and propel his reputation. His name would be whispered when he walked into a room: "That's Judge Mender who wrote that piece on Chase Peters." He would be feared and respected.

When he left Richard's office, Judge felt a gnawing in his stomach and a salty, dry scratch in his throat. He had stopped into an empty bar on lower Seventh Avenue to order a scotch on the rocks and smoke a cigarette. It was not the kind of place high society would be caught dead in. He needed the distance to reflect. Like his hunt-loving father before him, Judge was going big-game stalking. Judge Mender was twenty-seven years old and was about to bring down a rising star in Manhattan society.

Chase Peters was a comer. He was a charming and handsome homosexual who enjoyed easy entrée into Manhattan's junior society. He attended Brown with many members of the set. He was connected, through his family, to the current White House and was making a name for himself as a party planner for the gilded group. He produced a few good parties for the more press-friendly heiresses and quickly vaulted to the upper tier of that rarefied group. "You must use Chase Peters for your next event," one would say to the next. "He gets it. Do you know what I mean? He gets it." And that was all it took. Chase threw away the invoice for the rich girls, got a few mentions in the right press and then spiked the price for the next level of climbers who would pay the big bills.

Judge Mender was the first to mention Chase Peters in print. That was the part of his job Judge enjoyed most. Discovery. Judge thrived on the charge he got when unearthing a new rising star on the scene. His job depended on it, yes, but he relished the access Jet Set provided. Judge's interests were well-suited to the magazine's readership. Socialites and celebrities were easy fare, shooting fish in a barrel. It was his attraction to bona fide artists that Judge indulged by means of the Jet Set business card and assuaged the early guilt of puffing up the trust fund set. If he fell in love with the work of an artist, he would take her to dinner and turn in a story about the hot new painter. If he was excited for the release of a new book, he would invite the author to lunch. Judge reveled in the ease with which he rolled with the cognoscenti.

It was a mention in Judge's column which brought Chase Peters out of mass and into the beau monde. Chase Peters was now, by all accounts, a force to be reckoned with. None other than Palm Beach real estate heiress Victoria Newton had made the introduction. Judge met Chase at The Union Club for drinks one night, which turned into a raucous stumble up and down town and finally into Chase's bed. He ran into Chase many times on the benefit circuit last season and on a few occasions over the summer in Southampton. Judge wasn't surprised when he spied him table dancing at Les Caves in St. Tropez. Judge had begun preparation on a feature story on Chase for the magazine over a month ago, a positive and glowing fluff piece. Then the grumbling began.

Judge heard the first rumble from the indomitable Victoria Newton herself. "Who is this Chase Peters? Who does he think he is?" she fumed over the telephone last week. Victoria hired Chase to decorate her annual Southampton party after he was mentioned in Judge's column. Yes, she had introduced the two of them, but it took the imprimatur of Jet Set to trust him for such an important event. Victoria Newton's party kicked off the summer season for the junior set and Chase was hired to make the event buzz, which by all accounts he succeeded. Judge wrote up the glamorous night in his column as the best party in months and ran half a dozen pictures of Queen Victoria and her court. But Victoria was less than pleased with Chase's behavior the night of the event and incensed when his bill arrived in the mail.

"He not only begged me to seat him next to Simone Lambert — and by the way, what party planner asks to be seated? Who does he think he is, Maxwell Jones?" She barked through the receiver. "Anyway, he not only slithered in beside Simone but then proceeded to make out with her on the dance floor, before snorting an eight ball in the bathroom, mind you, and then going home with Andrew. God knows what happened when those two disappeared. And then! -— hold onto your hat -- mailed me a bill for twenty thousand dollars!" she enunciated sharply. "He's finished as far as I'm concerned."

Judge laughed at Victoria's presentation of the evidence against Chase. None of those offenses, by itself, was enough to get anyone kicked out of a black tie party, especially in Southampton. The sum of the small parts, however, at a Victoria Newton event, was merely another Saturday night scandal in this world. But the misstep and insult of bedding her current boy interest, Andrew Christopher, and then having the nerve to charge her full price for the party. And it wasn't the amount that incensed her. It was the notion that Victoria was not as press worthy as the other, thinner heiresses who received Chase's service for free. It all added up to ungrateful bounding and if there was anything worse in her mind, Victoria Newton couldn't find it.

Once Judge's investigation into Chase's background began, the dirty details started popping up like weeds in a well-tended garden. School chums from Brown, business associates and, most damaging, spurned lovers joined in the current talk of the town. There was one particular incident -- allegedly involving a scene with a hustler in a bathtub -- that was so debilitating and scandalous that Judge could only listen and surreptitiously repeat; it could not be written.

Judge stood at the dingy bar staring into his drink. He took out his cell phone and lingered on the directory for a moment. He scrolled down through the illustrious names. He wanted some advice, but she wouldn't have it. Judge was a long way from his mother and Ophelia, Alabama, further than time, than distance, than education. He was in another world now and there was only one person he could turn to in this new reality. The uncertainty gnawed at him. He was unsure and he wondered that his instincts would fail him. Until now, he had always been an excellent calculator with a scissor-quick ability to see all sides of a situation, a crucial tool in his acceleration through the magazine and social worlds of Manhattan. Never in his life had he been wrong or misguided, nothing he could remember anyway. He had always done it on his own, but now he was in thin-aired altitude with much more at stake.

He knew what he was going to do. He would seek the counsel of wisdom and age. He stubbed out his Marlboro in the ashtray on the bar, threw his head back and let the half-full glass of fuel splash down his throat. He wiped the sides of his mouth with his sleeve, picked up his cigarettes and headed out the door into the thumping city.

The pieces had come together. That was where the day had begun. Professional benchmark followed by heavy booze and God knows what. He savored the juxtaposition as the warm water washed away his sin. Judge was startled by the sound of the shower curtain sliding open and turned to see the naked man from his bed stepping in beside him.

"Mia left," Caleb said as he pulled the shower curtain shut. "It's just you and me now."

Judge narrowed his eyes and cracked a crooked smile.

"Sorry man, I've got to get to work," and slipped around the curtain and into a towel. He got dressed and rushed the befuddled Caleb out the door dripping wet and pulling his clothes on as Judge shut the door unceremoniously behind him. Judge laughed at the thought of the half naked cater-waiter running into his neighbors in the hall. Then the pain in his head reignited the nausea in his stomach and the body would not be so easily bum rushed. He shuffled into the kitchen to ingest the stale coffee from the night before that would get him out the door. His head pounded harder and he searched for anything to dull the pain. There was nothing medicinal in a cabinet anywhere but a tiny roach of a skinny joint propped up in the overflowing ashtray. It was too short to light. He burned his fingers. He pulled on his coat and walked out the door.

It was just after noon when Judge made it to his desk in the brightly-lighted electric pulse of the Jet Set newsroom. The unforgiving fluorescent light and loud whir of his colleagues chatter were not helping his head. He turned to his cubicle neighbor, Leah, who was busy typing a story into her keyboard.

"Leah?" He managed through smoke-cured tonsils. "Do you have any more of that Emer'gen-C. I think that's the only thing that will bring me back to life."

"Yeah, I think so." She stopped typing and fished in her desk drawer. She found a one-dose package of turbo Vitamin C powder and handed it to Judge. "I'll get you a glass of water and how about I order us a couple cheeseburgers?"

"You are bucking for a promotion, baby," Judge said, "or perhaps a marriage proposal. Which do you prefer?"

"How about a little uninterrupted silence to finish my piece?"

"You got it," Judge said with a smile.

"Oh wait," Leah blurted. "A Meredith something something from the Metropolitan Opera called to say that your tickets to opening night would be at Will Call. I put the invitation there on top of your inbox. I swear that is the most money invite I've ever seen."

"Oh great," Judge said sarcastically and lifted the heavy cream-colored envelope, his name swirled elegantly in calligraphic splendor. "I suppose she cc'd Richard so he'll be expecting me there. What a drag. I thought I was going to get out of that."

"What's a drag is that that event cost most schmos about two grand a piece and you waltz in with your free tickets. I bet you a hundred bucks you don't even cover it, not even one sentence."

"I will say it was the chicest turnout for an opera opening in ages. The luminaries were luminescent." Judge lifted his chin and pointed his nose to the ceiling.

"That's nauseating, wait, oh yeah, there it is. I just threw up in my mouth. And the opera?" Leah pressed.

"Nobody gives a damn about the opera," Judge practically spit out of his mouth. "The Jet Set reader wants only to read about who was there and what they wore. Give me a break."

Judge ran his finger along the gilded edge of the invitation. The truth was he was thrilled to be attending opening night. The Metropolitan Opera season would open with Cavalleria Rusticana and Pagliacci. Standard operas, sure, but this was an exceptional circumstance: Not only would the crème of New York society turn out in their finery, but Placido Domingo was to sing Canio in Pagliacci – Enrico Caruso's most famous role – and in the doing, Domingo would surpass Caruso's record of seventeen opening nights at the Met. Judge held the invitation as proudly as a diploma. He had exerted an extra degree of charm on the PR girl in the Met's publicity office to get that invitation.

"I'm just saying," Leah continued, "that with all this access you have, it isn't unthinkable that you might actually absorb some of this expensive culture you are exposed to on a nightly basis. I would kill to..."

"Yeah, yeah, yeah," Judge said teasing. "You'd kill to cover my beat: the opera, the ballet, the plays, the openings, the capital C culture."

Judge slid the invitation back into the envelope and ran his finger over his name so masterly rendered. "You will one day, baby. One day this could all be yours."

Judge raised his hands, palms up to indicate his work and the treasure of the trade that littered his gift-filled cubicle. "Until then, I've got to sit through a fucking opera tonight and pretend I'm enjoying it because I'll be tucked up in the goddamn president's box jonesing for a scotch and a cigarette."

"You don't fool anybody with those gifted clothes and that affected accent, Judge Mender. You're still a hick from the sticks lost in a New York swirl."

"I know," he said and flashed a devilish grin. "Ain't it grand?"

He turned and fished for a cigarette in the flattened pack on his desk. Judge's cubicle was an orgy of detritus from his professional and personal life, which were as intertwined as the pieces of a natty rope. He was paid to socialize. And then they sent gifts. It was something he could have never imagined. He looked over it again with wonder. His desk was cluttered with slides from various parties, edited and un-edited pieces for the magazine, business cards, scraps of paper with names and numbers crumpled and strewn, three ashtrays overflowed with ash and butts. The cork board on the wall was plastered with thank you notes and photographs of Judge with rich men and beautiful women and artists and celebrities. Invitations mounded and fell to the floor. Emphatic invitations on expensive papers so thick they could stand in for a burglar's credit card and pick a lock. There were piles of gifts in each corner. Gifts from fashion houses, champagne makers, home furnishing companies, cigar makers, perfume companies. One casual glance revealed a robe from Porthault, a tin of Osetra caviar from Petrossian, Absolute bottles, two black cashmere sweaters from Prada, old-fashioned glasses and decanter from Tiffany's, all carelessly on the floor, spilling out of boxes.

Judge picked up the phone to check his voice mail. Twenty-five messages and it was only mid day. There were the usual calls from ambitious socialites telling him how fabulous he was last night, all hoping their pictures would be chosen for his next party coverage page. Not that they would ever be so blatant as to mention that, in fact, would demur the fact if they were actually selected, but nevertheless, they called and hoped to be one of the anointed on Judge Mender's Seen page. Then followed the calls from the eager publicists, imploring him to attend their next event. Then the embarrassment of calls from the unknown and un-connected, cold-calling to invite him to their events, parties he would never acknowledge, must less attend and calls that would never be returned.

After deleting twenty worthless messages, he copied down the names of the five calls he would return. He began at the most important – the members of society that he favored at that moment -- and spent the first half hour listening to their accounts of the night before. These re-tellings, combined with his own badly scrawled notes, would make up the crux of his coverage on the event. He had to wait for the photographer's pictures to confirm his feeling, but generally, he already knew whose pictures he would run. Lucy Shining was a given. He would run her picture every column if he could. But after a stretch last spring in which every one of his columns ran big, smiling pictures of Lucy, Richard had summoned Judge to his office.

"I know you have a thing for Lucy Shining, but do you think you could hold running her picture to just once a month?" his editor had said half-joking.

"I didn't realize. I'll pay more attention."

"The magazine has to be seen as discovering new social stars as well fawning over the old guard's progeny. Find some new girls. I want to see the next Lucy Shining."

The editor waved his cigarette wand and dismissed Judge.

Judge pulled a pile of Jet Sets from a tray on his desk and flipped through a few of the summer issues to his column. Lucy Shining didn't follow the flock abroad, so he hadn't run any photos of her all summer. He flipped through the first two fall issues. He hadn't run Lucy at all last week, and only once the week before.

Judge was entranced by Lucy Shining. She was – in his opinion -- the perfect combination of woman: unapproachable wealth, devastating beauty, natural sex appeal and unmitigated cool. He became lightning charged in her presence and often determined a party's success by her attendance. In the past year, Judge's column had made Lucy Shining the current star of New York society, and she barely recognized him when he said hello. He figured by running her picture often enough, she would have to notice him eventually. But all of last year he had circled from a cool distance. He was determined to break through this season. None of the other girls excited him anymore. It seemed Lucy Shining was immune to his charm.

He returned to his voice mail and made a couple of calls to prod anecdotes from trustworthy sources. It was the usual routine when he was trying to get a particular angle from someone. The sources fell into three categories. There were the ones who would say anything and everything: usually these were the publicists. They would blather endlessly in hopes of getting one of their clients in print and they were usually the most disposable and unreliable. The next group was comprised of those who didn't care what they said and would offer up a little nugget that was amusing, or useful, or scandalous and this is where Judge got most of his news. The third group was the privacy obsessed and they were loath to confirm or deny any tidbit he'd managed to unearth. These sources, of course, were the most valuable and most reliable. And the most difficult. If he could get a bit from any one of them, the column was made. Today, he had landed on one such particular spot.

Chapter 13

Victoria Stokes

"Sweetie, you are never going to believe who had the nerve to call me this morning." Victoria Newton barked into the telephone receiver. She stood in the kitchen of her grandly-decorated apartment on East Sixty-Third Street, her expensively-colored blonde hair in a bun, a plush, navy bathrobe cinched tightly about her robust figure. She wore silk slippers with her initials swirled in bright red silk thread. An imperious air was in place even here in the private enclave of her kitchen. She wore a serious expression on her natural face. Victoria employed the drama of makeup only at a gala. She was a natural beauty in the fresh scrubbed Newport school, burnished by weekends in Palm Beach.

For Victoria, last night was fun and games at the Waldorf; this morning was all business. She was on the telephone with the first of many co-conspirators of the new day, recounting the events of the night before. Victoria first called Sweetie, which was not only a term of endearment, but the name of one of her closest and most trusted allies: fellow heiress and Palm Beach neighbor, Millicent "Sweetie" James. Victoria rustled through The New York Post, scanning Page Six for any boldface name she knew.

"You won't believe it. The flower from the Bronx, Lily von Reynolds." Victoria said this as if it were the name of some disfiguring disease.

212

"Oh nooo," cooed the voice on the other end of the phone.

"I mean, can you believe it?" Victoria puffed. "I practically ignored her last night, flitting around me like some annoying gnat, begging for attention. How can I be any ruder to her? Her climbing is appalling."

"Why do they all alight on you?" Sweetie asked. "They all seem to target you."

"I have no idea. I am not nice to them," she barked. "Anyway, hold on."

Victoria set about dialing her voicemail, pressing through the prompts, skipping previous messages until she landed on the offending call. Sweetie waited patiently, listening through salutations of messages on Victoria's voicemail. "Hey Tory. It's me.."

"Ms. Newton, this is..." "Victoria. You were radiant last night..."

"Okay." Victoria said. "This is it."

"Good morning, Victoria. This is Lily von Reynolds. I just wanted to call and tell you how wonderful it was to see you last night at the Animal Rescue Fund. You looked so beautiful in that Oscar. I wanted to talk to you about the ballet committee, so could you please give me a call when you get a chance? Did you say you were going to the St. Luke's benefit tonight? I hope so. I love hanging out with you at these things. Oh, well. Hope to see you there. Otherwise I'll talk to you soon. I am so glad you agreed to be on my committee. It is going to be such a great party. Bye now." Click.

"Can you believe her?" Victoria said voice rising. "'I love hanging out with you?' like we're old school chums or something. Can you believe the familiarity? Why did I agree to be on that stupid committee of hers?"

"Why did you? I thought you couldn't stand her."

"I agreed months ago, one of the first times I ever talked to her. She approached me at Geneva's Shahtoosh party when I barely knew who she was. She bombarded me with so many names I thought I would need a broom to sweep them all up. I thought she was innocent! I thought she was somebody! Little did I know that she was some conniving little tramp from the Bronx with ambition. Do you know she didn't have any of those people confirmed on the committee until she got me on board? The scheming! I found out she was calling all over New York telling everyone 'I have Victoria Newton confirmed for my Palm Beach party.' I should have squashed that bug when I had the chance."

"You have made her, Tory. Look where she was six months ago and look where she is now. I mean, that Town & Country cover was shocking."

"I know. I know," Victoria said deflated. "I have no one to blame but myself. Do you know Sally Banning sat me right next to her at her Colony Club luncheon last week? Not to worry. I frosted her, but good."

"No!" Sweetie shrieked with delight.

"I couldn't believe it! Fortunately, I had Elizabeth Pilgrim on my right and she can't stand her either so we had a good round of it."

"Oh, that Lily must have loved it, though." Sweetie felt suddenly slighted. "Why did Lily von Reynolds get invited to Sally Banning's luncheon at the Colony in the first place?"

"Oh, you know," said Victoria, "the same way she gets invited to everything. Her husband gave a steaming wad of cash to Sally's theater thing and so she had to invite her. I put the kibosh on that, though. I pulled her aside and gave her my research."

"No!" Sweetie squealed, "What did you tell her?" assuaged now, she wanted the rest of the story.

"I told her the truth!" Victoria pronounced absolutely, like a pontiff with the righteous word of God on her behalf. "I told her she was a little immigrant from Queens who won a scholarship to Princeton, married some New Jersey gangster, polished up her act in finishing school and was now flitting around the Manhattan social circuit showering money and joining committees. Besides. There is no "von" in the Bronx, much less New Jersey!"

Sweetie squealed again.

Victoria chuckled. She liked the way that came out.

"Anyway, Sarah learned her lesson. She told me she wasn't going to Palm Beach for Lily's ballet benefit and neither am I. Now if I can only get Elizabeth to bow out. I mean our names are already on the invitation, and that's unfortunate, but all the more effective when we don't show up, don't you think? Hold on. I have a call on the other line. Let's see who's calling me."

Victoria checked the caller i.d. Jet Set Publications.

"Oh, it's Judge Mender. Boy, have I got a scoop for him."

"What are you going to tell him?"

"I think it's time for a little exposé on a certain little flower from the Bronx."

"Victoria. You are deliciously cruel."

"Not cruelty, Sweetie. Truth. I seek the truth! I can't stand fakes! Not in jewelry, not in society. Goodbye, Sweetie darling."

Victoria clicked over to the waiting call.

"Judge Mender, darling, you brilliant man," she trilled in falsetto. "You cut such a dashing figure last night in that new dinner jacket from Ralph. And your tan! Is that left over from St. Tropez? I don't believe the Waldorf ballroom has seen such southern charm since Truman Capote."

"Yes, and I should never forgive you for standing me up at Cinquante-Cinq for lunch that day."

"Darling, please, I gave you my first dance last night and that is usually reserved for a man I'm meant to marry."

Judge sensed a slight dig in the air. Was she implying he would never be marriage material for the regal Miss Newton?

"Well, that's true." Judge did not remember dancing with her. "I hope I didn't step on your toes."

"No, darling. We danced early in the evening, before the liquor soaked your socks. I told you last night, but I have to repeat. Your column on the scene in St. Tropez was divine. You made me regret that I never made it over from Monaco. Did Mia Wilson really spend the weekend on Puff Daddy's yacht? What a tart!"

Chapter 14

Maxwell Gloats

"Where are the goddamned silver horns?" Maxwell Jones boomed.

Judge followed the darting dapper man into the back of his warehouse, sipping a coffee and smoking a cigarette. Maxwell tapped his pen on the surface of the clipboard in his hand and it made an awful, pointed, pop, pop, pop, penetrating his head and re-igniting his hangover. He needed to talk to Maxwell about the Chase article. He came here for advice but Maxwell was puffed up and clucking about his business. Judge took out his cell phone to check his office voice mail. He found a chair in the middle of the room and took a seat as Maxwell strutted and stirred.

"If those very valuable candelabras were left at the Waldorf last night," Maxwell boomed, "someone in this warehouse is going to be very displeased."

Julie, Maxwell's blushing, blond assistant -- fresh from Princeton and eager to please -- ran around a pile of equipment like a day-old chick darting for cover. She pulled and poked in boxes and bags, lifting and shuffling the heap of boxes and trunks from the previous night's party, all the aftermath of glamour waiting to be stored on shelves.

"I swear, I swear, I swear Mister Jones," she pleaded, near tears. "I swear they put them on the truck last night. I think I swear."

"Find them, darling pie. I am waiting." Maxwell pulled out his mobile phone, scrolled to 'Waldorf' and pressed a button. He walked away from the frantic Julie, out of ear shot and waited for the rings.

"Hello, Siro? Maxwell Jones here. Good morning. We had another circus last night, eh? Thanks for your hard work and your talented team, can't do it without you."

Maxwell walked in between two walls of steel shelves soaring twelve feet above him. The shelves were packed neatly with cardboard boxes, each declaring its contents in enormous yet elegant black magic-markered script: Décor Principaute Limoges, Décor Alexandrine Limoges, English Ivy White, Promenade Bernardaud, Vintage Bernardaud, Reed & Barton Grand Baroque, William IV Table Service. The shelves created a Pharaoh's tomb, a vault of treasures to make any table a royal affair, if only for one night. And the right price.

"Sure, sure, don't mention it," Maxwell continued. "You know I'll always take care of my friends. Did that strapping bartender get his extra little bonus, what was his name, Caleb? Good, good. He was quite popular with the women and the men. I think I might have to steal him away from you. Sure, sure. Have him telephone me this afternoon, will you? Thank you, Siro. Listen, one other thing. Did my gorgeous little darling of an assistant leave off the silver horn candelabras last night? I figured as much. I will send Louis over right away to get them out of your way."

Maxwell adjusted a box marked "Finger bowls."

"Okay, thank you again, Siro. I will talk to you soon. I think we have another one in two weeks. I'll have to check the schedule. It's small, some cancer thing. I'll be in touch. Goodbye, now." Maxwell put the phone away in his jacket pocket, ran his hand over a box in front of him that read "Summer flatware", smiled and walked back toward Julie and the mountain of equipment.

"How are we doing, Julie?" Maxwell teased. "Any silver horns present themselves?"

Julie turned around, eyes brimming with tears. "I, I, I, can't find them, Mister Jones. I think they were stolen. I'm so sorry. I'll pay for them."

"Very well, then. I will need a check for one hundred thousand dollars, made out to Maxwell Jones, Inc." he delivered haughtily and made his eyes wide in an exaggerated motion and glared into her watery eyes. "Should you call your father of shall I?"

"Oh my god! Mister Jones!"

Judge looked up from his note pad and laughed. Before Maxwell could break character, the girl burst into tears and ran off the storeroom floor toward the bathroom.

"Oh well," Maxwell said. "If she comes back, she'll have a job. If not? Time to find a new assistant. I'll have to poach Conde Nast again. How draining."

Maxwell motioned for one of the crew. "Manny, could you put all this away? Except for the Garrard Tureens. We will use them tonight for the Opera Party. Everything is all checked in except for the silver horns and they were left at the Waldorf. Send Louis over to pick them up immédiatement. We don't need them in Siro's way all afternoon."

"Yes, sir." Manny shouted as he disappeared behind the mountain.

Maxwell walked through the giant warehouse like General Patton, admiring the monument commemorating his success and importance.

He turned sharply toward the front of the building and accelerated toward the direction of his office. This was the best part of his day, overseeing his possessions and surveying his property. He felt successful and confident in this storeroom. What other event planner in town had his own store room in Soho the size of a football field? Hell, his closest competitors didn't even own their own equipment, much less real estate. This was all his and he was pleased. After twenty years in the business, he was at the top of a competitive field. He extended much effort and labor to get to this place where Manhattan society regarded his work as the gold standard. A Maxwell Jones event guaranteed glamour, beauty, originality and most importantly, press coverage. He acknowledged often this was a career made of hard work and luck, yes, but he also knew his personality, his charm and his handsome face had opened those doors wider. His hard work, talent and connections merely kept him at the party.

"Judge!" he shouted back over his shoulder. "Are you coming or do you want Manny to put you in a box and store you away until you are needed?"

Judge closed his phone, stood and put his note pad in his breast pocket. "Coming, mom."

In the office Wanda the receptionist flipped through The Daily News. She didn't bother to rustle when they came in, just kept her head in the newspaper.

"What trash are you reading about this morning?" Maxwell said and poured a cup of coffee. "Did you get any milk today, oh I see it."

"Some floozy is saying she had an affair with Richard Gere," Wanda said.

"Who cares? Tell me more."

"She met him when he was in town doing that dumbass gangster movie and now says she's pregnant and doesn't want any money, just recognition."

"Oh sure," Maxwell said. "Recognition in court. Any messages?"

Judge laughed. He had no use for the other columnists in town. They lived on celebrity gossip and he thought of them alternately as hounds or rats. He did not consider himself in their company and most of New York agreed. Judge was the gentleman journalist. He did not wallow with the rest of them.

"Yeah, they're on your desk," Wanda said. "Your wife called. She and your daughter made it to Palm Beach already. No news, she says. Just said to tell you they made it." Wanda looked up from her paper and into Maxwell's eyes, deadpan: "They made it." She returned to the paper and continued reading.

"Any other messages, dear?" Maxwell pursued.

"No business, of course, just gossip." Wanda said, turning the page. "From the usual suspects: Mrs. Whitmore, Mrs. Menton, and Mrs. Bushhog."

"Ha!" Maxwell laughed. He appreciated Wanda's Queens-bred irreverence. Luanne Bushwell was one of the richest women in New York and president of the board of the New York Public Library. "Please tell me you call her Bushwell when she calls." He followed Judge into his office and closed the door.

"I call her ho' bag, when she calls," Wanda said aloud to herself as she turned another page of the paper. Ho' bag Bushhog, calling? Shall I connect you?"

Until Judge called and said he needed to talk to him, Maxwell had planned to spend that morning as he spent every weekday morning after a big event during the season, talking to his ladies. If he produced the event, reaping his praise, if it were a competitor's job, dissecting the disaster. He collected the gossip: relaying the generic, filing away the juice-filled.

The previous night's party at the Waldorf was the unofficial start of the New York social season. After three summer months of parties in Southampton, cruises to Sardinia, table hopping in St. Tropez and grouse shooting in Scotland, New York society was back and itching to dress up and be seen. Last night's Animal Rescue Fund at the Waldorf was the first fundraiser of the season and the well-heeled herd arrived ready to graze. Corrina Samuel of Palm Beach, and her best friend and neighbor, Serena Robertson, had in five short years, pulled together THE party of the early season. Against all odds and even lesser interests, the two had managed to bring what was once considered a regional party for beach goers in Palm Beach in the lackadaisical spring, to a must-attend party in Manhattan in the very competitive fall. Of course, the two women had two beautiful, young daughters fresh out of college who were making successful inroads on the junior social scene. The daughters invited the junior set, and suddenly the party was an institution on the calendar.

The old guard had put away the summer, pulled autumn out of the mothballs and attended last night in high style. Kisses were exchanged like old time reunions, never mind that most of the group had seen each other all summer. The complaint that there were never any new people or new places to go never held. When any one of this group managed to venture somewhere new, they always ran back to the comfort of the enclaves: Aspen, St. Tropez, Monte Carlo, Palm Beach, Northeast

Harbor, Newport, Southampton, and finally, the mother ship, Manhattan.

Maxwell usually spent his mornings listening to the varying interpretations of a singular event. As Manhattan's most established and trusted events planner, he had blurred the boundaries between servant and guest. He was now, in his fifties, a seated guest at these events, and usually at the most prominent table, the host's. Last night he was seated between Corrina and Joan Rivers, the evening's emcee. So it was with an odd mixture of delight and bemusement that he listened to these morning-after reports. He was in the unique position of being seated with the served as well as the servants. He knew the story on both sides of the curtain and for as long as he had been in this business, this was the story each side ached to hear: the other side's. Society dames wanted to know which bartender or cater waiter was arousing which one of her friends. Bartenders wanted to know which dames were accessible and who was generous with the money.

"So, Judge, my boy, how are you feeling this morning?" Maxwell said a little too loudly for Judge's ear. "Wait, it's two o'clock. How are you feeling this morning?"

"Ha, ha." Judge said dismally. "I should think you would know, introducing me to that waiter who had a tasty scotch waiting every time I got back to my table. Were you trying to render me useless? What have I ever done to deserve your wrath? I almost lost it in the bathroom of the Starlight Roof. Very nice."

"It was never my intention to get you drunk, my dear boy. I wanted you to test drive the new server and let me know what you think. I am considering stealing him from Siro." Maxwell tapped his pen on his desk. "Sooo? What did you think?"

"As a waiter?" Judge was slightly confused. "He was fine. I certainly have the hangover to prove it, so yes, I can recommend his talents."

"Not those talents, you twit." Maxwell leaned back in his leather chair and put his Belgian loafers on the desk. "I saw you leave with him – and that anorexic fish, Mia Wilson. What do you see in her really? Ugh, I do not understand bisexuality, let alone poor taste. Don't bother denying it, and don't worry, none noticed but these eagle eyes. So tell me about Caleb. I think he makes a good addition to the stable. I hope you didn't ruin him."

Memory pulsed through Judge's brain, his mouth opened and filled with saliva. "Caleb? uh, Maxwell. Was that his name?" Judge cringed as he waited. This made his head hurt even worse. He tried to keep his nocturnal wanderings darkly hidden behind the velvet curtain. He danced with the most beautiful girl and made a show of leaving with her. He wondered if he was losing his touch or if comfort in this world was making him lazy.

"Caleb." Maxwell pronounced with measured glee and waited for the obvious. He sat up right and threw his feet to the floor, tapping a little dance under his desk. "Putting it together…" he sang.

"Well, let's just say," Judge said after a pause, deciding to confirm Maxwell's suspicions in a trade for the advice he'd come calling for. "If we are relying on my memory to assess his talents, we are in trouble. I can only say he was a fine mess in repose amongst the sheets this morning. Oh, wait. He did try to join me in the shower." Judge knew the little treat would titillate Maxwell right out of his shoes.

"Brilliant!" Maxwell shouted to the ceiling. He lowered his voice, Wanda would think he was mad. "I knew it. Tell me every detail."

"God, you're a horny old goat. Why did you ever marry that woman in the first place if all you want to do is talk about naked boys?"

"It's a generational thing, Mr. Impertinent," he said haughtily. "I had to marry. You know very well how difficult it is for a southerner, much less a man of a certain age here in high society. Now, tell me every detail or you get no news from me this morning. I'm sure you were too drunk to recall anything for your column. And I have got some juice. I should charge you a kickback, you know. You really are the worst at party coverage, you worthless lush."

"The story's finished. Not to worry, I gave you laurels ad nauseam. You will be very pleased." Judge shifted in his chair and took a deep swig of the quickly cooling coffee. "I have come to you this morning for a little counsel. It's about the Chase Peters' story. It's happening."

"Good," Maxwell said a little too quickly. "He was a slithering little snake last night. Didn't you think?" Maxwell forgot his lust for a moment when there was court intrigue afoot. Chase Peters had poached a big name client from him and was focusing his ambition on Maxwell's territory. Of all the other party planners around town, none worried Maxwell so much as Chase Peters. He was smooth and connected and, to Maxwell, dangerous.

"He actually runs around the room inserting himself into picture poses with these famous girls," Maxwell said. "It is sickening to behold. I mean, don't you think he actually looks reptilian? What with that nose, those beady eyes, that slicked back hair?"

"I guess so," Judge said uneasily. "He's never rubbed me like he does you."

"He was shameless last night, absolutely shameless. The way he smiled and bowed to Corrina was embarrassing. He talked to her as if she were Brooke Astor for Christ's sake."

"Do you mean he showed respect for her position?" Judge asked curiously of this delicate point. He had walked that same line before, balancing on the edge of respectful homage and playful banter.

"Respect for her position?!" Maxwell boomed. "Corrina Samuel is a desirable, vivacious woman in the prime of her life! She doesn't want to be treated like a grand dame dowager, especially by a handsome younger man. She wants to be flirted with, treated like a woman! He came up to her and practically curtsied while pressing his new business card into her hand! So obsequious! What a bounder! I cannot bear him."

"But do you think it's fair to knock him down? This story will kill his career, at least with the clients he has now. And he'll be blackballed socially."

Maxwell checked himself. He didn't want to turn Judge off by making this too personal. He redirected. "Judge, my boy, Chase Peters is an affront to everything society stands for. He's a shameless bounder. He's transparent. He is not one of us, you and I. Sure we were born far from the crystal chandeliers of Park Avenue, but we were raised right. You exhibit a natural charm and grace that society finds titillating and welcome. Hell, that same charm is what I've built my career on. This Peters boy is a varmint and he offends. I repeat, he is not one of us."

"I guess you're right," Judge said, gathering strength. "He does have an embarrassing propensity for being pushy and vulgar."

"Now, you're talking. You're first instincts were right, trust them. This story is going to make you famous and very popular with the right people. I guarantee it."

"I got it. I know what I'm going to do."

Maxwell smiled broadly and boomed, "Oh forget all that. It's making my blood pressure rise. Calm me down, Judgie boy. Tell me what you remember of Caleb's -- what did you call them? Assets?"

Chapter 15

Scarlet Floats

Scarlet Goodman actually hummed as she walked beneath the gilded arches of the Plaza Hotel lobby. She would have whistled, but whistling, along with chewing gum, was something her mama told her that ladies did not do in public. I guess a lady wouldn't whistle anywhere, she thought, but humming is okay. She smiled at the doorman as she exited. She smiled again at her shoes atop the hotel logo swirling in the portico carpet. The autumnal buzz of a crisp blue Manhattan morning pulsed up through her shoes, reverberated through her body and set her honey blonde bob to tingling. She wore a suit of Chanel lineage, pink with chocolate brown trim. Scarlet saw the outfit in Vogue months ago and knew it would be her welcome-to-New-York-look. She had torn out the page and taped it to her vanity mirror at home, and it was now her traveling companion, affixed to a mirror in her hotel room.

That morning she got dressed with the same excitement as for a Mardi Gras ball. She clasped on pearl-and-topaz earrings and added the matching necklace as well, then slipped into her three-inch chocolate brown heels. It was the exact look from the magazine, just as the magazine's stylist had created it. Scarlet Goodman may not have been to the manor born, but she made a picture perfect facsimile.

Scarlet surveyed the vista now stretched out in front of her and the famous hotel. No general on a battlefield could have looked more convincing or confident. Busy men and women brushed past her at the top of the wide stairs. The passers-by excused themselves curtly, but to Scarlet it all sounded like how-do-you-do. She lifted her gaze higher, her eyes widened to take in the whole scene. The sun shone brightly from a sparkling blue sky and blanketed her with dazzling light. Her own sparkling blue eyes looked left to where the gold statue of General Sherman protected the edge of Central Park. The trees behind him seemed to Scarlet like troops awaiting their orders to march gallantly forward. Sun flashed off the statue and Scarlet remembered the Chanel sunglasses in her pocket book. Her eyes wandered from Sherman to The Pierre across Fifth Avenue and, next to that, the Sherry Netherland and F.A.O. Schwartz and Bergdorf Goodman and then, back to her side of Fifth, another Bergdorf and the Paris Theatre. She took one slow step down, towards the arched water sabers of the Grand Army Plaza fountain, and felt a sense of arrival. In her mind she heard the footman announce: Miss Scarlet Goodman of New Orleans.

She scanned the scene faintly noting the soaring architecture around her and the early plumage of turning leaves accompanied by the applause of flapping flags of the hotel above her. But it was the choreographed staccato bustle of people that riveted her wild diamond eyes. People came and went from every corner and every crevice. Pedestrians crisscrossed the tableau in front of her like dancers getting into position in an oversize ballet. They came from cars and taxis and the sidewalk and the subway. They filled the stage, taking their positions and just as quickly moved on and were replaced in the next act. They were dressed for their roles as varied as balls on a pool table, scattered and colorful at the break careening off the sides and falling into pockets of the subway entrances.

"Excuse me, Miss, said a voice below her. "Can I hail you a taxi?"

Scarlet jumped a tiny bump and looked down the stairs at another doorman in a blue blazer with gold epaulettes. He looked to her like an officer in a far away romantic war.

"Oh, no sir. Thank you," she said as she descended the stairs. "This is my first time in New York City and I wanted to take it all in." She stopped at the bottom of the stairs and extended her tiny hand. She lightly touched the brass name tag on his broad chest. "Good morning, Sergio. My name is Scarlet Goodman."

"Well, good morning Miss Goodman," he said as he tipped his officer's cap. "Any relation to our fashionable neighbor?" he said as he motioned with a gloved hand toward Bergdorf's.

Scarlet followed the motion to the sign on the white granite building. "Oh," she said. "I'm not sure. I'll have to call my mother in New Orleans and ask. Can I get back to you tomorrow?"

The doorman laughed and tipped his hat again and smiled with a nod, "Miss Goodman from New Orleans. Welcome to Manhattan."

Scarlet crossed the street and joined the ballet on the plaza, passing the fountain and scurrying across Fifth Avenue she found herself staring up at the soaring entrance to F.A.O Schwartz. She delighted in recognizing the names of places she'd heard about all her life but never realized that they were actual brick and mortar realities. She thought the toy company was a catalog, not a real store, yet here it was on Fifth Avenue across from The Plaza Hotel.

She took out her cell phone and called her mother to tell her the discovery. "It's a huge toy store right on Fifth Avenue. I know! Oh Mama, listen. There's a place next to The Plaza called Berg…" she turned around and read the name. "Berg….dorf," she pronounced slowly, "Berg…dorf Goodman. The darling man at the hotel asked if I was related. Do you know anything about that? Okay, ask Aunt Mary. Goodbye now, I'm going inside. It's so exciting. I'll call you back."

Scarlet closed her phone with a snap and popped it into her pocket book. She slowly approached the door and squealed with delight when the toy soldier man boomed, "Welcome to the world's greatest toy store!"

"Thank you!" she beamed. "I've never been here before."

"Well, you are in for wonderful experience miss." The toy soldier man smiled and Scarlet could see that he was younger than she. And cute, she noted. She smiled at him and said, "Thank you very much."

The toy soldier turned to watch her as she pushed through the revolving door, her pink skirt snug on her bottom as she pushed on the revolving door. Nice ass, he said to himself before turning back to greet a group of twelve little girls accompanied by a couple of mothers, brood mares with a herd of fillies. "Welcome to the world's greatest toy store!" he boomed.

Once inside, Scarlet couldn't believe her eyes. The store was big and bright and loud and colorful like a parade float. She almost lost her balance as she stood looking up at the toys hung from the ceiling, mouth as wide open as her big blue eyes.

"I can't believe I'm here," she said out loud.

"I know! Isn't it amazing?" A little girl from the group behind her was standing next to her, repeating the same performance in half size. "I wish I lived here."

"Me too," Scarlet whispered and hugged the little girl around the shoulders. "It's amazing."

She roamed around the first floor of the store and then out the back door and found herself on Madison Avenue. She kept on humming as she stood at 58th Street. Scarlet then took a right and began walking south on Madison Avenue. She thought to herself. This is what real society ladies do, she assured herself as she adapted to the pace of the migration on the sidewalk, not knowing that she was walking in the wrong direction.

Scarlet Goodman made a reservation at the Plaza because that was the only hotel she could think of when she thought of New York City. She was raised on the Eloise books and that was the place she knew she had to stay. There was never any question in her mind that there might be another hotel. When the decision was made and the date circled on her calendar, the only thing left was to raise enough money to get her journey started.

She decided to leave New Orleans and go home to Lafayette and put together the greatest yard sale the town had ever seen. She spent days working on the colorful signs and put them up all over town. She made little table cloths in bright colors to display the merchandise. She and her mother cleaned out every family member's garage, closet and attic. The sale was a great success. She even sold her Honda Accord to her cousin. All told, Scarlet hit Manhattan with over twelve thousand dollars. Plenty, she thought, to get a nice apartment and some furniture. So if she splurged her first few nights on a room at the Plaza, it was alright. She had to make the right impression, even to herself.

When she called the only person she knew in New York, Harrison Jackson, he howled with laughter when she said where she was staying. "Only you, Scarlet Goodman, would take a room at The Plaza." Harrison was the plump yet handsome son of a grand New Orleans family and a friend of Scarlet's from college.

Scarlet met Harrison her freshman year at Tulane. He was a senior and he'd been ensnared by her bright eyes, perky beauty and practiced manners the first time he saw her at a mixer at the SAE house. His fraternity was hosting the girls from their sister sorority -- Kappa Kappa Gamma -- and Scarlet had just pledged that fall. They dated on and off that first year, but Scarlet was a virgin and Harrison wanted more than she would give. When the romance petered out, they remained close because Scarlet would not let him disappear once she'd figured out what he was and what that meant. His friends whispered that she wanted his five million dollar trust fund, but to Scarlet his social connections, both at Tulane and in New Orleans proper, were what made her blue eyes dance.

In the year that they dated, Harrison took Scarlet everywhere she wanted to go and introduced her to everyone she wanted to meet. Scarlet was on scholarship at Tulane, the prize from the Miss Magnolia Sweet Water pageant and much more valuable to Scarlet than a rhinestone tiara. Upon arrival at Tulane, she had never met anyone like Harrison Jackson, much less his friends and family. The houses, the parties, the people, each discovery became a revelation to her.

The highlight of her social ascension in New Orleans came during Mardi Gras when Scarlet was Harrison's date for Rex Ball on Mardi Gras day. Scarlet knew that the krewe of Rex was the most prestigious of all the Mardi Gras krewes and was made up of the most socially prominent families in New Orleans. Scarlet was perturbed when Harrison told her that only men could ride the Rex float in the parade. Riding the Rex float was the fantasy with which she had danced as a little girl when she thought of Mardi Gras. It was only after Harrison took her to Fleur de Paris on Royal Street in the French Quarter that her spirits returned. He insisted on buying her the most expensive gown there to make up for her disappointment. The seasoned sales ladies were grandly polite helping her select the right gown for Rex. It was only when she ducked behind the dressing room curtain to change did they raise their plucked and painted eyebrows in recognition of the skill of the Jackson boy's ambitious little tart.

On Mardi Gras night, Scarlet and Harrison arrived at The Municipal Auditorium for the Rex ball. Scarlet was confident that she could hold her own against the royal court. She was determined to outshine the Rex queen and her maids, even when Harrison told her that the court's gowns were custom made and would be in the Empire style of Josephine. Undaunted, Scarlet collected praise from every one she met on the dance floor, but couldn't help envy the court in those majestic gowns as they descended the great stair and were announced to the throng. The following day's newspaper accounts heralded Scarlet as the prettiest girl at Rex and therefore of all the krewe balls. She was featured again in the next day's Picayune, her photo bigger than those of the actual queen and she smiled inside and out at her triumph. She had never felt so important and desired in her life and thus had her first taste of the elixir that would lead her to New York. That evening Scarlet embarked on the search for the Holy Grail, that mysterious golden vessel adorned with jewels that was paraded before the eyes of an untested youth.

Harrison Jackson moved to New York when he graduated from Tulane to join the wolves on Wall Street for a little big city training before returning to run the family business. Scarlet kept in touch with him through weekly phone calls and long, flowery letters on beautiful, perfumed stationery. Harrison humored her and fueled her fantasy of high society grandeur. He supplied her with made-up anecdotes to accompany the names she read about in the society columns. Scarlet followed the exploits of the social animals through Jet Set, Suzy and most importantly, The New York Post's Page Six, which she read a day later at the Lafayette Public Library. Now that she was in Manhattan, Scarlet bought The New York Post to scan the hard copy of the column. It's so much better hot of the press at a corner newsstand, she told herself.

Scarlet plucked her cell phone from her pocket book and pressed "1", her hotline to Harrison.

"Harrison, I read in Page Six that Sally is divorcing Jules Mahar." Scarlet would report.

"Really? I didn't see that." Actually, Harrison never read Page Six and more often than not received his information from Scarlet.

"Yes! do you know them?" Scarlet would ask excitedly.

"Oh sure. I sat next to her at the Church Street Benefit. She's a little homely, if you ask me." Harrison lied. He never sat next to her. He was at the benefit and so were the social Mahars, but Harrison, being unconnected in New York and a single ticket buyer to the charity events, was always placed at the worst table in the back corner of the room with the other unconnected, but ambitious patrons of the Charity of the Week Club.

"Harrison. I want to join all the right committees now that I'm here." Scarlet announced matter-of-factly as if she were seeking a gym membership. "Who do I call?"

"Uh," Harrison stammered. He had no idea who to call to do such a thing, but he knew enough to know that you don't just stroll into town and call up someone and ask to be on a committee. In New Orleans, it had been easy for Harrison to indulge Scarlet's fantasies. His name was as famous there as any in any city. Harrison provided cover for Scarlet's early gaffes and once saved her from complete and total social ruin, a series of events of which she was completely unaware. If Scarlet wanted to go to any New Orleans party or ball, no matter who gave it or how exclusive, the Jackson name could procure an invitation. And Scarlet had used that entrée like a limitless credit card.

"It doesn't work that way in Manhattan, Scarlet." Harrison finally said after a minute.

"What do you mean, it doesn't work that way?" she chirped. "I've written down the charities that I want to join. Who do I call to get on their list?" Harrison could almost see her wide eyes blinking through the telephone and he smiled to himself. Her innocence and ambition was a seductive tonic, and he enjoyed her dependence on his guidance.

"Well, Scarlet," he said slowly and without condescension, "most of these committees, the good ones anyway, are made up of very connected people who are old friends. Old friends who went to pre-school together, boarding school together, university, weddings, holidays, etc." he said calmly. "It would be like someone from Biloxi strolling into New Orleans, calling up one of the Mardi Gras krewes and saying, 'Hey, I want to ride on your float this Mardi Gras'. It doesn't happen that way."

Scarlet winced at the resonance of her own experience. Harrison was mildly cognizant of the prick he'd just inflicted. In his desire to help her he found it necessary, at certain intervals, to remind her of the ground rules.

"Oh." Scarlet said, a detectable wind being let out of grandly-colored sails. "But," she recovered, "aren't you friends with any of them? Don't you know them?"

"Uh, sure." He stammered. "I mean, I know who they are and some of them know who I am, but I don't know any one well enough to..."

"Aren't you on any of these committees?" she interrupted.

"Uh, no, Scarlet," he confessed. "I buy a ticket and show up. No one knows my family up here. It isn't as easy as it was in New Orleans."

"Well, don't you ever talk to anyone at those things?" Scarlet was getting perturbed and her practiced lady-like composure was cracking. "I mean, what do you do, stand around with your thumb up your butt?"

"It's not like that, Scarlet," Harrison said defensively. "Those people are a tight-knit group. It's not easy to penetrate. What am I supposed to do, walk up and introduce myself? They certainly don't approach me. You usually are confined to your table mates and your dinner partner, whomever that may be."

"So you are telling me you don't know one person, not one person I can call?"

"Well, there is this one guy, Roger. I mean, I met him at the museum benefit, and I see him at a few events."

"Great," she said calmer. "What's his number?"

Harrison searched his desk for the man's business card.

"Good," Scarlet chirped. Full sail and back on course. "Goodbye, Harrison. I'll call you back."

She hung up the phone and dialed the numbers then stopped and flipped the phone shut. She looked up and down Madison Avenue as if the solution would find her on the sidewalk. How could she have put so much faith in her New York future in this unworthy person? Harrison Jackson, what a worthless turd, she thought. She had spent this whole time thinking it would be as simple as dialing up Harrison and getting the job done just as he had managed in New Orleans. Now she knew his fantastic reports from the front lines of society were just that. She had to think of a new tack. She hadn't come all this way to let this little set back knock her down. She would have to do what she had done so well in New Orleans. In New Orleans, Harrison had the luxury of not caring. His name gave him entrée, but it was she who navigated. It was she who guided them to the right parties, with the right people. She knew who was who and which people were the ones to be seen with. Harrison always seemed not to care, but he did come through for introductions. She had propelled them to the top of that social register, and she would be the one to do it here, in New York. It might not be as easy, she thought, but it can be done.

She scanned her brain, her brows wrinkled, her lips protruded. "Moomba!" she said aloud.

She reached into her bag for the newspaper and flipped directly to Page Six. She scanned the page until she found the article.

Moomba Mamas. The uptown girls can't get enough of the Moombarita, the specialty drink at the downtown lounge hot spot. At Monday night's Karaoke fling, Lucy Shining, Rhea Brown and a bevy of other Park Avenue princesses took to the stage for a rousing rendition of Aerosmith's Walk this Way, only to be joined by real rock royalty, Liv Tyler who stood in for lead singer and father, Stephen, tossed hair, slurred lyrics and all. The uptown brigade has made Moomba the epicenter of the Uptown Downtown fusion.

Scarlet flipped open her cell phone and hit redial.

"Harrison, it's me. Listen. You're taking me to Moomba tonight."

"Moomba?" he said with surprise. "Do you know how impossible it is to get into that place?"

"Listen, Harrison," Scarlet hesitated. She hated to be bossy with him and drop her Miss Magnolia Sweet Water cover, but sometimes he needed a kick in the right direction and this was one of those times. With fortitude and tightly exhaled breath, she said sweetly with extra sugar, "I really want to go to that club. I've been so looking forward to this, seeing you, seeing New York, making the scene. I want you to work it out, Harrison. I really want to go and I really want to go tonight!"

"Scarlet, it's Monday night."

"I know," she said with sweetness concentrate. "Isn't it exciting?"

"Alright, I'll make a few calls and see what I can do."

"Good. What time should we go?"

"I don't know, ten?"

"Ten? Is that too late?"

"Too late? I don't think so. I guess we'll find out tonight." Harrison knew from experience that nobody went to Moomba as early as ten o'clock, which is why he agreed to go. They would be able to get in the door at that hour and maybe even into the impenetrable upstairs. If they arrived after eleven there would be little chance of even getting in. The upstairs would be out of the question. "Ten O'clock sounds right. I'll swing by and pick you up at nine-thirty".

"Yea-ness!" She squealed into the air above her." Oh my god! What am I going to wear? Listen, I've got to go. I'll talk to you later."

Scarlet hung up the phone, and confidently approached the first attractive man she made eye contact with on the bustling sidewalk.

"Excuse me, sir. Would you be so kind as to tell me where I might find Barney's New York?"

The man, first annoyed by this disruption of his commute, found placation then desire in the siren spark of her electric eyes. After turning her around and sending her in the right direction, he kept pace with her, watching her ass and dreaming of a mid-day romp with an exotic creature, then day dreams dashed as Scarlet scuttled through the revolving door of the fashionable store.

Chapter 15

Moomba Found

Scarlet Goodman stepped gingerly out of the taxi as Harrison held the door. She huddled behind Harrison, clutching his arm as they approached the entrance to Moomba. Red velvet ropes on stanchions marked off a little four by six foot box in front of the door. She looked at the window covered by thick curtains and couldn't see anything. Harrison walked up to the rope and said hello to the doorman. The man smiled and looked over Harrison's shoulder at Scarlet standing there, blonde hair and blue eyes twinkling. She sparkled on the gray Greenwich Village sidewalk. He winked and unhooked the rope and stepped aside.

"Thank you," Harrison murmured.

"Thank you sooooo much," Scarlet cooed.

"What separates Moomba from other clubs?" Scarlet asked in the cab on the way downtown. Success, Harrison told her. The club had become the hangout for the New York and LA crowd, which jaded New Yorkers loved. As much as they disdained the other coast, they loved the Hollywood connection, the Chateau Marmont of it all, and they loved sitting next to, yet snubbing, hot young actors, he explained. Moomba was the place the junior society was calling home at the moment. They came in jeans and their slum gear on an off night and they came in dinner jackets and ball gowns after a benefit. Moomba was the current gathering place for the trust fund set. They owned it and lorded it over Hollywood. Many a night they would run around dancing and drinking and smoking and completely ignoring the latest Hollywood It boy. Not only did Moomba draw the right crowd, it turned away more people than it let in, Harrison told Scarlet. Ten fold. All of this exposition had amped Scarlet up to blast out of the gate. Her little filly legs pranced and stomped. Harrison decided not to mention the real party room upstairs. He didn't want to face her disappointment when they were turned away.

They entered through the parted curtains, and Scarlet was all eyes, a porcelain doll blinking in the dark; her eyes seemed to illuminate wherever her gaze landed. She wasn't sure she would be able to recognize anyone because she'd only ever seen the girls in magazines, never in the flesh, and it was very dimly lighted inside. She adjusted to the low candle light, and took inventory of the room and was deflated to find it almost empty. There were four young men in suits at the bar and a few other patrons hovering at small tables and one couple lounging on a sofa against the back wall.

"Where is everyone?" She whispered to Harrison.

"It's early. What will you have to drink?"

"Oh, a champagne cocktail please. Thank you." Scarlet was busy taking inventory. Her eyes followed the lines of the room as Harrison crossed in front of her to catch the bartender's attention.

She spotted a set of stairs that seemed to lead nowhere. They rose about eight feet, votives lining each step and stopped abruptly at a landing with a red velvet curtain.

Harrison turned with her drink and said, "Well, here we are. Welcome to New York." He clinked her glass.

Scarlet unconsciously clinked back.

"There, go get that table." She motioned with her fantastic doe eyes in the direction of an empty table.

"This is a good spot," she said as she settled in and shrugged off her new mink capelet.

At that moment, the group of men in suits, they must have been Harrison's age, she thought, attractive -- bankers, maybe -- left their perch at the bar and started walking toward Harrison and Scarlet. Scarlet's eyes widened as they approached and turned and walked up the half set of stairs to nowhere. The front man was the most fashionably dressed. Harrison should get a suit like that, she thought. The troop leader arrived at the curtain and poked his head through, turned and whispered something to the others, then turned and faced the curtain and waited. Scarlet was riveted. She looked behind her at the people at the tables and sofa behind her. Were they paying attention? Did they know what was going on? She saw them all turn, much more surreptitiously than she had, but they all clocked the maneuvers on the stairs to nowhere.

Suddenly a man appeared. He stepped from between the part in the curtain like a magician onto a stage and Scarlet's big eyes fluttered. She saw the well-dressed suit whisper something to magic man and motioned with a thumb over his shoulder at one of the other suits. The magician looked the fingered suit over and shook his head and disappeared back into his Ali Baba cave of curtains. The suits stood shuffling and whispering for a moment and then the fingered suit guy turned and walked back down the stairs, a look of disgust visible even in the darkened room. The others filed off one by one until stylish suit gave up the mission and followed them back to the bar. They didn't stop to retrieve their drinks, they walked out the door and on to the street and into a realization.

Scarlet grabbed Harrison's arm. He stiffened and felt his stomach clench knowing what was next.

"That's where they are," she whispered. "That's the VIP section."

"And you just saw what happened to those dorks."

"They were guys in suits," she said confidently. "We look fabulous."

"Can we have one more drink here before we go up?" Harrison wanted to sound optimistic for Scarlet, but he had no intention of going up those stairs. He'd done the dance once before with some guys from work and in an exact reenactment of the scene they just witnessed, had been turned away with a "Not tonight, fellas," from the same snotty doorman. The only difference between his group's humiliation and tonight's players was that on Harrison's night, a Friday, the main room here was packed with people who watched every move and smirked when he and his group returned to the bar. He admitted that tonight's players were smart in making a hasty exit, only mild humiliation to be found in a waiting taxi.

Harrison went to the bar to fetch another round of drinks, and Scarlet watched as more groups of people climbed the stairs. The next attempt -- two model girls -- glided right in. No surprise, she thought, as did the next group of two black clad boys and another model looking girl. Then two girls approached. They looked like secretaries who seemed to Scarlet as if they usually wore purple, but now had on black outfits, approached and were turned away by magic man.

The native dance was repeated again and again for the thirty or so minutes Scarlet and Harrison sat there. Roughly twenty-five percent of the attempts were successful, Scarlet calculated. She liked her odds. She finished her cocktail and stood up.

"What are you doing, Scarlet?" Harrison slumped deeper into his chair.

"I'm going upstairs. Are you coming?" She straightened out the fabric on her Cavalli top and pulled it snug over her jeans. The salesgirl at Barney's — her name was Jade -- had steered her away from the silver sequined cocktail dress she really wanted for tonight. "No, no, no, honey," she said. "If you're going to Moomba, you have to dress like a model hooker on stilts. Sequins are way too office Christmas party." Jade made her buy some ridiculously high heels by someone named Louboutin and cost her six hundred dollars. She guaranteed that this outfit would get Scarlet in. But I've already gotten in, Scarlet thought. Did salesgirl Jade know about the stairs to nowhere? Of course, she did, she thought. Girls like Jade knew everything about places like Moomba. Scarlet picked up her new little Dior bag and walked up the stairs. As she approached the curtain, she didn't know what she would do. Should she poke her head in, or just stand and wait? As her new expensive shoe hit the landing where the curtain was, the magician peeked through and smiled. He pulled back the curtain and nodded her in.

"Hey," Scarlet smiled. "How are you tonight?"

"I'm great, Gorgeous. How are you? Come in."

"Oh, thank you so much. I have a friend with me." Scarlet turned and motioned for Harrison to come up. He bolted upright in his chair. The rocking table nearly spilled his drink. He scooted up the stairs and joined Scarlet on the landing.

245

"This is my friend, Harrison Jackson. I am Scarlet Goodman." She extended her hand. "What is your name?"

"I am Shripiel. Where're you from, honey chile." The magician imitated Scarlet's accent.

"We're both from New Orleans. What about you Shree Paul?" By this time the stairs were filling up behind Scarlet and Harrison.

"I'm from India. It's nice to meet you, Scarlet Goodman. Now get on upstairs."

Shriepel stepped aside and let Scarlet and Harrison continue up the stairs. It wasn't a stairway to nowhere after all, she thought. Wouldn't Jade be proud?

"Lucy Shining!" a voice from a table left of Judge lobbed over his head, loud enough to rise above the Snoop Dog rhyme and land in Lucy's ear. "You look fucking amazing!"

Lucy jerked her head in Judge's direction and tipsily decided the declaration had come from him. She smiled and slipped through the crowd between them. Judge sat comfortably squeezed into a banquette facing the room where he kept an eye on the evening's coming and going. Lucy appeared in front of him, dancing eyes and smirking lips. Lucy had apparently shaken her entourage and he thought she looked more comfortable entering this scene alone than he would ever be. She definitely looked more beautiful tonight, if that were possible.

Judge stood up to greet her, to say hello, and if she was receptive, invite her to join his party. He had never been so familiar as to kiss her hello before and withheld that desire. Lucy, without signal, stepped on the little black box of a table, teetering over a decadent display of champagne glasses and empty Dom Perignon bottle, an Absolute bottle, a plate of half-eaten steak frittes and two ashtrays overflowing. She lofted skyward in one step and into position Arabesque, without toppling a glass or flipping a plate, then fell forward into Judge's arms pushing him downward into his seat. Straddling him, she playfully assaulted him with big, dramatic kisses all over his face and neck. Judge was unchecked in his surprised delight and full-throttled laughter. He had seen her almost every week over the past year and she'd not once given him more than a faint smile. Now she bounced on him like they were old friends and lovers. He looked around and saw that people clocked the commotion.

"I'm sorry everybody," Lucy said loudly to Judge. "I didn't mean to crash your party." She slid off Judge's lap and squeezed in between him and Samantha Denson. "Sorry, Sammy. Did I spill?"

"Good to see you, Lucy," Samantha said.

"Why are you all here tonight?" Lucy yelled. "And why are you all dressed up?" she squeezed Sam's hand and kissed her cheek. "Hey pretty lady."

All of the guests at Judges' table were dressed in gowns and dinner jackets. Lucy was definitely on her way to drunk. Judge thought she had never looked sexier.

"We were at the Met earlier," Judge said.

"The Metropolitan Opera House?" She mocked in a fine British accent. "How very upper crust."

"Hey, it wasn't terrible." Judge brazenly brushed her hair out of her eye.

"I know, sweetie. I'm just fucking with you. What are you drinking?" Lucy grabbed the glass from his hand and took a big gulp. "Yuck. Scotch."

"Whom do I have to kiss to get a drink in this establishment?"

Suddenly, as if by design, which was the case, a tall, orange drink appeared in front of her. Lucy grabbed the glass with both hands as if it were hot chocolate après ski.

"Oooh, I love these Moombaritas." She took a long pull from the straw and shouted. "Yummy!" She looked up to thank the waiter and was surprised to find the owner, Jeffrey Winston, standing there.

"Jeffrey, Darling!" She bounced to her feet, leaned across the table, and wrapped her arms around him. "Thank you for my Moombarita, sugar pie."

"Thank you for coming," the owner said. "Can I get you anything else, Beautiful?"

"Just keep 'em coming. We're going to get drunk tonight."

Judge shook his head and wallowed in a pleasant state of disbelief.

Jeffrey nodded at Judge, "Hello, Mr. Mender."

Judge snapped back into character, returning the nod, "Hello, Mr. Moomba."

"I'm still waiting on my article," said Jeffrey.

248

"I'm still waiting on my scotch," said Judge derisively.

"Oh, you two stop talking about business or I'm out of here," Lucy said. "I want to sing some karaoke tonight. Who's joining me? Judge? A little 'Don't go breakin' my heart?' You have to love that song."

"Maybe later, Lady. I need a few more drinks before I can act that fool."

"Jeffrey! Get this man drunk. I must have a karaoke partner immediately."

"On the way," the proprietor said. "Later, Lucy. Later, Judge."

Jeffrey turned toward the bar and muttered under his breath, "Prick."

Upstairs at Moomba was starting to vibrate and the walls hummed and the low lights flickered. The magic hour approached, which is never a point on a clock, but rather a convergence of elements. The hour, the drinks, the people, the music, and the spirits were confluent and those in the room who appreciated such moments welcomed its arrival and smiled at each other knowingly. Anything that happened now would be icing, superfluous.

Leo Di Caprio arrived amid a posse while the proprietor ejected the group seated next to Judge and Lucy. Lucy glanced over and smiled at the actor, but made no other notice. Sam Ronson spun between karaoke sets and it seemed the room had been aching to dance. Lucy danced her original jig on the table top, but was now taking a smoke break, talking to Sam and Rhea Brown, who just arrived with Mia Wilson. Several people left and more joined the table and now, to Judge's surprise, Chase Peters sat across from him.

"Lucy, darling! Judge! Hello! What a night, eh?" Chase yelled above the opening guitar riff of 'Sweet Child of Mine'.

Chase wore an impossibly tailored dark suit that fit like rich skin. A scarlet bow tie danced under his chin and a pochette flopped insouciantly out of his jacket pocket. His auburn hair was slicked back in a style that evoked Evelyn Waugh -- with a smirk on his lips to match. Judge felt his cheeks heat but looked Chase square in the eye and nodded. "Hello," he mouthed.

"Hey, Chase," Lucy yelled. "Dance with me." She jumped over the table again, this time toppling someone's empty glass and landing on the other side with Chase. He grabbed her hand, preventing an embarrassing Lucy spill and the two started dancing in place. There is no dance floor at Moomba, just a small walkway between two rows of tables in the narrow room. When someone started dancing, those nearest either had to join in or move because at that moment the space was a dance floor. On this night, the patrons started dancing early and in earnest. Lucy, hands in the air and head thrown back, sang loud and unabashed.

She's got a smile that it seems to me

Reminds me of childhood memories

Where everything

Was as fresh as the bright blue sky

Chase's presence momentarily disrupted Judge's joyride, and he clicked into reporter mode. He surveyed the room, taking notes of who was there. He started to write tomorrow's column in his head. Would he be able to remember all these names? There was Crown Princess Victoria of Sweden huddled with countryman Marcus Shenckenberg and her little brother, Prince Phillipe. Sean Lennon was dancing with Liv Tyler and Bijou Phillips. Several of the social girls cavorted at Sam Ronson's table, gossiping and drinking and smoking. Sophia Copola and Marc Jacobs were slunk in a deep sofa across from them, barely discernible to Judge through the fence of legs and asses in front of him.

Judge's eye landed on the face of a girl he'd never seen before. She was extraordinarily beautiful and fresh. Beauty is not rare in this world but this girl was curious and alive. Judge saw electricity in her eyes. In contrast to the cool blasé of most of the girls of this class whose eyes were snake slits of ennui, this girl seemed almost telekinetic. He watched the girl's face as she watched the dancing, throbbing crowd. She watched Lucy dance. Judge watched her expression. There was a pure, innocent pleasure he rarely saw in Manhattan, and never at Moomba. She was not like the other girls in the room. She shone like a little lost star. In a room full of gorgeous women, one of them the future queen of Sweden, this girl's presence stood up and shouted, quietly. He laughed out loud at the little girl with the big searchlight eyes and awed expression. He followed her eyes as she surveyed the room again. Her eyes brightened wider, if that were possible. He looked for what she saw.

He scanned the room to the right, toward the bar and landed on Victoria Newton. She had entered the door wearing a big pink costume of a dress, hair high and jewels glistening in the low amber lighting. She stood under one of the halogen down lights and her enormous diamond necklace and earrings sent out distress signals. Judge stood up and waved to catch her eye across the loud and darkened room. She looked perplexed. Victoria was only a few years older than Lucy and the other girls of her set, but her carriage and demeanor placed her in another

251

time and place. Victoria looked as if she had stepped out of a Sargent portrait into the raucous room. Discomfort flickered across her tight-lipped smile and stiffened in her statue-still stance.

Moomba was not Victoria's kind of place. She didn't particularly like the uptown downtown fusion. She read the same Page Six article Scarlet had and instructed her driver to head down to the trendy club after the Met opening. Sweetie James was standing behind her with Andrew Christopher.

Victoria smiled at Judge and stretched her neck to inventory his table. Lucy Shining, good. Samantha Denson, good. Chase Peters, yuck. Judge read the look on her face and knew she would not cross the room. He made his way around the table, through the fallen branches of legs and shoes out to the aisle of dancing fools toward Victoria.

Lauryn Hill blared through the speakers and all the white people in the room – there were only white people it seemed -- started bobbing gangster-style, and rapping along, then dancing. Judge could barely make it through the elbows and asses pumping and bumping around him.

It's funny how money change a situation

Miscommunication leads to complication...

Judge bounced with the beat as he tried to reach Victoria. The room was so tightly packed one wondered where he would go if there were a fire. There was certainly no easy exit. Judge bounced up next to Rhea Brown and Mia Wilson. The two grabbed him and rubbed him into a sandwich between them. He laughed and rubbed them back, his hands on Mia's ass in front of him and Rhea's behind him. He looked for Victoria and saw her bobbing her head, trying to find a beat. Judge heard himself laugh harder than he thought possible in the thumping madness of the room. He untangled his body from Mia and Rhea and continued his swim against the current.

A drunken model in a band-aid size mini skirt grabbed his neck, pulled into him and shouted in his ear:

You might win some but you just lost one

You might win some but you just lost one

Judge laughed again, less patiently, but still in good humor. He danced his way up to Victoria.

"Hello, Empress," Judge shouted as he kissed her cheek. "I see you all stayed for the end of the opera."

"I saw you sneak out with Samantha Denson after the first act. I am afraid that girl will turn you into a delinquent," she scolded. "So this is the famous Moomba. What a dump! It's almost as depressing as Doubles." She said referring to the private club in the basement of the Sherry Netherland hotel. She kissed him on both cheeks and bopped her head again, this time she added a little shoulder bounce which reverberated in her strapless bound bosom. "I see you're doing time with Chase Peters. Doesn't his true story come out soon?"

"Very soon, the next issue." Judge shouted with a smile.

"Well done!"

"Hello, Sweetie! Hello, Andrew!" Judge said loudly over Victoria's bouncing shoulder. The two smiled nervously and wide eyed. The preppy sidekicks lapped up the circus around them. They stood safely behind Victoria's voluminous gown like little children peeking from behind nanny's apron, safe in the folds of that enormous pink fortress.

"Is that Princess Victoria over there?" Victoria asked. "What's she doing talking to that dumb model boy?"

"They've been sharing state secrets," Judge said. "He's a Swede, you know." Judge said.

"Really?" Victoria said. "How dull. I forget now that she's at Yale that she will actually rule Sweden one day. How nice for her."

"Would you like me to clear a path?" Judge offered. "We can say hello."

"Oh no. If I could even make it through that god-awful tribal dance, I would have to pass that wretched mink, Chase Peters," Victoria said. "I can see it all from here. Thank you."

She took the room's temperature for a few more minutes. She stood forthright and accepted air kisses from a few of the girls on their way to the ladies room. Suddenly she snapped to attention.

"Well, I've seen it, now goodbye," Victoria said as she kissed Judge on the cheek, gathered up the folds of fabric of her dress and turned toward the stairs. Judge wondered if Andrew was expected to pick up the ends and carry it like a train.

"That's it? Karaoke will start back up any minute now. You aren't going to sing us a song?" Judge asked.

"Oh hell no," she laughed. "I've got to get home and get out of this dress before I explode. Tell Lucy I said hello, though she'll hardly register. She's in rare form, I see."

"Everyone is," Judge said hazily looking over his shoulder at Lucy. "It's a good night.

On the visitor's side, on the other side of the dance aisle from Judge's table, Scarlet sat on point as if she were watching a championship tennis match. Her eyes were glued to every movement. She had studied the players from the program and now loved matching names to faces. She was delighted that they had gotten there early. She watched attentively as the princess procession paraded by. She recognized many of the girls immediately, and deducted who the others were by their associations. She kept a tally in her head of who had come and gone, who sat with whom, who snubbed whom and who crossed the room for whom. Judge's cross to Victoria did not escape her notice. The little girl from nowhere was brilliantly accurate in her observation and deduction, making more prescient prognostications than a native. And this was her first night. It was a wonderful game to her, and she would have surely scored in the ninety percentile had such a score been kept.

Scarlet wondered where they had been that they were all dressed so beautifully. She would know soon when the columns came out, but oh how she longed to be inside the circle now, full of knowledge and exclusivity. Had they been at a dress-up party at one of their houses on Park Avenue, or at some fancy ball at a museum? She'd seen the star player Lucy Shining come in the door and Scarlet had not missed a move. Harrison thought Scarlet had gone into a trance. When Jeffrey the owner took Lucy her drink, Scarlet grabbed his sleeve and said, "I'll have what Lucy Shining is having. And do you know who the boy is she's sitting with."

"Judge Mender," he said. "That prick from Jet Set magazine."

"Ooh,' she said in tiny shock, both at the crude remark and the positive i.d. of her favorite columnist.

When Lucy bounced up to dance for the twelfth time that night, Scarlet holstered her nerve, stood up and jostled her way through the asses so that she was dancing right beside her. Chase Peters turned around in an ecstatic display of sweaty athleticism and liberal libations and wrapped his arms around Scarlet and pulled her close in an adapted tango move. Scarlet squealed.

"Hi! I'm Scarlet Goodman," she shouted in his ear.

"Hey, Sexy. I'm Chase Peters."

"Oh, I know who you are. I just read about you in New York Magazine."

"What's that?" he yelled in her ear, slurred, smoky breath and a smile.

"I just read about you in New York!" she yelled louder.

"Oh yeah, wasn't that nice?" He shouted back, "Do you know Lucy Shining?" He turned and pulled Lucy closer.

"Lucy, this sweet thing is Scarlet Goodman," Chase shouted about the music. "Isn't she gorgeous?"

"Hey, Gorgeous," Lucy shouted and kissed Scarlet on the lips, turned around, threw her hands in the air and danced away. Scarlet smiled and threw her arms around Chase in the same way she'd seen Lucy. She wanted to freeze the moment, make it last, keep dancing and laughing and meeting fabulous people and being a real New Yorker. She had no idea where Harrison was, but she knew he was watching.

Chapter 17

Jet Set Exposed

Victoria Newton padded to her front door, holding the coffee cup tight and sure. The doorman stood at attention, arms outstretched with the morning's papers. She accepted the bundle, thanked the doorman, closed the door and walked to the kitchen. This was her routine. This is where her days began. She opened first The New York Post to Page Six. The headline story read: Chastened by Jet Set: Icarus Falls to Earth.

Victoria smiled and reached for the telephone. The day had begun.

Judge sat at his desk in his cluttered, smoky cubicle quietly reading the Page Six article to his mother in a tone so hushed she could barely hear him. "Jet Set magazine has squashed the social climbing career of yet another striving hopeful. Society editor and man about town Judge Mender has lowered the boom with a scathing account of a life society party boy Chase Peters would rather have kept secret.' What do you think?"

"I think I feel sorry for Chase Peters," his mother said.

"Mother, that's not the point. Didn't you hear my name?"

"Oh, yes, honey," she changed her tone. "Congratulations, Judge."

"It's huge, mother. I'll send you a copy. Listen, love you. I have to go. I have three lines ringing. Love you. Goodbye."

Judge hung up the phone and picked up the next line. "Judge Mender."

"Ha," he said quietly. "It's just some little story, it's nothing really. Ha, ha. You think?"

Maxwell was about to break routine. One of the secrets to his social standing was that he never called anyone, but rather waited for society to call him. He certainly would never deign to call a journalist let alone a society reporter, but Judge was different. He had known Judge for less than a year, but he felt an extraordinary connection to him. They were both southern, yes, but it was more than that, Maxwell reasoned. He empathized with Judge's awkward journey from country mouse to city rat and wanted to know him, in fact, had entertained a notion to seduce him, but Judge had made it clear that they were to be friends. In spite of the fact that Maxwell was old enough to be Judge's father, Maxwell moved in close to Judge in a short time and courted him as a new confidante. He dialed Judge's number.

"My dear boy, you've done it!" Maxwell trilled into Judge's ear. "You've absolutely skinned the snake. The title! The Talented Mr. Peters! Oh he'll die to be associated with that movie."

Maxwell picked up the advance copy of Jet Set Judge had messengered over. He flipped to the flagged page which held the article. He began reading Judge's words while employing a booming, dramatic stage voice.

"Chase's arrival in Manhattan -- after graduation from Brown -- presented an opportunity for the exploration of one of the world's oldest professions. Long before party planning was an option for making money, Chase found that he had a God-given talent for hustling business. Whispers which began at school about his questionable business dealings, turned into cocktail standard among his schoolmates who now found themselves in New York. Making new friends in the bright big city came naturally to the gregarious bon vivant. His congenital charm and considerable trust fund notwithstanding, the future society darling seemed to seek the company -- and investment -- of well-heeled company."

"It is brilliant!" Maxwell shouted. "You must be so pleased. He must be so annihilated. Everyone is talking. Rejoicing! It is a complete coup. The pen! The pen! It is so mighty."

"I thought you'd be pleased," Judge said listening to the words read out loud for the first time. He felt a panic in his stomach. "God. It's really out there now. He'll be shattered. Congenital charm. Considerable trust fund. That's alright for a phrase, I guess. I guess he can't try stealing your clients now."

"Honey, he'll have to steal bread from Madame DeFarge," Maxwell gloated. "Of course, if he still has his little black book, I suppose he could return to the days of wine and hustlers, I mean roses. I hope he doesn't kill himself. That's all we need, another martyr. Oh, before I indulge in this one second more, you have to tell me, are you or are you not joining me in Miami Beach for Christmas?"

"I want to," Judge snapped back to the conversation. "I have to face my mother's wrath, which I have been postponing. She's going to be disappointed when I tell her I'll be coming home to Dixie for the first Christmas in two years and spending less time at home than she thought," Judge said. "Oh, I'm going to follow the flock to Palm Beach and stay at Victoria's for New Year's. Will you be going up there from South Beach?"

"Miami Beach," Maxwell corrected. "Of course. You can ride with me. That way Jet Set won't have to rent you a car. It's the least I can do for this tasty little story. You are becoming quite a little member of the social migration, my boy, Southampton and Saint Tropez in the summer, Palm Beach after Christmas. Are you sure you shouldn't insert a bunny hop to Aspen for Christmas Eve?" Maxwell chuckled. "So, back to the story at hand. Have you heard anything from poor Chase?"

"Chase Peters?! Are you kidding? He wouldn't call me, would he?" Judge was startled at the notion. He hadn't thought much past the publication date. He was solid in his decision to write the damn piece. Now that it was out there, he thought he was done with it. The panic expanded.

"What happens when I see that fool?" Judge blurted.

"I wouldn't put anything past him, personally. I have been so shocked by his behavior in public that lord knows what he's capable of now that he's been exposed. Maybe you should make Richard pay for a body guard. I can see it all now, 'Crazed and disgraced, party boy Chase Peters attacks Jet Set bon vivant Judge Mender with a polo mallet."

Judge howled with laughter. Only Maxwell would find the most obscure reference of ridiculous and make it hilarious.

"You think he's going to use a polo mallet as a murder weapon? That's original. I didn't think we thought him that original."

"Not original, dear, ambitious. He knows everyone who's anyone would first reach for a polo mallet. He'll want that in the papers when they arrest him."

"You are a twisted old queen, Maxwell. Twisted."

Chapter 18

Scarlet Rises, Victoria Reigns

Three weeks is an era in the life of the perpetually social and such time had passed since the Page Six mention and the Jet Set issue with Chase Peters' feature hit the newsstands. As Judge saw it, he was the toast of his little slice of town. He'd received the requisite praise from the social set and a few surprise calls from old or lost acquaintances. What surprised him most were the calls and letters from the old guard. Everyone in Manhattan, it seemed, loved a takedown. Even those who feigned nonchalance reveled in the game supposedly beneath them. In a town where the press can make anyone a celebrity overnight, the collective joy in an exile surprised him. Fame could be so easily achieved in spite of a lack of talent or circumstance of achievement. Fame was, as always, bestowed on fortunate accidents of birth, indescribable beauty or exposed scandal. The exercise had been much easier than Judge imagined.

With the publication of the Chase story Judge had proven himself a protector of the sanctity of Manhattan society and it had welcomed him into the fold as a gatekeeper, of sorts. The reaction of those he courted completely surprised him, and he opportunistically reaped the benefits. He was recognized everywhere he went because he only went to the kind of places that laid Jet Set out like the Bible. He was given the best table and comped dinners at his favorite restaurants; he was courted by the upper levels of society and would have his pick of guesthouses in Southampton and Litchfield County the next summer.

Of course, he hadn't heard from Chase Peters. Maxwell told him that Chase had taken leave of the city. Reports from friends found him hiding out at a friend's house in Palm Beach. Chase left the temporary control of his business to his cousin, but after the story, there was no business.

Judge, for his part, felt no remorse. Chase had gotten a little too familiar after the night he fell into his bed. He vowed to never do that again. He valued discretion above all and didn't want to be reminded of it every time he went out on the town. In the final analysis, it turned out to be relatively easy to take down someone that everybody secretly disliked. Would the next one be so inconsequential he wondered?

An invitation to a Victoria Newton dinner party was a sought out and rare occasion and Scarlet Goodman clutched the engraved card to her chest like a Faberge egg. Scarlet had been in Manhattan for three months now and this was the moment she had dreamed of. She found an apartment on Seventy-second Street and flew back to Louisiana to bring her teacup poodle Precious back to New York. She learned right away that she had to be in the 10021 area code and she looked at her address on the envelope with pride.

As the season progressed through the fall, Scarlet read the columns and magazines and knew which benefit committees were right. She directed Harrison's money to those charities and her fantasies took flight. In record time, she was listed on some of the circuit's best committees alongside names she used to only read about. Her name was on the committee lists for The New York City Opera, The Winter Wonderland Ball, The Frick Gala, and the biggest prize, the season-ending New York City Ballet Spring Gala, Dance with the Dancers. It gave her much pleasure to find her name on the committee list of an invitation. One day, she knew, she would be listed as a vice chair, not just a committee member and then, finally, a co-chair of an event. Co-chairs were comprised of the top tier, the most popular girls in Manhattan. Sally Banning, Elizabeth Pilgrim, and Victoria Newton were listed at the top of the most sought after invitations. She intended to be listed among them.

Tonight Scarlet Goodman was going to a dinner party deep inside the compound and she could not wait to get there. She glided into the back of the Lincoln Town car she had ordered with an affected accent she copied from Victoria: "Sixty-third Street. Between Park and Madison," she instructed the driver.

Scarlet held the invitation in her open palms like a dove, occasionally running her finger over the lettering. She had been seated next to Victoria at a luncheon for breast cancer at Oscar de le Renta's showroom the week before. Scarlet was elated at how quickly they hit it off. After only a few minutes of conversation, Victoria asked for her address and informed her of her upcoming dinner party. Scarlet knew exactly who Victoria was, even before she moved to Manhattan. She had followed her every move through Jet Set and, next to Lucy Shining, was the one person she wanted to know and imagined herself becoming friends with, going shopping with, sitting next to at the manicure station, and having their hair colored. This was the vision of Manhattan life she had dreamed of.

"One Twenty-Five East Sixty-Third Street, Miss," the driver said, penetrating her thoughts and halting her flights of fancy.

"Oh, thank you." Scarlet popped the invitation into her pocket book and waited for the driver to open the door.

"What time shall I return, Miss?"

"Oh, who can say? I'm sure we'll be drinking cocktails and talking for hours. I'll call you when I'm ready," she purred in her best Victoria Newton. She walked through the open door being held by the doorman.

"Scarlet Goodman to see Miss Victoria Newton," she announced to the doorman, a little too loudly.

Her hungry eyes gobbled up the decor of the lobby. The room wasn't as fancy as she'd imagined but still well appointed and slightly austere. The room was covered in dark wood and expensive draperies and white marble floors. The elevator walls were made of the same old wood with shiny brass plates and knobs. The floor was covered by an embroidered carpet, and Scarlet traced the outline of the intricate design with the toe of her Chanel spectator. The low, amber lighting made her feel like Lily Bart as the car climbed steadily through the floors to Victoria's lair.

Scarlet felt butterflies hatching in her stomach, the unfurling wings made her nauseous. Her practiced bravado was being swirled upside down as the butterflies flitted inside her. When the elevator reached Victoria's floor, her confidence had withered in contrasting proportion to the climb. When the door opened, she stepped out nervously into the hallway which had four doors. The doors surrounded her like security guards and Scarlet felt utterly unnerved. She turned to the doorman.

"Victoria is on the left," the doorman said. "Number one."

"Thank you," she whispered as she pressed the doorbell. Scarlet took a deep breath and pulled her performance together. She tugged the hem of her black Chanel jacket. She adjusted the pearls at her neck. She touched the edges of her hair and smoothed the sides. She took another deep breath, lifted her chin and pulled her lips into a confident pout. She rang the doorbell and folded her hands in front of her.

Victoria opened the door in a flash and Scarlet's eyes widened as the door swung open.

"Darling Scarlet Goodman!" Victoria boomed as she pulled Scarlet nearly out of her heels, yanking her into the brightly lit room. "You little pecan tartlet, I am so glad you could come. Please come in. I think you must know most of the people here."

"Thank you for inviting me, Victoria," Scarlet said smoothly and double kissed Victoria's rosy cheeks.

Victoria led Scarlet around the room, presenting her to the dozen or so guests. As the introductions were made, Scarlet began to realize that this was not an A list crowd. Sure, she recognized the faces and names, but these were not the girls whose company she sought. These were not the profiles in Jet Set. She smiled and sighed relief when she was introduced to Sally Banning. She collected a glass of champagne from the server at her left. "Thank you," she whispered.

Victoria dished out more introductions and returned to her post at the door. Scarlet landed with Sweetie James. Scarlet knew that Sweetie was considered more of an understudy to Victoria -- rather than a player herself — so she put on a placid smile and let Sweetie pepper her with small talk. Scarlet was now free to take in the apartment.

Victoria Newton's apartment was grand beyond her years. At the age of thirty-one, Victoria possessed the air and bearing of a dowager princess. She was regal and steadfast, a great ship dropping anchor among the sleeker yachts. She wore blond, straightened hair, a perpetual Palm Beach tan and simple clothes set off by dazzling diamonds. Her apartment was a similar statement. The furniture was solid, classic and strong. The colors -- yellow stripes, red accents -- were lorded over by well-lighted portraits of imposing ancestors. With a sprinkling of silver, from the framed photographs to the tea service, Victoria's Newport/Palm Beach lineage permeated the room. Whereas other girls of her age and station experimented with bohemia and the treasures of Marrakech during these pre-marriage years, Victoria lived in the comfort of her class. There were early American antiques, with a splash of Louis XV, chintz from ceiling to floor, and a caramel-skinned maid waiting quietly within reach. Victoria Newton's apartment on Sixty-third Street was exactly what Scarlet Goodman had pictured when she imagined herself at a society dinner party. Victoria wanted it that way. She liked things in their place: whether apartments or people made no difference.

Scarlet excused herself from Sweetie and walked into the dining room. The table was set in high style. There were three small, tightly packed vessels of Leonides roses in the center of the table with low votives twinkling in the lowered light. Scarlet felt warm and content. She lingered at the table, reading the name cards. It wasn't an undesirable gathering, she thought. They were Victoria's Southampton crew. It was a respectable crowd, but not one to be written up in Jet Set, she reckoned. Scarlet's hope returned. She continued reading the name cards at the table. She found her place card next to Carlton Cushing on her left. Where had she read about him? Oh yes, he is the committee chair for The Museum of the City of New York. She had never managed to crack that invitation list, much less the committee. Scarlet discovered that the museum party was strictly Old Guard; newcomers were patently ignored. She looked at the name card on her right. She held her breath and at the same time the door knock announced the final guest. As the door opened, Victoria bellowed.

"Judge Mender, you're late, come in and tell us all about your latest character assassination."

Scarlet squealed inside. She read the name on the card at her right. Judge Mender. She held the back of the chair to steady herself. She felt lightheaded and triumphant. Scarlet saw her face in the shiny surface of the plate in front of her and saw her future as clearly as a photograph. Years from now when she looked back on her life, this would be the night that changed everything, the night her dream was placed squarely in her hand. This is the night that will change my life, she said to her reflection. And she was right.

Chapter 19

Lucy Shining & The Wonder Ball

The Winter Wonderland Ball at the New York Botanical Gardens in the Bronx had, in two short years, risen to the place of prominence -- for the junior set -- as the party of choice for the Christmas season. The fact that the event stood alone in a time when most charities were reluctant to compete for guests with holiday plans, made the event's eminence indisputable. The host committee was comprised of four of the most influential social girls of the moment who limited the committee to their closest friends. The committee, in turn, was expected to keep the invitation list equally exclusive, much to the dismay of the Garden's board who actually hoped to raise money by inviting more than a mere two hundred guests. But the girls would have none of it. They envisioned a winter ball where everyone wore their white gowns and white furs and weren't forced to see or talk to people they didn't like or know. Victoria Newton was this year's event chair, along with Sweetie James, Sally Banning and Elizabeth Pilgrim, and she sat in her kitchen this morning dialing numbers to check on final details.

"Judge Mender, it's Victoria Newton, where are you?" she barked into the phone after being surprised to hear him answering his cell so early. "I didn't expect you to answer. I was going to leave you an extremely long message. Are you awake?"

"Well, good morning Miss Newton," Judge said, ignoring her insinuation. "I actually went to bed early last night. To what do I owe the pleasure this morning?"

"Well, darling, it's time for the Winter Wonderland Ball and I'm up this morning making my rounds like a goddamn publicist. I just got off the phone with Maxwell Jones and he assures me he is going to create heaven on earth for this party, at a considerable discount, I might add."

Victoria, in all her millions, was known around town for her frugality and while that fact may have annoyed designers and jewelers, it delighted benefit boards city wide.

"You know the theme of this thing is white! white! white!" she boomed. "Maxwell says he will clean out the worldwide market for white flowers to transform the Garden's Crystal Palace into a winter white fantasy. I am so glad he agreed to do our little party. You know our budget is nowhere near what he commands. Anyway, he says you are spending Christmas with him in South Beach before you join me in PB. You'd better be careful down there with all those minky minks. I don't want you to be too exhausted when you get to me."

"I've told Maxwell that I'm expecting much rest and relaxation," Judge said. "He assures me that will be the order of the day."

"Oh, I think you are in for a surprise on that front, Judie Poo," Victoria said archly. "I hear his parties in South Beach are legendary. Do you now that he won't let his wife or daughter near that condo? They've never even been there. They don't even have keys! I hear it is strictly boysville."

Judge was surprised to hear how much Victoria knew about Maxwell's private life, a life he thought Maxwell guarded like a mistress and kept below the radar. He tried to deflect. "Oh, it can't be all that indulgent. I imagine those reports are mostly myth, like everything else that surrounds him."

"Oh, I hope not," she sighed. "Of course, there is his deep, dark buried scandal from years ago. I've never gotten the whole story, but my mother alludes to it occasionally. You know it's heavily guarded if this nose can't sniff it out. Ha!" Victoria loved to laugh at herself. It was rare that she met anyone more amusing. "Although," she paused, "he did manage to prevail. I mean, look at him now."

Judge pressed his memory. He had heard intimations of Maxwell's past, but the subject never came up with the man himself and Judge, uncharacteristically, did not press. He made a notation on a post-it on his desk. Maxwell. Scandal?

"I live for scandalous stories about homosexuals; they are my favorite dish. But darling, that is not why I am calling." She exhaled. "What do you need from the Botanical to cover this thing? You are getting the exclusive, of course, as you demanded. We expect many pages in the magazine with glossy, full color photos of our gorgeous girls. The board will decapitate me if you do not fawn."

"You're getting it, Victoria," Judge laughed. "You're getting it. All I need is a seat for me and a pass for my photographer."

"Well, you are seated at my table, of course. That grungy photographer of yours doesn't need a seat, does he? I'll tell them to make a plate for him in the kitchen."

"Ha," he laughed. "That's fine. He never sits. Now, you are sure there will be no other press there, not even photographers?"

"Absolutely no other press. As for photographers, Patrick McMullan will be there, but that's no problem for you, is it?"

"No, he's fine. But I must insist that he not sell the pictures to anyone else before my story runs."

"Will do. So what are you wearing? Who do you want to sit next to? Those are my stock questions of the day. I suppose you'll be forgoing the white Gucci gown with the white fox cape?"

"Yes, I won't be able to get it from Milan in time," he laughed. "Who is at your table that I will tolerate?"

"Well, I could list them, but who are we kidding? You stop listening after I say Lucy Shining."

"Oh, good," he said unchecked. "Lucy is at your table?"

"Yes, and I've got you next to her. Try to contain yourself. If she shows, that is. You know how notorious she is for blowing off the big parties." Victoria paused. "Actually, maybe you could help me."

She paused again. This was the final item on her check list of elements of a successful party: A-List hosts, well-selected committee, controlled guest list, Maxwell Jones décor and catering, Peter Duchin Orchestra, DJ Tom Finn, Jet Set exclusive and the attendance of Lucy Shining. Victoria continued nonchalantly, "If you could be bothered to swing by and pick her up, she would have to come. Will you do that? I'll arrange it all if you consent."

"Of course," Judge said, suppressing his own delight and answering with mimicked nonchalance. "That would be nice. Let me know what she says, where and when and all that."

"Gorgeous. I'll let you know when I have it all decided. I'll send the car to you first, then to hers, then on to the Bronx."

"The Bronx," Judge moaned. "Can it be true that we are going to a party in the Bronx?"

"Please, don't even get me started. When I was getting flack from the old farts on the board about how tight the guest list was, I said, 'Listen. Do you have any idea how difficult it is to get these people out to a party in December, much less haul them up to the Bronx in white gowns? The guest list must be exclusive if you want this to be a great party.' I mean, I should really get some humanitarian award for this. Don't you think?"

"Absolutely," he laughed. "Your charity knows no bounds."

"Okay, I'm off. Many calls to make before I'm sainted. Will I see you at the Cipriani thing tonight?"

"I'll be there."

"Okay, darling. I'll call you back with the details for the car. Goodbye, Love."

When the day of the Winter Wonderland Ball arrived, Victoria had arranged all the details for Judge's pickup and delivery of the elusive bird known as Lucy Shining. Victoria sent a note on her personal stationery -- engraved by Mrs. Strong, of course -- outlining in telegraphic detail a timeline for the evening's pursuit of happiness:

7:45 PM	Eilat Car Service arrives
8:05 PM	Driver picks up Lucy
8:25 PM	Arrive at Botanical Garden
8:30 – 9:00	Cocktails & Merriment
9:00	Dinner & Dancing

Judge set the stiff card on his bureau and poured himself a dose of the trusted tonic of confidence. This was as vital to his routine as a clean dinner jacket and freshly pressed shirt. A double shot of The Famous Grouse neat allowed him to walk into this world with his chin locked in place: From the first time Jet Set sent him in to cover a society event, Judge relied on the soothing effects of Tequila to get him out of the anxious panic in his apartment and through the bright light of the grand portal. He threw his head back and finished the contents in one slurp. He set the glass down and checked his reflection in the large mirror against the wall. As much as his tuxedo had come to feel like a uniform to him, he was always surprised and pleased by what he saw. He ran his hand through his slicked wavy hair. He raised his chin and crossed his arms over his chest. Courage! This was his routine. He would be alright.

When Judge descended to the lobby of his building, a black-suited driver stood waiting beside an equally sleek, black Lincoln Town car. Judge slid into the cold leather darkness and the driver closed the door. Judge was surprised to find a chilled bottle of Dom Perignon and two flutes resting in a pewter bucket in the middle of the back seat. The driver said,

"Compliments of Miss Newton. One Sixty-Eight East Sixty-Eighth Street and then the Botanical Gardens, sir?"

"Yes, that's fine." Judge had no idea where Lucy lived or how to get to the Bronx. He sat back and trusted that all was arranged and he merely had to follow directions. After a brisk ride uptown through light traffic -- he was surprised when the driver said, "One Sixty-Eight East Sixty-Eighth Street," and opened the car door.

Judge, startled, said, "Oh, sure, sorry. I'll be right back down." He walked into the lobby of the building and said, "Judge Mender to see Lucy Shining."

"Oh, she's expecting you, sir. Go right on back. Take your first left past the elevator and up the little stairs. Her apartment is at the top."

Judge noted the informality of the doorman and the directions. He imagined that Lucy Shining would live in the penthouse of the grandest building overlooking Park Avenue. This was a nice building, he noted, it was just not over the top grand or pretentious. He reconsidered. It is exactly where she would live. He climbed the little flight of stairs, nervously pulling the cuffs of his sleeves. He was glad he'd taken a double shot of tequila. Judge knocked on the door and, when swung open, found himself face to face with Lucy in her kitchen. This is the back door, he thought.

Lucy stood in the half-opened doorway fidgeting with an earring. Upon seeing her, Judge had to control the urge to laugh out loud. The invitation, the pre-press, the talk of the town was the Winter Wonderland White Ball. White. White. White. Judge had heard it a million times from Victoria and Maxwell. "White in the Bronx, how hilarious, how decadent, how indulgent," Maxwell crowed. Now with all that direction, here stood Lucy Shining in a royal purple gown of the simplest cut in silk charmeuse. The dress was a halter top style she'd tied casually behind her neck and the rest of the fabric clung affectionately to her lithe frame. She was tan and sexy and gorgeous without jewelry -- save a gold ring -- and she had no idea she was to be the thorn in a white bouquet. She had probably never seen the invitation and just as certainly did not participate in the girly gossip that told them all to follow orders or be embarrassed.

"Hey, Handsome," she said as she leaned in to kiss him lightly on the lips while attaching another dangly earring in her right ear. "I'm almost ready. I can't believe I'm going to this thing. I really hate them, you know, but when Victoria called and said she was sending a car and the devastating Judge Mender to fetch me, how could I say no? Would you like a drink?"

"Sure, what have you got?"

"It's all in the 'frig. Make yourself at home. I swear I'm almost ready. Make me a vodka soda with a splash of cran. I'll be right back."

Lucy disappeared through the double doors connecting the kitchen to the living room and beyond. A black cat poked his head around the corner, gave Judge the once over, dismissed him and walked out of sight. Judge opened the refrigerator and found nothing but two large bottles of Kettle One in the freezer. He hastily made two drinks. He wanted to get a glimpse of the apartment before she rushed them out the door.

"I have your drink," he yelled toward the bedroom and started surveying the apartment. The place was photo ready, he thought. He would kill to get this story. It was one of the most beautiful, yet most comfortable, apartments he had ever been in.

The colors were dynamic but not overwhelming: rich reds, vibrant oranges. It all felt very citrus. The furniture was modern but not stark, dark and rich, warm wood accented by plush fabrics in geometric prints. The layout was a large, expanse of a room with alcoves of comfort. There were seats gathered around tables here and large pillows huddled around low tables there. There was an absence of bric-a-brac that he thought almost masculine.

"Oh, thanks," she said, appearing suddenly from around the corner. "The place is a mess, but snoop around. Check out the entryway, I just had it repainted. Not sure if I'm sold on the color, though. Never been too keen on yellow." She turned, drink at lips, the long, train of her purple gown swooshed behind bare feet as she disappeared again.

In a flash, she was ready. The drinks were hurriedly finished and glasses dropped in the sink. Lucy flipped a coral-colored pashmina over her head and around her bare shoulders and shut the door tightly behind then. When the pair descended to the lobby, Lucy turned to Judge and said, "I don't need a coat, do I? It's all inside in this garden party, right?"

"I would imagine. It is December, after all."

"Right," she said as they approached the doorman. "Hello, Gino. I'm pretty fancy tonight, don't you think?"

Gino beamed. It was obvious that she was the happiest part of his day.

"You look very beautiful, Lucy," the doorman said. "Have fun."

"Oh we will," Lucy said to Gino, then turned to Judge: "It's not going to be too stuffy or serious tonight, is it?"

"I've heard it will be fun," Judge said. "If not, there's nothing that a little heavy drinking won't fix."

"You see, Gino," Lucy laughed. "That is the way to win a woman's heart. Get her smashed on your first date. Goodnight."

The driver whipped around the back of the car and opened the door and Lucy slid in. "Champagne," she laughed. "Fancy, schmancy."

"A gift from our hostess," Judge said slightly embarrassed as he slid in behind her. "Very nice touch, don't you think?"

"Absolutely," Lucy smiled. "Miss Victoria thinks of everything."

Judge popped the cork and Lucy squealed. Judge laughed again and poured them each a glass.

"To fancy people," Lucy said.

"To fancy people," he answered and narrowed his eyes. Was she fucking with him?

After a couple of blocks, she settled back in the seat and stared out the window.

"New York is so beautiful in December," she sighed, a hint of melancholy seeping into her tone. "I love the city at Christmas time. So many people talk about getting out of town and I wonder. Where else would you want to be? I mean, yeah, it drives me crazy and I have to get out. I have to escape every once in a while because it gives me perspective. But New York is my home. Although I do get restless seeing the same people, the same parties, the same bullshit. I get tired of all that, like everybody else. I guess that's why I'm always searching, trying something new. I mean, I just got this new apartment because I was bored with the old one. I would never want to leave New York, I just need a different perspective every once in a while. Something different, something exciting. And it did the trick. I have a whole new outlook now. This is where I want to be at the moment."

Judge felt a pang of contempt infect his light mood. How easy it was for her. He felt how different life was when you had money. Serious money left no room for fear. He hated her for a millisecond. Judge had never seen her sober before. He'd never been sober around her either. They were acquaintances in a bottle. This was all new, this soberly getting to know someone. Had he ever been here?

He pushed the thoughts away and stared at her as she continued talking to herself. He wondered if she knew she was talking out loud. She looked very sweet sitting there across from him. He looked out the window and for the first time that season, noticed the holiday decorations in lighted windows and doors. He smiled in spite of himself.

The car turned north on Park. After another block, she said:

"Judge, I have to talk to you about something and when we're done, we won't have to mention it again. And please know that it won't affect our night."

This serious tone was something he never imagined coming out of her beautiful mouth. Judge turned away from the window to look at her, but she continued staring at the blur of Park Avenue whizzing past like a film projector out of sync.

Then suddenly, she said in the same tone. "Why did you write that mean story about Chase Peters?"

Judge sat back in his seat. He was stunned. No one from this group ever questioned him. They were terrified of him. He didn't know what to say.

"I never read it, actually," she said. "I was talking to Rhea Brown today, telling her I was going to this thing with you and she read me a piece of it. Why would you do that? Rhea thought it was hilarious and said all of New York loved you for it, but I still can't understand why. Why would they love it and why would you write it?"

He searched his brain. Here was the confrontation he had managed to avoid. He flipped from superiority over this little rich girl to defense of his actions. He only came close to this conversation with his mother, and he rushed her off the phone.

"Honestly, Lucy?"

"Yes, tell me." She turned and looked back out of the window. He was relieved not to have to look into her eyes. He turned toward his side window and did the same. His head was turning inside out, thoughts crisscrossed mangled and tangled. A long suppressed nausea rose in his throat. He had fought his insides over the story a thousand times. He had changed the angle back and forth. He had edited and added so much at one point he started over from scratch. He finally had to concentrate only on the style and ignore the content. He did not sleep the night before he turned the final draft into his editor. Was the story an attempt to squash a competitor? Judge and Chase were both Extra Men, as they say in this circle. Every society girl, hostess and dinner party needs an Extra Man. They prove invaluable and are invited everywhere. Have tuxedo will travel, is the motto. Or was it fear of being discovered? He and Chase clicked immediately over a bottle of scotch. Their tryst was something Judge seriously regretted, more so when he saw that Chase wasn't discreet or distressed at about it all. Judge envied his confident swagger that was Chase's birthright. He was from this world, yet Judge was more popular inside the walls. Yet Judge knew his popularity stemmed only from his column and if he weren't covering this world, he would never been accepted so quickly. Chase had everything, the whole stacked deck. Judge held only one card.

"Ambition, I guess," he said after a swallowed pause. "My editor wanted the story and it was my time. I had reservations, sure, but I wanted to write it."

"But, why? What did he ever do to the editor of Jet Set magazine?"

"He isn't discreet. He pissed some people off," Judge said suddenly clear-headed now but a little too haughtily for his own liking. "Some very important people, and that's what the magazine does. It reports on this little slice of humanity who thinks it is the most important people in the world, and Chase Peters got on the wrong side of the right people."

He was at first pleased with that response, it was the one he had practiced in his mirror and was indeed the thesis of his piece. But then doubt seeped in and he thought how stupid that sounded and how stupid she must think him now. He continued, "I know this won't sound any better, but it would have been written with or without me, and well, I wanted to prove my worth to the magazine."

"I don't really know him that well," she said. "just socially. He's always nice."

He'd be here now instead of me, Judge thought. If I hadn't written the thing, Chase Peters could be sitting here with her instead of me. He relaxed in rightness. The nausea backed into remission.

"Still, I wouldn't have thought that people out there disliked him," Lucy continued talking to herself in the window glare. "But, like most of the people I see around New York, I probably wouldn't recognize him out of costume in the day time. Most of those people are just a kiss hello at a party." She paused in thought. "Do you ever notice that New York is really two cities? One day and one night?"

He laughed to himself. The subject of Chase was over and disposed of.

Judge's New York day and New York night were about as opposite as any two worlds he could imagine. By day, he slaved at his desk under the constant fear of being fired or exposed as a fraud. He lived in fear that his career was just timing and luck and any day his editor would see through his cloud of charm and get rid of him. Compare that fear to the ass-kissing worship he received when he went out on the town. Dressed so elegantly in his black tuxedo and southern manners, he was treated like royalty by the world he covered. He was seated at the best tables, spoiled with expensive gifts, introduced as a person of means to incredibly rich and important people. There was a distinct difference in his night and day. She had no idea.

She turned to Judge to see if he agreed, then she stopped, sharp in a thought.

"Would you ever do that to me?" she blurted. "Would anyone at the magazine ever do that to me?"

He was startled and disturbed that she brought the subject back up and was about to dismiss this topic when he looked at her face and his anger fallen away. He discovered the most vulnerable Lucy he had ever seen – or any of these fancy girls for that matter -- and it brought him immediately back under her spell. The confident exterior armor was in her lap, unconsciously revealing the little girl he imagined she used to be. He felt a new layer in his appreciation of her. This was another side, the innocent side and all he wanted to do was embrace her. This feeling was almost husbandly. He wanted to protect her from this ugly reality of her world that she seemingly never knew existed.

"No, Lucy. You are not Chase Peters. And I wouldn't allow it, even if they tried."

"Okay then," She turned, armor re-fastened. "Because if you did, I would cut your balls off." She shoved the empty glass toward him. "Pour me some more shampoo, hot stuff."

Judge laughed nervously and poured her another glass. His mind was spinning and he did not want to think about Chase Peters anymore or ever again. She reached in her purse and pulled out a skinny little joint and waited for a light. He knew that the soon to be smoked pot would erase the uneasiness in the seat between them. Judge inhaled deeply and cracked the window to blow out the exhale. A few seconds later, Lucy leaned up to the front seat, "What's your name, driver?"

"Jerry, miss."

"Jerry, please turn on that radio and let us hear some music. Try 98.7. We're going to a fancy party and we want to sing all the way there."

Whitney Huston came out of the speakers as the driver turned up the volume.

"I love this song," Lucy shrieked. "Come on, Judge, sing it with me."

Judge laughed and stared at her. "I don't know the words."

"That's okay," she smiled and put her hand on his shoulder, "I'll go solo."

> *It's not right but it's okay*
>
> *I'm gonna make it anyway...*

Judge watched Lucy wrap up in the music. With the marijuana, the champagne and the seat dancing they missed the ugly part of the drive through the Bronx and were deposited deep inside the Botanical Garden when the car stopped and the driver hopped out to open the door.

"Whoa!" Lucy said as the door popped open. "Are we here? Who knew the Bronx was so close to my house?"

Judge turned, startled again to see the driver holding the door. "Oh, we're here. " He slid out of the Town Car and extended his hand to Lucy.

"I can't imagine this thing can measure up to the party we just had in that car," she said as she put her hand in the crook of his arm. "But let's do give it a whirl, darling."

"Wow," Lucy said as she looked up at the atrium of the Crystal Palace bathed in white lights. "Is all this just for us?" She squeezed Judge's arm and pulled close to him. It was frigid cold and he thought, I should have told her to bring a coat.

"It's not right, but it's okay," Judge said as he took Lucy's hand.

They were late. The hustle of arrivals had subsided and the phalanx of photographers waited for Lucy Shining. Victoria had given the exclusive coverage of the party inside to Judge and Jet Set, but arrivals were fair game. The photographers from all of the fashion magazines and wire services were in place and waiting for Lucy. Victoria Newtown stood at the end of the row, the general overseeing her troops. From where Judge stood, she looked like a grand white apparition, or maybe Saint Peter in drag, and though the swirling yards of glistening fabric obscured her feet, he knew that she impatiently tapped her shoe.

Victoria wore a beaded sleeveless white top over a full white organza and tulle skirt with elbow length opera gloves and a white mink cape around her bare shoulders. For the first time, Judge notice that all of her gowns were the same cut, just different fabrics and different colors, depending on the party and the season. He'd seen her in this look in pink for the Met opening night, in yellow for the ballet opening and in red for the Animal Rescue party. How funny, he thought. Why have I never noticed that before? He was suddenly blinded by the flash of the cameras and Victoria disappeared on the other side the glare.

Lucy turned to Judge and said, "I'm about to sprint this. Hang on." She grabbed Judge's arm and barreled through the runway of lights.

"Lucy!" The photographers shouted.

"Lucy! Over here!"

"Lucy. Please stop for Vogue!"

Lucy pulled Judge along, yanking him out of his doobie-champagne haze. The photographers continued snapping and flashing and yelling her name, but Lucy dashed past until they reached Victoria.

"Hey, Victoria," Lucy said as they got closer. "Let's get inside. It's freezing out here." Lucy pulled Judge, past Victoria, but Victoria would have none of it.

Victoria gently stepped between Lucy and Judge, slipped her gloved hand around Lucy's slender waist and pulled her to her side. "You look absolutely gorgeous, darling." Victoria covered Lucy's cheeks with big showy air kisses, her voluminous white gown almost cocooning the purple reed-like silhouette of Lucy like a Calla Lily. The photographers swarmed and flashes filled the cold, dark night like heat lightning.

Judge stepped quickly out of the frame and admired Victoria's skill. She knew that if this party was to be considered a success, the photographers needed this picture. He also knew Lucy was the rarest bird to catch on film. That is why Victoria arranged for him to pick her up and hand-deliver her, he realized. He suddenly felt a little uneasy at his role in this scenario, but then shook it off. He had ridden here with her, next to her. He could hand her over to the greater cause with little regret. Besides, he would be seated next to her at dinner and the night already held such promise his usual dread of these things was replaced by an unfamiliar anticipation. He had basked in her undivided attention and no matter what happened the rest of the night, he was already further along than any of the competition for her favor.

He focused again on the scene. He had to put that car ride behind him. I am here to work, he thought. I am the exclusive journalist here, he reminded himself. He focused again on the flash bulb orgy in front of him and looked at Victoria again with professional admiration. There was no way she was going to let Lucy Shining slip past this photo pool, not after all the work she'd done to get her here. Judge clocked his own photographer rushing to get the shot.

Victoria finally released Lucy and the two walked over to where Judge stood.

"Well, I'm glad you two finally made it. I thought maybe you'd gone to Queens instead." Victoria leaned in and kissed Judge on the cheek. "Hello, darling. Thank you for coming to our little party. And thank you for escorting the divine Miss Shining. Was everything in order? The car on time, I hope?" Victoria knew the answer to that question because she checked with the dispatcher of the limo company and knew exactly what time the car picked up Judge, when he arrived at Lucy's and what time the two left her apartment. The final report came when the car entered the Garden's grounds.

"Oh, yes, Miss Newton. Everything was as it should be," Judge said. "The champagne was an especially nice touch." Judge smiled at Lucy as he put on his grand inflection voice. This was the voice he employed when talking to the ladies of the old guard and when he met Victoria in public.

"Yes, thank you Victoria, it was very kind." Lucy mimicked him. "Can we go inside? I'm freezing."

"Absolutely," Victoria barked. "You need some meat on those bones. There is no frilly food at this party. We're eating meat and potatoes tonight. You are at my table and I'm going to see to it that you eat a square meal, even if it's the first one you've had in days. Follow me."

Lucy put her hand back in Judge's arm. "I guess mama Newton caught us for being late."

"Too bad she can't banish us to the kid's table," he said with a smile.

"Thank god you're here with me." Lucy said as they entered the main room of the glass ceiling-ed hothouse of the Botanical Garden's Crystal Palace.

Judge and Lucy stopped short and stared. Their eyes grew as wide as their mouths as they entered the room and felt transported into another world. The interior of the atrium was transformed into sheer fantasy. When the order said white it had been enforced. Maxwell had outdone himself, again. Judge knew that the recent competition from Chase Peters had ratcheted up his game. Maxwell sensed that a new threat could be around the corner and perhaps not so easily disposed of. He treated this junior event like a coronation and worked his minions like slaves to put this party up as one for the ages. He'd crowed to Judge

288

for weeks on the phone about how this party was going to be the death of him. He said he worried himself skinny to stay within the confines of the committee's meager budget, and though he'd never admit such to Judge, absorbed a hefty chunk of the cost to make sure there was an evening of absolute enchantment during Victoria's reign.

There was a palpable electric current in the room and it pulsed through Judge and he felt his hair tingle. Judge didn't know if it was due to the chill in the air or the magic of the décor or the fact that they had all trekked through the urban jungle to a party in a hot house in the dangerous Bronx. Whatever the chemical combination, Judge felt giddy for the first time in a long time. His chronic cynicism of these events melted away as Lucy squeezed his hand and whispered in his ear, "Wow."

In the expanse of the glass-enclosed atrium, the symphony of sounds boiled over into cacophony: The clatter of long-lost friends who hadn't seen each other since the night before chattered and clucked; the orchestra -- attempting to soothe over it all -- played a bit louder than usual and the trumpet player blew with gusto; the ebullient squeals as girls greeted dresses, declaring one more beautiful than the next matched the rich, deep laughter from a group of young bankers and brokers, unabashed in the early joy of making money for nothing; the clink of glasses and plates being bustled from crate to table sounded like little bells in a Christmas cantata.

No sooner had Judge and Lucy found their table in the wake of Victoria's skirts did Maxwell slide astride Judge and plant a jaunty peck on Lucy's cheek.

"Lucy Shining and Judge Mender. You are the most ravishing couple in attendance." Maxwell boomed as all in earshot nodded in agreement.

"Why thank you, Maxwell." Lucy said as she accepted the second kiss on her left cheek. "Did you create this delightful room just for us?"

"I am afraid I must take sole credit for this, my child. I worked my fingers to the bone, well, someone's fingers to the bone, at any rate. I must say though that it was merely a canvas awaiting your serene arrival. Lucy Shining, you have never looked more radiant in your life."

Judge wanted to laugh. Maxwell was rarely obsequious to the junior set. Now here he was fawning over Lucy.

"Why Mister Jones, you flatter me," Lucy replied in a terrible southern accent. "I'll say I must declare any radiance I exhibit is the fault of this strapping young buck at my side," she continued in her awful drawl. "You see, he got me intoxicated on expensive champagne in the car riding up here." Lucy slid her arm back through the crook in Judge's and said, "Maxwell Jones, may I present Judge Mender."

Judge bowed slightly. "How do you do, Mr. Jones?"

"I'm grand, my dear boy, absolutely grand." Maxwell leaned into Judge's ear, opposite Lucy and whispered, "Follow me to the bar."

Judge turned to excuse himself to Lucy but found there was no need. She had been engulfed by a covey of girls, clucking and touching. Judge turned to follow Maxwell, but jerked his head back at a sparkling little bird of a woman standing demurely on the outside circle of the group around Lucy. She shone among a sea of shining girls. Her beauty and her sexy gorgeous gown arrested Judge. Who is she? he wondered. Her body language telegraphed that she wasn't a close friend of any of the girls, yet she stood there waiting to be introduced. It would have seemed incredibly awkward if the energy of the night weren't so fantastic or her beauty was any less riveting. Her presence added a brighter star to the firmament. Judge racked his brain to place her. He knew he knew her, but... then suddenly, Scarlet Goodman! My God, he thought. Did she look like that when we met?

Judge turned back around and followed the back of Maxwell's figure as he bobbed and weaved though the tightly arranged tables of eight. Judge focused directly on Maxwell so that he wouldn't have to lock eyes on anyone and stop and small talk. He was grateful to Victoria for the champagne because it had made Lucy giddy and rolled over the awkward scene in the car, but now he really needed a scotch and he knew Maxwell would have a nice, single malt stashed behind the bar. He finally made his way through the maze of tables and found Maxwell perched at the bar with a striking and familiar bartender pouring two glasses of Oban. "Thank you Caleb," Maxwell said so that Judge could hear him. "Your favorite single malt, if I remember correctly?" Maxwell said as he raised his glass.

"You don't forget much, do you Maxie."

"Judge," Maxwell scowled.

"I'm sorry," Judge teased, "Mr. Jones." And the two clinked glasses.

"Well," Maxwell smacked as he set the glass down, "before I commence on any gossip or pry the details of your joy ride through the Bronx with the richest girl in Manhattan, there is one bit of information I have been waiting weeks to hear."

Judge set his glass down on the bar and gazed over Maxwell's salt and pepper head to the hundreds of yards of white tulle crisscrossing the glass ceiling and the thousands of tiny white lights intertwined inside. Then his eye focused on the glass ceiling where hundreds of tiny votives in miniature hurricane lamps sat outside melting perfect circles in the snow. His eye followed to the center of the room where there was an enormous crystal chandelier surrounded by a dozen, smaller versions which illuminated every table in soft elegant light. In the center of each white covered table stood a crystal vase, four feet high, filled with Yoshino cherry blossom twigs which were at the exact perfect point of bloom and each table shimmered with the thinnest layer of gossamer fabric set with white and crystal and silver table settings.

Judge returned to Maxwell's anxious face, which had followed his inventory around the room.

"Maxwell," Judge said softly, reverently. "It is the most magnificent room I have ever seen. I expect to see Marie Antoinette come floating in with her sheep."

Maxwell hooted with delight. "Do you honestly think so? I mean, I knew it was gorgeous, but, Judge! the competition is so fierce these days. One can't just rely on one's reputation anymore, or the stock room for that matter, even when one's stock room is the grandest in Manhattan. One must strive, one must dream, and one hopes . . ., soar."

Maxwell now allowed his gaze to retrace the same path Judge's had just traveled. There was a mixture of relief and pride in his eyes and Judge felt proud of him. He knew how Maxwell had worried over this event and now it would be the talk of the town.

"Well, it looks like you've sewn up the next generations' weddings all in one night," Judge said as he took a long swig on his scotch. "They'll be beating down your door after this extravaganza."

"Oh I do hope so," he beamed. "I've taken a shine to these youngsters. By the way," he continued. "When did forty years old become Junior Society? I see a few familiar faces that haven't been junior since God was a boy. Every benefit that boasts a junior committee states clearly that junior equals forty and under. A decade ago, forty year olds where at home with their wives, husbands and three squealing spawn. Now they are here wearing scandalous gowns and dancing on tables."

"I suppose since this group of girls is about to hit thirty, they decided that forty would be the new cut off," Judge said.

"Well, I'm not one to tell truths and puncture illusions," Maxwell said slyly, "but some of these guests' birth certificates would exclude them from even that criterion. Judge darling, it is the end of an era. We are going to hell. I just hope I get paid before the bottom falls out or the good lord smites us down."

Maxwell turned back and picked up his scotch glass and looked back at his masterpiece glowing and twinkling before them. "If only our sweet southern mothers could be here to witness their prodigal sons sitting in all this high cotton."

Judge looked at Maxell and laughed heartily and finished his scotch. "If only."

Judge squeezed his way through the tight tables and chairs, excusing himself to the backs of guests as he inched toward Victoria's table, happy and content that this night was taking flight. The orchestra played A-train as the straggling and intoxicated guests reluctantly found their seats. No one wanted to sit down at their assigned table as the cocktail half hour expanded into a full, loaded hour. The waiters scurried around the room beseeching the flock to kindly take their seats, but they were being ignored wholesale.

Victoria stomped across the empty dance floor to the bandstand and curtsied to the conductor, Peter Duchin, who handed her a microphone. "Take your seats, gorgeous people. Now!" Only then did the jubilant swarm begin the slow buzz to their seats. The din of conversation would have been deafening if not for the sweet sound track of nostalgia provided by the orchestra. To Judge it looked like a scene from a 1950's cotillion. Everything was perfect, he thought, and wondered if the alcohol and Lucy were clouding his judgment. The dresses, the hair do's, the tables, the waiters, and especially the orchestra were rendering the room timeless.

He looked closer and the present came sharply into focus. Cleavage reverberated everywhere. The fronts of the dresses were cut so deep, there was real hope in the men's eyes that breasts would be revealed. Each expensive gown was cut lower than the next and Judge was sure that some of the girls had employed tape to keep the dresses in shape and on the body. So there they were, Judge mused, waltzing into the past on a perfect winter night in New York, with hard bodies bronzed from tropical climes all to raise money for the hot house in the Bronx. It was a fantastic scene and Judge took a deep breath.

When Judge arrived at Victoria's table, all he saw was Lucy, alive, beaming and floating on a white cloud under the cherry blossoms. He sensed for the first time that this buzz was beyond champagne and scotch. He stopped short to shake the realization and was stopped by Victoria's gloved hand.

"So!" Victoria demanded. "First impressions?"

Judge stared at Lucy as his eyes began to haze. "Absolutely mesmerizing."

"Mesmerizing? Hmm, I guess that'll do." Victoria said as she released him to find his seat across from her. She turned to Sweetie James. "Mesmerizing, he says. I would have settled for a stunning or even an unprecedented, but mesmerizing will do. Fucking poets."

Sweetie laughed then hugged Victoria snuggly. "I agree with Judge. It is absolutely mesmerizing." And the two heiresses surveyed the room, content that the night was a success.

Suddenly, Victoria straightened her back and her eyes narrowed into little slits. Lily von Reynolds was walking toward her.

"Sweetie!" Victoria whispered. "The flower from the Bronx has found her way home!"

Sweetie turned and saw Lily making her way through the tables, her eyes locked on Victoria.

"How in the hell did she get in here, and what the hell is she wearing? She looks like the Wicked Witch as designed by Bob Mackie." Victoria fumed. "I personally returned her check to her with a note saying we were completely sold out."

"Victoria! Darling! What a night!" Lily was upon them. She had abandoned her husband at coat check. "This is the most beautiful room I've ever seen in my life. Congratulations!"

Lily wore an enormous white gown, about two inches of fabric short of a hoop skirt, with a long sequin and crystal beaded cape sweeping the floor behind her. She wore opera gloves and her dark hair was piled high and held in place by a tiara.

"How…. I mean," Victoria stammered. "Hello, Lily. I wasn't expecting you. I mean, I didn't see your name on the guest list."

"Oh, I know. I am such an idiot. Oh, hello Sweetie," Lily said as she kissed Sweetie on the cheek. She then took aim at Victoria. Victoria pulled back.

Lily continued, "I sent our check in too late and it was returned, so I called Harold Barnes, you know, the President of the board, and he told me not to be ridiculous. Of course I was welcome. I offered to pay at the door and he insisted that we attend as his guests, gratis. So, here we are. I can't get over how gorgeous you look."

Lily stood waiting for Victoria to return the compliment. Victoria stared above her, looking at the chandeliers.

"I guess we were the last to arrive," Lily continued. "Those photographers went crazy when we got out of the car. I have never seen so many flash bulbs in my life."

"Your dress," Sweetie said. She was dying to know, as was Victoria, but Sweetie knew Victoria wouldn't flatter Lily with interest. "Whose dress is that? Zang Toi?"

"Escada!" Lily said with pride. The PR girl said they made it just for me. Isn't it divine?"

"It very original," Sweetie said diplomatically, afraid to look in Victoria's direction for fear they would spill.

"Well, gorgeous to see you. I must go find my husband. Goodbye, girls."

"Goodbye, Lily," Sweetie mumbled as she and Victoria watched the caped wonder navigate the tables back to her seat.

"Can you imagine!?" Sweetie said stunned.

"Ridiculous." Victoria said and squinted to take in the dress from the back. "Her husband must have written some fat check to get her in here gratis. I just can't believe what money can buy these days. Oh, well," she snapped. "That little tramp is not going to ruin my night. Just please, Sweetie, keep her away from me. Wait, did she drop her scepter?"

The two women erupted in laughter, holding each other for support.

Judge returned to his seat to find Lucy relaying some animated story to Rhea Brown and her date, the tennis pro Frankie Haynes. What the fuck is he doing here? Judge thought.

"Judge! Gorgeous!" Rhea yelled above the din.

Rhea wore a sequined white Halston column of a dress with a slit down to her navel and her tanned, tangerine breasts were half exposed. Judge admired her torso before greeting her lips, and she offered a straight-on full tongue kiss. He laughed as he pushed her back.

"Are you already drunk?" he said. "I think everyone here is loaded to the gills." He cast a half-cocked look toward Frankie. "Aren't you here with your tennis pro?"

"Yeah," Rhea said as she wrapped her slender arms around Judge's neck and pulled her body up close, connecting with him from head to knee. "Who cares? You know I'd dump him in a minute if it meant one night with you, big daddy."

Judge laughed heartily, disentangled himself from her drunken embrace and took his seat beside Lucy.

"Hey babe," Lucy said as she leaned over to kiss his cheek, "These two have been keeping me busy and getting me very drunk."

Judge looked down to see Frankie's hand resting rather high on Lucy's shimmering purple thigh and he shot a look deep into Frankie's eyes and said, "I think you're mauling my date, dude."

Frankie looked down at his hand and said, "I didn't realize you were together, dude." Mimicking Judge's lapse into dude-dom. "Lucy forgot to mention it." He slowly, seductively removed his hand, "I just saw you with the old flower decorator and assumed that's who you came with."

Judge looked at Frankie in the eye and smiled deep and cocksure. "Well, everyone makes mistakes." He leaned over and kissed Lucy on the cheek and whispered, "Sorry to abandon you. Maxwell needed to be complimented on the room."

"Oh, it is so divine. Everyone is talking about it. There is such a wonderful vibration in the air. I know that sounds queer, but it's true and I'm a little short of vocabulary tonight." She took a big swig of her drink. "It's like we've been lost in a cold, dark wood and drunkenly found our way to some enchanted castle in the middle of the black forest, and this little party was created by fairies and waiting just for us."

Judge listened rapturously to her and was moved by this revelation. This was the Lucy who delighted in the wonder of a mystical night in Manhattan. He was first impaled by the sexy, smart-ass Lucy, but this new reveal fit the room and his mood and it seemed to lift him out of his chair. Their absorption in each other during dinner completely annoyed Victoria. Each time she tried to lob a conversation across the table it got snagged in the cherry blossoms. Lucy and Judge were aware only of each other. They talked only to themselves and laughed and snuck cigarettes from under the table cloth. Judge slipped their waiter a twenty to keep their glasses liquid and for once, attention was paid.

After the dinner plates were cleared, Lucy was the first to break from table and head to the dance floor, pulling Judge with her.

The Duchin Orchestra was the evening's first act, tapped to enhance the arrivals and lift the room into an elegant and timeless space. For the serious, post-dinner dancing, DJ Tom Finn was de rigueur for a junior event. Victoria ordered Finn to start his set.

Lucy and Judge danced and drank and drank and danced and snuck cigarettes in the kitchen with the staff and danced some more. Judge's jacket and hair were soaked through with sweat and he kept dancing. The night had landed on some confluence of perfect timing. Maxwell had spread stardust across the room. The dinner was insignificant because the drinks flowed like a rushing river. First, the orchestra, then the DJ hit the right balance of sentimental journeys, eighties rehash present pop and classic funk. Molded by the sure hand of Victoria Newton, the guest list was the perfect combination of old and new. Every face told the other the glee that danced within, even curmudgeon-in-training Harry Little was drunk, dancing and laughing.

Victoria stood glowing in the center of it all. Wherever there was a gathering, whether at a table, at the bar or in the center of the dance floor, the grand swan was positioned to soak up her praise. And she should, Judge thought. She deserves recognition for creating this little slice of heaven by sheer force of hurricane will. And she will be rewarded, he noted.

It was getting close to midnight and Judge knew Victoria would leave soon. She never stayed late, even at her own parties she would gather herself and stroll out the door. He wanted to talk to her. When he sensed her final goodbye, he excused himself from Lucy and landed beside her.

"Congratulations, Miss Newton," he said as he kissed her cheeks chivalrously. He was very drunk now and he wanted to be sure to dish out the attention he had withheld earlier. "The evening is a smashing success."

"Well, I am so delighted that you were able to attend. I see my little carriage ride arrangement has certainly landed you in a favored spot." Victoria nodded over her shoulder toward the shimmying Lucy on the dance floor.

"Yes, I have enjoyed my carriage and dinner companion immensely," he slurred. "Thank you sincerely for the town car and for this wonderful night. Goodnight." And he kissed her again and turned and walked away, grinning.

Victoria grabbed the back of his arm and pulled Judge back into her. She leaned into his ear and said, "I want you to mention that our little flower from the Bronx crashed my party." And Victoria pointed to Lily across the room, her tiara gleaming under a light. "And whatever you do, do not run a photo her. Can you remember that?"

"Absolutely," Judge slurred. "Consider it done."

She released his arm and he turned and stumbled away. Victoria watched in amazement as Judge went back in the direction of Lucy and turned to Sweetie at her side. "I hope he sobers up before he writes up the party. He should say it was a stellar success, a gorgeous winter garden party with the exception of one pesky, little weed."

Victoria took one more glance over the revelers on the dance floor and those gathered around the tables laughing and singing. "I don't remember when I've seen everyone so drunk. Ha!" she laughed out loud. "Good for them. Good for me."

Judge returned to the dance floor to find Lucy dancing with the most beautiful creature in a white beaded gown with a pale blue chiffon scarf at her neck. In his drunken state he thought it was Daisy Buchanan and momentarily looked for Tom or Gatsby. The creature turned, full of smile and beautiful blue mirrors for eyes and Judge saw that it was Scarlet but couldn't get past his delusion of Daisy.

"Hey Judge!" she squealed and popped into his space, shattering his illusion, she kissed him on the cheek. "It's so good to see you again. Isn't this the most amazing party ever?"

Judge smiled and nodded.

"I'm Scarlet Goodman, we sat next to each other at Victoria Newton's dinner last month," she yelled above the music, hot in his ear.

"Of course," he yelled. "I'm a little drunk. You'll have to forgive me."

"I could dance all night!" she said swinging her arms. "This is the most fun I've ever had in my life."

"Me too," Judge said honestly and slipped past her to snuggle behind Lucy. "Hey, Gorgeous. Miss me?"

Then it was time. Daft Punk. The unmistakable opening riff of the junior's anthem blared through the speakers.

One more time...

Squeals from the back of the room accompanied a great movement as the party en masse moved from the elegant tables to the dance floor. Rhea Brown lead the way, shaking her ass and punching the air with her arms.

Music's got me feeling so free

We're gonna celebrate

Celebrate and dance so free

One more time

It seemed as if the entire room, those who could still dance, now abandoned their seats and conversations and reassembled on the dance floor, shaking the foundation and shouting the lyrics to the glass ceiling.

Lucy turned around and kissed Judge passionately on the mouth. She pulled back and looked into his eyes. She was visibly drunk and her eyes had turned into little slits. "Please take me home, babe." She draped her arms limply across his shoulders and nuzzled into his neck. "I'm very happy, but I'm very drunk."

Judge looked around the room. It was time to go, he reckoned. He decided to take the least popular egress and get Lucy out of the public gaze. He and Lucy had been sneaking into the caterer's kitchen all night to smoke cigarettes after security stopped being polite about their sneaking smokes under the table. He knew they could go through there. Judge ducked behind the plastic wall of a tent, and guided her through the kitchen. He took out his phone and dialed the driver and instructed him to pick them up there, fifty feet from the main entrance where photographers were still waiting. Safely in the car, Lucy fell fast asleep on his shoulder.

The car glided down the FDR highway where the street is level with the East River, and Judge imagined he and Lucy were in a small, cozy vessel headed out to sea. The lights of Queens blinked across the water in the clear, cold night and Judge pulled Lucy closer and buried his nose in her hair. His heart pounded at the kiss memory. He closed his eyes and wished he could fall asleep with her wrapped in his arms, but his brain paced. The night behind them bounced in his head. He closed his eyes and wanted this fragile pleasure to last longer. The driver signaled right and coasted onto the East 63rd Street exit.

The car arrived at the awning of Lucy's building and Judge looked into her beautiful, peaceful face.

"Lucy," he whispered. "You're home."

She stirred and snuggled deep into his neck. "No," she purred.

"Lucy, come on. You're home. Let's get you upstairs."

"Carry me, hero," she whispered sensually in his ear.

"Alright, hold on."

He slid out of the car and told the driver, "I'll only be five minutes." Judge didn't believe for a second what he was saying and the driver silently agreed.

Judge lifted Lucy up and into his arms. She draped her long, smooth arms around his neck and resumed her nuzzle. The doorman held the door as Judge carried her down the hall. "Thank you, Gino," Lucy purred. "You're working some late hours tonight, baby."

The doorman smiled nervously as Judge carried his feather light trophy down the hall and up the stairs through the unlocked door of her apartment. He carried her into the bedroom. He put her in her bed, gown and all and began the demon struggle within his drunken brain.

"Lucy," he said. "Are you awake?"

He gently stroked her face and she began to breathe deeply, just shy of a snore, his fantasy vaporized.

His head adjusted as he turned off the lights in her apartment. With each flip of a lamp switch, he returned to the task before him. Tonight he had to write the report of the night they'd just experienced, so the revelers could confirm their suspicions that they had a spectacular evening and the uninvited could curse the air that they missed the greatest event of the season. He struggled with the careening thoughts in his mind and returned once more to gaze at her in the low light of a single lamp. Lucy drifted deeper into drunken sleep. The beautiful princess from the ice ball lay frozen in repose and Judge leaned back down and kissed her on the lips and whispered, "I think I love you."

Judge left her there, locked the back door of the apartment and quietly slipped down the stairs. He said goodnight to the relieved Gino and slid back into the now less romantic Town Car.

As the car glided through the still, dark night down Fifth Avenue toward his apartment, Judge took out his note pad and began to scribble bits and snatches of the night behind him. If he wanted to get out of town early to visit his mother in Ophelia and Maxwell in South Beach -- all before joining Victoria in Palm Beach -- he would have to turn this story in tomorrow, which meant no sleep tonight. He took out his phone and dialed Maxwell. He could help him. He would surely have it all down in every detail. No answer.

Judge's evening was just beginning. Suddenly the glow of the magical night extinguished. While the guests were merrily kicking up their heels at Moomba, or blissfully falling into dreams, he was going to be chained to his laptop. He would have to hack out the report that would make them all feel the altitude of what they were almost sure was the greatest night they had ever experienced. The magic was fading and he was alone.

Act Three

Season in the Sun

If society fits you comfortably enough, you call it freedom.

Robert Frost

Chapter 20

Into the Shining

April 1, 2000

Judge took a deep breath of new air drifting through the open windows of his apartment. The heavy curtains, which until now had been his security detail against intruding sunlight, were drawn wide and the warmth of streaming sun bathed the room. He sat still and content as he followed specks of dust particles floating past on the gentle air stream. It was the first day of April. The sun varnished the room, filling him with a sense of the new and possible. The wooden furniture shone, the mirror gleamed. His watch on the bureau flashed like a theater sign announcing a new production. There seemed to be a klieg light presenting this day.

There was a smell in the air he couldn't place. He lay on the sofa and the rays of sun felt good on his face, his arms, his legs. He could see tiny buds on the Ginkgo tree outside the window. Thank God, he thought. I can use some spring about now. He had been confined to bed rest by the doctor, not for any physical injuries from the assault, those were healed, but for exhaustion and dehydration. The doctor told him not to work or drink or go out for two weeks and he would release him from the hospital to the comfort of his own home. The events of recent weeks had taken an edge off Judge and for the first time in his life he felt like he knew what vulnerable was.

He picked up his old stand-by book, a collection of the works of Tennessee Williams, and settled into a crook in the corner of the sofa. The prescribed two weeks had passed and though he was feeling his old self physically, he wanted more time. Again there was the familiar and comforting scent wafting through the window. It reminded him of college for some reason. He slid off the sofa onto the floor and picked up a pile of CD's on the floor next to the television. He found Widespread Panic. He put in the disc and forwarded to track four.

Travelin' light...is the only way to fly...

Judge saw himself and Russ, driving up I-85, hell bound for Athens, Georgia drinking Jack Daniels and smoking joints and listening to Widespread. The road trip turned out to be as much an experience as the concert. That was long before he knew what this life was. Russ. The two hadn't spoken since the last night he was in town. The Walkers sent an incredible flower display to his hospital room. Russ left a slobbering message on his voicemail about that last night and how sorry he was about his assault, but Judge hadn't called him back. He hadn't called anyone back. He took time off from work and went into his cocoon. His old life in Manhattan did not exist for him these two weeks and his yearning for Ophelia increased with each sunrise.

The cell phone rang and stomped on his thoughts. Judge crawled back to the sofa with every intention of turning the damn thing off and keeping it off the rest of the day.

Lucy Shining calling.

He couldn't help himself. He flipped open the phone, "Lucy Shining calling," he said, "What's up gorgeous?"

"Hey, babe," she said. "It's this day that's gorgeous. Where are you?"

"In my house. Where are you?"

"I'm on the street where you live. Get out of that house and let's have a picnic on the river."

"A picnic on the river? Are you serious?" He leaned out the window and saw Lucy standing on the street looking up at the building, not knowing which window was his. "I see you. Want to come up?"

She searched the windows and spotted him leaning out and a giant smile covered her face.

"Hey, handsome," she said into the phone, looking up at him. "Buzz me in, but pull it together. This gorgeous day's a waistin'"

"Your southern accent is terrible," he said and walked over to the intercom.

"Then I'll just have to keep on practicin'."

He buzzed her in and looked around the room. Anything embarrassing? Good thing the maid came on Thursdays.

Judge opened the door and waited for the elevator. The door slowly rumbled open, and Lucy jumped like a rabbit out into the hall.

"Surprise, lover boy."

"I'll say."

She quickly walked the length of the hallway, timidly arriving into his open arms. She kissed him softly on the lips, holding back as if she were afraid she would re-injure him. She pulled away, searching his face for scars and something more. Satisfied that he was healed, she kissed him again and said, "Come on, get ready."

"Alright, give me a second."

He followed her into the apartment and she dropped her bag and went over and bounced down on the sofa. "So this is the famous bachelor pad. Nice."

"It'll do," he said, no longer embarrassed that his place was inadequate for a girl of her class. He was surprised by this new confidence. "Can I offer you anything to drink?"

"Got any champagne?"

"Yeah, what are we celebrating?"

"This gorgeous day, sweetie pie. I'll open it, you get ready. I'm playing the role of girlfriend today."

"Well girlfriend, it's in the 'frig." He laughed as he pulled on some sneakers and fished around his desk for his watch, wallet and keys. "Okay, I'm ready."

Lucy came out of the kitchen with two flutes full of champagne. She handed him one and looked into his eyes and smiled. Without a word they clinked glasses and turned them up.

"Let's re-cork it and put it in my bag," she said. "We can get some little cups at the deli. Oh, grab a blanket, it might be damp."

He searched the closet for a cotton blanket and took the champagne bottle, wrapped it inside and put it in her big bag. "I'll carry it."

"So gallant," she said, smiling.

They stopped at the corner deli and picked up sandwiches and a salad, a bottle of water and asked the counter man for two plastic cups. "Oh, and another bottle of champs, please."

"We'll need to go next door to the liquor store for that, babe," Judge said.

"Oh yeah, the liquor store," she repeated.

He couldn't place it, but something was different about her today. There was something in her manner. There was a complete unfiltered sweetness to her today, the same that he had first noticed in the car on the way to the Winter Ball.

They walked west down Tenth street to the river. Judge hadn't been on this street since the night of the assault and there was nervousness in his gait. When a group of thug-looking teens passed, Judge felt a flash of panic. Lucy felt his arm tense where she held him. She sensed this shift in his comfort and nuzzled closer to him. Judge felt calmer in her presence. He looked over his shoulder to see the group walking on away from them unaware of his existence.

The boardwalk by the river was unusually crowded for the afternoon hour, due to the first warm day of the year, but not as many as would have been on a Saturday or a Sunday, he noted.

"Where do you want to sit?" he asked.

"Oh, let's go down to that big park on the water."

"It's quite a walk."

"That's okay, I can take it," Lucy said, then suddenly, "How about you? You back in fighting shape?"

"I'm as good as I ever was."

She dropped down his arm and took his hand and he was surprised and happy. He usually despised hand holders, smugly displaying their affection on the street. Handholding was like a leash around a man's balls, he thought. But this felt okay, it felt right, comfortable, and not leash-like at all.

They found the park and settled on a smooth little patch of grass yards away from a few kids kicking a soccer ball. They spread the blanket, unpacked the bag and sat down with the picnic between them. Judge poured them each a glass of champagne and they touched the cups. "To this gorgeous day."

She pulled the cup away from his lips and locked on his eyes. "To us," she said and kissed him.

Judge's mind raced. He was not going to make a fool of himself by falling for this act again. Things were so good between them. He didn't want to spoil it by clarification.

"Lucy..."

"Judge, I have something I want to tell you."

He stared at her and waited, the two of them, so cocky and confident, suddenly silent and fumbling.

"When we were in Palm Beach, by the water on New Year's Eve..."

He didn't say anything. He didn't want to move. She was going to humiliate him again and not even know her own power.

"You said you loved me."

"Lucy, I ..."

"Let me say this before I chicken out. I've been thinking of how to say this ever since I got back from Africa."

He closed his mouth and braced himself.

"You told me you loved me and I teased you away."

He nodded, then lowered his head. Pain rising, hot on his face and neck. Chest swelling, lungs swelling, bracing for the blow. She touched his chin and pulled his eyes back to hers.

"I told you not to love me because I was afraid. I know about your reputation and to tell you the truth, I thought you were gay. Everyone warned me not to get involved with you. They said you would hurt me. I thought I could handle it. I thought we could just have fun and then, well, just go on like we have been, casual, but a lot of fun. But I can't do this anymore. I was miserable in Africa thinking about you. I couldn't wait to see you. But you never called and I..."

"I wanted to Lucy, I..."

"And then that amazing night at the Frick when it was all so incredible. I thought we were having such a good time and then you split on me. I mean, we had this amazing evening and then poof, you were over me."

"I thought that's what you wanted." He remembered how incensed he'd gotten over her flirtation with Caleb. He was drunk and the sight of them together had pushed him over the edge. He vowed to get over her. He would not be a fool.

"I know it's my fault. I pushed you away, but then, that horrible day in the hospital. You don't know how I cried over what happened to you. Then when you came to and it was just you and me in the room, you were so sweet and you needed someone, and, well, I wanted it to be me. It was a different side of you and I ached that I couldn't stay with you. I've wanted to call you since then. I called the doctor and he said he had ordered bed rest and you shouldn't be tempted or disturbed or there could be terrible repercussions. Did you get all the packages I sent you?"

"I got them. Thank you," Judge smiled at the boost the deliveries had brought him: hand-painted cards, baskets of exotic fruit, a loopy African mask. "I'm sorry I haven't called. I've sort of taken a sabbatical inside my own apartment. Contemplating the meaning of life and all that mid-life crisis shit." He lowered his head and picked at the label of the bottle.

"I know," she said and slipped into a small smile. "Just when you needed me most."

He looked at her with surprise.

"I'm sorry," he said, lowering his head again.

She didn't mind his downward gaze now.

"That is why I came to you today. I can't let another day go by without telling you this. Every day since you left the hospital has been a lonely waiting game. I couldn't take it anymore. I had to see you today."

He looked up at her eyes which welled with tears. He put his hand on her cheek.

"I love you, Judge," she blurted almost as if admitting a crime. "I love you. I want to be with you. Not just at a party or when we're drunk, but now. I woke up this morning and this day was so incredible and I felt like there was a hole in me. There was no one there to share it with me and it hit me. You are the one I want to be with. So here I am, if you'll have me."

Judge felt a wave of relief, but was it comforting? He thought this is what he wanted to hear. Here presented before him was the ultimate trophy in an arduous and exhausting hunt. He wondered how his luck could be so unending. His earlier peace and acceptance now fading, he closed the curtain and was resolute.

"Come here, you sappy little girl," Judge said with a smile. "I loved you the first time I saw you."

Judge leaned in and kissed her.

"Judge, this is going to sound crazy, so don't say anything."

"Crazier than what you just said?" He smiled. His head seemed ice clear as he felt every cell of his body spark and dart up and down his nervous system. He never knew what it felt like, he realized, so why should he deny this? Hadn't he followed every opportunity thus far? Couldn't he be what she wanted, said she needed? He felt his heart swell in his chest and his breath slowly pushed through his throat and across his lips.

"Yeah, hold on." Lucy took a deep breath and looked down at the blanket between them. "I want you to marry me."

She cocked her head in the way that had first knocked him down and slowly lifted her eyes to his.

"When you were in the hospital, I had my own crisis and realized that you are the one I want to be with and if something had happened," she choked and her eyes welled wetter with tears, so close to spilling from those green ponds. One tear escaped and rolled down her cheek and under her chin. "I would have never known what it was like to really love you or even to say those words. I want that now."

The word echoed up like a stone thrown in the Grand Canyon. Marry, marry, marry, marry. Starting loud then getting softer and softer until he could no longer hear it. He was stupefied.

"Don't leave me hanging here, Judge."

"Of course," Judge laughed. "Hell yeah. I'll marry you. Let's go right now."

"I'm serious, Judge."

"So am I," he shouted above her head toward the river. "I will marry you, Lucy Shining."

"Thank god," she smiled with a sigh and put her head on his shoulder.

Chapter 21

The Announcement

Page Six. *We hear that society journalist/playboy Judge Mender mixes more business with pleasure than a body has a right to, but he just may have set the bar so high that no one will ever match. He is engaged to none other than reigning It Girl Lucy Shining. Our spy tells us she popped the question and he accepted. Uh, yeah. Can you say instant billionaire? We'd hate this guy if he couldn't soon buy and sell us. Congratulations, Lucy and Judge.*

Victoria Newton received the morning news from her doorman with her usual appreciation and gratitude due the man who made the most important part of her daily ritual a reality. She closed the heavy wooden door quietly and shuffled to the kitchen, newspapers tucked under her arm, coffee cup guiding the way. She put the papers down, as she did every morning, with The New York Post on top and perused the cover. What trash this paper is, she thought, as she noted every morning, and slowly turned the pages, deliberately extending the anticipation of her favorite reading. She turned to Page Six and scanned all the bold-faced names, dismissing the political, barely acknowledging the celebrity. She wanted to read about those she saw every night. And today, two names struck her, hitting her in the face like a cream pie with a hidden brick. Victoria Newton fell onto the stool, grazing its edge and landed with a thud on the tile floor.

Maxwell Jones finished his morning inspection of the previous evening's aftermath and strolled the aisles of his treasure-filled warehouse. He entered his office in a particularly jaunty mood and poured himself a cup of coffee. "What's the news today, Wanda?" he asked of his receptionist.

"You tell me, you tight-lipped turtle."

Maxwell flipped around, off guard, and looked at Wanda who was holding up The New York Post, opened to Page Six and folded over to highlight the particular article. Maxwell narrowed his eyes and stepped closer and, then, recognition. "Oh, that. Well, that didn't take long."

"You mean to tell me you knew about this and didn't pop a peep?" Wanda asked incredulously. "Since when did you become so discreet?"

"I only found out yesterday." Maxwell said as he took the newspaper from her hand. "I can't believe it's in this rag already. Jesus! Does this thing have a desk at the CIA? Where the hell do they get their information?"

"Your boy is marrying Lucy Shining?" Wanda asked, still unable to process. "How? Why? When?" I can't... I don't...When...?'

"It happened on Saturday," Maxwell said. "Remember how gorgeous it was on Saturday? Evidently, love was in the air and the white doves circled. Believe me, I am as shocked as you are. All of New York will be. You are in good company. It is simply unbelievable." Maxwell took the paper and walked into his office.

"But isn't he a homo?"

"When has that ever stopped a man from getting married?" Maxwell said with a wide grin and walked into his office.

"Hey," Wanda shouted after him. "Give me my paper back."

Maxwell closed his door, sat down at his desk and pulled a bottle of Maker's Mark out of his bottom drawer and poured a long shot into his coffee. "Jesus Joseph Mary and Diana Vreeland. I cannot believe this is in the paper already."

Maxwell put down the paper and took a long sip of his spiked coffee.

Chapter 22

A Flea Market Affair

"Wake up, Judge."

"Humph?"

Judge discovered the alarm clock through the unfamiliar filter of waking in a bright room, his own. The device dared to display the ungodly hour of 8:00 AM on a Saturday.

"Good morning, babe," Lucy whispered in his hear.

She placed a steaming coffee cup on the bedside table as she slid back into his bed.

"Rise and shine, gorgeous. Come with me to the flea market. Drink your coffee and seize this beautiful day."

"Are you crazy?" he said opening his eyes and immediately closing them again. "It's eight in the morning."

Judge pulled the cover over his head.

"Please, Judge. I want you to go with me and then we'll get a nice breakfast somewhere."

"This early morning enthusiasm is not your best quality."

"Come on. It'll be an adventure."

"Adventure," he pulled the cover down. "I can't wait."

Judge pulled Lucy close and nuzzled in her neck. He was unfamiliar with being so content and it surprised him every breathing minute. He was at ease with her. He could forget with her. He hadn't loved someone in so long – perhaps never -- and this feeling felt new to him, unequaled. He wanted her still and that surprised him. Yes, they were only two weeks together, but this time with Lucy was a strange new world. He loved her at first sight, circled her from a distance for too long and worshipped her up close for the past year. The past two weeks felt like a languorous lifetime.

Lucy spent every night at his apartment since that celebrated day by the river. He discovered Greenwich Village anew with her hand in his. They escaped from their worlds. They were expatriates in their own city. He barely worked, checking into his office by phone under the guise of working from home. He took her to his favorite places in the Village. Panino Giusto on Hudson for coffee and croissants in the morning, steak frittes at Titou on West 4th Street, sesame chicken at Mama Buddha on Hudson, beer and burgers at Chumley's on Bedford and book shopping at Three Lives on West Tenth. The proprietors -- or friendly staff -- would fawn over Lucy as if he had brought her home to mother. Lucy loved him more as she soaked up these strangers' affection. New York was new to her too. She had never felt such familiarity in her hometown and loved the way Judge seemed to be at ease in these places. She thanked God she had made her move toward him and he accepted. She told him so every other sentence.

Now, they wandered the rows of the flea market on Sixth Avenue, and Judge was surprised at how Lucy marveled at this junk. He had never been a habitué of flea markets or thrift stores and didn't understand the draw. Yes, he'd found the Church Mouse in Palm Beach, but that was part of that trip. Like space cakes in Amsterdam his senior year in high school. He didn't expect to try that again until he returned to the Netherlands. But God, was it packed. Where did all these people come from? The smell of roasted peanuts and cotton candy reminded him of the Lee County Fair he'd gone to as a child. The place began to feel familiar to him and after a while, he settled in and rolled in the off-beat charm. He followed Lucy and let her treat him to her strange attraction to this world. Lucy kicked into an odd trance of auto-pilot as she hummed a little ditty and led him through the aisles of vendors. It was overwhelming to Judge. How did anyone know where to look? What to look for? It all looked so confusing. But, not to Lucy.

"There's my favorite man up on the right. He has the greatest stuff. I once bought a New Orleans street sign from him. I don't know what I did with it, now that I think about it, but at the time I couldn't live without it. It was Carondelet Street. I love the way that sounds. Carondelet Street. Is that in the French Quarter? Hey Berryman. How's tricks?"

"Hey Lucy," the man said. "I've got something special for you today."

Judge snapped out of a daydream with the sound New Orleans and thought of Scarlet Goodman and the story that was about to hit the newsstands. What a galaxy away that confusion seemed to him now. He hadn't thought of any of that anguish which had caused him such pain. How wonderful and dangerous to be so consumed with distraction that all the other things in life fell away. He knew that he had to tell Lucy, but he didn't know how. He'd thought of nothing these past two weeks but her and their present and their future. He wanted to tell her about the Scarlet article. He had to tell her.

"Lucy, I ..."

She walked into the booth lorded over by an old lumberjack man.

"I come here every week I'm in town. Berryman has the best stuff."

"Lucy, I wrote a story on Scarlet."

Judge was in his head, but mumbling aloud. It started out as a nice easy fluff piece. What happened? It changed. She changed. I changed. How can I tell her? Victoria doesn't like Scarlet? That will sound so stupid and spineless. Maybe I am. Scarlet's become a Chase Peters? No.

"Look at this! I love this!"

The man handed Lucy a small wooden bowl, very primitive with scratches and scuffs. It was about the size of a dessert plate, rich and dark with a painted red rim that was worn, chipped and faded.

"Isn't this amazing?"

"Amazing? It looks like a hundred year old dog bowl."

Judge looked at her and saw her genuine delight in the thing. She could afford anything in the world and here she stood before the bearded lumberjack hoping against hope that he would part with the beat up bowl. She had the luxury of buying anything she wanted, she didn't need to be sold. Wasn't the value more important to her than price?

Judge exhaled and stuck his toe in the deep end.

"It's great, Luce," he said. "Hey, you know Scarlet Goodman?"

"It's so gorgeous. Feel the weight. Isn't it amazing?"

"Yeah," he held the bowl and felt its weight. "Wow, it doesn't look that heavy."

"I know. I love it."

"So Luce, Scarlet Goodman. Do you remember her?"

She turned the bowl over in her hand and held it up to her face.

"You know, the girl you met at the Frick?"

"Who?"

"You met Scarlet at the Frick Party. I ran a photo of you with her in the It Girl issue?"

"How much do you want for it, Berryman?"

"A hundred dollars."

"You're crazy," Lucy said laughing.

"A hundred dollars?" Judge said.

"A hundred dollars," Berryman said.

"I'll give you sixty and you'll love me," Lucy said.

"Sixty dollars for an old bowl?" Judge asked.

"Sixty-five and not a penny less," Berryman said with a wide tooth-missing grin.

"Sixty-five and not a penny more," Lucy said and handed the man the cash and slid the bowl into her big hobo bag.

"I love you," she kissed Judge. "We're going to live together soon and this is the first piece for our new place. I'm going to serve you cereal in it every morning."

She laughed and pulled him out of the booth and into the bustle of people seeking bargains and treasures.

"Oh Judge, I'm so happy. Are you happy? Yes, I see it, don't deny it."

She kissed him again and his head emptied as his heart pounded.

Ring. (Telephone)

"Sorry, babe. That's my phone. Hold on. Hello? Hey Rhee. Judge and I are at the flea market. Shut up, he's enjoying it. Aren't you, Judge. Yeah, hold on. Judge. It's Rhea. She wants to throw us a little pre-engagement thing Tuesday night at Moomba before I leave for Singapore. Just a small party, she swears. You do swear don't you? She swears. For what that's worth. Yeah, we can make it."

We, Judge thought. He leaned in and kissed her again. He allowed the Scarlet story to float away when that unease was consumed by pleasure that he didn't think he possessed or was capable of mustering. Scarlet Goodman and her fate were a million miles away.

Chapter 23

Last Night at Moomba

"Judge? Judge Mender?"

Judge indulged trappings of a new life, allowing decadent thoughts to dance around in his head. Lucy was leaving the next morning for Singapore for two weeks. Rhea, Frankie, Mia, and Jack made up the little party at Moomba and Jeffrey, the owner, peppered the table with attention and Dom Perignon. It was just after midnight and the room was filled with fancy people. Princess Arianna was seated behind them with her entourage and the minor British royal offered congratulations to the happy couple.

"Judge Mender?"

This time the voice was accompanied by a tap on his shoulder. Judge turned around to find a preppy, bland banker boy calling his name. It was Scarlet Goodman's friend, he thought.

"Yes. How may I help you?" Judge was too content to be annoyed.

"I'm really sorry to bother you right now. I'm Harrison Jackson, a friend of Scarlet Goodman's. We met at the Frick party. I need to talk to you for a second."

"What is it Harrison? What can I do for you?"

Judge was about to offer Harrison a glass of champagne when he noticed concentration in Harrison's eyes. There was urgency, a sternness that was out of place in merry Moomba. It reminded him of something. He couldn't say what it was, but the look in the young man's eyes disturbed him. He's probably my age, Judge noted, but he looks so much younger. Maybe it's that dorky suit and that slicked down hair.

"What is it, Harrison?"

"Do you think we could go downstairs?"

His first reaction was to say, no, but he said, again, "What is it, Harrison?"

"The story you're writing on Scarlet Goodman is a lie," Harrison whispered in Judge's ear. "There is not one ounce of truth to it and if you run it," he hesitated, "my father will sue you and Jet Set for libel."

"Let's go downstairs," Judge said then turned to Lucy, "Excuse me, babe." and nodded to the others, "Ladies, I'll be right back. Hold my spot." The women were in a state of champagne giggling and barely noticed his departure. Frankie and Jack were discussing a barely-clothed brunette across the aisle from them.

Judge bounded down the stairs in a storm of irritation and anxiety. Snippets of conversations popped in and out of his head. Victoria, Maxwell, Richard and the phone conversation with the woman in New Orleans came and went as the joy of the minutes before faded quickly with his descent. Harrison and Judge found a table in the middle of the room. There was no one on this level, not even a bartender.

"I'm really sorry to bother you here," Harrison began. "I didn't know how to reach you and Scarlet says you come here a lot."

"Did Scarlet send you to talk to me?"

Judge was not pleased to be in this situation. He had dealt with this before. Subjects of his features -- whether they cooperated in the story or not -- always got skittish when the date approached publication time. He had spent much time avoiding relatives and friends of a subject after an interview. In some cases, even the attorneys got into the act. Scarlet had cooperated with the story and, though he was sure she had no idea of the shift in the angle, had probably sent this Harrison to make sure it was positive.

"No, absolutely not. She has no idea that I'm here. She has no idea what you think you know."

Judge stiffened.

"I think you need to get to your point, Harrison. If you hadn't noticed, I was in the middle of a celebration."

"Sorry about that. It's just, well, Scarlet is one of my closest friends; we dated in college. I'm her only real friend here in New York and I have to protect her."

"Spit it out, dude."

"My aunt says you have talked to some people in New Orleans," Harrison said, gathering courage. "and you were asking about an incident in Scarlet's past."

"Yes, that is true."

"You've heard a story that she used to..." Harrison paused, obviously in pain. "There was a story going around New Orleans that she was a prostitute."

"I know all this Harrison."

"All that winter, people ran around town saying that some girl on the social circuit was working the parties, working the men, and taking money and..."

"I'm getting bored here, Harrison. Tell me you didn't pull me away from my girl to tell me what I already know?"

Judge fished in his pocket for a cigarette, but the pack was empty. Harrison reached in his own pocket and pulled out a Marlboro red and handed it to Judge. Harrison leaned in and lit the cigarette. Judge inhaled deeply and blew a sword-like flume of smoke over Harrison's right shoulder.

"It wasn't Scarlet. It was her younger sister, Caroline."

Judge cocked his face and lifted his right eyebrow.

"What?"

"It was her little sister, Caroline," Harrison continued and now the words flowed fast. "Scarlet never heard the stories and I never told her because, well there was nothing anyone could do. Her sister came to New Orleans for Mardi Gras and got into some trouble with some of my buddies, two in particular. I confronted Caroline with my information and made her promise never to tell Scarlet. I gave her some money to disappear back home and Scarlet never heard a peep about it. I lost a good friend over it, and made him swear never to let anyone find out about it."

The words raced by now, river like. Harrison expanded in confidence and defense. He then said softly. "Scarlet is a sweet girl from a small town. She was blinded by the party scene in New Orleans, and she was a little too ambitious. The girls of my set were jealous as hell of her and they spread the story that Scarlet had slept with several of my friends and taken their money. It was common knowledge that I had spent a lot on her. She bragged that I bought her dresses and jewelry. Her family didn't have any money and, well, I was in love with her, maybe I still am, if you want to know the honest truth. I want to make her happy. That was my mistake, I guess, and that is why the story was so easy for people to believe. She was naturally pretty and charming and they only wanted to bring her down. I was constantly protecting her and defending her. The story was squelched immediately. My father even got involved to nip it because he really felt for Scarlet. It turned into a mildly scandalous story of that winter, then it died. Until now."

"Why should I believe you, Harrison?" Judge stammered. "You just admitted that you're in love with her."

"Because it's the truth," Harrison said unyielding. "And can I ask you a question?"

"Yeah," Judge said, his heart sinking, head pounding. "What is it?"

"Why would you want to write something like that anyway? I mean, you just made her dreams come true with that It Girl thing and now, this. Is it because she's not one of these snotty New York girls?"

Judge retreated one final time into righteousness. "Because she wants it so badly."

"Jesus, you sound like an old lady." Harrison spit with anger. "That's what they all say. I want to know, is that so terrible? Is that such a crime? Yeah, maybe she's a little hungry, but if she wants it and it means so much to her, isn't that exactly the kind of person who should get it? And besides, it's a pretty nice life. Who doesn't want it? I mean, don't you? You seem to be having a pretty good time, running around swilling champagne and destroying people."

Judge looked at Harrison in the eye and jumped up from his seat.

"I have to go."

Judge mounted the stairs three at a time and hurried to the table and pulled Lucy aside. She was sickened by the look on his face.

"What's wrong, Judge?" She brushed her hand through his hair.

"I don't know, food poisoning maybe. I just got sick in the bathroom. I'm going home."

"Hold on," Lucy said sweetly. "I'll go with you."

"No," he said firmly and she sat back in surprise.

"I'm sorry. I need to be alone right now. Call me later." Then, he added under a thin smile, "I don't want you to see me all sick and puking. I'll call you in the morning. Don't worry." He kissed her forehead. Judge turned and scooted away.

"I love you," she said confused. "But," she said quietly and watched him bolt out the door and down the stairs. "I'm leaving for Singapore in the morning..."

Harrison stood smoking next to the door.

"Are you going to kill it?" Harrison asked when Judge rounded the door at the bottom of the stairs.

"It's too late. It hits tomorrow." Judge said frantically, looking at the floor. "I've got to go."

He pushed past Harrison, hitting his shoulder. Judge stopped and turned to him, "I'm sorry, man. I..." and he walked out the door.

Judge walked out of Moomba into a sudden beating rain. It was an unusually warm night for April and the rain was cool on his face as it soaked his shirt, his pants, his underwear.

Water collected in his loafers. It squished and splashed inside his shoes as he hurried across Seventh Avenue toward his apartment. His head spun and he felt drunk, disoriented. He wasn't drunk. That was the problem. He wished he were drunk. He wished he were high. He wished he were anything but wrong. How could I have been so stupid? How could I do that to Scarlet? How could I have not seen the truth? Victoria played me.

The sudden realization was a stab in the neck. Victoria had proven that the old guard never loses and he had been the pawn he so desperately tried to climb above. In his desire to please he'd gotten careless. Scarlet's story would hit the stands tomorrow and all Judge could think about was escape. Escape from New York, yes. Escape from this career, from this society, from this life. He wondered who would find him if he killed himself. Lucy would be gone. Maxwell? He doesn't even know where I live. How many days would his body lie there, in that lonely apartment until someone found him? He walked on, west on Tenth Street, the rain pounding harder. Why can't I get struck by lightning? Why was there never any lightning in Manhattan? At least that would be unique. Original. Sudden. Why was there never any lightning in Manhattan? He considered walking to the waterfront. Maybe the thugs would finish him off.

Judge found himself in front of his apartment, key in hand but unable to put it in the lock. He buzzed his apartment as if there were someone there to let him in. He looked at his watch. It was almost one A.M. He didn't want to wake Chinese girl who lived next door, so he stopped. He opened the lobby door and sat down inside on the cold radiator box. He waited for something. He waited for somebody. He needed a voice. He needed to hear someone or something say, Go on. He stood up, no voice was coming. He climbed the stairs, one step at a time, pulled both feet even, and then climbed another. He dripped wet, so completely drenched that puddles marked his trail. The rain had gone through him and now followed his misery, evidence that he was there, temporarily. Would it evaporate by the morning? Would there be any trace of his remorse when he awoke? No. He knew the answer. Like every other twinge of guilt, he would suppress and erase it by morning light. Then the story would begin again, undaunted. He reached his door and decided that he would own this misery, this failure, this defeat. He would not let it go. He picked up the phone and dialed Scarlet's number. He had to talk to her, to confess, to warn her, to prepare her for the jolt in tomorrow's Jet Set. The phone rang four times and the voice mail picked up.

"Scarlet. It's Judge Mender." He imagined her there, bolting out of the cover to breathlessly answer the phone. But she did not answer.

"I, I need to talk to you," he pleaded. "As soon as you get this, call me. Please. I..., just call me. I'm sorry."

Because she wants it so badly.

Didn't they all want it? Didn't he want it? Didn't Victoria want it? Didn't Rhea want it? Even in some way she would never admit, didn't Lucy want it? She seemed to hold it back with one hand while she beckoned with the other. What was the difference? It had to be more than technique, didn't it? Was it the simple fact that Scarlet's desire was too transparent it doomed her? Was it that simple? Or was it simply girls being girls, reliving throughout life and on a grander scale the petty

335

alliances from grade school? Hadn't he played the same game? Hadn't he seen in Chase Peters something unseemly, yet familiar, and squashed it as carelessly as any of Victoria's crusades? His own desire for entrance into this club had been just as strong. He read the same map as Scarlet from as far away. Only he had been given the key. His entrance was smooth, undetected. Yet had he not exulted in each exclusive invitation, each private club, each guesthouse or dinner? Only his exultations were hidden. He didn't wear them on his face, in his eyes, in his voice. Scarlet had made the mistake of showing her hand, her elation, her desire. She was unguarded, un-jaded, unabashed and girls like Victoria, and himself, he saw now, were turned off and pushed to the point of penalty. How could someone be so crass? he'd thought. So with little provocation from Victoria, he'd committed murder. She'd pushed him to the edge and put the gun in his hand. He'd killed Scarlet's dream, which was just as devastating as taking her life. It meant that much to her and he'd killed it.

He hung up the phone and looked at himself in the mirror. The room was dark except for the light in the hall. He left the front door open and the light illuminated half his face. The effect was sinister. His eyes were ablaze. His hair was matted slick to his head and his cheeks shone wet. This mirror where he preened and basked in all his glory now returned an evil matched only by Dorian Gray. He punched the mirror where his face was reflected. To his surprise he wasn't cut. The pieces fell on the floor, clanging brittle on the wooden floor, then quiet again. He turned his back on the fractured mirror and began removing his slick, spongy clothes. He left the pile of wet clothes on the wooden floor and they slowly expanded, a black wet blob with a skinny stream of water which followed the gentle slope of this old room.

Any other time when he felt this dead, he would smoke a joint. He would squelch the pain and fall asleep. Not this time, he told himself.

Tonight you are going to feel this. Tonight you are going to burn and churn through the night and know what this feels like. This is your sentence and this is your time. He got into bed soaking wet, the sheets clung to his body and he lay there, dead to himself. He did not sleep.

At daybreak, he slumped inside the descending elevator, stumbled out onto the street and slowly walked to the corner newsstand. He picked up the copy of Jet Set and flipped to the article. He prayed, grasped, pleaded to God that somehow it would not be there. Or at least maybe there would be an omission. Richard was notorious for his last minute edits and maybe this time Judge would welcome his hatchet.

Jet Set Chronicles by Judge Mender

Je suis la Goulue.

She's a very pretty girl. She's a pretty girl in a neighborhood chock full of pretty girls. She is blonde in a neighborhood of salon-perfect blondes. She wears Chanel in a neighborhood where it is as common as plaid skirts at Spence. What is uncommon are the eyes. They sparkle and shine like little flashlights outside a diamond blue window, trying to determine what is inside.

She sits in a corner banquette at La Goulue, waiting for this meeting, the meeting which she knows will change her life. Her eyes dance at your arrival and it is flattering to think that the shining eyes are for you. The eyes are almost too intense. They seem to want something badly, something more than you can give her. Is this Circe's revenge? She rises to greet you and you fall under her spell.

This is a very auspicious beginning. Much like the beginning she enjoyed in her first few months in Manhattan. Meteors have shined less brightly and traveled less distance than this little goddess.

New York society is the launch pad for many an ambitious girl on the move, but this story begins down south in New Orleans where a little voodoo, a tidy sum of questionable financing, shrewd maneuvering and a rapacious appetite will start the projectile in the direction of Manhattan.

"Je suis la Goulue, je suis la Goulue", she says between dainty, yet voracious bites of tuna tartar. Scarlet Goodman is fascinated by the story of Louise Weber, the most outrageous dancer of turn of the century Paris. Weber was a muse of Toulouse Lautrec and the queen of the Moulin Rouge. The girl had a penchant for draining the drinks of men at Moulin Rouge, earning the nickname La Goulue, or The Glutton. With borrowed clothes and new persona, La Goulue became one of the most scandalous self-creations of Montmartre, being painted nude by Renoir by day and dancing the cancan into revelrous night.

Alleged New Orleans debutant, Scarlet Goodman, supposed daughter of one of the crescent city's founding families has ascended Manhattan society with the speed and pinpoint precision of a golden bullet. After a

mere four months in Manhattan, she found her name listed prominently
on the Frick Museum's junior committee alongside such old guard scions
as Victoria Newton, Lucy Shining and Elizabeth Pilgrim and heralded as
one of this magazine's own It Girls.

While Scarlet Goodman arrived on these shores with more borrowed
money than connections, there is one connection she probably now
wishes had been buried a little deeper in the Vieux Carre. It appears that
little Scarlet Goodman of Lafayette, Louisiana and now, Manhattan has
more in common with La Goulue from Montmartre than her namesake
Scarlet O'Hara. But borrowed clothes are just that. The Glutton has
foregone Montmartre for Manhattan.

Judge couldn't read anymore. He threw the magazine in the garbage can on the corner and stumbled to the closest tree and hung on for support. He vomited forcefully and heard a girl scream as the projectile hit the ground. "Gross," she said.

"Fuck off," he muttered.

He stumbled back into his building and rode the coffin-like elevator to his apartment. How can I call her now? Scarlet never returned his call last night; she must have gotten the message too late. She would never call now. He'd written the cruelest story of his short career based on two sources, Victoria and her friend in New Orleans. And it wasn't true. Harrison told him. The conversation roiled in his brain. He couldn't stop the loop. I'll certainly get fired. Will I get subpoenaed? Am I going to jail?

Chapter 24

The Photo Reveals

Scarlet knew the schedule for the new Jet Sets like she knew that redbud trees bloomed after jonquils in the spring. She knew that the new magazines hit the newsstands in New York on Wednesdays, a week before the subscriptions hit mailboxes here and the rest of the country. This fact was one of the things she loved about being in New York. Being the first with the news was a small victory, a slice of power that she didn't flaunt but kept close. And this Jet Set. This issue was her issue. Judge Mender interviewed her way back in January and told her it was for the May issue. She had tried to put the publication date out of her mind because she knew that her desire would make the passage of time unbearable. The April issue had delayed a lot of the anxiety. That issue with the It Girls was such an unexpected phenomenon that it had knocked her own feature story off the radar in her mind. It was like she was competing for Miss Louisiana and suddenly somebody crowned her Miss America. She leap-frogged over all the other state contestants and was now walking down that runway, rhinestone crown blinking in the spotlight.

Scarlet began this morning in a methodical trance, as if a camera filmed her from above. She crafted every movement like an actress, holding each minute in an eternity, a photograph so future generations could feel the import of this event, this moment in time when she would arrive at the confluence of her dreams. She took extra care selecting her outfit: a pink pea coat over a camel cashmere sweater and chocolate brown trousers. She slipped into brown suede Belgian loafers and found her big Chanel sunglasses and slipped them into the pocket of the pea coat. She walked solemnly to the door where Precious waited and selected the pink leash with the brown polka dots and bent down to snap it in place around the pup's pink collar. She entered the hallway and pretended it was the red carpet, photographers yelled her name as she politely smiled but did not stop to pose.

Once on the sidewalk in front of her building, she quickened her pace, Precious darted to and fro on tiny legs echoing her racing mind with little mince-y steps on the sidewalk. She spotted the newsstand and imagined a halo of light, the effect of a particular sunbeam streaming directly onto the newsstand, calling her name. Mario would be waiting with the issue and he certainly would be expecting her this morning, she thought.

"Good morning, Mario. Isn't it absolutely beautiful this morning?"

"Good morning, Miss Scarlet," he answered subdued. "Looks like spring has sprung."

The vendor handed her an issue of Jet Set but could not look into her eyes.

"Thank you, Mario," she said as she handed him a five dollar bill folded neatly in the palm of her hand. Precious barked.

"Good morning, Precious. Are you taking good care of your mommy this morning?"

"Oh, she's a perfect angel today, an absolute sweetheart." Scarlet stepped back and picked up Precious and nuzzled in her curly fur. "See you tomorrow, Mario."

Scarlet set Precious back on the sidewalk and began walking toward her apartment. She decided that she wanted to experience this moment in private. She clutched the magazine to her chest and quickened her pace, the imaginary camera crew jostled to keep up with her.

The moments between the newsstand and her arrival in her bright kitchen passed unnoticed and unaccounted. She could think of nothing but the story which lay waiting for her inside the pages. She unleashed Precious and sat down at the kitchen table next to the big picture window looking south over Manhattan. The cover was especially beautiful, she thought. Who is that model? She identified the blue and green checked Marc Jacobs dress immediately. It was the one she loved when she saw the slides of the runway show on the internet. I wonder how much it is going to cost. Then she thought of the call she received from the designer's publicist setting up an appointment for her to come by and borrow some clothes. That is the one I will choose, she thought. It is perfect for a little lunch at Goulue.

Scarlet opened the magazine and scanned the table of contents. The stories all look so interesting, she thought. Society Girls flock to Tuleh. Saint Tropez in the Age of Puff Daddy. The Second Coming of La Goulue.

Scarlet set the magazine down and scrunched up her nose. The Second Coming of La Goulue? What is that about? She ran her finger back down the list. Page 56. She flipped to the page, her heart pounded in her tiny chest. She opened the book to page 56 and there was a full-page color photograph of her dancing at the Frick with Harrison. Harrison dipping her and the fabric of her dress pulled aside and there, in a full page picture was the blurred out, but unmistakable visage of her exposed, bare breast.

Scarlet shrieked and Precious ran under the sofa. "Oh my god! Why would they run that picture?!"

Her cell phone began vibrating on the table. She picked it up and saw that it was Harrison calling. He can wait, she thought. She pressed the button to send the call to voicemail and then the phone announced that there were now two missed calls. She pressed the button and read the name Judge Mender. The time said the call came in at 1:15 in the morning. What is that about? she wondered. She set the phone down. Nothing was more important to her at that moment than the magazine in her hands. The mighty Judge Mender will have to wait. So will Harrison.

She couldn't take her eyes off the photograph. She glanced down at the text, but her eye kept peeling away the blur to see if she could see her nipple. She lifted the magazine to her face. Her nose touched the page. She looked at the picture like she wanted to crawl in. Harrison wore the strangest look on his face, leering into the camera, one eyebrow cocked like a devil. What is that look? she thought. Harrison has never made that face before. How drunk was he that night? She exhaled deeply and set the magazine back on the table. It's okay, she thought. It's just a picture. She took a deep breath and began to read the story.

Chapter 25

Myths & Muses at NYC Ballet Gala

The New York City Ballet's Dance with the Dancers Gala marks the end of the junior social season in New York with a rowdy and decadent exclamation point. It was the last event before the crowd moved off the grey island in search of blue sky and sand. The summer would begin in Southampton with Victoria's annual bash and clambakes on the beach at Flying Point. The flock would spend July in St. Tropez spewing magnums of Cristal at Les Caves and pecking over Mille-Feuilles de Poisson at Cinquante Cinq. A few would cruise over to Tunisia, while fewer still would take to the bogs outside of Edinborough for grouse shooting. They would reassemble back in Southampton in August to kiss the summer goodbye and migrate back into the city by the start of September where it would all gloriously begin again.

But tonight was the City Ballet Spring Gala. This party had the characteristics of the last day of school. The fact that the dancers from the corps de ballet attended amped the sex appeal of the party through the roof. Dancing got dirtier, drinking got sloppier and some fantasized they would bed a principal, or at least a member of the corps. The older set attended, but at this party they were strictly sideline; the juniors ruled this night.

This year's theme was Mythology and Muses and Rhea Brown was ring master. Yes, Sally Banning and Mia Wilson were her co-chairs, but this was Rhea's party and everyone knew it. She had personally called most of the guests and threatened them with banishment if they didn't come to her party in full drag. "If the invitation says "Dress Gods and Goddesses, Muses and Saints" you better fucking wear gods and goddesses, muses and saints," she told Judge when he complained that he didn't feel comfortable in costume. Rhea arranged for the designer Farkam Kahn to dress her friends and there had been a wild dress party the week before at the designer's studio that ignited their crowd for this night.

In spite of her efforts at dressing him, Judge left the skimpy Apollo costume hanging on his bathroom door, donned his trusted tuxedo and took a taxi to Lucy's. She arrived from Singapore late last night, and he had talked to her only briefly that morning as she slid back into bed. She wanted to sleep off the jet lag so she could enjoy that evening. He confirmed the arrangements later on her voicemail and left another message from the car on the drive up Madison Avenue. When the taxi pulled up to the covered entry of her building, he paid the driver and let him go. He wanted to spend a few minutes with her before they hit the party. He wanted a few minutes alone with her after her two weeks out of the country. Tonight would be their first big public appearance together since Page Six trumpeted their engagement. Rhea told him Lucy had been upset with her for spilling the engagement to the editor, but Rhea rationalized that the news would get out soon enough. Why not let her curry favor with the influential columnist by giving him the scoop? Judge found his life unbearable at the office because of the news. His editor sensed that Judge wouldn't be long in the position and wanted to iron out the wrinkles before Judge ascended to Mount Olympus. It made Judge sick to see him squirm. He couldn't decide which was worse: the editor's bitchy remarks and unreasonable demands or this new sniveling and scraping for favor. He figured he would have to get accustomed to this new perspective.

It was now three weeks since the news story about their engagement, and Judge had noticed a distinct change in people's attitude toward him. He was sought out at every event before, but now people treated him differently. People who had never returned his call now left messages on his voicemail. Victoria sent him an embarrassingly expensive flower arrangement and invited him to her Southampton house the first weekend of the season. He was astounded at the suddenness of it all. Lucy, thank god, was not aware of any of it. Maxwell had almost been unbearable, but he was the one relief Judge had.

Judge managed to completely ignore the after-effect of the Scarlet story. The May issue had been on the stands for two weeks now, and it had not caused the sensation he'd feared and, maybe, secretly hoped. The news of his engagement had drowned out all other stories in New York society. The beau monde could hardly bother with the speed bumps of a little girl from New Orleans who'd been knocked off her pedestal. The magazine's attorneys swooped in and took care of the legals. Judge was advised to reveal his sources in New Orleans and it would be the jealous goats who would take the heat if any legal action threatened. He gave the attorney one name in New Orleans. He did not betray Victoria.

He was relieved that Lucy had been in Singapore for the past two weeks and he never brought up the story with her over the phone. He panicked in the beginning, but now, like every time before, time washed the panic away. He never heard back from Scarlet after his frantic phone message and figured that she left town. He pushed away the sloppy mess with the comforting thought that once he was married he would no longer have to write that kind of story again. In fact, he was planning to quit Jet Set as soon as he and Lucy returned from their honeymoon. He would look for another job in the meantime, but he hardly thought the prospect difficult. All in all, he couldn't believe how easy he'd gotten over the Scarlet incident. He was thankful that no one had witnessed his breakdown that night after Moomba, especially Lucy.

He said hello to Gino as he strolled confidently past the doorman of Lucy's building and was halfway down the long, narrow lobby when Gino yelled after him. "Miss Lucy's not here, sir."

Judge turned and looked at the doorman. "I'm here to see Lucy Shining."

"Yes, sir. I know. She left about a half hour ago with a pretty girl and a handsome fellow all dressed for a fancy party."

Judge walked back toward the door. "A half an hour ago? Did she leave a message for me? For Judge Mender?"

"No sir, she didn't say anything at all." The doorman lowered his head and lowered his voice. "She seemed a little strange, if you don't mind me saying. Not her usual flirty self."

"No, no, not at all," Judge said. "Strange? Do you have any idea why?"

"No sir, like I said. She didn't say anything. Not even hello or goodbye, which is not like Lucy at all. That's the strange part."

Judge walked past the doorman and out onto the sidewalk and flipped open his cell phone and hit redial. No answer at home. He dialed again. No answer on her cell phone.

"Uh, thanks Gino. If she comes back..."

"I'll tell her you stopped by. I sure hope she's okay."

"Yeah, I'm sure everything's fine." He stared up at her window.

Judge walked absently toward Park Avenue. He called her cell again, no answer. He called Rhea Brown.

"Hello, Rhea. It's Judge Mender."

"Hey, Judge, What's up? I'm so late. I am seriously going to be an hour late for my own party. You better not be calling to cancel."

"Have you talked to Lucy?" he blurted.

"Yeah, I was talking to her this morning. Have you tried her at home?"

"Yeah, I'm here now. She's not here. I was supposed to pick her up to go to Lincoln Center. The doorman said she left a half an hour ago. Upset."

"Upset? What the hell does the doorman know? He's a little too nosey, if you ask me."

"Rhea!," Judge blurted. "What were you talking about to Lucy?"

"Nothing, just gossip that she's missed while she's been in that God-forsaken Shanghai town and what she was wearing and what I am wearing. Have you seen the gown..."

"What gossip?" he interrupted.

"Let's see. Mia is fucking Frankie again even though she's dating Jack. I hate her, I have to tell you."

"What else?"

"Oh, and Scarlet Goodman."

"What about Scarlet Goodman?" Judge felt his stomach flip.

"I read her a little of your story. Brilliant, by the way. What a fake, she turned out to be. I cannot believe she is such a hooker. I mean, we're all hookers, but wow. Such a shame really. She had star potential. I don't have to tell you that, though. That picture in the It Girl issue, Jesus. You fucking made her Judge. But then, that last photo of her tits..."

"Rhea, stop talking!" he shouted.

"Why? What's wrong?"

"What did Lucy say about the story?"

"Nothing. She just said she had to go and that she'd see me at the Dance with the Dancers."

Judge needed to sit down. There was never a bench in this city when you needed one. Would he look ridiculous sitting on the curb in a tuxedo? He paced back and forth on the sidewalk. "She didn't seem upset at all?"

"Not really. She just got off the phone fast, but she does that all the time with me. She says she hates my gossip, but everybody says that and they don't mean it. I mean, everybody likes gossip. Judge?"

Judge snapped the phone shut and frantically waved for a taxi which screeched to a stop. Judge jumped in the back seat. "Lincoln Center, please."

He slumped in the seat and looked up at the tops of the buildings along Park Avenue. God please let her be there.

Judge jumped out of the car and ran across the Lincoln Center plaza, the cathedral-like atmosphere bathed in light and the center fountain erupted in a riot of dance.

Judge swung the doors wide of the New York State Theater and furiously scanned the crowd but didn't see her in the lobby.

"Judge Mender! So glad you…"

He didn't stop at the press table but hurried through the jostle of arriving guests picking up their table assignments and clucking their initial hellos.

He stopped at the top of the stairs of the great hall and the cocktail portion of the event was in full swing beneath him. He surveyed the noisy crowd in the promenade below for signs of Lucy.

Most of the guests had heeded Rhea's warning and arrived in full mythology drag. There were yards and yards of purple and gold and red silks with fanciful embroidery and mirrored paillettes sewn into every piece. There were plumes and tiaras and crowns and turbans, never had he seen so much head gear. Maxwell Jones dressed the two statues at both ends of the hall with purple and gold togas and topped them with gigantic golden crowns. Yards of purple, yellow and gold fabric flooded down from the ceiling creating an illusion of Mount Olympus. Gobos projected the constellations on the fabric in a fantastic multi-colored night sky. Judge immediately recognized Pegasus and Crux, the southern star. Maxwell doesn't miss a trick, he thought.

It was easy to see who had attended the dress party; the inner core group set the style tone and huddle together in a tight clique at the bottom of the stairs. The DJ played some hip hop song Judge didn't recognize and a few of the younger dancers from the corps de ballet were already on the dance floor.

Judge descended the stairs, his need to find Lucy matched only by his need for a drink. Judge grabbed a flute of champagne off the first tray which passed and just as quickly returned the empty glass. He made tracks for the bar and ordered a scotch on the rocks.

He spotted Victoria first, surrounded by a sea of lavender silks and headdresses. Her cousins were in town and the three Palm Beach blondes were dressed identically to compliment Queen Victoria's gown. She was resplendent complete in a golden robe clasped at the shoulder with an enormous diamond brooch. Her head was adorned with a bejeweled crown. Judge thought, is she supposed to be Zeus? She waved a peacock feather fan. She nodded towards him, and he started in her direction. As he approached, he could see that Maxwell was in her group. He looked perfectly ridiculous in a purple and gold jacket, gold pantaloons, and golden curly-toed slippers.

"Well, look everyone. If it isn't the future Mr. Shining," Victoria boomed.

"Ha ha." Judge tried to smile. His heart pounded and his armpits squeezed a sponge down his sides. He knew he wouldn't calm down until he saw her.

"You look regal, Victoria," he managed.

"Thank you, Judge. I see you couldn't be forced into a get up like the rest of us. I never pictured you for a poor sport. Although I'm sure your other half will arrive and make up for it and put us all to shame. That Lucy seems to love a costume. Where is your fiancé, Mr. Mender?"

"She'll be here soon. I had an errand to run first." He took a thirsty gulp of scotch.

"Well, I want to be the first to host an engagement party," Victoria boomed like a judge to her jury. "The season's ending, perhaps we should do it at the Southampton house the middle of June. Will you all be around?"

The group around her all nodded that they would and Judge searched the crowd and didn't answer.

"Judge, darling. Is the middle of June good for you and Lucy?" Victoria asked, eyes blinking for a response.

"June? Yeah, yeah. That'll be nice," he mumbled.

"Judge, darling," Victoria pursued. "Are you sure nothing is the matter? You're sniffing around like a crack head looking for a fix."

"What?"

"Nothing another stiff drink won't fix. Right, my boy?" Maxwell stepped forward and took Judge by the arm, and turned him in the direction of the bar. "Excuse us please. Can we get anyone anything from the bar?"

"No," Victoria said. "Andrew went to fetch us some drinks hours ago. He should be back soon, if he hasn't fallen in a hole somewhere. I really should get a leash for that boy." Victoria craned her neck to see where in the world Andrew could be.

Maxwell led Judge to the side of the bar that was least populated. He turned and put his hands on Judge's elbows.

"What is wrong with you?" Maxwell said, searching Judge's eyes. "Victoria is right. You look like you're on drugs or something. This is not the time to flip out, darling. You are on the brink of greatness."

"Maxwell. Something is wrong. Lucy may be done with me." Judge stammered. His knees buckled, but he caught himself on the bar. He was about to collapse.

Maxwell looked around to see if anyone had heard him. Judge wore sweaty beads on his forehead. His eyes darted nervously around the room.

"My god you're sweating. Are you ill? Do you have a fever? Did you stay up all night again?" Maxwell put his hand on Judge's forehead.

"I'm not sick, Maxwell," Judge said and pushed Maxwell's hand away. "Stop touching me."

"I'm sorry," he said, shocked by the violence of Judge's touch. "You are beginning to worry me."

"I told you what was wrong. Lucy is done with me!"

"What are you talking about? The girl worships you. She's over the moon for you, Judge. You have hit the jackpot of love."

"She wasn't at home tonight," he blurted. "I was supposed to pick her up and she wasn't home."

"Is that all? You've told me a thousand times that girl is nothing if not capricious. Come on, Judge. What is happening to you? I've never seen you so unglued. This is not your most attractive side."

"Maxwell, If I lose her, I'll kill myself."

"Well, to die young and gorgeous. That's the dream I guess. Exquisite corpse and all. Overrated if you ask me, though. I'm quite enjoying my middle passage. But alas, you won't have to die tonight. Look who's making a grand entrance."

Judge turned and saw Lucy standing at the top of the blood-red stairs. She was in full glorious costume, and she radiated light and heat. She wore a gold gown with beads and sequins of the same color which shimmered as she moved like a diamond bracelet on a sun-drenched beach. Her hair was slicked back and meticulously coifed to look like a crown with crystals and jewels woven on strands of golden hair. The effect dazzled. It looked as though a spotlight had landed on her and heralded her arrival. The crowded room nearly hushed when she came into focus. She wore a thin veil and though only her eyes were uncovered, Judge could see that she was not smiling. She had chosen as her inspiration Polyhymnia, the muse of sacred poetry. She called Judge last week after she'd done a little research. She was excited about this party and said she was going to make him proud.

She looked more beautiful than he had ever seen her. Judge smiled, a momentary relief came over him as he unconsciously stepped in her direction. But she was changed. She was not the lighthearted and spirited Lucy. She looked older, matured, a serious beauty. Although the effect of the golden gown and hair made her look like a goddess who had kissed the sun, her expression was ice princess. Judge felt his stomach flip.

Then, rounding the corner and joining her at the top of the stairs stood Scarlet. Scarlet wore an identical gown interpreted in silver and wore the same effects as Lucy in her own short blond hair. A trail of sparkling jewels formed a garland. If Lucy was Polyhymnia, Judge reasoned, Scarlet must be Melpomene, the muse of tragedy. The two outshone the constellations projected on the ceiling and Judge marveled at the complete picture before him. His heart pounded, his throat closed and his breathing dammed in his throat.

Scarlet glided astride Lucy and the two joined arms and walked together, muses descending into the masses. Judge noticed now that Scarlet was changed too. The innocent sparkle in her vivacious eyes was gone. Her eyes looked more narrow and feline. She held her head to one side and her chin was slightly tilted upward toward the constellations. As the pair approached the middle of the stairs, one of the younger male dancers from the corps rushed up the red carpet to meet them and fell face down at their feet in worship. Another dancer at the bottom of the stairs started applauding wildly. Soon the room erupted and applause rose mist-like up the stairs enveloping the two creatures in repose elevated above the crowd.

Judge rushed toward them, but he was not alone. The crowd of friends and admirers surged toward them as they descended into the throng and Judge could not reach her. He was swimming, pulling his body forward with his arms, desperately trying to get up stream, but the surge was too great. He was drowning, gasping for air. He had to reach her, to touch her, or he would go under.

He struggled to penetrate the tittering crowd where Lucy and Scarlet landed to harvest their praise. The pair of sparkling muses stood statuesque beside Victoria. The bombastic Zeus barked her approval.

"What an entrance! What a moment! Did the photographers capture it?" Victoria shouted above their heads. "Lucy, Scarlet, you are too gorgeous and grand to be believed. Now tell me, what are you supposed to be? I don't know beans about mythology."

Judge couldn't believe what he was hearing, but he didn't care now. He had to talk to Lucy. He slipped between eager guests and outrageous costumes, pushing and pulling his way to the center. He came face to face with her and he froze when he saw the look in her eye.

"Lucy. I came by your house, I ..."

Lucy turned from Victoria and let her eyes land on him. She looked dead into his eyes and her frozen façade did not crack. Behind the transparent silk veil, there was a curtain of calm over her face and the flicker in her eyes that had first captured him was gone.

She looked at him and the revelry of the room evaporated. It was if they were alone in an empty room, all white walls and no furniture, no carpet, nothing to blunt the words that were about to hit him from every direction.

"How can you be so charming and smart and conniving and evil all at the same time?" she said in a calm, steady voice, the pale yellow veil shuddered slightly with each word. Victoria looked at her with surprised eyes and turned to look at Judge.

"I tried to understand your choices once before," she continued. "But I don't know who you are. I cannot love a man who does what you've done. I am embarrassed for you. Please leave. I can't look at you."

Lucy turned her back to him, and Judge stood face to face with Scarlet. Scarlet made no expression. She stared at him and then followed the pull of Lucy's hand.

Victoria absorbed every detail and immediately deducted the truth. She looked at Judge who was trying to save face, but it was impossible. A tear trickled pitifully down his cheek and he cried after her, "Lucy!"

"Judge, don't." Maxwell was at his side. "Come on. I've got to get you out of here."

Judge stood frozen yet his body ached as if shrapnel were penetrating his organs. The gathered flock followed Lucy's lead and turned their backs to him. He felt the doors close and realized he could no longer save himself.

Maxwell pushed him through the crowd and up the stairs. The stage that had just promoted Scarlet's triumph, now exclaimed his shame. Judge turned one last time to find Lucy. She shimmered in the crowd below him, clustered with Scarlet and Victoria. Victoria put her arm around Scarlet's waist and fawned over her gown. Lucy looked up and caught Judge's eye and a single, glistening stream rolled down her cheek. She unfastened the veil and mouthed goodbye.

Maxwell pushed Judge further up the stairs. Judge's eyes stayed on her face, not wanting the final moment to end. Maxwell scanned the room below them, searching everywhere to gauge the damage. They did not see him until Judge bumped into him, chest to chest.

"Excuse us, sir, so sorry," Maxwell fluttered, "My friend isn't feeling well…"

Maxwell froze when he looked up and into the grinning, triumphant eyes of Chase Peters.

"Hello, Mr. Jones," he said with a courtly flair. "And hello to you, Mr. Mender."

Judge barely lifted his head, "Get out of my way, Chase."

"Why certainly. You two on your way out so soon?" Chase continued as he passed them and descended the stairs. He stopped and flipped his head over his right shoulder. "I thought you two at least would congratulate me on my genius interpretations of muses for this little party."

Maxwell turned around and said, "What the hell are you talking about, you silly twit?"

"Lucy and Scarlet, of course" he said with glowing confidence. "I've started a couture collection out of my little studio. I called Lucy last week and begged to dress her. She brought along Scarlet at the last minute. It was hectic, but we pulled it together, don't you think? You see, I needed a little good PR and what better canvases than those two gorgeous press darlings. It seems like a smashing success, if I know my applause meter. I do hope your photographer caught it Judge. That is, if you still have a column. Oh well, good luck." Chase bounced down the stairs back into the embrace of the Jet Set.

The odd couple shuffled through the lobby until Maxwell pressed Judge through the doors onto the plaza. Judge, catatonic, was pulled toward the fountain. He found the edge as the water leapt into the air, lighted from below. This spout that for years had applauded artistic triumph -- and perhaps inspired declarations of love -- now laughed at Judge and danced mockingly behind him.

"My god that was the most dramatic thing I have ever witnessed. It was better than Traviata! You children certainly love to put on a performance. And such a public display as I have never seen! My god! I have said it a thousand times, yet I shall say it again: your generation has no sense of propriety whatsoever. Oh, but what a show! Who knew that Lucy Shining was such a diva? It was so well done, my boy, so very well done. I'm sorry, Judgie, but it was really quite marvelous. I hate to seem glib, but you must admit it was quite a performance. And Chase! I did not see that coming. I warned you though. I told you he was an opportunistic little snake. How long did he lie low in the reeds to pull that stunt? My my, what a night. I am so glad I did the décor. They will talk about this one for ages."

"Maxwell. I just lost Lucy."

"You must go home at once," Maxell snapped as he stood before Judge in the ridiculous costume, a genie from a bottle there not to grant him three wishes, but to show him his future.

"You have to leave, Judge. You cannot be seen here."

Maxell motioned over his shoulder toward the terrace above them. Guests from the party began the slow trickle onto the gallery to ignite cigarettes. Laughter and smoke peppered the clear night air. It would be mere minutes until the ripple turned torrent and then the opera would be complete. The throng would point and whisper and Judge's shame would follow him into the street. Judge looked up at the buzzing balcony and shook his head. He leapt to his feet, violently shaking his head as if bursting the surface of water. "Tell me what to do!"

"Go home," Maxwell said sternly. "There is nothing more you can do tonight. It's merely the second act. I am afraid the opera must play out. Go home. I'll call you in the morning."

"Can we go to Bemelman's and get a drink. I really need to talk right now, Maxwell."

"I'm very sorry to say it, Judge, but no. You wear the scarlet letter. You have been out played. You are an outcast right now and I cannot afford to be seen with you. I've already risked my reputation by escorting you out. I must return and save my own hide. In fact, there's Rhea Brown now. I will join her grand entrance."

Maxwell took a step back and yanked the lapels of his costume. He looked deep into Judge's eyes.

"Go home. It will look better in the morning."

Maxwell turned and crossed the plaza and scuttled toward the lobby. Rhea hurried across the plaza without seeing Judge and through the open door being held by Maxwell. The two exchanged kisses and Maxwell offered his arm to mount the grand stairs. Judge's eyes followed them through the wall of windows. As he ascended, Maxwell turned one final time and raised his hand in a small wave hidden from Rhea. His golden slippers flashed on the red stairs as he disappeared into the revelry of the last party of the last month of the dying Manhattan social season.

Judge sighed near expiration. He turned toward the street and noticed one last dashing black figure crossing the plaza. Harrison in his evening clothes charged toward him. Judge stood still deciding too late to turn. Harrison headed directly toward him and lifted his arm in a speedy blur. Judge felt the power on his face and fell backwards, splayed on the granite ground in his worn-out tuxedo. Harrison never stopped moving. He walked toward the glass wall of doors and into the carnival. The exits on the balcony above him opened and Judge heard the familiar refrain blare from the speakers:

> Music's got me feeling so free
> We're gonna celebrate
> Celebrate and dance so free
> One more time

Judge slowly found his feet. He groaned and wobbled and dusted the dirt off his black pants and touched his face where Harrison's fist had been. The connection was the opposite side from his first attack. Harrison must be left-handed, he reasoned.

Judge faced the back of the plaza now, and he felt miniature before the grand arches of the Metropolitan Opera House. His black silhouette dwarfed by the great hall where nine months ago he sat in the president's box on opening night, that night when Domingo ascended into record. Judge left that performance to follow Rhea and her troupe into a year-long ride unlike any he knew he was likely to know again. That September night felt years away from here. He looked up and tried to find the stars. The comedy is ended. Pagliacci, the clown. Domingo had sung Vesti la Giubba so beautifully that September night. He heard the plaintive arioso behind him, above him, surrounding him.

Recitar!...mentre preso dal delirio

Non so piu quel che dico e quel che faccio!

Eppur...e d'uopo...sforzati! bah, sei tu forse un uom?

Tu se' pagliaccio! vesti la giubba e la faccia infarina.

La gente paga e rider vuole qua.

E se arlecchin t'invola colombina, ridi, pagliaccio...

E ognum applaudira! tramuta in lazzi lo spasmo ed il pianto;

In una smorfia il singhiozzo e'l dolor...

Ridi pagliaccio, sul tuo amore infranto!

Ridi del duol che t'avvelena il cor!

(Go on stage, while I'm nearly delirious?
I don't know what I'm saying or what I'm doing!
And yet, chin up! I'll try harder. bah, you think you're a man?
You're just a clown! on with the show, man,
And put on your white-face.
The people pay you and you must make them laugh.
And if harlequin should steal your columbine, laugh,
You're Pagliaccio, and the world will clap for you!
Turn into banter all your pain and sorrow,
And with your clowns' face hide grief and distress...

Laugh loud, Pagliaccio, forget all of your troubles,
Laugh off the pain that so empoisons your heart.)

Judge laughed sadly and turned toward the street to find a taxi, to go home, to go to bed, to begin anew. Tomorrow was another day – how true -- and tonight was behind him, as was the season. Judge felt the warm wave of absolution crash behind him, the obloquy falling from the balcony above held by the unbreakable dam of his imagination. The spectral voice followed him across the plaza and into the night air, defeat so suddenly and definitively delivered wafting faintly sweeter now. He felt the wave of relief again. The same relief he'd discovered in the hour before Lucy beckoned outside his window, now surrounded him but did not drown him. He recalled that crucial day when he'd fallen back into the same lie, the same pursuit and it had ruined him, or at least the life he thought he had to live. Now he looked out at the plaza before him, a curtain drawn open with candor and peace. His pain ebbed. His head cleared and he walked slowly forward, a foal on wobbly legs, gaining strength in small increments and wildly curious.

The End